I HEARD YOU TAKE ACTION

ELIOTT McCORMICK

COPYRIGHT © 2024 BY ELIOTT MCCORMICK

All rights reserved. No part of this publication may be reproduced, stored or transmitted in any form or by any means, electronic, mechanical, photocopying, recording, scanning, or otherwise without written permission from the author. It is illegal to copy this book, post it to a website, or distribute it by any other means without permission.

This novel is entirely a work of fiction. Unless otherwise indicated, all the names, characters, businesses, places, events and incidents in this book are either the product of the author's imagination or used in a fictitious manner. Any resemblance to actual persons, living or dead, or actual events is purely coincidental. Any research undertaken for the novel was conducted solely through open source channels.

FIRST EDITION

Cover Art & Illustration by David Provolo
Edited by Kieran Devaney

For my parents, and M.H.Q.

1.

Past midnight in late April, fire shot into the sky outside Sherbrooke.

I learned this during an indifferent conversation about my future: hungover the following morning, I was eating in a soiled McDonald's on Sainte-Catherine, my molars stuffed with a rubbery breakfast sandwich.

"I really don't care what happens," I told Patty, my roommate, who asked what I wanted to do after university.

"Graduate and then get some office job," I continued, looking out the window onto the street. "For what?"

I was too exhausted for optimism because we'd been out on successive nights. Patty had recently befriended a real estate agent who ran a high-priced poker game downtown. That was Friday, when sometime past two a.m. I correctly guessed that a puffy financial services manager had a bad hand. His tell — a thumb and index finger in nervous intercourse — became obvious as he recounted the improbable conquest of a Brazilian model.

It felt great to leave that posh apartment with a wad of traceless cash. And I knew how this distinct satisfaction — arrived at by taking five bills from someone who twice referenced a Harvard MBA, and smaller amounts from three others whose vague careers likely placed them near the margins of organized crime — would never be approximated by an office job on René-Lévesque. It's not like I could have boasted about this win to my parents, either, who recoiled at what the law looked down upon. Besides, nothing remained of my victory: I spent these winnings at a trashy club on Saturday.

"I know," he said, "forcing laughs at the shitty jokes of some fat co-worker…"

"There's no pop in that kinda life, you know?" I said, despairing at a colourless existence that would neuter the only skills I was proud of. My mood turned when Patty got up and began to waddle in imitation of a secretary at the business where he interned.

"I just gotta find some way to make a living that doesn't make me want to kill—"

My phone began to skate across the grease-stained tabletop. An unknown number convulsed for my attention, so I picked up and was met by a breathless voice on the other line: our old neighbour revealed the cottage had become a husk.

"Fuck!" I high-jumped from my seat, inadvertently closing our conversation.

"What?" Patty asked, looking on with rare concern. I ran outside to hyperventilate on the corner.

I dialed Dad, as he answered more reliably than Mom. I dialed Mom, in the faint chance she may pick up. I dialed the landline, as perhaps they weren't at the cottage and had returned home early. I called the neighbour back, but he didn't answer: instead, I was received by his wife, whose muffled sobs over the breaking line confirmed what, in that area of the lower stomach where truth is revealed, I already knew.

It wasn't arson, according to the local investigator, who believed some antiquated electrical system was the culprit. I neither challenged the verdict nor took interest in it. Why would

I? My parents were both dead, while their bodies — twin lumps of sunken organs, found twisted together in bed — I was spared having to identify.

I had no brothers or sisters and my lone uncle lived in Ottawa, but we hardly spoke. Family friends and neighbours made immediate contact to offer their support, which I received with muted appreciation. There are only so many sympathetic shoulder squeezes I could stand before my body began to resist. As I said to an old girlfriend, who stared at me through moist eyes at a pub we attended after the funeral, there was nothing anyone could do.

What about the house? It needed upkeep: the foundation was creaky, its kitchen hadn't been changed in decades, the roof had holes and its pitted driveway resembled the scarred cheek of someone who suffered from teenage acne. But it was mine, at least, and any cosmetic improvements could be undertaken in time.

I could touch upon my emotional wellbeing, but descriptions of grief's stages are imprecise. Language does not convey the blast of nothingness one's brain experiences whenever it's reminded that what was will never be. The next few months, which I can no longer remember, were a fugue in which I did little but watch sports and spit tobacco juice into a cloudy water bottle.

And it was through sports — the one constant in my brief life — that everything changed. Because nothing happens just as a matter of will, and it's possible that what follows wouldn't have occurred if not for chance: of certain things happening in just such a way that other, more dramatic events were their consequence. But when the principals in any story are liars, thieves and men with no moral center, the expectation shouldn't be a blissful ending.

It's fitting, then, that my criminal career started at a fight.

2.

There are gonna be some studs there tonight," Patty assured me. "Some real fucking studs."

"That right, Patty boy?" I sidestepped a drunk college boy, recently kicked out of a nearby strip club, whose pants were at his ankles. He put his hand on my shoulder as I passed and smiled.

"Big time. You're gonna see a couple potential world titlists. Studs, dude."

We were walking to a boxing show at Métropolis. Patty was given tickets by someone at a downtown gym he'd started training at. Already, he was an expert.

Smartly dressed, my oldest friend wore new white sneakers and jeans that tapered at the ankle, with a green golf shirt whose collar he'd turned up. In contrast to his bedroom, everything about Patty's physical appearance was clean, and he had a brilliant understanding of which parts of his life needed to be organized so the gratification of his physical urges could proceed unimpeded. Blue-eyed with light-brown hair, he benefitted from sharp cheekbones and clear skin.

I also had a polo shirt on (tight to accent my good health), jeans and white Nike sneakers, which I worried about dirtying each time my serviceable high school track skills were employed to leap a sidewalk puddle.

On Sainte-Catherine's southwestern corner sat the Notre-

Dame-de-Lourdes Chapel. Though I stopped attending church, I had once visited on a school trip and the altar's craftsmanship was such that even a self-assured young man could acknowledge its mastery. Presiding over its apex was a golden Mary, her arms extended downwards in humble welcome, doubtless annoyed by the neighbourhood's sins: on the pavement below a group of cackling drunks had congregated.

Clusters of people walked in both directions. Swaggering Haitians slunk by as Chinese university students chattered excitedly. Young Americans with maroon faces, their distinctive voices carrying in the air, stumbled past in search of downtown bars, and coolly dressed Francophones sidestepped tourists. On my right, seated on the wet cement slabs across the street from the church were two Haitians. The woman, who had toothless upper gums, was nearly seventy but outfitted in clothing suited to a thirty-year-old. She was speaking with a taut-looking younger man whose sideways red hat exposed his wary eyes.

We walked by Saint-Denis, where I had gotten drunk for the first time, and then Sanguinet, where an ex-girlfriend now lived. Next, we passed Pussy Palace, a massage parlor we visited as eighteen-year-olds. Made reckless by youth, a friend's aggression resulted in his unconsciousness under its fluorescent sign outside. Two skinny, mustached men stood around smoking menthols.

Then came Sainte-Elisabeth, on whose corner sat a four-theater cinema where lone patrons could absorb orgies on large screens. In its vinyl seats had congealed enough genetic information to populate a small city.

"Remember when Mal-man dropped his lollipop and then sucked the sticky shit off?" Patty asked. I laughed at the memory. Years ago, a group of us had skipped high school in search of a transgressive story. One porn-going friend fumbled his candy there and (for show, I guess?) made the improbable decision to return it to his mouth. I remembered a lone man sitting in the theatre's front row when we entered. He left immediately.

"We can stop if you want?" Patty asked. "First load's on me."

"Only if being poor gets us tossed from Célestes," I said. Corps Célestes was a legendary strip club we'd graduated to after first finding our way in the cheaper, lower-tier spots further east on Sainte-Catherine.

"I was there the other night with Ken and Halfpipe," Patty started, referencing in the latter instance a friend whose crotch had ballooned during our visit to the Palace. "Anyway, Seamus Helmer shows up, sits down with us and starts telling stories. I'm barely listening as the guy says he took down twenty-three girls last year at St. FX," Patty said, laughing. "Twenty-three. Keeps emphasizing the number in that monotone voice of his. It'd be possible if his breath didn't smell like he gargled with butt sweat. So I'm treating the guy like he's Evan Stone, listening to his 'process' for wheeling, and when I get up to take a leak, I turn around and see he's been staring at a signed Jordan jersey in a glass case along the wall. I didn't have the heart to call him out."

I laughed. "Why was he there with you?" I asked.

"He's been in the boxing gym, sucking up to the guy who runs it. Probably heard he was gonna be there."

"Sucking up to him how?"

"Guy who owns it, Eddy, is a serious guy around here. And Helly's always desperate to know the right people."

"And serious people see through him," I answered. "Did he show up, Eddy?"

"Yeah, and he basically told Helly to fuck off when he started asking too many questions. We got talking and I mentioned we'd be going tonight. I'll introduce you. You'll like this guy." I nodded as we passed Hôtel-de-Ville and had to sidestep scaffolding and traverse the coned walkway that had been set up Sainte-Catherine.

Homeless were asking for money. The nose of one man, outfitted in a tattered brown tee shirt, and with a face too red for April, had swollen to twice its natural size. Mapped out over its bridge were streets and highways of purple capillaries. His eyes seemed injected with red dye that had only since faded, and they blinked slowly as I passed. "Got any money, sir?" he asked in French.

"Sorry, I don't," I said, holding my hand within the pocket to prevent a shock of coins. There is a process of desensitization that occurs as one ages. If one is perceptive as a child and finds their feelings hurt by any injustice, they will live with a terrible burden, for the world's suffering is inexhaustible and there will never be a moment in which one can look into their surroundings and find them free of problems. To cope, the body eventually numbs.

"Your pockets go empty?" Patty asked, his tone somewhat mocking.

"Get me back into that poker game and I'll treat these guys like I'm Trump."

"Most of the people get fired on that show," he answered.

When we finally reached Métropolis, there was a group of high-heeled women outside checking their purses for tickets. The alpha, taller than the others with dark hair and skin whose tint approached orange, wore a suit jacket whose open neckline revealed the contour of a silicone-boosted breast. They spoke accented Québécois French and eyed us as we walked into the theater.

Inside the venue, orange, blue and purple lights centered on the ring. Two amateurs were fighting: they circled each other and threw punches that rebounded off the other man's arms and shoulders. From our distance, each blow appeared to land soft, and whenever a punch finished near the face, sparks of applause reverberated off the venue's walls.

The floor was becoming full, and pockets of people peered down from the gondolas above. Tables had been set up close to the ring and were populated by organized criminals — obvious and over-tanned — and their prostitute dates.

Breasts bulged from halter tops and tight pants gripped waists that tapered into thick legs. The hair was violent, whether oil black or a retriever blonde. They walked aware of being watched, planting both feet to accent the movement of their hips. An olive-skinned girl whose lower half had the inverted structure of a spinning top glanced at me as she passed. She sat down beside a man with tribal tattoos.

Patty slapped me on the shoulder. "More puss in here than Célestes."

"As many meatheads, too," I said.

Soon, a square-jawed man in his mid-forties came over to where we were sitting. Of average height, with short dark hair, he wore a checkered jacket that sheathed his rounded shoulders. Suffocating the man's wrist was a gold watch. Standing behind him were two younger men and an attractive blond woman about his age. He said hello to Patty, making a joke that I didn't hear, before turning my way. Patty introduced me to Eddy. I reached out to shake his hand and felt the cold edge of a pinkie ring.

"Sacrament!" Eddy started, shaking his head. "This guy pulled you out of the apartment tonight?" he asked, aware we were roommates. Patty laughed.

"He promised me action," I said.

"I own the gym where he comes in," Eddy said, pointing to Patty without looking at him. "He's training like a madman, ostie!" Boxe Montreal was a subterranean gym on Sainte-Catherine I had been to once. Two world titlists had started there.

"Patty's talking like he's Roy Jones," I said. At this, Eddy laughed as though I'd made one of the funnier comments he ever heard. Patty howled with disingenuous force.

"Ed, this guy wanted to rub one out at Pussy Palace on our—" Patty started, before being cut off.

"—If a guy like Jones were here tonight, who'd you match him against?" Eddy asked.

"I'd put him in with someone he'd stop," I said. "Get him some rounds and give the fans a reason to come back."

"That right?" he asked.

"I guess. Figure out what's most interesting about the fighter and use that to suck people in," I said.

"That's smart," Eddy said, tapping his temple as he turned to the blond woman. "You guys looking forward to the World Cup of Hockey? Might be the only thing you see all year."

"We're going to games one and two," Patty said, pointing to me. "Gotta get it in now with that fucking lockout coming—"

"What are you doing these days, Teddy?" Eddy asked.

"Still in school. One more year."

"And then?" he asked.

"No plan yet."

"I may have something for you," he said, handing me a business card. His full name was Édouard Robichaud. Underneath was the name of a holding company.

"Whizz with the numbers, this guy," Patty responded, pointing to me with his finger.

"You have work at the gym?" I asked.

"I might, but you're not an office guy," he said, "I can tell." Before Eddy could reveal more about me, the blond woman pulled him from behind.

"He's the new Big Gerry?" I asked. Patty smiled and shrugged his shoulders.

The first several bouts featured prospects of varying potential. A tattooed local from Laval was making his professional debut and at least one hundred people were here to watch. They cheered each time he landed a punch, and his opponent — a weathered Portuguese man with an Easter Island-shaped head and a record of 21-37 — dutifully fell midway through the second round after absorbing a punch whose impact was greater than its force suggested.

I realized the productions that had taught me to love boxing — famous black and Mexican men fighting for golden belts at Caesars Palace, their matches verbosely narrated by tuxedoed whites — couldn't exist without shows like this, so far away from the legitimizing imprimatur of American media. Suddenly, boxing felt real.

Prowling the venue in a fitted suit was a tanned, muscular man holding a succession of conversations with three people in tow. This, Patty told me, was Calix King, Pugilistica's owner and promoter. One of those trailing him was a short blond who saw Patty and came over to sit down. Véronique Faubert was a fourth-year marketing student at Concordia, earning placement credits doing public relations work.

"I know nothing about boxing," she confessed, her attention moving from Patty to me. He introduced us and I shook her hand, returning at once to the ring. They continued to talk while, in front of me, a cagey Arab fighter started to find his target, locating the forehead of a doomed Pole.

"So you guys grew up together?" Véronique asked, tapping me gently on the wrist with a program.

"From the womb," I said.

"Cheating off this guy got me through high school," Patty said. Véronique laughed.

"Where are you from?" I asked her.

"Tadoussac," she said. I'd been there once on vacation with my parents. It was where the Saguenay River met the St. Lawrence. "Ever been?" she asked.

"A long time ago. I saw the whales." She smiled and started to say something, only to be whisked away by the promoter's fingers.

Our eyes followed her as she walked over to the promoter,

who was speaking with a group of businessmen at one of the side tables. "I heard some things," Patty said. He was unsure of where the money to found Pugilistica came from, but knew that King, who appeared to be in his early forties, had been a real estate agent before entering boxing. "I heard the money was Russian," he continued, speculating without basis that King had been financed by a local gangster.

At once, Métropolis turned black as the co-main event was scheduled to start. It featured a leathery Mexican and a young Haitian boy from Montreal North who had one of the most impassive faces I'd ever seen. They were both welterweights, but Octavio Linares, whose sagging midsection folded over his trunks, was clearly a more natural fit for lightweight and had been moved up to serve as cannon fodder for Ferdinand Guillot.

"What is this *shit*?" I asked Patty.

Linares showed a wolfish toughness through the first four rounds. Sporting a mustache that looked like hair springing from a caterpillar's back, he pressed forward, bobbing his head and shoulders to confuse Guillot. He did so without enough athleticism to deter the younger fighter, as the Montrealer landed repeated punches to his midsection and head, drawing his hometown cheering section out of their chairs. "Technician!" the black faces yelled, urging their man to finish the job.

But Linares was too ornery to cede the ring. A veteran whom I suspect knew he was there to lose, Linares wanted the fight to unfold on his terms and, towards the end of the fourth, Guillot threw a lazy jab that he'd anticipated. The Mexican appeared to lift himself out of his shoes and landed an overhead right on Guillot's left eye, following this punch with a left hook that blasted the younger man's cheek. Guillot staggered backwards and made a protective shield of his fists before shimmying his way out of danger as the round ended.

I watched Guillot walk back to his corner. His chin was still up, as if to suggest he wasn't injured, and the boxer sat down on his stool where he was set upon by his trainer—a white-haired Québécois—who was wagging his finger in the fighter's face. Guillot mounted a half-hearted defense of himself before nodding in agreement, while, in the other corner, a stoic older Mexican man gave instructions to Linares, who appeared tired as he took labored breaths. The Mexicans were here to improve Pugilistica records, so what advice might a trainer offer a fighter whose fate was preordained?

In the fifth round Guillot mounted a barrage. He looked reenergized, perhaps embarrassed at having been caught, and began to walk Linares down. The lazy jab he employed to lull opponents into attacking him so that he could counterpunch had disappeared. Each body part was now moving in concert and the disparity in athleticism became stark. However shrewd he may have been, Linares didn't have reflexes to mitigate Guillot's speed and started getting hit to his abs and forehead. Guillot knew he was in full control, but rather than launch himself at Linares I could see him preparing for a knockout, measuring distance to throw a conclusive power shot.

Near the end of the fifth, Guillot rocked Linares with an overhand right, which vaulted him backwards into the ropes. Badly hurt, the Mexican pulled his hands towards his face, but in doing so exposed his midsection. Guillot immediately threw three left-handed shots at Linares' right abdomen, the third of which pushed his liver into its supporting organs, and the Mexican collapsed to the floor, where he flopped like fish upon a boat deck.

The referee set himself upon Linares and immediately waved his hands skyward to stop the fight. At this, Guillot's section erupted. The Mexican's trainer stepped into the ring with a look of calm concern, having seen countless men felled by similar punches, and held Linares' head in his hands with an endearing tenderness as the fighter began his slow recuperation. In the ring's other corner, the victorious Guillot — his face still blank — threw his hands up and climbed the turnbuckle closest to his supporters. He pointed both arms at them and flexed a triumphant bicep. This prompted another "Technician!" chant and I could see the black breasts of one fan bouncing with each syllable.

I refocused my eyes on the people at ringside. Photographers joked on the ring apron, officials held roving conversations and patrons bought drinks from overworked servers. Everyone seemed at home, even me: I'd lost track of time, but my phone revealed that it was now ten-thirty. I could have remained in place for another two hours.

Ten minutes later, with every floor seat occupied and the gondola filled, our main event started. It featured two svelte local fighters, one young and white, the other black and old, who locked into a ten-round struggle in which each man landed several hundred punches. Standing directly in front of one another, they bombarded one another's faces in the absence of shields.

The crowd swelled as the fight wore on, and I — usually too self-possessed — felt myself being swept away in its crescendo. A furious exchange as the eighth round closed brought the theater into a state of ecstasy as fans jumped to their feet and screamed encouragement. With his back against the ropes, the black fighter absorbed a power shot that thrust his face from left to right. Rather than bicycle out of trouble, he shook his head and smiled, knocking his gloves together to indicate that he wanted more, and in the bravado expressed by this moment my sense of time and circumstance became nothing as I merged with the fighter into a realm where individuation gave way to instinct. Infused by the vitality that was the source and reward of his vigour, I was with the black fighter when he pounced forward with an uppercut that gave his opponent a glimpse of the ceiling; I then entered the body of the white fighter, badly hurt but obstinate in his wish to go on, who absorbed this blow and threw a desperate right hand that staggered his opponent. My immersion ended only after the ten second warning came and both fighters were standing in the middle of the ring, egging the other into coming forward. With each cocky salvo the beating heart of Métropolis became louder. They both landed clean shots and continued brawling after the bell sounded.

I didn't remember getting up but was standing now, clapping and wild-eyed, having forgotten myself within the swell. I turned to Patty, also absorbed by the drama. "This is amazing," I said to him. "Is it always like this, the atmosphere, I mean?"

"I think so."

For the first time since my parents died, it felt as though my world, once gray, had become technicolor again. A throb and lifeforce had been exposed — one I didn't know existed and to which I was desperate to return. These men were living elementally. For a brief moment, so was I.

3.

When he was forty-six, a bleeding ulcer preceded my father's anal cancer diagnosis. The consequences of this development — beyond the initial grappling with mortality felt by the husband and wife, and, to a far lesser degree, their teenaged son — was a series of chemotherapy treatments that did little to prevent the conquest of his digestive system.

My father's dim prospects for a healthy resolution changed when he learned of a novel stem cell treatment in Boston. Of course, it was far too expensive and wouldn't be covered either by the provincial health care system or his work benefits, so my parents took out a home equity loan to pay the treatment's costs. They received small amounts of support from friends and a work fundraiser, but accountability for the fee was mostly theirs. Until their lives were extinguished by bad electrical work, my parents were making quarterly payments on a schedule that was set to go on for some time.

But it worked. As his treatments matured, the tired, emaciated man barely capable of absorbing a morning newspaper transitioned back into his former self, and whatever poison remained in his system retreated before the ingenuity of his American doctors. How close my father was to death, only to be given another chance, before being robbed of a second act through an avoidable tragedy, is an irony that may have tortured his mind in the milliseconds before his last breath.

I thought about this the morning after the fight, having returned to their house to receive any mail, when I found hidden within the stack of paper a quarterly hospital invoice. A natural procrastinator, I wasn't interested in opening it this morning, and instead went to the fridge in search of a drink. There was a lone bottle of tonic water on its second shelf. This was among the last items my parents bought — any perishable purchases having expired soon after them. When I opened it, the pop felt thunderous in our soundless house.

The following day I met the Dean of my program. When I arrived at her office, located in the far corner of a twenty-second floor high-rise (outside of which, tacked to a bulletin board on the wall, were student printouts attacking the Iraq War), she rose from a tidy desk to greet me. A small, fit woman of about fifty in a dark suit jacket, Diane Sutherland gestured to the chair in front of her desk, and I sat down.

"How are you?" she asked. "I want to reiterate how sorry we all are here about what happened."

I had no idea what she knew of my academic record and general underperformance. Several times throughout undergrad I was encouraged by professors to participate more. "You have a very good style," one of my English professors told me in first year, having made her approach one day before class as I stood alone in the hallway. I smiled at her suggestion and promised to contribute more. This never happened.

The Dean clasped her hands together and leaned forward "We don't expect you to complete all of your courses right away," she said. "Take as much time as you want."

"Thank you. I'm going to take the year off." I wanted to finish school but had no motivation to complete it.

"Of course. There's no rush, given what you've been through. One of my parents passed when I was seventeen, so I have a small sense of what you're going through."

"Thank you," I repeated, not knowing what else to say.

"So, what's next, Theodore?" Diane opened her arms when she said this, as if to indicate that anything was possible. The world could be mine, her bearing suggested.

"I've been settling their affairs, so that's keeping me busy." This wasn't true, as those responsible for disbursing the will weren't answering my emails.

"Do you have a lawyer?" she asked. I told her that I did.

"And the future, Teddy?"

"What about it?"

"Do you have any sense of what you want to do? Some professors really spoke highly of you." Her question — asked with a concern that bordered on maternal — stunned me by its forgotten relevance.

"I really don't know, yet," I said. "I've got this other stuff to deal with first."

Beside Diane was a picture of her family. Her two sons looked as if they were a few years older than me, smiling from underneath Adidas ball caps on a beach. Burnt-red cliffs placed the image somewhere in Prince Edward Island.

"My older son also has a degree in History, too. He teaches at a private school now." Diane's voice rose an octave when she said this, tendering his lot as an option for me. I smiled but had no interest in teaching the Confederation to bored teens.

"In any case, if you need anything, don't hesitate to reach out," she said, passing me her card. "I wish you the best, this year and into the future." We shook hands and I thanked her before getting up to leave.

When I walked outside, Concordia staff was setting up for the first day of classes. Students standing outside the main doors were talking about their course loads with an excitement I never understood. I hated school: a place of grandstanding, interpersonal awkwardness, competitive animosity and punishing boredom. I never wanted to come back here, but Diane was right: I *did* have a future — one I hoped would have nothing to do with anything learned in university. What the hell would it be?

"That broad from the fight, Véronique, she liked you." Patty and I were sitting in Peel Pub one hour before Canada and the United States would play their first game of the World Cup of Hockey. Montreal bubbled with the influx of people: hotels were full, self-important hockey media people seemed everywhere and I spent a small part of the afternoon at Dorchester Square, watching adults in jerseys getting drunk before the game.

Downstairs, every seat was taken. Seven-dollar pitchers appeared out of nowhere, as though provided by a conveyor belt whose supply couldn't meet demand because, furnished by a separate conveyer belt, were inebriated hockey fans, who clung to the staircase for support as they waited for the opportunity to load their organs with trans fats and alcohol. There was cause for the excitement: an NHL lockout was coming and there would be no more professional hockey this year. Even more, after winning Olympic Gold two years ago, Mario Lemieux was playing again for Canada, for once in his hometown. Every twenty minutes, tables of Anglo drunks would rise to sing the national anthem. A man in his forties, his blowfish cheeks already cherry red, chugged a pint glass for the surrounding tables goading his alcoholism. Our beer was warm, but we continued drinking.

"Did you guys ever…?" I asked.

"No," he said, shaking his head in regret. "We worked together on a group project once, but fuck all happened. So you got a bill from the hospital?" Patty asked, looking past my head to the backside of a black server.

"Yeah."

"For how much?"

"I was too much of a pussy to check," I said.

"Won't be on you to pay," he responded, shaking his head. An American couple in blue jerseys had arrived and were booed by the bar.

"You don't think?"

"Fuck no, but it don't matter anyway," he said, "'cause even if there's some bullshit, I may have an opportunity to help you make some money. Legit cash."

"Doing what?"

"Remember Eddy, from the fight? Took a shine to you. Told me at the gym he may have some work."

"In one of his clubs?"

"No." Patty took a long sip of beer, eager for my intrigue.

"Okay, so?" I asked. He looked around to see if anyone could overhear our conversation (if they could, no one would remember), and then leaned in to where he was a few inches from my face.

"Working as a runner. I told him you were smart, good with numbers, and he talked about giving you a half-sheet, since he just lost a guy—"

"Lost how?"

"I don't know," Patty said. "He moved or something."

"What's a half-sheet?"

"Taking action," he responded, as if this was common knowledge. "They call Eddy 'the Executive.'" From there Patty began a monologue.

At the top of any gambling ring was someone who served as its bank. This was Eddy's "office." The job I was being offered was to find bettors and supply them with logins and passwords to access a website operated out of Costa Rica. Depending on who won and lost, I would have to pay out or collect their money every Friday. As most people lost, I would get to keep half of the money, while the other half would go to Eddy — hence the "half-sheet." If someone won, Eddy would supply the money to pay them out.

"But you're responsible to make that money back if you go into the red," Patty continued. "So you don't get another dime until you pay back what you owe the office for covering when you get beaten on the money. But you can do that real easy. Again, these fucking clowns always lose. You may have a bad week once in a while, but it's quick to come back from."

"And when guys don't pay?" I asked.

"You work out a payment schedule, I don't know," Patty said, looking away. "I don't think guys are getting their heads cracked anymore, it brings too much heat. So?" he asked.

"Won't they be fucked without hockey this year?"

"Still got football, still got college sports. So?"

"So what?" I said, taking a slow sip of beer.

"Are you interested?"

I shook my head. "I don't know shit about that stuff. Why don't you do it?"

Patty looked down for a moment. "He knows about your situation and wants to help. This guy's a moneymaker," he went on. "Anyway, offer's on the table but the shelf life's short."

"Not for me," I said, "thanks though."

Patty looked down. "It's a ticket to do whatever you want," he answered. "What else you gonna do this year? You got all the time in the world. Or are you worried about the morality of gambling or something? You're no angel, so who gives a fuck?"

His point was substantiated by a past decision: on the wrong side of midnight two years ago, light punched the pupils of my weary eyes.

"Have you had anything to drink?" the police officer asked, leaning into the six inches of window I'd opened.

"One to three beers," I said.

Bloated and bleary-eyed, this was my response to a cop who pulled over the car I was driving not far from my parents' house. I was nineteen then, piloting a drunk friend to a downtown bar for last call, having just been cut off from a local pub after slurring "Teo Fluwee" to a bartender who asked if I had a favourite hockey player. Once behind the wheel, I hit a median.

What do I remember most? While the handcuffs were uncomfortable and the ride to police headquarters ominous, it was the intensity of the policeman's flashlight — that merciless fucking light — that returned in my sleep.

After telling my parents about the arrest (they received the news with downcast eyes and thoughts never fully expressed), my next disgrace came standing before a judge. It would be boilerplate — given Quebec's uncompromising impaired driving legislation — so I didn't expect a surprise on the day of my court appearance. I had been waiting for two hours as the judge went through various charges facing other defendants that day (one small, skinny man with a pubic hair mustache who was accused of stealing quarters from gumball machines across downtown, arrived in the prisoner's dock dressed in a Corona jersey, smiled to the two overweight women there to support him, and said, "Bain oui," when the judge asked if he was prepared to live legally again).

This experience — immaterial by criminal standards — was bad enough to discourage further interaction with the law. As a kid our age was in the process of being thrown out for dumping a pitcher over his head, I motioned for Patty to get up. The puck would drop in twenty minutes and lines at the Bell Centre moved like desert caravans. It was time to go.

Thirty-two cunts had taken over a thousand people hostage. This is what dominated my world on Wednesday morning. Not the previous night's game (Canada beat the US on goals by St. Louis and Sakic), or tonight's (we were playing again against Slovakia), but Beslan, North Ossetia, a place I'd never heard of until that morning, when "Knowledge Day" in a remote Russian town had turned apocalyptic.

"Storm that fucker and slit their throats," Patty said, coming into the living room. He sat down on the ragged La-Z-Boy that faced our small TV. Children had been jailed in a gym, their escape blocked by terrorists in suicide vests. Patty's strategy seemed unwise.

"You message her yet?" he asked me.

"Nah," I said, obsessed by the coverage on CNN.

"You gonna?" I didn't even respond as Patty got up to leave. "Peel again tonight bud," he said, walking out the door. I continued to watch throughout that morning and afternoon, stopping only for the game. That night, Canada beat Slovakia 5-1 and Patty and I got drunk afterwards, battling for each drink at an overstuffed bar on Crescent.

Throughout Thursday the Russian government held unsuccessful negotiations with the terrorists, and when I woke on Friday morning the siege had ended: with idiotic recklessness, government forces stormed the building. Over three hundred innocents were killed. One of the hostage takers had been lynched by the Russian parents.

Rather than message Véronique, that Friday night Patty and I went to Corps Célestes. We were led through the narrow hallway by a bearded bouncer to a table at the back reserved for university students the club assumed were poor. After sitting us down, he said, "And for me," holding out his hand in expectation of a tip for escorting us less than twenty meters. I ground a fist into my pocket and found a five-dollar bill, which I gave to him with less hostility than he deserved. Unimpressed, he nodded and walked away.

While none of us had any real money, Patty ordered a round when the waitress came by. The club was full, with men of all ages in small to medium-sized groups (with the exception of a few horny loners plotted around pervert's row). One Asian man was rebuffing the attempt of a droopy white girl to go for a lap dance, while elsewhere, roving packs of strippers (thick cheeks swallowing their thongs) searched for marks among the clientele.

A short, brown-haired dancer walked by and Patty took control of our table.

"See that chick?" he started. "Two weeks ago I'm here on a Saturday afternoon and she saunters over to have a chat 'cause there's nothing going on. Starts telling me all about the club, the life, whatever. We're shooting the shit, having some laughs, and I'm putting off having to go for a lap dance. Anyway, she tells me that some of the clientele pay for piss."

"What?" I asked. The whole table laughed.

"Guys pay for piss. These zeros fork over cash for it. Even two bills for a jar, she said."

"What do they do with it?" I asked. He pretended to drink from a pint glass and began giggling uncontrollably. I wasn't offended by the idea but nor did I laugh — it depressed me to think of some loser returning to a mouldy apartment and placing a jar of urine on the upper shelf of an empty fridge. Did the john label his purchases? Did one glass taste different from another?

I sat back and watched every aspect of the club for a few minutes, lost in its details.

"Going for a dance?" Patty asked.

"Not in my budget."

So many times I'd stumbled into one of these booths, where

thick-legged dancers with grainy nipples, stretched over silicone balls, pushed their groins into yours for twenty dollars a song. Because their premise is to objectify women for your pleasure, moral logic condemns them as fallen places for stunted men. Whatever one's beliefs, it was impossible to spend any time here without these considerations becoming obsolete.

As we were talking, a teddy bear-shaped drunk was thrown on stage. He must have been getting married, because several of the strippers began to assault him. Spanks of his bare ass became whips, and soon he was duct-taped to a pole. The strippers began to pinch his nipples and groin as the crowd oooh'd appreciatively. In his helplessness, I couldn't decide whether he more closely resembled someone being crucified (minus the horizontal piece of wood), or a damsel, tied to a tree on a remote island, whom the hero must save before a golden-tongued villain destroys the world.

Pleased by his degradation, the lead stripper pulled his pants down to reveal a miniscule penis shrouded by a knot of black shrubbery. The crowd laughed as derisive fingers pointed to his dick.

"What's the point of this?" I asked.

"Guy's gotta be humbled before he ties the knot," Patty said, extending his hand to receive a beer from our server.

"You thought any more about what we talked about?" he asked.

"The half-sheet stuff?" I asked. Patty nodded.

"Probably not for me." Patty said nothing as we both took sips of our beer. On stage, the abused man had left (his asscheeks having turned tomato red) and a languid dancer embraced the pole.

"You like that girl?" he asked, pointing to her.

"I wouldn't say no."

"When's the last time you took down?" he asked, likely knowing what the answer was.

"It's been a while."

Patty put his hand on my shoulder.

"Why don't we correct that?" he asked. Two dancers arrived at our table and asked to sit. I tried not to stare at near-perfect spheres bursting from a pink bikini. They belonged to a white Québécois, tattooed across her arms and back.

"I'm Annie," the one closest to me said in French, smiling as she provided her hand.

"Teddy."

"What brings you in tonight?" she asked. I laughed at her question, and she giggled along with me.

"So a dance, then?"

"I'd love to, but maybe later."

"Okay," she replied, feigning a smile as she got up to leave. Beside me the other stripper was sitting on Patty's lap. She was leaning into his ear, trying to entice him towards the back room. Patty whispered something and she nodded before moving towards a table of older men. As new bodies came onstage, I noticed a group enter through the front door. Eddy was in front, shaking hands with staff.

"There's your boy," I said. Patty's knowing smile implied he knew Eddy would be coming in, and the group made its way around the stage to a nearby booth. When he saw us, Eddy waved. Another table was being moved close to theirs, and two other men, who had been sitting close to the bar, joined their group.

"You know they'd be here tonight?" I asked Patty.

"He may have mentioned it."

Patty got up and walked over to say hello. I watched as he leaned in to make several jokes that Eddy's group started laughing at. Patty then motioned for me to come over. Drawing a breath, I got up from my seat and approached the table. Before I had the chance to speak, the largest of his guys gave me a knowing pat on the shoulder, indicating that I should sit down. I moved in beside Eddy, who squeezed my forearm. From close, I detected expensive cologne.

"How you doing, man?" Eddy asked, pouring me a drink. Just extending beyond the border of his wrist was a tattoo.

"Got your eye on any of the girls in here?" he asked, before I had a chance to answer.

"A couple," I said. We were speaking French.

"Listen," he began, putting his arm around my neck, "I know Patty talked to you. And I know you've had a rough time lately, ostie. I've got an opportunity for you — if you want it. It's a low-risk thing," he went on. "Not what you think. I just need smart, reliable guys. Patty said you're both. And you seem like it, because I like to think I can read people. Anyway, this is real, real good money if you stay on top of things."

"What happened to the last guy?" I asked.

"He's got an issue with the government, but it had nothing to do with work. Guy has fucking mental problems and wouldn't leave his ex alone. Anyway, I don't want to keep you, okay? Enjoy your night and let me know if you're interested." I thanked Eddy and we shook hands. When I got back to our table, Patty smiled.

"He's interested," Patty said.

"That his crew?"

"Some of them. There's no pressure in any case," Patty said. "I thought it just might be a good chance to make some dough."

On stage, an immaculate girl appeared just as I felt a tap on the shoulder. It was the dancer I'd spoken to earlier. "Come back for a dance, baby," she said, taking me by the hand. Later, I told her. I needed to get some money.

"It's all paid for," she said, smiling as she gestured towards Eddy's table. She pulled me upwards and away from our table. Patty slapped my ass when I passed him.

"Have fun, lad," he said.

I followed her into the back room where she led me past booths of strippers being groped by men finessed from the floor. We walked towards a door on the other side of the champagne room — one I didn't know existed, and which opened to a small hallway with rooms on either side. She slid back the final door to reveal a small living room.

"Have a seat," she said, proceeding to disinfect the couch. When she finished, Annie turned around and slowly walked towards me, taking off her shirt. Without removing her thong, she straddled my thighs and started massaging her chest with my hands.

"Are you feeling alright?" she asked.

"I'm okay, how are—"

"—Eddy said you deserve some good treatment," she said, shrouded by a cloud of perfume. "Just relax. Think about nothing. When guys think about nothing…"

Annie pressed my fingers between her legs, leaning in to kiss me as she cupped the back of my head. She then pushed me back against the synthetic leather and got down on her knees, pulling my pants away to reveal a rising shaft that she brought to full maturity before fitting it into her mouth. Eventually, Annie pulled out a condom and applied it with her lips. From there, she leapt on top, wedging herself into me as she clutched my shoulders.

We carried on through various positions. She dug her hands into my back with such force that I told her to stop; I then turned her around so we could fuck against the couch, each of us panting with such intensity that I soon forgot myself as a wellspring began its release. When it was time, I withdrew. She exhaled and produced a cloth from her bag to wipe the moisture from our bodies. I fell back once more against the couch and laughed.

"Thank you," I said to her.

"Thank Eddy."

4.

I woke up hungover and it took me several moments to remember what happened the night before. Patty bounded into my room while I remained facedown on the gnarled bedsheet. He slapped my back to toast the night's success.

Later that morning, I went over to my parents' house under the pretense of having some work to do. When I walked into the empty house, my head veiled by an imaginary mist, I threw a bag of clothing onto the kitchen table and sat down on our couch. There were sports highlights on, but I couldn't focus and instead stared at the ceiling, doing my best to tone down a rising anxiety that had become a staple of these mornings. After an hour I fell asleep and woke up in the quiet darkness of our living room. With great effort I stumbled into the bathroom, where I clutched the wall for support as a thick orange stream rebounded off the toilet water.

On my way back to the couch, I noticed the same bill I'd been avoiding sitting on the coffee table. Rather than open it, I went to the mailbox outside the front door, where I grabbed the stack and re-entered the house. I sat down on the sofa and began opening the letters. Most of it was nonsense, though I did receive a note of condolence, addressed to my parents (who did the letter writer believe was their audience?). Within the mound was another bill from the bank. I ripped it open to assess the damage. In large bold print was a quarterly amount that was past due.

Eleven thousand, two hundred and fifty dollars.

What the fuck? How could it be this much? The bill's due date had already passed, so I opened the next letter to see the total balance. In eighteen font lettering it read $225,000.

"Fuck you! Fuck you! Fuck you! Fuck you!" I screamed into the empty house.

Our old brick townhouse sat on a sloping street north of Sherbrooke. We had a small backyard, divided between a large deck my dad installed one summer when I was ten, and a garden patch in the far right corner where my mother grew tomatoes.

My bedroom looked out onto the street. When I was young and sent to bed early in the spring, before the sun had gone down and whichever NHL playoff game I was watching had ended, I would perch myself on the windowsill and stare at the children still playing, hating my second-floor imprisonment. It was from this room that my father would call me whenever dinner was ready, and I would rush down the stairs, taking a seat at the table, where my parents would talk about work, extended family members, politics, and other topics that I would close my mind to until the conversation returned to hockey, as it often did whenever they tried to pique my interest.

They were older when I was born, and this, I suppose, explains why I never had a sibling. Both teachers, my parents had met in university, but I was still unsure of why fifteen years passed before my arrival (perhaps there were romantic detours along the way). The result was a glut of attention each night, when my mother made her usual walk up the creaking stairway, entered my room and read from the edge of the bed, her black hair falling down to the pages of whichever Roald Dahl novel we were working through. We carried this routine through for years — my understanding of the world expanding through the imaginative powers of an old British writer, whose story of a young boy poaching pheasants introduced me to a world beyond my Montreal bedroom. From there, my reading became more independent when it expanded to Scott Young's hockey books, and I had no idea the person who conceived Bill Spunska also produced the man whose music flowed through the old kitchen speakers whenever my parents made dinner.

Our house was older, and its basement wasn't finished. Inside the doorway on its main floor was a newly renovated washroom on the right. Sometime after I was born, my parents opened the boxy main level so that our kitchen looked onto the living room, which, in turn, faced the backyard. We had a fireplace with a TV overtop, and a spacious bookshelf — filled with titles from their university days, Joyce and Woolf and all of that. In the corner of the living room was a piano no one played (my mother failed in her attempt to culture me when she said I couldn't play hockey unless I practiced, so, as a ten year old, I sat at its keys each afternoon, miserably pounding the same note with my index finger).

Behind our house was an alleyway. I would escape into it, hiding underneath the overhanging trees as I waited with short, shaky breaths, petrified of being located by one of the kids whose task it was to tag me. On either side of us, the second-floor windows of neighbouring homes kept watch over our movements, hiding worlds behind their walls.

Until I was a certain age, my parents forbade me from walking down to Sherbrooke. I would do this anyway, looking behind me to ensure no one saw my turn onto the busy road, where I would make a thrilling two-block tour before turning back up towards the rink. In the summer, when on long afternoons sun blasted the street's sidewalks, I would take refuge under a tree and watch the older women in flower dresses and tiny shorts emerge from the shops and cafes, intrigued by whatever histories were buried in their heads.

So much of my life was squeezed into the streets south of Monkland. From secret kisses beside the College to scheduled fights after school, and then, later on, our nightly escapes, when we'd meet with friends who also succeeded in sneaking out. A hodgepodge of tongues and skin tones, I always saw NDG as an enclave distinct from the city that overshadowed it, enhanced by our association with Montreal but independent of its cultural sweep. It was where my best memories occurred: those only possible in childhood, when consciousness hadn't yet become burdened by memory, and true vitality — experiencing the miracle of *just being there*, running barefoot through a sprinkler or playing baseball in the summer heat — felt like a lightning bolt.

Every day after school I played street hockey with the same kids nearby. There was Wade and Ben, Jonesy and his small, temperamental brother Pete, Ryan, Pierre-André, a local bully named Bobby, Rajeet and his younger sister, Kamalpreet (who had natural talent and could have turned into a fine player if only her family had the means and interest to enroll her), and two dozen other local kids, including Patty, who sometimes tended goal and would smash his stick whenever someone scored on him.

Day after day, year after year, we carried on with this routine. Then we arrived in high school, where we'd meet in a nearby park on Friday nights to drink booze stolen from our parents' liquor cabinets. I had people over the first time mom and dad went away for the weekend, and we got so drunk in my living room that a near-unconscious Patty had to be dropped off on the lawn in front of his parents' house. The next morning, his father came over to speak with me about the dangers of alcohol abuse. But Patty's father never told on me, which I always respected him for, and when my parents came home neither had an idea of what happened in their absence.

When I first started watching porn — at probably eleven or twelve — I would always do so when they went to bed or left the house. That's how — unexpectedly, unforgettably — I introduced myself to the eternal habit on a soft September evening which ended in a gray pool that settled into the folds of the bathroom's carpet. When, after cleaning myself off, I emerged from the shower, feeling lighter than I ever had and desperate to tell Patty (when I did, he claimed to have already been jacking off "for years"), my mother was walking up the stairs with a glass of water. As usual, she had fallen asleep on the couch watching television.

"Goodnight Ted," my mother said, clueless to the life-altering event that had taken place. Every night from then on I made the same trip into that bathroom. How could they not have known what I was up to?

"Your parents took out a home equity loan against their house, and their estate is still indebted to the bank. So you're going to have to sell the house to pay the remaining balance."

This verdict was delivered by a manager at our local bank. I remembered coming here as a kid and being told to sit in the corner, where a generous teller would sometimes produce a lollipop to encourage good behaviour. Waiting in that branch, with its gray and blue tones, felt longer, even, than being at church, and I couldn't remember if Bruce, the man who sat across from me, was around back then: overweight, his thinning hair and droopy neck placed him somewhere in his mid-forties.

"What? So even though they're both dead, the last thing they owned is going to get repossessed?" I asked.

"Not repossessed, per se, but…"

"Is there anything I can do?"

"Well, yes, of course, you can come up with the money." He looked down, in regret of his answer.

"And I owe two hundred and twenty-five grand?" I asked.

"Yes. Payable in quarterly installments of eleven thousand, two hundred and fifty. So forty-five grand a year, total."

"What happens if I can't come up with it?" He explained that after a certain time the bank would repossess the house and keep the sale's balance to pay our debt. The money that remained would be folded into my parents' estate and disbursed to me whenever the clowns responsible for settling it did their jobs.

"Jesus Christ," I said. There was no way I could come up with even a fraction of this amount. "One of those payments is already in arrears, right?" I said. "If I don't pay it soon?"

"The interest will just keep compiling. You know," he started, looking up from the computer, "if you sell, you can pay off the debt and make some money."

"I don't want to sell," I said, furious at this absence of logic: the payments on our house would have continued had my parents not been microwaved by bad heating boards. Why, in death, should they get fucked again? I took a breath so as to not lose my temper, gripping the chair's sides until my fingertips hurt. From my seat in his small office, I could see that two girls I'd known from high school were waiting to speak with a teller. They'd noticed me. I had a faint memory of being at a party with one of them years ago.

"What about asking relatives?" he suggested. "Might be a good way to raise some funds?"

"Again, no," I said. He looked down at the notes on his desk. "What I mean is, that's not really an option," I explained. "I don't have any relatives to call on."

"What about their wills? They had pensions, right? Have they been paid out?"

"The people in charge of that aren't doing anything for me,

man. They won't even answer my emails."

"Sorry to hear, but if you can work that out, it will help with some of these payments," he said. "Either way, once you make a decision, let me know and I can help settle the paperwork."

Bruce showed me the door, where we shook hands and he gave me a sympathetic shoulder squeeze. With my head down, I walked out without acknowledging the girls (I couldn't bear another explanation of how things were going) and was met by a cloudless sky outside. From across the strip mall parking lot I noticed a Money Mart offering "cash today." In front of its storefront window were two people who appeared upset with one another. A sun-beaten man in the sort of khaki pants you could unzip into shorts was wagging his finger in a woman's face, his other hand in possession of a crumpled piece of paper. I spat on the ground and kicked a crushed bottle of coke. Then I remembered there was still another way.

"You want to get with Eddy?" Patty asked, taking a bite of his sandwich. Back at the apartment, he was lying on our ripped couch, waiting for a talk show paternity reveal.

"Right away."

"I thought you turned him down?" he asked, still staring at the television. Patty pulled out a tin and began to pack it.

"I reconsidered and need to talk to him now." Patty wasn't listening to me from his position on the couch. Onscreen, Maury Povich was teasing his studio audience with the coming test results. I walked over to stand in front so he couldn't see.

"Fuck, okay! Why so urgent?" he asked, spitting into a blackened bottle.

"I need to pay a debt or they're gonna take my parents' place," I said, extending my hand for the tin. I snapped the chew into place and placed a pinch into my lower gum.

"Wow, really? The treatments for your old man?" he asked. I nodded. "That's a good spot," he said. "Hold onto it for a while and when the market goes up you can sell."

"Just fire him a message, okay?" I said, indifferent to his financial advice. "I can't let this slide, or I'll end up in a doorway on Sainte-Catherine."

"Alright bud, no problem." Patty got out his phone and started texting. I sat down and looked out of the living room window onto Drolet. Across the street, a homeless man, new to our neighbourhood, was screaming about someone having stolen his shopping cart.

In a rising voice that undermined the seriousness of the information he was delivering, Maury revealed his results. A mulleted paternity-denier began insulting the crying woman who maintained he was the father.

Five minutes later, Patty's phone buzzed. "Wally's on Sainte-Catherine," he said, looking up. "Three this afternoon."

5.

"He's a motherfucker, the guy. No? Never did nothing for nobody."

"Remember that showdown outside Célestes, where the dealer — that fat kid with the fake Lambo who talked like his uncle was President of the Middle East — started talking shit to him?"

"Got his dick nearly shot off." Laughter was followed by sounds of rehydration.

"I have a problem," I said. Eddy and I were sitting in a booth at Wally's, a downtown sports bar. Several of his men were in the adjacent table, talking about somebody they thought was set to be released from jail. On the TVs, Gary Bettman was speaking to reporters about the pending lockout, his head bobbing along to another verbose explanation. It didn't look like there would be an NHL season this year, but no formal announcement had been made.

"What is it?" he asked, not breaking eye contact. I explained that my parents' debt would have to be paid in order to keep our house. When I told Eddy of the amount, he winced. Behind him, the NHL Commissioner had exited and some TSN analysts were parsing Bettman's newspeak.

"You don't want to let that thing go, eh?" he said. "I don't blame you. It's all you got left. I'm sorry that happened, man, ostie." Eddy shook his head.

"I'm not giving that house back." I responded. Eddy looked from his drink to me.

"Exactly, fuck 'em. Whether it's the government, the hospitals…" Here he stopped, overcome by the unfairness of it all. "They tax you every way they fucking can, sacrament. When my mom died, they tried to take away her house, too."

"Yeah, well, that's not going to happen here," I said. Our waitress returned and I took a long sip of the cold beer she provided.

"So," he continued, "do you want a loan?"

"Not exactly. What we talked about the other night…"

"The half-sheet?"

"Yes."

Eddy paused for a moment. "You want to do it?" he asked, finally.

"I do."

"Are you sure?"

"Yes."

"Are you reliable?"

"I am."

"You going to be everything Patty said you would be?" As Eddy's posture straightened, his pecs pushed outward over the stomach, folding his golf shirt onto itself. I nodded, yes, meeting his eyes.

"How much is the debt again?" he asked.

"Two hundred and twenty-five grand." Eddy whistled.

"If you handle things right, you'll be able to pay it back. As for the *how*, you can talk to Karim about that." Eddy nodded to one of his underlings — a short, slim Arab, likely a few years older than me, dressed in a black Dolce and Gabbana tracksuit — who was seated by the bar.

"I think you can do this," he continued, "but no fucking around." Here Eddy's tone changed. "Karim has a sheet, too, so talk to him about what not to do. I need to see weekly returns, okay? So you gotta learn how to lay off risk. And you gotta be able to collect. But if you do it right, you'll have more than enough cash on hand. In the meantime, get yourself a legit source of income. To start, I'll put you on my payroll at the boxing gym. You can't be making big purchases, though. In fact, don't make any big purchases at all, it's stupid, so stay quiet — but if you're going to pay that debt off first, you won't be doing that anyway. If you gotta collect and a guy doesn't have it, make a plan for him."

"Thanks Eddy."

"You got it, bud. But can I rely on you?" he asked, a final assurance of servitude.

"Absolutely."

"You can't be careless with this shit."

"I won't," I said, "I'm careful."

"You ain't gonna be talking too much?"

"Never." Eddy extended his hand for me to shake, staring into my eyes.

"One sec," I asked.

"Yeah?"

I pointed to the TV behind him. "What about this?" I asked. "That's gotta be a huge slice of the business, no?"

"We're gonna be creative. Just 'cause hockey's not on don't mean these guys won't be betting. I got a couple of ideas to work out. Okay tough guy, Karim's going to talk with you now." Eddy patted me on the shoulder and got up to leave, motioning to Karim, who came over and deposited his small body into the booth. He called the waitress over, pulled a handful of cash from his pocket and paid the bill Eddy left, asking first for two more beers. "What's up, bro?" he said. "You're good with the numbers, right…?"

The next day, I spent the entire afternoon watching college football. I would have around twenty-five bettors underneath me, and for the first week I'd watch the lines to get a sense of how they moved. My duties would start the following Friday, when I'd pay people out and collect from those whose opinions had met reality's bulwark. The bets were registered on a website we gave gamblers access to, and I could see that ten thousand was already in play for the first slate of Sunday NFL games. Most of the bets were small, but one man, whom Karim referred to as a whale "with half a fucking brain," came in for over five thousand.

"Premium Sports Betting" had a simple green and yellow interface that even a novice bettor could navigate easily. By selecting a sport in the left column and moving to its specific page, bettors could wager on most events (the priority for guys here, he said, was hockey and football). We had updated odds posted every day (and sometimes on an hourly basis, like during NFL Sundays). A bettor's credits — which corresponded to the amount of money he had in reserve, and which we would adjust when they needed more, even if the gambler was in debt — were displayed on the screen's top right corner. There was even a mechanism that allowed you to make sophisticated parleys by picking multiple outcomes, with the odds changing beside the hypothetical bet as its degree of implausibility grew. This, I was told, was the third iteration of Eddy's site, which twice previously had been shuttered to stave off police investigations.

"Bets'll be coming in all day, bro," he told me. "You just gotta keep track of things. If you can get into a situation where there's too much action on one side, we'll lay some of that shit off." His explanation for how this would occur was unclear and involved placing a bet with someone else under an alias. For now, my best hope was for everyone to lose, as Eddy promised they usually did.

To monitor our risk exposure and ensure it remained balanced, Karim recommended hedging for half-sheet guys. This way we wouldn't get devastated by one side of the ledger, like in instances where everyone won by taking the favourite. Richer bookies like Eddy could afford not to obsess over risk because they had enough in reserve to pay off losses. For us, a more conservative approach was required.

Patty was along for the first Sunday of the NFL's regular season. Our plan was to meet Karim at Wally's later, but during the afternoon we'd watch from our living room. Of the thirty-five registered bets, twenty-two were losing. We had a couple beers and listened to beefy men in suits scream at one another during the halftime intermission.

"How many guys you got on the sheet?" Patty asked me, dripping black saliva into his spittoon.

"About twenty-five."

"You gonna recruit more?"

"That's what Eddy wants."

"You should start taking action at school," he said. "We both know a hundred guys who'd wanna wager with you." He was right, as that afternoon at least five friends came over to watch football before moving on with their days. All were betting through the province's parley system, whose odds were terrible and required you to place multiple bets because of antiquated match-fixing laws.

As the afternoon wore on, bets started coming in on the four o'clock games. The action was moving too far on one side so I texted Karim about whether to lay off with another bookie. He messaged back to say we'd wait.

By seven-thirty, the four o'clock games were over, and we

were up by twelve thousand when Patty and I went down to Sainte-Catherine. In the same booth where I sat with Eddy yesterday, Karim greeted me like we'd grown up together. He had a new tracksuit on: black with green and red trim, and a golden chain that stood out against his white Armani tee.

"Day's going well," he said. "No problems so far. A lot of shit'll be coming in during the last couple quarters when guys wanna chase."

We sat down and had dinner. Clustered around the sports bar were divorcees drinking beer and watching football. Spontaneous conversations started whenever a notable play or injury provided conversational opportunities to combat loneliness. Friends of Karim's came and went throughout our meal. They would meet us for an hour or two, talk about their money problems, the girls who didn't want to fuck them and those who couldn't get enough, and then depart for a vague appointment.

"You know what comes next, right?" Karim asked me. "Depending on what happens with the Monday nighter, you'll have a lot to collect on Friday." Karim smirked while he said this.

"You ready for that?" he asked.

"Ready for what? Why you smiling?"

"We're giving you a guy for the first week, okay? He's going to help you collect. Wait until you meet this dude," he said, laughing.

"I can do it on my own, no?"

"You'll have to eventually, bro. For now, we'll give you some muscle. The guys you're picking up from are nothing to worry about, but they need to know we're not fucking around when you show up for the first time, okay? This legend you'll have with you…" he said, smiling, "I don't even know shit about hockey but this guy—" Karim laughed to himself.

It was now past eleven, but I kept remembering this didn't matter: I didn't have anything to wake up for, and while Patty did, it didn't stop him from ordering another round. His speech had become laboured.

"Let me know if you need help," he said, having overheard our conversation about collecting. "I'm here for whatever you need. You owe me, anyway," he continued, with a boozy, jack-o-lantern grin.

"What for?" I asked.

I could see Patty organizing his thoughts. "You owe me a chance," he said.

"At?"

"Making money. You wouldn't be here without me."

"I'm only here 'cause of one reason…" I said, pointing towards my wallet, where a picture of my parents popped out of a credit card slot. "When the debt gets paid you can take this over, 'cause I'm only doing this shit until it's taken care of." Patty took a slow sip of his drink and nodded, looking away. To my left, Karim was texting a girl he wanted to meet up with.

"Come on bud," I said to Patty. "Let's go home." I paid the tab and we left.

Our sheet made ninety-three hundred for the weekend. Of this, I would earn half. I felt a moment of deep satisfaction when, after depositing the cash on Wednesday morning (paid early to me by Eddy as a welcome gift), I explained to a halfway inquisitive bank teller that these were proceeds from several large items belonging to my dead parents, which I sold for cash (he said nothing further after "dead parents").

On Thursday the NHL initiated its lockout. The league was arguing with its players about instituting a salary cap, but I cared nothing about these details and was only concerned insofar as it would make our jobs more difficult. There was endless talk on television about spats between "arrogant millionaires" and the immediate futures of players who wouldn't have a league to play in this year, but I tuned most of this out: there were more immediate things to do.

That Friday, I had to collect and pay out. This involved driving around with Maxime "The Woodchipper" Doucette, who, with some effort, squeezed himself into the passenger's seat of my small sedan that morning, thanking me for picking him up at his Ville-Émard townhouse. I had no idea what sort of arrangement he had with Eddy, but Maxime was likely making a few hundred dollars to spend a couple hours sitting in the car beside me. He sipped from a Tim Hortons cup.

"Excited to play tonight?" I asked on our way to the first stop. The regular season for Maxime's semi-pro league started today.

"Not really," he answered in French, yawning as he leaned back in the chair, "but I'll be ready by game-time." Maxime, who occupied every centimeter of my passenger seat, looked like a grizzly bear occupying a wood stump. Unshaven, with a goatee and short black hair, he stared out at the road, his eyes partly covered by an Expos hat.

"Can I ask you something?" I began.

"Of course, buddy."

"Are you nervous, knowing you gotta fight?"

"A little bit, but it's a good nervous, you know?" I didn't. "Makes you feel that pop. I've been in hundreds of 'em, man. Yes, it's risky but I'm probably not going to see any shit tonight I haven't before."

When we pulled up to our first stop in Kirkland, the gambler was already outside, pretending to busy himself with yard work. A skinny man in his early thirties, he came down the driveway and approached my car in short, tight strides. I rolled down the window and he leaned in towards us. His face was drawn and creased at the eyes, as though belonging to someone older. I could smell his morning coffee.

"Next time, can we meet in a parking lot?" he asked.

"No problem," I said. He produced an envelope from inside his sweater.

"Twenty-one hundred," he said, handing it to me.

"Thanks." I was about to drive off when Maxime nudged my shoulder.

"Count it," he said, softly. The bettor had turned to walk up his driveway. I moved my hands through the stack of bills. He was short.

"For fucks sake. Hey!" I called out, motioning for him to come back. He looked like someone caught coming out of the shower.

"You're short two bills."

"Are you sure?" he stammered. I flipped through his envelope and handed him the money.

"I had no time to hide it," I said. Beside me, Maxime smiled.

"Fuck, sorry, honest mistake buddy," he said, looking back to his house. "I don't have it now, but I'll get it to you this week."

"This week?" I asked.

"That a problem?" he asked. I couldn't tell what level of threat he represented and then remembered Maxime was beside me.

"Why not today?"

"What? Come on?" he said. I could sense Maxime's body flex beside me. "That was never the way it used—" he began.

"—You got the slim envelope," I said. "It's not a lot. Try for today." I said this in a soft voice, one I hoped would communicate a firm expectation.

"I'll message you," he answered. The gambler turned around to walk inside. I watched as he closed the front door of his townhouse.

"He may have been testing me," I said to Maxime.

"You passed," he said, taking a sip of his coffee.

"Having you here didn't hurt." Maxime slapped me on the shoulder. I pulled a tin out of my pocket and offered it to him. He smiled for the first time.

"Holy Christ bud, right when I needed a pinch, calice!" he said, gesturing to his empty coffee cup. "I always finish with one." Maxime started packing the tin, offering it to me before he took a tumor-sized mound. The dip was fresh and moistened the tips of my thumb and middle finger.

That morning's other collections took us across the West Island. The other bettors paid in full, and several times I saw their faces change from annoyed resignation to forced friendliness when Maxime came into view. One of the gamblers, Stu Boudreau, had gone to my high school. A football player, he was a few years older than me, and I remembered how he walked the hallways in expectation of people getting out of his way (Stu possessed an anger particular to Canadian football players who loathed their secondary place on the sports hierarchy). While I think he still lived in NDG, Stu asked to meet at a Tim Hortons in Pointe-Claire. When we arrived at the parking lot, he was waiting in a City work truck.

"Waddup man?" he said, getting out of his car. "I *heard* you take action now! Who the fuck told me that?" he asked himself, scratching his head. Stu looked from me to Maxime.

"How ya doin'?" I said. Stu handed me his envelope, looking back again towards Maxime. Probably twenty-four now, he was forty pounds heavier than in high school and appeared to be on steroids. None of this registered with Maxime: lost in a tobacco bliss, he didn't even look at Stu.

I counted the envelope's contents. When I finished, Stu began to speak — looking toward Maxime, hopeful he was listening.

"So no hockey this year, eh," he said.

"Nope."

"Then I better be good with the football," he said, smiling.

"You should be an expert," I said, "from what I remember."

He shrugged his shoulders. "Win some, lose some," Stu said, looking from me to Maxime. "Can't lose too much though, or I won't be allowed back at Célestes!" He then began a story about being thrown out of the champagne room when two strippers fought over the privilege of having sex with him.

I hated myself for pretending to laugh at his story. "You'll always be allowed back, but you need bread to truly enjoy it. Anyway, thanks bro," I said, eager to leave. Stu signed off, walking back to his work truck. I rolled up my window.

"That guy's a pussy," Maxime said, still staring forward. "Anyway, you need a spot they can come to," he continued. "A cafe or something, makes things easier."

"Doesn't that make it easier for the cops to see who's coming and going?"

"Only if you're not careful," he said.

I told Maxime that my dad had taken me to see him during his QMJHL days. He asked whether we still went together, and I told him what happened. Maxime covered his mouth and nose in the manner one did when told of something terrible.

"I'm so sorry, buddy," he said, shaking his head. "What the fuck man?"

"All good," I responded. "That's why I'm here." I told him about the debt and my plan to pay it off. Maxime slapped my shoulder in approval. From there, he kept me entertained throughout the rest of our ride, and seemed to come alive as the morning moved closer to his game, inventorying the best opponents of his career: from names I'd known in the NHL to semi-pro legends I'd heard about from friends familiar with the league he played in. He had an eight-year-old daughter,

Angélique, whom he shared custody of with an ex-girlfriend. She wasn't with Maxime this weekend.

Our last collection was in Laval. The bettor lived on a winding street of Versailles-plagiarized mansions, each a monument of gray rock and gaudy trim. When we arrived there was a Porsche SUV in the driveway, but I saw no evidence of its owner. The house had one of those anvil knockers I was unsure of how hard to hit, so I clacked it twice against the expensive door and could hear heavy feet walking in my direction. When it opened, a large, Mediterranean-looking man with a stubbled chin appeared.

"Hold up bro," he said, his tone icy.

"Sorry."

"You're his new guy?" he asked.

"I am." He didn't have an envelope and looked behind me to the car, where Maxime was sitting.

"Who you got with you, bro?" he asked.

"Maxime Doucette."

"One sec," he said, turning back towards the kitchen. He didn't appear to be working or perhaps had a job that kept him at home. In the kitchen's distance, I could see a distrustful poodle staring at me. When I shifted my weight, it began to bark, its fur fading into the kitchen's white ceramic backdrop. The dog was ridiculous. Soon the man reappeared to provide the envelope. I began counting but he cut me off.

"It's all there, bro," he said, looking down at me from his elevated position.

"It is?"

"You don't believe me?"

"I believe you."

"Tell Eddy to loosen up his lines," he said.

"I'll pass on the message."

"I'm kidding, bro," he continued, "maybe it's you who's

gotta loosen up. What's your name, anyway?" he asked.

"Teddy." He held out his hand for me to shake. A golden pinkie ring pushed against my finger.

"Sil," he said. "Thanks for coming, bro. Tell Eddy hi and that Mikey's looking to settle up."

"I'll let him know." I turned around and walked back to the car. In the driver's seat I went through his envelope. Everything was there. I nodded to Maxime.

"You gotta get home. Pre-game nap soon, no?" I asked him,

"After I eat something, yes."

We drove back to Longueuil in silence. In several hours, Maxime would be driving in the opposite direction for his game against Laval, and when we got to his house — its driveway dominated by a large pickup — I pulled a hundred-dollar bill from the envelope and handed it to him.

"This is on top of what Eddy's giving you."

"No. Thank you, but no, T. Just give me a pinch and I'm good, bud."

"Then I'm giving it to the next homeless guy I see," I said, holding up the bill. He smiled and snatched it from my hands.

"What are you doing tonight?" he asked.

"No plans."

"Come to our game," he said. "We'll go for a beer afterwards. I'll leave a ticket for you."

I pulled the tin from my pocket and handed it to him. Maxime protested but I assured him there was an entire log at home. He laughed and took it from me, emphasizing his exit with a tap on the hood of my car.

"Great to meet you, bud," Maxime said, turning towards his house, where he would sleep in preparation for the night's violence.

6.

I hadn't been in the Colisée de Laval since playing in a high school hockey tournament five years ago. A 'House of Pain' banner — the arena's pirate flag — hung from the rafters, and when I arrived, pushing my way through the bikers and beer girls selling Molson Dry in a saturated, excited lobby, there were already fifteen hundred people here for the warm-up. I had never been to one of these games and knew the league only by its reputation. This was the first night of its regular season — one where, in the NHL's absence, the St. Lawrence Senior Pro League (SLSPL) was the only game in town.

Laval wore yellow and blue, while at the other end Saint-Jean went through its opening drills in orange and black. I walked the length of the arena, ducking underneath low support beams to find a seat near where Doucette was warming up. I noticed him at once. He was the largest player on the ice — with rounded shoulders that filled an overstretched jersey — and its most spastic. Toward the warmup's end, after striding the length of the red line to sow fear in the other team, Doucette began shadowboxing by the boards before barrelling off the ice, drawing jeers from a group of locals — all dressed in ski-doo jackets — who'd been taunting him from behind the glass.

Once the game started and there appeared to be almost four thousand people in the small arena, I took a seat close to the Saint-Jean bench. The Laval fans seated behind appeared to forget about the game, leaning over the railing to shout insults at the players, some of whom spent most of the period turned around, chirping back at their tormentors. The degree to which fans felt emboldened to insult people who could shitkick them was always hilarious to me, and one of the principal terrorists, likely in his sixties, too old to be doing this sort of thing and conspicuous in clothing that didn't have a racing logo on it, insulted Maxime through his cupped hands. The Woodchipper didn't respond.

Doucette took only two shifts in the first period and moved with surprising agility for such a big person. I could see him yelling at his teammates to hit harder, and even from the bench he was a difficult figure to turn away from. Francois Coude, the Laval heavyweight who had once played a hundred or so games for the Los Angeles Kings, was his obvious target, but to the dismay of the violence-oriented fans they didn't meet during the first period: Coude was playing on the second line and trying to score.

"First game of the fucking season and no fight in the first fucking period," a man beside me said to his friend in French.

When Saint-Jean returned to its bench for the second period, a group of Laval fans leaned over their bench to insult Maxime in French. Every so often, one of his teammates would turn around and exchange with them.

"Fuck you Doucette tabernak, you twatty fucking ostie cunt!"

"Spot-picking trash should be bouncing in a whorehouse, sacrament!"

In the second period things became hateful. This came as a relief to the throng of boys to my right, several years younger than me and each with a lollipop-sized chunk of dip in their lower gums, who were yelling "ostie pussy" at Maxime. Two fights broke out in the first minute, even if they were uneventful: frustrating tussles between middleweights (one, a fat brown-skinned man whose gruesome strides the fans laughed at whenever he attempted an honest shift) that resolved without any punches landing. These were mere appetizers.

Five minutes later, Maxime and Coude found themselves opposite one another for the first time. They may as well have been the only two people in the world at that moment, and when Doucette spoke to Coude from within inches of his face, the same boys elbowed one another so as not to miss what they'd come to see. In what must have been an eternity for both men, they crouched low on the faceoff, in sham expectation for the puck to be dropped. Coude had fought three hundred and seventy-one times before, many of these against men on Maxime's level, but I felt afraid for him in this moment: the Woodchipper could hurt you.

Once the puck was dropped, both men removed their helmets and circled one another. Maxime's face had twisted into a psychotic glare, while Coude wore a look of resigned seriousness. The courting began in Laval's defensive zone and ended at centre ice, where they met and grappled. Maxime eventually freed his left to land a barrage of punches on Coude's face. On the fifth blow, which ended squarely on his jaw, the former NHL heavyweight turned stiff-legged and fell to the ice. It was unclear whether he lost consciousness.

As Maxime was escorted away, his shoulders still flexed in rage, one of the Laval middleweights (believing himself beyond Maxime's anger), said something insulting to the Woodchipper, who punched him in the shoulder. This drew a crowd and some pushing ensued. Maxime eventually made his way to the box and yelled at Coude from across the ice. Around me, the fans were laughing, ecstatic there was something to be mad about.

Inspired by the violence, a dozen or so fans started taunting Maxime from behind the Saint-Jean penalty box. The Woodchipper seemed to have regained his composure and didn't move, while several feet away the referees and timekeeper discussed which penalties to parcel out. This took longer than it should have, and fifteen minutes elapsed between his fight and the resumption of play.

Minutes later, there was more excitement when the group bothering Maxime got a reaction. They were standing at least fifteen feet away (and far enough out of range that if he somehow scaled the glass they could escape), each with both hands cupped around their mouths to amplify the insults. Perhaps it was his past they referenced, or a member of his family, but Maxime turned around and began talking back. I couldn't be sure of what he was saying, but the Woodchipper started pointing towards the exit as an instruction for them to wait outside after the game. This went on for several minutes until Maxime turned around and sat down. Upset their conversation had ended, his critics began inching closer to the penalty box until a security guard came over and pushed them back up into the upper seats.

With two minutes left in the second, Maxime took another shift. (He had been given a five-minute major and additional ten-minute misconduct for pushing one of the refs after he tried to attack Coude). He played little as Saint-Jean fought its way back into the game, receiving no challenges as the skilled forwards on his team scored three goals to make the score 5-3.

Late in the third period, Maxime had a fine moment. With his team leading, he earned a rare shift and showed some modest skill when he unloaded a slapshot the Laval goalie caught in his trapper. For this he received a sarcastic cheer from his throng of haters. The Woodchipper responded by aping a Degeneration-X salute and the referee then dismissed him from the game.

"Doucette won't take shit from any of these goofs," a familiar voice said behind me. It belonged to Sil, whom I'd taken money from earlier that afternoon. Behind him was a smaller man, wearing a black tracksuit.

"Hey Sil, hockey fan?"

"This guy cleaned me out this morning," he said, speaking to his friend. "My buddy sponsors the team," Sil went on, directing his finger to an advertisement on the boards for a local strip club. "I come every once in a while. If the Woodchipper's in town I can't miss that shit." He was sipping on what appeared to be a rum and coke.

"He's worth the ticket," I said.

"Well, I don't pay, bro," he declared. I returned to the rink, as Saint-Jean had just scored to make the game 6-3. With a minute left, and the outcome beyond doubt, Laval's coach sent out a line of goons and the crowd's mood improved once it realized there would be more fighting.

"I've known Ed for a long time. He's a good guy," Sil said, as one of Saint-Jean's forwards pretended to suck his thumb before the Laval bench. "He needs good people around him," he went on. "And he's gonna need good people around him." Across the rink, Maxime had emerged from the changeroom and was taking pictures with fans. "You're in a tough business, and competition's gonna pick up," Sil said.

"How's that?" I asked. The puck was dropped, and four players started fighting. After one of the Laval middleweights was pummeled, people started throwing beer cups at the Saint-Jean player being led off the ice. There had been, I think, six fights tonight, and the game provided enough violence to offset any disappointment about seeing the home team lose. We watched in silence as the tussling continued.

"Some guys'll be coming out soon," Sil said, now close to my ear. Before I had the opportunity to respond, Maxime had appeared at my side and put his hand around my shoulder. I could feel the Laval fans — whose attitudes towards Maxime had softened, now that they weren't separated by glass — look on with envious respect.

"Chipper! How are those knucks?" I asked, pointing to his hand.

"Still there," he said. Across from us, Sil shifted his weight, so I introduced them. The Italian was only a couple of inches shorter than Maxime, but fatter, with loose skin that sloped from his chin into the neck, like an inverted sail. In contrast, Maxime was gladiatorial.

"Nice scrap tonight," Sil said, "Coude picked the wrong guy."

"I picked him," Maxime responded.

"Well, looks like you guys won 'em all tonight. Anyway, we gotta go, Teddy," Sil said, nodding to Maxime as he shuffled by. The fans loitering around Maxime moved out of Sil's way.

"We picked up from that guy today," I told Maxime. His eyes became wide.

"That fuck in Laval? He say something to you?"

"No, just announced himself. Said something about competition picking up soon."

Maxime shook his head. "Let's go for a beer."

Mid-pint with Maxime and some of his teammates at a Laval bar, I received a message from Patty. "Véronique was asking me about you again. Send the girl a message…"

After a few introductory texts, we agreed to meet the following night at a Spanish restaurant on Saint-Laurent. Stepping out of my cab, I was met by a bachelor's party. The lads were drunk, parading in front of them a tubby thirty-year-old in a beige bodysuit, over top of which a red thong was stretched. They were making comments at the girls who passed.

I entered the restaurant and was welcomed by a dark-haired hostess who led me to our table, on whose surface sat a red candle. Within minutes a waiter appeared. I ordered a drink and enjoyed the atmosphere. There were a few other couples on dates, leaning in to speak with one another, tables full of friends and a lone drinker, staring forward in rumination over past misdeeds.

Ten minutes later, Véronique appeared. I watched as a bearded patron glanced at her backside while it maneuvered through the aisles. We hugged and she sat down, though only after excusing herself for being three minutes late. Véronique's body, moulded and refined by the gym, was firm from within her black dress, and the candle illuminated her face as she spoke. She had flawless, creamy skin and ample lips that always seemed on the verge of smiling. Her blonde hair had been tied back, which emphasized high, rounded cheekbones that made a subtle ridge over her cheeks. The contour of her eyes — dark green, lubricated and fully opened — were tracked by a thin film of black eyeliner.

"How are you?" she asked, smiling. "I wasn't sure if we were ever going to meet up."

"Been busy, but wasn't because of a lack of interest," I said.

She smiled. One could get away with anything if your story was sad enough. A waiter appeared and she ordered a cocktail. I asked Véronique about boxing and whether she'd stay on with Pugilistica.

"That was only for a school credit. I won't be back."

"Was it a good experience?"

"Yes…" she said, organizing her thoughts. "I learned a lot, but boxing isn't really my thing. It's upsetting. Seeing people beaten. I don't enjoy that." As a young girl she saw a hockey player knocked unconscious during one of her father's family outings (the league Maxime played in had a team in her hometown). He convulsed on the ice as a halo of blood formed around his head.

"Is boxing as messed up as people say?" I asked.

"Hard to say. I wasn't really close to it. I just helped organize events and tried to get the word out for each one. So I don't really know. Lots of interesting characters. It's very different."

"Go on…" I said.

"There was this judge…" she said, stopping herself as she smiled and shook her head.

"Oh yeah?"

"I can't believe I'm telling you this," she said, "but there was this judge — he's still around — who started talking to me more and more at the fights. An older guy. I don't know how he got my number, through the media contact guide, maybe? Anyway, out of nowhere, he started sending me pictures of his dick. Can you believe that?"

I burst out laughing and then stopped myself. "Jesus Christ," I said, shaking my head. "What'd you do?"

"I never answered. Eventually he stopped."

"You give this guy your number, or what?"

She laughed. "He probably got it off the company flyers we used to pass out at the fights."

"You ever tell your boss?" I asked.

"I was going to if he did it again."

"Sorry you had to deal with that."

"Whatever, he's an idiot. But beyond him, with boxing, there's just a lot of people I'm not used to being around, you know? People who…" here she smiled and paused.

"What?" I asked.

"Nothing. I don't know. I'm talking about people you see at the events. Tough guys, those types. But maybe I'm just reading into things. I really don't know. I'm not a prude or anything, but it was just kind of eye-opening. I never met those people growing up. Aren't you…?"

"Aren't I what?"

Véronique didn't finish her question. "You seem pretty interested in the company," she said, smiling.

"I liked the event, that's all. Good people watching." Véronique laughed when I said this.

"That's for sure!"

She asked about my dating history, and I told her about my two previous girlfriends, doing my best to speak about them with a vague respect. "So," she began, "would you say you're not a person who has to date?"

"No, I don't *need* to. I mean, it's worthwhile when you're with someone you like. Otherwise I'm fine to do my own thing. What about you?"

"I don't *need* to either," she said. "But, like you, if there's someone I like then I think it's worthwhile." Véronique told me that she once dated a player on the Concordia men's hockey team — pausing, mid-sentence, to tell me that she didn't gravitate towards hockey players — but that their relationship ended when he graduated and left Montreal to play minor pro somewhere in Europe.

"Well, *I* played hockey," I said, to which she laughed. I hadn't come close to the level of her ex-boyfriend and was dismayed by this.

"You're what, a numbers guy, not a hockey player?" I failed to hide my discomfort.

"What I mean is—" she began.

"I'm not really either, I don't know…" The waiter came over with our drinks. I stared at the floating ice cubes in my glass.

"You just need something to get excited about." She said this with an enthusiasm I couldn't quite understand.

"I guess. Hey — what else did Patty tell you about me?"

"Well," she began, "beyond what happened — and I'm so sorry, I kinda figured you wouldn't want to talk about it — but that you got a new job."

"I did." I took a sip of my drink and waited for her follow-up.

"That sounds kinda risky?" Véronique said.

"I have a big debt to pay, or I'll lose our house." Véronique's eyes glowed overtop of the candle.

"Patty told me that. Well, hopefully you can take care of it."

"What about you?" I asked. "What's your plan?"

"I want to do some traveling after I graduate. Want to come to France with me?" she asked, laughing at the idea.

"Of course," I said, smiling at her now without a trace of self-consciousness. Sitting cross-legged on the chair in front of me, bent over as she scooped cheese from the plate of chips I'd ordered, Véronique appeared at ease. Her black dress stood out against the restaurant's green and yellow — colours that became softer as the night aged. There was less pressure to make conversation and we took satisfied sips of our drinks.

By now it was nine-thirty, and while there were still tables eating dinner, the restaurant was transitioning into a bar. My forehead began to glow as I ordered one last beer, nodding in agreement with Véronique when the waiter appeared to ask if this would be our last round. I felt content, as did my date, who was giggling with greater frequency. "I need to stop," she said, "or else I'll be lying in bed all day tomorrow and I can't have that."

While I hoped things would unfold with an organic logic, I wasn't going to ask her back to my place (Patty was having people over) or my parents', and could only hope that she'd suggest one more at her apartment. It was now half-past ten and the waiter appeared with a bill for more than most people made in a day. She offered to split but I paid in full. Véronique thanked me and we walked outside, where partygoers made friendly gestures as they passed. I asked if she wanted to go for one more somewhere else. She smiled.

"I would love to, but I have things to do tomorrow and don't want to be too hungover."

"We can do it again soon," I said.

"Yes, for sure."

We stood in the street for a moment, smiling at one another. She grabbed both of my hands and pulled me into a hug, thanking me once more. I wished her a good night's sleep and from there we resolved to meet again as soon as we could.

I didn't want to get drunk with people Patty met that week and instead cabbed back to NDG, where I entered a quiet house and slowly walked up the creaking stairs, employing the light-footed technique I once relied on so as not to disturb my parents. Brimming with a happy sentimentality, I sank into bed and reached for my headphones. The ceiling lapsed in and out of focus as I closed my eyes and returned to an old obsession. The next morning's final memory of a fine night was the comforting surge of endorphins I experienced during Kanye's *All Falls Down*, whose third verse implanted itself in my memory, where it vibrated over and over, and over again.

7.

The bets came early on Sunday morning. Everyone identified the same weak line that I had pointed out to Eddy over text and picked the Packers (Green Bay's opponent, the Bears, were quarterbacked by the underwhelming Rex Grossman). As this was the Sunday Night Football matchup, it would be the day's biggest game. Otherwise, most gamblers chose the moneyline, with some less-than-savvy bettors parlaying multiple outcomes to increase their payout. While this was a bad strategy that didn't work, for the easily tempted, an absence of logic didn't mean the absence of action.

Life has few stories less interesting than a gambler's near misses — often recounted bar-side, the storyteller's beaten eyes glistening from boozy consolation — when a fumble, empty-net goal, missed free throw or pop fly conspired to rob them of a life-altering windfall. In the early days, before serious bettors began engaging with bookies, and when, just out of high school, we used the government's parlay system, this conversation would always be followed by the aggrieved man producing some crumpled ticket from his pocket.

The men betting with me today were either graduates of this system or long-time bettors who called their bets into a traditional office. I was dying to know what their lifetime success rates were, and — in the likely event they mostly failed — why they kept coming back.

Since most of the money went to the same teams, I wondered when our handicappers would alter the lines. If everyone bet the Packers and they won, my sheet would be carpet bombed. But if we adjusted the odds to make betting on Chicago more attractive and the Bears won, it would re-balance the teeter totter and distribute our risk more evenly. Of the two dozen people with me, about twenty had wagered and more action would come in before dinner.

Still at my parents', I called Patty to see if he wanted to watch the game and we met again at Wally's. Other people began to file in as the afternoon turned into evening, Karim among them, and we monitored the action together as more bets came in on the Packers (every hour, one of Eddy's underlings would text me updates on a separate cell phone of our betting balances and where the action was moving). For reasons I couldn't understand, our website — whose interface loaded slowly on a Blackberry I used for non-work communication and internet browsing — still had the same odds posted, even though we needed to move action towards Chicago in the event Green Bay won. I texted Eddy about this. He said they were "working on it," but why was this not done automatically?

Twenty minutes before game time, Eddy messaged back to say that a change had been made, and I verified the updated line on our website. Chicago was now paying eleven to one, but fifteen minutes passed without a bet being registered. Five minutes to kickoff, with the odds now at thirteen to one, someone (a person I didn't know, who hadn't wagered the previous week) registered a five thousand dollar bet on the Bears.

"Look at this shit," I said to Patty, absorbed in his nachos. "Some guy just put five dimes on Chicago."

"They see that line and get greedy," he said, pausing to secure some wayward cheese. "Easy fifty K for you though." I shook my head in disbelief of this business. Unlike drugs, with the army of police oversight and real possibility of getting shot, I put up no money of my own for this, provided no product beyond an interface on which to register a wager, and then collected money from people incapable of scaling back their greed.

The game would undermine my confidence. Playing behind a young quarterback who single-handedly lost their season opener when he threw a game-ending pick, the Bears defense intercepted Brett Favre twice and returned a fumble ninety-five yards just before halftime. I felt a pit growing in my stomach as the third quarter ended, and then anxiety when, in the fourth, the Packers offense punted on its first possession, was intercepted on the second, and then turned the ball over on downs with 1:18 remaining. The mysterious bettor, who made a lone wager all day, profited sixty grand from a five thousand dollar prediction on Chicago. In my second week on the job, I was beaten on the money.

It was hard getting out of bed the next morning. With yesterday's loss, I owed even more to Eddy (beyond what he gave me to cover the first two missed quarterly payments) and was now fifty-seven thousand, five hundred in debt.

This was to be the first shift at my 'official' new job as a manager at his gym. When I arrived that morning, the third cardio kickboxing class of the day had just finished and sweaty, middle-aged people were slowly walking back to the changerooms. Elsewhere, several young boxers, none of whom had appeared at the Métropolis event, hit heavy bags.

Eddy had a relationship with Pugilistica, whose fighters were allowed to train here for free. There were posters on the wall advertising the company's most recent cards, and framed photos of the company's boxers. When Patty speculated that the

Pugilistica had been financed by Russian criminals, he was perhaps only half-wrong.

Eddy asked me to meet him at ten, but he hadn't arrived yet. I sat down by the ring corner and looked at the pictures along the wall. The largest of these featured Olivier Rioux, a handsome young middleweight who was the company's biggest star. Beside him were images of the city's immortals: Durelle, Gatti and Hilton, as well as a glossy signed photo of Leonard-Duran. Twenty minutes later, Eddy arrived and pointed towards the office, where I sat down in a chair opposite his desk. He pulled a laptop from his bag and didn't appear bothered by yesterday's results.

"Do you have a piece of Pugilistica?" I asked. "I was looking at all those pictures."

"I've known Calix for years," he said in French, without looking up. "But no, not really. Anyway, it happens," he said, without me even broaching the subject. "We all took a bath on that game, sacrament, but there's nothing you could do. Well, almost nothing…"

"What did that guy know to put five dimes on Chicago?" I asked, rapping my cell phone against the table.

"You gotta be wary of a guy who only takes one game, ostie," he began. "It means he's done his research. The guys that bet the whole board, thinking they're going to run up some parlay, that's where we get over."

"Do you know this guy?" I asked. Eddy did.

"He can bet. Makes all his money gambling. On games, stocks, he's a real quiet guy. Still, he got a bit lucky yesterday."

"So what do I do?" I asked.

"You're down how much?"

"Thirty-five. Most of the wagers on Green Bay were small. Nothing over twenty-five hundred."

Eddy smiled. "Welcome," he said. "You'll get to know their habits better. Most guys have a limit, but you're not gonna see many individual bets that size. Usually a dime or two at most, but the guys on your sheet usually bring in smaller action. But next time, monitor the risk better. If you're vulnerable anywhere, lay some of that off, okay?"

"Okay." It felt like I was being lectured by my father.

"Guys'll be betting this week, so you're gonna make back some of that thirty-five," Eddy went on. "Otherwise, you're in the red until that gets paid back in full, you understand?" I did. "Come by the office on Friday morning to get your cash to pay out," he said. "You'll feel better by then."

8.

The playoff baseball bets wouldn't start until the following week, but by Friday I'd made only a few thousand back on my debt. When I arrived at the gym that morning, Eddy wasn't there. One of his underlings, a bulldog-faced Québécois named Maurice, took me into the back office and provided envelopes to distribute, including a bulky one for the person we owed sixty-five thousand to. I took the package and left to complete the drop-offs, not realizing it would have been easier to also collect on the way. (I was putting off this second task since I didn't have Maxime today. He was leaving early for a game in Jonquière.)

Handing money to winning gamblers was easy — laughter when I produced the envelope and a joke about things "being tense at the end." The final drop-off was for the biggest winner, who lived in an expensive townhouse on a spiraling Westmount street. I knocked several times on his door, but no one answered. Standing idiotically on the front stoop, I noticed a camera in the right corner over his door pointed in my direction, so I knocked again and could hear feet on the other side. The mail slot opened and a voice likely belonging to a man in his forties said, "Just slip it through." With some effort, I pushed the package into a pair of disembodied hands. "Thanks very much," he said with an odd dispassion.

The rest of my morning was spent picking up money and I had to visit seven bettors across the west end. Knowing who I was collecting for, none protested, and my route even took me through a doctor's office, where the young secretary who passed me the envelope, clearly ignorant to what it contained, smiled and wished me well. All of the counts were correct, and I placed them in a secret slot Eddy had me build into the glove compartment of my sedan. My last collection was at Sil's. He owed twenty-five hundred and would surely complain about some wrongdoing. Only now, I didn't have Maxime to discourage him.

I knocked on his door and Sil opened it at once. The curtains were drawn in his front window, and without saying hello he checked behind me to see if I was alone. At once he became relaxed and delivered the news I expected.

"I don't have it. I'll need another week, bro," he said.

"You don't have *any* of it?" I asked.

"No." Sil looked at me with the dumb, stubborn eyes of a dog refusing to cede its bone.

"When can you get it?"

"I told you, a week." He was starting to loom overtop of me.

"There's going to be a vig."

He smirked when I said this. "You just learn that word? Fuck your vig." I calculated my odds. Sil was advantaged by three inches and fifty pounds, and my last fight ended with temporary brain damage.

(I *have* been beaten up in my life. I was provided this experience two years ago, when a trashy patron at a downtown bar who thought I shoved him from behind (it was in fact a stupid college boy in search of the washroom) delivered six punches to my head. Though drunk myself, I remember the anxiety produced by this scenario, my sorry attempt to fight back, the thudding feeling of his knuckles cracking against my skull and then a slow, peaceful return to consciousness when the temporary black space into which I'd escaped was replaced by glossy bar lights and the concerned faces of friends. Before that, I'd fought several times as a child along with several minor incidents on the ice that resulted in little more than a swearing and some shoves.)

"Fuck the vig?" I asked. My face was getting hot.

"I've been a customer for years, bro. First time I was ever short. He'll be fine with it."

"I don't know about that," I replied.

"You're new to this. Trust me."

"We'll be in touch," I said, moving slowly away from his front stoop. With a joyless smile, Sil closed the door.

The shithole highway was packed along the way home. In the distance a hatchback had blown out its wheel and it took fifteen minutes to move half a kilometer. I thought about Sil and the stubble on his fat chin when he told me any payment would wait. The car in front of me was breaking every five meters, as if the driver had hiccups. I yelled in frustration.

"Sil had nothing," I said to Eddy when I got back to his office. Karim was sitting in a chair outside the door. He extended his fist for me to bump before I walked in.

"What? Why not?" Eddy said, looking up from the local real estate listings on his laptop.

"Said he needs a week and refuses to pay a vig. Said you wouldn't care because he's been a loyal customer."

"Where does that leave you?" Eddy asked.

"What do you mean?"

"What do I care about his reasons, tabernak?" Eddy asked, annoyed by the explanation. "You can't collect your money, Teddy? You going to let this guy make a clown out of you?"

"No…"

"Let him slip and he'll be a fuck forever," Eddy said, leaning forward on his desk. "How much are you in the red now, ostie?" he asked. "Over fifty K? And you're gonna let this fat asshole slip? How are you gonna pay back that debt, bud, the one on the house? That's why you're here, right?"

"Yes. So what's next?" I asked.

"What's next? What do you mean? You're a smart kid, right?"

"Yeah, well…"

"He thinks you don't have the heart for this," Eddy tendered, leaning back in his chair.

"So?"

Eddy's face hardened. "So? So what? You want to drag the stone or carry the whip, Ted? Handle this." He passed an extendable baton across the table.

I messaged Sil and told him we needed to meet. Later that night, he would be at the same strip club which sponsored Laval in Maxime's league, and I knew Sil wouldn't be alone. But Maxime was unavailable and Patty, who sometimes escaped whenever a bar fight broke out, would be useless in this scenario. On Eddy's instruction, Karim would come with me. I told him to wait in the car.

"What if he fucks around, bro?" Karim asked, concerned in my passenger seat as I drove us north along the fifteen.

"He won't, not in there at least," I said. "He's going to threaten me, but it can't go beyond that inside." Karim scrunched his face, uncertain of my logic.

"His buddy owns the club, they can pull you into a back room. What the fuck are the bouncers gonna do?" he asked. I told Karim of my plan and he relaxed, looking out the passenger's side window.

When we arrived at Panorama, I handed each of the bouncers fifty dollars and entered alone. It was a medium-sized club with only one stage, large and perfectly square. Pervert's row was contoured by a junior hockey team, and through a forest of limbs I could see Sil towards the back, sitting in a booth with two other men. Before they noticed me, I pulled over two dancers who were trawling the open floor.

"I'm going to meet a few guys in that back booth over there," I said. "If you entertain the two guys I'm *not* talking to for a half hour, I'll give you $150 each." I showed them the money. "I'll give you half now and leave the other piece with the coat check girl, but you can't take no for an answer, okay?"

"Why would they say no?" the taller of the two women asked.

"They're cheap, but I'm covering for them. You just can't tell them I've paid for it, okay? It's a little game we're playing." Both women agreed and I provided their halves.

"Just give me thirty seconds first." They nodded and I walked over to where Sil was sitting.

"My guy," he said. Sil's hateful morning eyes had turned arrogant. "We got something else to go over, bro?" One of the men with him had been at the game. The other, steroided and small-eyed, wore a black tracksuit zipped up to his chin.

"How are ya boys," I said, addressing all three. "The vig starts today. Gets added to the principle. Or we go with a schedule." At this, Sil laughed.

"*You're* expecting money from me? Now?"

"Whether it's today or a week from now." One of Sil's friends started to get up, but the dancers appeared and sat down before he could.

"Not now, girls," Sil said, but each had already wrapped her hands around one of his men.

"They just made a couple of new friends," I said. "You wanna talk here or someplace else?" I asked him.

"I don't want to talk at all. What the fuck's the matter with you?" he asked.

"Nothing, but the message stays the same. No breaks. That's all I came here to say."

"What are you going to fucking do about it?" he asked.

I turned and walked away. Both strippers continued to fondle his friends, and after leaving their money at coat check I reached the parking lot, where a group of guys my age were smoking. A hand appeared on my shoulder. Sil spun me around.

"You don't leave me, you little mick goof. You've been doing this for, what, two weeks?" I could feel his hot breath on my neck.

"Get your hand off me," I said, slow and deliberate. In the corner of my eye, I could see Karim getting out of the car. The group of smokers was watching us.

"You wanna free fuckin' hospital stay?" he yelled. Sil grabbed me by the neck and attempted to throw a right hand, but I ducked and punched into his beer keg stomach, whose fat I grabbed and twisted. Sil grunted and let out a short yelp, like a cat whose tail had been stepped on, and at once time appeared to slow down as we tussled in the parking lot, his fat body pressing against my arms. When Sil tried to stabilize my shoulders, I kicked him in the shins. He screamed, released his grip and then started reaching into his pants. Before he could produce whatever object was concealed, I pulled the baton out of my pocket and cracked the side of his jaw, my hand swinging like an orchestra conductor. This produced a musical, hollow pop, and his dumpy body fell to the ground, where Sil clutched his face and began to whimper. "Oh shit!" I heard one of the university kids say. I kicked Sil in the stomach and reached into his pocket, where I found a wad of cash and removed part of what he owed. He could barely react as Karim prepared to kick him in the ribs. I told him to hold off.

"He's done," I said, looking down at Sil. "*You* did this, you stupid fat cunt," I screamed at him before turning to the group.

"You saw him come after me, right?" I yelled at them. They all nodded together.

"Your stories better not change," Karim warned, turning

around to meet the group. I showed them a hundred dollar bill. "Show me your driver's license," I demanded. The leader hesitated for a moment, so I reached into my pocket. He pulled out his wallet, gave me the card and I memorized his name and address.

"Stay honest," I said, handing him the money. As we were getting into the car, Sil's two friends came outside. Karim immediately got out from the passenger's seat and started waving a baseball bat, screaming at both to back away. I didn't want the bouncers to become involved so from behind the wheel I told Karim to come back. He made a few more threats to Sil's friends, now tending to the beaten man, and then climbed inside. Once we pulled out of the parking lot, Karim laughed all the way back downtown.

"I can't believe that shit," he said, over and over. "I just— I can't believe that shit."

I drove back to the Saint-Laurent supper club where Eddy was eating. He was in a booth when I arrived, surrounded by several women and a man I didn't know (his stupid face, flushed by wine, was that of a square businessman in love with his gangster company). I walked up to the table but didn't acknowledge his companions. When Eddy saw me, he removed himself and we walked to the bar's other side.

"How'd it go?" he asked.

"Things got physical in the parking lot."

"What do you mean?" he asked. I pointed to my pocket where the baton remained.

"I won't give it back to you now," I said, "but it came in handy. Told him the deal and he followed me out. He grabbed me by the neck, so I cracked him."

"Holy fuck, T," he said. "You went into the club alone?" I told him yes.

"Karim jumped in?"

"Didn't have to."

"Christ," he said. "I could be using you for all sorts of shit now." Eddy's lips were wet with wine, but I couldn't tell if he was drunk.

"We probably haven't heard the last of this," I said. Eddy scrunched his face in dismissal.

"He's a loser," he said. "Doesn't threaten my guys."

"What happens now?"

"He complains. Threatens to get his cousins involved. Probably something like that." Eddy took a sip of his drink, and I could see an older man trying to listen over his shoulder, so I lowered my voice.

"Who's he with? Guys they make movies about?"

Eddy shook his head. "They won't make trouble. Sil always has an excuse. Always has a story to tell. They know he's a dummy. Don't worry about blowback. He ain't gonna do shit."

"I'm not worried," I said.

Eddy asked whether I wanted to have a drink, but sitting with these people was an impossibility. What did I care about real estate transactions and the bitter gossip being passed between insecure adults? Instead, Karim and I went across the street, paid our way into one of Montreal's most expensive clubs and bought a five hundred dollar bottle of champagne. Surrounded by women whose names I never remembered, my body, drained of energy for months, felt like someone plugged it into an electrical socket. Swaying in the hallway outside the men's washroom, waiting for my opportunity to go in, I saw my swaying reflection in the mirror, smiled, and felt vital, for the second time in months.

9.

Véronique came over to our house the following day. Still hungover at five o'clock, my head floating in a sea of calm water, I spent the day watching college football. She offered to cook but I suggested going for dinner near my house. (I wasn't ignorant to the anger of some people in Laval, so we'd stay somewhere local.)

When she arrived, stepping through the front door, Véronique looked around the small foyer before giving me a hug. We walked into the kitchen where I put her things down on the kitchen table. From her bag she produced a bottle of wine, asking first if I could turn down the television.

"That's really loud," she said. I hurried over to the converter.

"Is this all part of your new venture?" she asked, pulling out a chair to sit down at the kitchen table. I told her that it was, hopeful my short answer communicated this wasn't a topic to fixate on.

"It must be hard to keep all of these outcomes in your head," she said.

"Everything's recorded, or else it'd be impossible."

"Who'd have thought a boxing match would have brought you there?" she asked.

"Or you here."

She smiled and poured me a glass of red wine. I took a sip and could hear my throat move in the empty house, whose bay window to our black backyard was like a mirror. Véronique looked around the living room towards the rows of books on my parents' shelves. She walked over to run her fingers along their spines before studying the family pictures.

"These are really nice," she said, pointing to one of our small family by the Chrysler Building. Seven years ago, we saw Montreal play the Rangers at Madison Square Garden.

We both sat down on the couch to face one another. Véronique began telling me about her week and an office conflict that made an otherwise dull job entertaining. Her married female boss had started having sex with a male student and details of their affair had been whispered between the cubicles. I don't know how much she cared about the story (perhaps she was only trying to fill the dead space), but my brain looped back for the climax, which I laughed at, as it involved two men at her office nearly coming to blows by a photocopier. Véronique giggled and I got up to pour us another glass of wine.

"Do you know who's going to win this game?" she asked, motioning to Georgia-LSU on television.

"Georgia's gonna steamroll them," I said, despite not being able to name three players on the team.

"So how does all of this work?" she asked.

"I'm still figuring that out myself" I said.

"What have you learned so far?"

"No offense," I said, "but I don't really want to talk about this." The conversation paused. "I'm sorry," I said, "but it's probably just better if we don't. It's more boring than you think. For the most part it's just about spreading risk around."

Véronique smiled. After another glass of wine we walked down to an Italian place on Sherbrooke I'd last visited with my parents. The garganelli was delicious, and Véronique leaned in to scoop food from my plate, touching my hand in the infrequent moments when conversation stalled.

We talked of music and movies. She shook her head when I

confessed my hatred for Usher's *Yeah!*

"Don't be so judgemental, Ted," she said, playfully. "It gets people moving. There's nothing wrong with that. Music doesn't need a deeper meaning. That song's about the dancefloor, man."

Véronique hated *Reservoir Dogs* (an ex had made her watch it), only liked certain parts of *Pulp Fiction* but seemed to have come around for *Kill Bill*. I asked whether she'd seen *City of God*, but, confusing the titles, Véronique said she'd read part of the book in a university philosophy class.

"Are you a religious girl?" I asked. We were on opposite sides of the province's linguistic divide but united by our mutual connection to Catholicism. She laughed at my question and explained her family's Sunday trips into church. Conservative clothing. Confession, refreshments and gossip afterwards. She started talking about her mom's reaction to the *Passion of the Christ*, which she described as a protracted torture scene. (I hadn't been to church in half a lifetime, and sometime in the last few years a childhood fear of my fate being one of eternal suffering should my sins go unconfessed had stopped making monthly rent payments in my head.)

"But do you believe in that stuff?" I asked her. Véronique shook her head from side to side.

"I think there are some good things in there. You don't have to believe *all* of it, right?" she said, maybe sensing my skepticism.

"But you," I continued, "do you believe in it? Heaven, hell, all that stuff?"

She laughed out loud. "What's all this?"

"I'm just wondering." I said.

"I believe in God, or something like that. Do you?"

"I don't know. It's in the back of my mind from going to church as a kid. But is it true? Rotting in hell for watching porn. I don't know."

"I don't know if that would land someone in hell," she said.

"I hope not," I said. She laughed again.

"I don't think you should worry about it so much," she said. "You're a young guy, there's still time to save you." Véronique laughed and I became embarrassed at how seriously I took her joke.

"I'm not worried," I answered, uncertain about whether this was actually true. "Just a weird thing to think about, I don't know."

"Are you thinking about this because of recent events, or your new line of work?" Around us the restaurant seemed to pause.

"Why?" I asked, afraid of her rationale. Véronique shrugged her shoulders without smiling, her posture one of benevolent challenge.

Our conversation turned back towards movies and television. We both loved *The Sopranos*. Season five had ended that June and I admitted to not having understood Tony's dream at the Plaza Hotel. Véronique had at least read some theory in a newspaper column about it representing his clouded judgment. Despite not understanding her explanation, I was impressed.

We shared three different entrees and when it was over I asked if she wanted to come back. Véronique agreed, blood filling her cheeks, and we walked home together, the air pregnant with a mutual understanding. We entered the front door and started kissing. I felt a throb in my groin, but when we reached upstairs and her clothes had been removed, revealing a body I would obsess about over the following weeks, my instincts were muted by a racing mind. Véronique tugged and caressed, pulled and prodded, but a paralysis that started in the brain had seized my body.

"Is everything okay?" she asked. "Take your time."

"Sorry, maybe it's the booze" I said, desperate for her to leave.

"No problem," Véronique responded, her eyes focused on

the ceiling. We were both looking for an exit, lying naked beside one another. She grabbed my wrist and squeezed it.

"I'll call you a cab," I said. She smiled, hugged me and then left right away. I spat at myself in the mirror five minutes after she shut the door.

I had no time to worry about what happened. The following day, Karim and I spent all afternoon in a bar, figuring out how to best balance our risk. We laid off some of our action on another bookie to help even things (an operator in Anjou whom Eddy had instructed us to use), and after placing a few bets I could relax.

He was excited today, having told me before I sat down that his girlfriend, with whom Karim had an uneven relationship, was pregnant. As I lamented the improbability he'd ever experienced what I did the night before, the corners of Karim's mouth stretched into a wide and easy smile, and I bought a shot to celebrate. It wasn't planned but he was still happy.

"How much of that debt you pay back?" Karim asked, grimacing from the Jack Daniels.

"Hardly any." I still owed Eddy for the first two quarterly installments, in addition to thirty-five thousand for that hermit in Westmount. I wouldn't make any profit for a while.

"You hear anything back from that fat goof in Laval?" he asked.

"Silvio?" I asked, turning my attention from the television towards Karim. "No. Will I?"

Karim shrugged his shoulders and pulled out a small bag of weed. "If he wasn't related to who he is, nobody'd look twice at that guy."

"He's got cousins, right?" I asked.

"They've given a thousand beatings, would have done the same shit you did," Karim answered, not looking up from the tapered bat forming in his fingers.

"And they're coming out soon?" I asked.

"That's what I hear. But they won't be starting problems right outta jail, bro." I'd never seen anyone roll a joint that fast and asked the waitress for another beer (I hated smoking: after a year-long flirtation at eighteen, I started to form memories unrooted from reality).

"Things will change out here soon, though," Karim said, looking up towards the television.

"How so?"

"The book. Sil's cousins are gonna want to take it back."

"What's the book?" On screen, two announcers were yelling at one another during the halftime show.

"The book is everything," he said, turning around to face me. "It's the system. You own the book, you own gambling, you own loansharking. But different guys own different amounts of it."

"What does Eddy own?"

"He doesn't own anything. What we're doing is independent. But there's probably an agreement that he kicks a bit up to the guys allowing him to take so much action." Still fine-tuning the joint, Karim raised his eyebrows as he said this.

"Allowed?"

Karim explained how the Italians controlled bookmaking across the city. There were other men with bigger offices than Eddy's, and figuring out which bettors belonged to whom required negotiation between those who decided these things. Karim talked about this knowledgeably, as though he'd seen this scenario before, and it occurred to me that I didn't know much about his life: how he'd gotten here and what Karim had done in the milieu. His experience in all of this was still a mystery to me: unlike so many of the young guys, Karim rarely talked about himself.

"So what happens when these guys get out?" I asked.

"That's the question, bro."

My sheet made just sixty-two hundred that day. Some bettors made bad choices, taking parleys whose likelihood of success was near impossible. When a carpenter from Kirkland (who certainly couldn't afford to wager) had dropped five thousand, he put down two more near the night's end. But while I had occasion to celebrate small victories, other men showed better instincts and each time a winning bet was registered I felt a sour twinge in my gut.

Thirty-one hundred dollars richer but still in substantial debt, I realized that if we could manage risk and ensure the teeter totter always returned to level, the money would be there each week, and, at the very least, we would profit from whatever juice we built into the line. I hadn't figured everything out, so early into my career, but I could see that none of these bettors stood a chance — their gambling constitutions were such that, despite contradictory evidence, each man believed himself possessive of some special insight — and it was our job to ensure the chance, however illusory, was always there.

But even with this insight, my sheet needed to start making more. Thirty-one hundred didn't feel like an achievement and was less than what Eddy expected every week. When I told him of the result, he grunted, unimpressed, and returned to his real estate listings. The informal probationary period was ending, and I had to attract more action in order to keep my sheet. An anxious pressure seized my body as I tried to fall asleep that night: to ensure Eddy didn't regret giving me the opportunity *and* paying off my debt, I had to find more bettors. I needed to find another way. I had to accelerate things.

Véronique messaged about seeing a movie on Thursday. I couldn't meet her again and made an excuse, promising to get together "sometime soon." I had no plan of ever doing so, however, and in time she would understand.

Instead, I went to a party with Patty. When I came awake the next morning, lying in the wrong direction on my childhood bed, my memory of the night was a black void whose onset had begun in a strange kitchen. There was a pit in my stomach, but groping attempts to reconstruct what the brain hadn't documented were useless, and so I stared bleary-eyed at the floor, where several feet away my pants lay crumpled. Cash was strewn across the carpet. I could see my cell phone flashing.

I picked it up. There were eight messages from Patty, and two from an unknown number.

"Where'd you go?" Patty asked.

"What the fuck happened with that girl?"

"Where are you?"

And then, an hour later:

"Why'd you try and go me?"

His other messages were incomprehensible. But there were other texts, sent between the two blocks of Patty's messages, from an unknown number:

"lets meet you fucking clown"

And then:

"fuckin pussy Ill break ur head"

It was already noon. I called Patty, who picked up right away.

"What the fuck, man?" he asked.

"What?"

"You fucking snapped last night and tried to go everyone. What happened with that broad?"

"What girl?" I said, now anxious for the first time (and annoyed, as I always became, when someone recounted what you couldn't remember).

"The one you were talking to. Looked like it was going okay then something happened, and her boyfriend wanted to tilt." A milliseconds-long memory played on the faded theater screen inside my head: yelling, pushing and the intervention of a strong arm.

"I have no idea," I said, "I don't remember a thing. But I got a couple of messages threatening me."

Patty paused for a second. "I've never seen you like that before," he said. "You were fucking furious. The boys were shocked."

"Yeah, I don't know," I said, lying back in bed.

"What about the guy who texted you?" Patty asked.

"What's he going to do about it?"

Patty laughed in a manner I wasn't used to, but I was too exhausted to continue talking. We hung up and I went back to bed.

10.

The following Monday, Pugilistica took control of Eddy's gym. Calix King was holding an open workout for the media and fans, as well as to create a sense of team in his fighters, who were individualistic by nature and worked out of disparate gyms across the city. Without exception, the fighters were friendly, and in the space of two minutes I had over half a dozen black, white and brown hands thrust into mine. Olivier Rioux — the boxer King seemed most intent on pushing — said hello like he had been waiting to meet me.

I was struck by the size of their hands. One Haitian lightweight I didn't know, who was at least five inches shorter than I, took my palm into his and I felt like a child interacting with an adult. I asked in French who he was slated to fight next, and he mentioned a local name I had little knowledge of. With the introductions done, I took a step back and became inconspicuous. In every corner of the gym there were fighters training: skipping, shadow boxing, practicing their footwork by moving forward in measured steps, and some distance away two younger boxers devoted themselves to heavy bags.

In the ring, Rioux began warming up, shadowboxing his way around its four corners. He would spar with a young Montreal prospect whose style would prepare him for a spring opponent.

With his sloped, narrow shoulders and compact midsection, Rioux had a fighter's body. His power stemmed from the ability to torque his legs and midsection. A puncher (in my definition, someone who relies primarily on power to win), whose greatest asset hindered the development of his other skills, at some point in his maturation a trainer should have emphasized the improvement of his footwork or punch selection, but this never happened. Today, he wasn't different than the fighter who had lost twice in the past, only older. A savvy opponent would prey upon the weaknesses that to me, a virginal boxing watcher, seemed obvious.

Rioux's career stalled three years ago when he lost consecutive fights in Quebec. In the first, he was knocked out by an experienced Mexican; in the second, he lost by majority decision to a local fighter Rioux was expected to beat. An aggressive, come-forward puncher, he fought in the firebrand style adored by Montrealers. This manner — cast in stone by the city's forebears, whose moxie and recklessness the native fans loved — had doomed him against Felix Diaz, who easily boxed around Rioux's artless rushes. It was a character-quashing event: to lose by stoppage is dispiriting for a young fighter, and Rioux was tepid in his next match, which he dropped by decision to a Quebec City-based fighter named Cedric Villeneuve. Repeated losses pierced his reputation and he descended from a man to fear into an object of pity. After taking time away from boxing, Rioux returned to earn a string of victories, and while none of these opponents were very good, he was at least fighting with his former confidence. A handsome action-fighter, King was eager to move him fast. (One Sunday morning that summer, I was walking down Saint-Laurent and passed a bus station whose exterior wall featured a close-up of his face. "This is the most destructive boxer in Montreal," read the French text, its point to juxtapose his handsomeness with a violence uncommon in pretty men.)

When the younger prospect got into the ring and they began

to circle one another, I noticed that even in sparring, where the objective is to work on one's weaknesses, Rioux still looked to throw power shots. He wasn't doing so maliciously—out of empathy for his inexperienced partner he'd taken a noticeable zip off his punches—but I realized it was the only way he knew how to fight. Rioux would lurch forward, often ignoring his jab, to throw the right hand even in situations where it put him off balance. The younger fighter began to parry these punches, swatting them away as he walked backwards.

When Rioux returned to the corner between rounds, his trainer, an oval-faced Frenchman named Joe Geraghty, congratulated him and threw a towel over his neck. There were no detailed instructions or criticism for omitting his jab and several times losing his balance, just a back slap and nod of encouragement. Even I, who knew far less about boxing's technical side than anyone in the gym, could see that Rioux wasn't receiving improper advice, and his faults were being enabled by the man whose job it was to eradicate them.

On the other side of the gym, Eddy was having what appeared to be a serious conversation with two brothers who belonged to a local bike club. Hands obscured mouths as Eddy looked down, listening to what I gathered was negative information. Once their conversation ended, the brothers turned around and left the gym without speaking to anyone.

As I watched the sparring, Eddy pulled on my shirt from behind. He wanted to talk in his office, so I followed him back and shut the door.

"I'm going to get a bit squeezed here, sacrament," Eddy started, sitting down in his chair. "I haven't told anybody else, and you can't say a word or guys'll start panicking and I can't have that. I'm telling you 'cause you can keep your mouth shut." I listened without saying anything.

"A couple of guys are getting out and they're going to want

some customers back," he went on. "This could mean less guys on our sheets, you understand?"

"Fuck, Ed, I'm still behind as it is." He held up his hands as if to say, 'what the fuck do you want me to do about it?'

"This isn't worth causing problems over," he said, "because then we're into a lot of bullshit and nobody makes any money."

"Are these guy's gonna make a problem for me?" I asked. He knew what I was referencing.

Eddy shook his head. "I don't think so. They have bigger issues, ostie, than that stupid fat idiot Sil…"

"So we need other sources of income, right?" I asked.

"Yes. And your sheet's gotta start bringing in more. I can't be seeing only three dimes from you."

It was obvious that Eddy — who was still processing whatever the bikers had just told him — didn't know what these sources would be. I was anxious about his ultimatum until something occurred to me. The bikers. That game I went to in Laval. The full house. Its angry fans. Everyone there to see a brawl. I snapped my fingers.

"Who's handicapping that league, the one Maxime plays in?" I asked. Eddy looked at me like I was an idiot.

"What? No one. No one bets on it. Why would they?"

"Why don't we start there?" Eddy laughed at this.

"On what? Take bets like it's the NHL?"

"We can get creative," I said, my voice rising. "There's a million things guys are gonna wanna wager on. You see the atmosphere there?"

"'Course. My buddy Andre owns Verdun. It's a gongshow. I've seen a million games. But it's a fucking pipe dream, T."

"Why? How? I'd say we take more action on boxing but there aren't enough events. And this league's going very week! Thousands of fans, every week in Montreal alone. They're playing to packed houses. It's a fucking circus, man! Gorillas throwing down every Friday and Sunday. And everybody's going there to see a tilt — or ten. We start setting lines on potential matchups, and you can't tell me people won't want to bet!"

"I don't know, maybe." Eddy looked down at his phone. Someone had just texted him and I was annoyed he didn't recognize the potential of my idea.

"Let me come up with a strategy, okay?" I said. "If we can take a piece of this, we can do it independently of the book. No oversight from other people."

"If it works," he cautioned, "they're going to look to get in on it."

"We can cross that bridge later," I said. "If it becomes *that* successful, we can think of a new angle. That league's a pure cash business. We start moving money through it, your friend benefits, too. More bettors, more fans, more excitement, more money." At this, Eddy smiled.

"I'll talk to Andre."

11.

Diane Sutherland had sent me an email to ask how things were going. With more pressing things to work about, I never responded, because at the beginning of October I moved back into my parent's house. So as not to put Patty out, I promised to continue making rent payments and would use our apartment as a place to sleep downtown. When I returned home with two bags of clothing, several neighbors knocked on my door to say hello, but after that first afternoon life became quiet again.

    I hated chores as a child. Whenever my father pulled me away from the television, I would sigh and give the ground a subtle kick. This would aggravate him ("Why don't you want to pitch in?") and I would complete the task with minimal effort before returning to my show. But after coming home for the first time — where I spent long, silent hours lying on the living room couch, listening to a vigorous breeze ripple our white curtains — I raked the golden leaves carpeting our front and back yards, washed every window and extracted dust from each room, including the wall of family pictures above the fireplace. I resolved to ensure the house remained clean. It was all the remained of Anna and Thomas Knox of Dunrobin, Ontario, and Kirkland, Quebec, and it belonged to me now.

Montreal was complicated. For decades, the Italians had dominated bookmaking, loansharking and had a South American drug connection that guaranteed their hold over the milieu long before the bikers' rise. The mafia had been a satellite of one of New York's five families, which in the 1950s sent one of their psychopaths north to bring Montreal's rackets under its control. This proxy status lasted for decades until a family from Sicily refused to take orders from the Calabrians. Tension between clans lasted for years, until some of the leading Sicilians went south to shore up heroin contacts in Venezuela while their men did away with the ruling class up north. The winners dominated Montreal for decades, leading mediation between the bikers, Irish and Haitian groups arguing over their right to sell drugs across the city. I wasn't sure whether Sil's cousins belonged to this extended network.

The bikers had long been one of Canada's two most dominant organizations. Many had strong relationships with the Italians and worked together on strip clubs, loansharking and drug importation. Who had the right to sell where was determined by territorial controls that required mediation whenever there were encroachments. There was frequent diplomacy because everyone's objective was always money, and those who survived the nineties longed to avoid police detection. There were over one hundred full patch bikers in the province and thousands of associates. Their authority was unchallengeable.

Where did we fit in? I didn't know how many guys Eddy had, but it was more than I saw every day. Beyond Karim, there were a dozen people who came in and out of his office, friends, criminals and local businessmen involved in real estate. Maxime was hardly there, but it seemed like Eddy had various enforcers whenever a debtor required encouragement. And while he didn't belong to any bike chapter, Eddy was close with many of their members. They came into the gym sometimes, faces I'd sometimes seen in the paper, and always without their patches. Eddy would close his office door when they arrived, and there were two brothers I had last seen in the boxing gym, bear-sized French Canadians — Pierre-Alexandre and Jean-Marc — who stopped to say hello whenever I met them at the entrance. They were the men I'd seen during the Pugilistica workout. It was from them, I suspected, that Eddy derived much of his influence.

"You know how many loans I got out on the street?" Eddy and I were sitting at a bar in Griffintown. Packs of young people flirted with neighboring tables, finding space for conversation whenever the militant hip hop didn't make speech inaudible. There was at least one group there involved in the milieu (obvious by the tinseled women, sitting gargoyle-like, at the ends of their booth). Young men stared at Eddy as he led us towards a back booth.

He was dressed more casually today than I was used to. The slacks and tie were gone but his outfit still spoke of money: leather brow loafers, acid washed jeans that had a light rhinestone pattern around the pocket stitching, and a white dress shirt, unbuttoned to the upper middle of his chest, where a golden crucifix rested in the slit between both pecs. Eddy wore a gold wrist chain and had spiked his dark hair.

"How many?" I asked.

"Depending on the week, five to six hundred K."

"That sounds like a lot," I said, taking a sip of my drink. Eddy raised his eyebrows in dismay that I wasn't more impressed. "How's it work?" I asked.

"I loan money for a few points. Depending on who it is, they might get a one to five percent vig a week."

"Who gets your loans?" I asked.

"Whoever can't go to a bank."

"Guys in gambling debt?"

"Guys in every sort of debt. People who own businesses need money. Bars, clubs, restaurants: whoever's got cash," he said, emphasizing the end of his sentence. "Think about this," he said. "You got a guy betting with you who's losing, right? He needs money to pay you back. So you give him a loan or extend his credit. Then he's into you for a vig. So you're making money on both ends."

"What happens when people don't pay?" I asked. "You send Maxime?"

He smiled. "Most settle up. Part of this is figuring out who can pay you back before any money goes out. That's why you gotta see what sort of business they have, whether there's cash-flow, if they have assets. If the person's got nothing, they get nothing. If they have something and don't pay when it's time, then you go a different way. But what happened to Sil happens less than you think." He smiled when he said this, and I didn't want to appear anxious by asking for more assurance that Sil's beating wouldn't cause an issue. I had been thinking about it more, and couldn't believe my comfort with the speed at which it escalated and the manner of its conclusion. Now, however, after the adrenaline had long worn off, I was wary of its consequences.

"So if you got five hundred K on the street at a three percent rate, let's say," I started, "you're taking in fifteen dimes a week, sixty a month."

"Sometimes more," he said. "Sometimes a lot more."

"That's pretty goddamn good," I said. "You could live on that alone." I didn't know what Eddy did with this money. Though he had a family (two young children and a wife I never met), he rarely spoke of them and spent every night in a bar or nightclub.

"That could be you, T. You have the head and heart for this work, ostie, just keep moving the way you are. But is that what you want?" He asked this with an interest I wasn't used to. (Like most alpha types, Eddy softened when there wasn't a room to dominate.)

"I gotta pay off my debt first, Ed. You talk to Andre?" I asked.

"I did."

Eddy described their conversation to me. Andre Bouchard — construction CEO and owner of the Verdun Hitmen — was initially resistant to the idea.

"He doesn't want fixed outcomes. Doesn't want you interacting with the players. Wants a piece of what we make."

"A piece?" I asked. "I mean, Ed, we can take bets regardless of whether he wants us to or not."

"Yes, we can" he said, "but I don't want us to, ostie. A lot of people are connected to that league, T, and he's friends with people I rely on. Gotta make compromises where you can."

I wasn't in a position to argue, but we could compromise only insofar as it didn't prevent us from profiting. I made this argument to Eddy.

"Next week you can start," he said. "Get the word out and we'll put some lines up on the site. You know who's playing, who'll be fighting?"

"I'll find out," I said. "But if he wants a piece, Andre needs to put us inside. New guys are moving in and out of these teams every game. So I need to know who's playing and who isn't. And I'm not going to be fixing fights, either. You can't fix a hockey fight. I mean, you can, but it's not like boxing. Unless someone gets really beaten up or knocked out, who wins is subjective, plus — unlike in boxing — this shit isn't scored by judges. No, we're gonna take action on matchups, the number of tilts, whether there's gonna be a brawl, the regular moneyline and over-under stuff." Eddy smiled as a waitress came over to our booth. He ordered two negronis.

"This could be good," he said. "We'll see how much money's there, tough guy."

"The show must go on."

On the second Friday in October, this was the advertisement luring hockey fans to the Verdun Auditorium. The poster featured a silhouette of two hockey players squaring off. A maxim of live entertainment, these words had a clever double meaning here. The "show" referred to the league's violent theatricality — an identify that wouldn't yield to the critiques of moralizing public officials. To support the SLSPL was to make a heroic and necessary refusal of civilization's blunting impacts.

We were three weeks into the regular season and Verdun was hosting Saint-Jean. These were the SLSPL's two most violent teams and would each have at least five heavyweights dressed, including, of course, Maxime — long one of the league's biggest names. Attendance had been excellent for the first three weeks: in part because there was no other hockey to watch with the NHL shutdown, in part because this was the wildest thing in sports.

I spent the previous week telling my bettors we were taking action on semi-pro hockey now ("it's fucking insane," Patty promised everyone we knew). It didn't take much to convince friends this would be fun (what young guy would say no to drinking cheap beer in an environment that didn't care how you behaved?), and our promotion introduced at least thirty new fans to the most unique show in North American sports. The Auditorium would be full: two weeks earlier, there was a stick-swinging incident in Saint-Jean that still needed to be avenged.

Bettors could wager on the moneyline, over/unders for goals and fights, fights per period, whether there would be a brawl and who would face whom. For the last category I put prospective matchups together from what I knew about the league, though I didn't have time to speak with Maxime beforehand (he was busy all week, working as a construction day labourer). As most of the wagers would be small, a loss was acceptable if it created a new market.

When we arrived at the Auditorium, not far from where my grandparents had lived in LaSalle, Patty and I moved through hundreds of people in the lobby: fans were buying jerseys of their favorite players, while slovenly adults with fat fingers carried tubs of poutine (held against their chests, urn-like), and girls in cut-off referee shirts poured hundreds of beers for the packs of men congregated on the floor. Everyone was here to see somebody get shit-kicked.

I picked up the two tickets Maxime left, and we walked into the arena. There was already a commotion at center ice in the remaining minutes of warm-ups. Patty laughed as we climbed towards the concourse level, where below us three players on either team were yelling at one another, with another being held back by a teammate. A group of fans were encouraging the players to fight but two referees came out from the dressing room area (they usually weren't on the ice during the pre-game skate) and kicked everyone off.

"This is gonna get nuts," Patty said, taking a sip of his beer. The Auditorium only had four thousand seats but there were at least twenty-five hundred people already here. By puck drop every seat contained a sitter. We were soon joined by a dozen of Patty's bar friends. Everyone was almost drunk.

I looked down at each team's first line on the ice for *O Canada*. Two of the players were having words from across the ice (Maxime wasn't starting the game, but I could see him on the bench, moving spastically in preparation of what was coming). Patty saw this too, and nudged me.

"These guys are going," he said.

The crowd cheered when *O Canada* was replaced by *Enter Sandman*. As both lines prepared for the opening faceoff, the wingers chirping one another throughout the anthem never arrived at the red line (the fans noticed this, of course, and stood up in excited preparation). Once the puck was dropped, four players simultaneously launched their gloves and helmets into the air and began circling one another. The fans around us started bouncing on the old concrete as four fighters came together and started exchanging bombs. Not wanting to be left out, the two centremen grabbed one another and were discussing whether to drop their gloves, while the defensemen on each team had rushed in, ready to become involved if necessary. There was so much happening that I didn't know where to look: one of the Verdun fighters landed a decisive uppercut, dropping his opponent from Saint-Jean. On the rink's other side, a Saint-Jean winger delivered right hands to a punchless opponent. The referees were trying to restrain one of the Verdun defensemen from jumping in to defend his teammate.

Around us, the chorus of guys we brought to the game were laughing, in disbelief it yielded such an immediate return. When the Saint-Jean fighters were led to the penalty box, local fans leaned over the glass to insult them.

As the referees took over ten minutes to hand out penalties, Maxime stepped onto the ice. The crowd booed when he skated to the Verdun bench, where Maxime pointed at the entire lineup, coaxing someone to step over. I could see Verdun's immense heavyweight, Stephane Lachapelle, prepare to scale the boards, only to be pulled back by his coach.

The fans started chanting "Lachey! Lachey! Lachey!" and finally Verdun's coach indulged them. When Lachapelle's skates landed on the ice, the Auditorium orgasmed, and Maxime skated over to Lachapelle and began speaking at him from within inches of his face.

"Fucking right!" Patty said. "Here we go. How many bets came in on this one?"

"A ton," I said.

I didn't know if they'd wait for the puck to drop, but one of the linesmen came over to separate the two heavyweights. This incensed the fans: it had been ten minutes since the line brawl, and with the initial meal digested, they were starved for something more substantial. When the play stopped, our game was still only one second old. When it resumed, time would stop again at two seconds as Maxime and Lachapelle dropped their gloves (Maxime having ripped off his own helmet to throw it the length of the ice). They circled one another as Maxime began shaking his shoulders, almost like a running back, to induce Lachapelle into a mistake. But he didn't bite, which forced Maxime to lurch forward and grab Lachapelle by his shoulder. The fighters grappled for several seconds, each trying to control the other's arms, before Maxime freed his right hand and started punching Lachapelle on the side of his head. He took the first few punches and started trading back, his fist finding Maxime's shoulder. The fans cheered as they anticipated a momentum turn but Maxime absorbed these punches, tied up his taller opponent's arm, and threw an uppercut that knocked Lachapelle's head back. He tried to grapple his way towards evening the fight, but the Woodchipper punched through the guard, landing another uppercut that buckled Lachapelle's legs. The Verdun heavy fell forward onto Maxime, who tripped under Lachapelle's weight, torquing the bigger man's body to soften his landing. As the referees tended to Lachapelle, Maxime got back to his feet and saluted the fans who were swearing at him in French.

"Fuck you Doucette, you cunt piece of shit!"

"Fucking loser!"

Patty was giggling beside me. He had just ordered a round

of beers for the five people he was speaking to at once.

"Nobody's fucking with you with that guy in your corner!" he yelled. I told him to keep quiet.

Across the rink, Maxime was entering the penalty box, where he was high-fived by three teammates. Some of the Verdun fans were banging against the glass. One, I thought, was mooning him.

I didn't know who was responsible for the stick-swinging incident and whether it had been avenged in the game's first few fights. With the bloodletting done, our game settled down and Saint-Jean scored three goals in the period's second half. At nineteen minutes, Verdun sliced in a loose puck to provide its fans with some hope before the intermission.

I looked at our section, which had swelled beyond what I expected. There were dozens of guys all drinking and laughing together. While only a few had bet, most would if we promoted this correctly.

"How many of these dudes wanna wager?" I said in Patty's ear.

"Most if you give them log-ins and shit."

At the concourse's other end was a group of older men. I assumed they were part of the milieu, given their look and command of the space around them. Speaking to a tall, goateed biker was a suited man who must have been Andre, the Hitmen's owner (we hadn't met, but I recognized someone from an article about the SLSPL). I wondered how many of the people he was standing with were moving money through the league, because it was a near-perfect system: the fans paid cash to get in, which its teams handed over to the players. Nowhere else in the hockey world could a well-known tough guy play a couple games for several thousand dollars (or more, depending on who they were, and how much revenue an owner stood to earn if they appeared). Beyond the Québécois guys, tonight there were players from Ontario, Saskatchewan and British Columbia and New York. All had been brought in to fight. With the right sort of arrangement, professionally organized, any gangster could hand a truckload of cash to a team owner and get legitimate money back through an improvised receipt.

Meanwhile, our group of young guys, oblivious to everyone around us, murmured about the collective hope that Saint-Jean would score a few goals to put the game out of reach (Verdun could then only salvage its remaining self-respect by brawling). When both teams returned for the second period, the penalty boxes were empty and Verdun began with its first line (one of whom, Marco Charbonneau, a former QMJHL superstar, had played two NHL seasons and was the game's best player). His line controlled possession by the Verdun goalie for almost a minute, cycling behind the net and hash marks, and nearly scoring when a deceptive snapshot hit the crossbar. But towards the end of an excellent shift, one of his wingers, hopeful for a point shot but too casual in his method, sent a weak pass to the blueline. It was intercepted by the defensive winger, who chipped the puck past Verdun's defenseman and towards the sprinting Saint-Jean centreman, now on a two-on-one. The puck-carrying center used his winger as a decoy (looking left to fake a pass), and the ruse worked, as he held onto the puck until the last moment before snapping a wrist shot over the goalie's shoulder. This made it 4-1, angering the home fans but pleasing all those whose hopes were ignoble. We had grown up in hockey and were familiar with its rhythms. Everyone knew what was coming next.

Saint-Jean put out its second line, knowing that to ice its fourth would turn the Auditorium into a killing field. Playing at home, Verdun had the last change, so Saint-Jean would have to adjust if Lachapelle reappeared. He did, alongside Myles Malarchuk — a fighter from northern Saskatchewan making his SLSPL debut, and who, two weeks ago, had been banned for life from the East Coast Hockey League. Putting his tough guys on was a strange move by the Verdun coach because the game wasn't over. Maybe he just sensed a beaten bench.

The crowd around me pushed towards the concourse guard rail. Across the ice, I could see the Saint-Jean players motion for certain players to get off once the puck was dropped. Maxime already had one leg dangling over the boards.

When the play started, Malarchuk took a baseball swing at the Saint-Jean centreman's thigh. The crowd spasmed and players on the Saint-Jean bench slammed their sticks against the boards. One of the forwards confronted Malarchuk, while the other ran off the ice so Maxime could replace him. The Woodchipper galloped towards Malarchuk, throwing his gloves so high that one went over the glass, and grabbed him by the throat. Maxime started punching with an unusual degree of anger, even for him: his hands were moving back and forth like a piston, while, just past center, Maxime's assaulted teammate limped to the bench on one leg. This wasn't the only fight. Beaudoin, another Saint-Jean heavyweight, was exchanging with Lachapelle by the far blue line, while their teammate, Daniele Gagnon, rushed Verdun defensemen Pierre-Marc O'Brien (a skilled player on at an unfortunate time) and began to strike him. Fans started climbing the glass close to where O'Brien's head was being pummeled and Verdun's coach screamed at the referees to pull Gagnon away. But the officials were occupied and didn't see what was happening in the far corner. I looked down at the Verdun bench again. One players' leg was hanging over the boards. If he jumped on, the benches would empty.

"Look at this," I said to Patty, motioning down to the Verdun bench, "if this guy goes…"

"Fuck yeah" he said, laughing. "Let's hope he does."

"They gotta pull this guy off…" I said, motioning to the corner where O'Brien was being beaten. But the referees didn't, and Cote, one of the Verdun enforcers, wouldn't stand for any more of this, so he leapt over the boards and rushed to the corner. Both benches emptied as waves of players began jumping over the boards, gloves falling to the ice as they looked for someone on the other team. The refs had no idea who to focus on, as there were at least eight separate fights taking place. Around us the Auditorium swayed, its occupants delirious.

"Fucking dust him!" one of Patty's bar friends yelled beside me. He had two beers in his hands, his head moving from side to side in a failed attempt to absorb everything.

Below us, the Woodchipper was still grappling with Malarchuk, both men exhausted. Beside them, two middleweights were punching one another and at center ice a furious fight emerged between two of the game's shorter, stockier players, who exchanged blows without any defense.

The referees had grabbed Beaudoin in the corner (he also managed to also beat up Cote, who had jumped over the boards to defend O'Brien). When he was being led off the ice, one of the fans threw a beer bottle that smashed against his helmet. Even from my distance I could see the spray rebound. Beaudoin attempted to wrestle his way into the stands, so a referee hurried him down the hallway.

On the ice, Maxime had recovered his wind and was skating around, looking for someone else to fight. He received no interest. Fans leaned over the glass by both benches, screaming at the Saint-Jean players. Elsewhere, the officials tried to break up existing fights or prevent new ones. (The percentage of players who don't want to fight — in the absence of some slight done to them which requires addressing — is always smaller than that of those who do, even in this league. In the arithmetic of hockey psychology, both teams were now even as Beaudoin had addressed Malarchuk's cheapshot.) One of the Laval middleweights brought his opponent to the ice in the brawl's last active fight. The crowd cheered in what I thought was a summary ovation, and for a second it seemed as if the sagging energy would discourage further brawling. But momentum's an interesting phenomenon, because just as the hostility appeared to have dwindled, fresh beef renewed its vigor.

By the entrance closest to us, I could see two players start talking. Words became pushes. Pushing matured into grappling and soon, several other players skated over to start a new, localized brawl beside the bench. There appeared to be around eight players punching and some of the guys with me started throwing beer cups at them. Drenched by wayward spray, a group of fans standing beneath us turned around and started yelling, but before they could engage with Patty's friends the on-ice brawl intensified. It was impossible to see who was winning through the storm of limbs, which somehow moved off the ice and onto the bench, where the interlocked hoard disappeared into the tunnel, traveling like a feuding rat king. Fans rushed down the stairs since most of the players were out of sight and fighting in the dressing room area's corridor. What we couldn't see was that a door was flung open to the parking lot, where the brawl continued on the pavement outside, sparks flying off the broken cement as punches from fully dressed hockey players flew in the October night.

Inside the arena, a few fights started in the stands, and one of the men Patty's friend hit with a beer cup started charging up the stairs. He grabbed a kid I didn't know (and who may not have been the culprit). A security guard ran in to break things up as another one of Patty's friends poured a drink on the man's head. He was struggling on the ground, his wet face in full grimace, as the group around him laughed.

"Fucking ostie pussy," one of the guys said, mocking the squirming man, now struggling to breathe.

I could see the guard straighten, angered by the arrogance

of a young Anglo, but the police had arrived, and he pulled the man away. Alcohol falling from his bottom lip, the heckler turned to high-five a friend.

I still didn't know what was happening with the players down the hallway, but a group of fans were leaning over the tunnel entrance. The security guards were pushing them back, one of whom was laughing as he spoke to a fan.

On the ice, things started to devolve again when two players began circling one another, perhaps ashamed they hadn't fought yet. The fans started calling for them to scrap, and so as not to lose momentum the person in charge of music began playing *Dragula*. Both middleweights started swinging.

"Fuckin' do 'em!" one of the guys beside me yelled. There were a handful of other players still out there, all too tired to be angry, while in the distance sirens yodeled over Rob Zombie. The crowd popped when it heard this. It was an ecstatic convulsion, like that which attended a shattering sound of glass, and then a bald outlaw's rush to the wrestling ring.

"What the fuck they gonna do with this game?" Patty asked me. I had no idea whether there were enough players to even finish. The final fight was done, and both teams were forced to opposite sides of the ice, resulting in a final, appreciative cheer from the crowd. The head referees explained infractions to Verdun's coach, who threw his hands up, upset that Laval wouldn't be penalized more for starting the brawl. When the penalties were announced, fans laughed at the ejections for "leaving the ice surface" before booing the ten major penalties against their team. A born showman, the Verdun coach held a wad of money up to insinuate the refs were in Saint-Jean's pocket. Every drunk in our group stood in disbelief.

"You think these guys'll be back?" I asked Patty.

"Are you fucking kidding me?" he asked.

When play resumed (probably forty minutes after the brawl

started), each team had only eleven players left. The style of game changed by necessity, and what had previously been a prison fight turned into a high-skilled men's league game. While the league was known for violence, it had legitimacy: those paid to score did it well, as most were past stars in the QMJHL, US college hockey, or in the minor pro and European leagues. Verdun batted in two goals to make the score 4-3. Its fans now wanted a win.

It was now past eleven, and though we'd seen only two periods the game had taken over three hours. This allowed more time for drinking. Not far from where we stood, the group I assumed was part of the milieu had grown, joined by several expelled members of the Verdun team, including Maxime. Patty noticed him and punched me on the shoulder.

Among the older gangsters — with whom the hockey players had a symbiotic relationship, as both groups received something important from the other — Maxime's teammates stood out for their shape and youth. The Woodchipper saw me from twenty meters away and came over to say hello. The young guys moved when he appeared, like a body of water parting before a crocodile. There was a bruise over his left eye.

"How are ya, big guy?" he asked, slapping me on the shoulder.

"What the hell happened outside?" I asked.

"Little skirmish, ostie, but cops broke it up." Maxime laughed when he said this. The eyes of twenty young men were watching him.

"No arrests?" I asked.

"Fuck no," he said, "just a friendly fight. Another one for the memoirs." Everyone laughed and a disembodied hand passed Maxime a beer. The fighter took a long sip and turned when a commotion started behind us. On the concourse, a group of Verdun players were confronting his Saint-Jean teammates.

"Tabernaaaaak!" Maxime said, turning around to walk in

the opposite direction. I grabbed him by the arm.

"Don't get into it here," I said. "Cops are horny to crack someone." Maxime paid no attention to me and moved towards the standoff. Players from both teams were chirping at one another, while the bikers appeared more amused than bothered. Maxime pushed his way to the front, where his head bobbed in aggressive discussion with the Verdun players. The concourse turned to watch, but before another fight began several cops appeared to calm the testosterone. The two groups left in different directions. Several police officers were speaking with the bikers. They seemed to know one another.

Maxime left with his teammates and gave me a peace sign as he passed. "We're going to the fucking bar!" he said to me. All the guys around me laughed together. "You coming?" he asked.

"I gotta see the end of the game," I said. Maxime smiled.

"Call me after," he said.

I promised to, and everyone watched Maxime as he passed. They had lost interest in the result and wanted to follow him out. I turned to the kid who insulted that guy on the ground (Shane, I think).

"You coming back to another game, bro?" I asked him.

"Fuck yeah," he said.

"You want to make a wager next time?" I asked.

"Fucking right."

"Will these guys?" I said, motioning around to the larger group.

"Abso-fucking-lutely," he said, swaying and red-faced.

"Good," I said, "get to know the league and you can clean up with the prop options."

From behind I felt a light tap on my shoulder. It was Véronique. Two other girls were behind her, neither of whom I recognized. At once a lump formed in my throat. I had no idea she had been there.

"Hey V, how are you?" I asked, my voice breaking. "I had no idea you came to this stuff?"

"I'm good. It seems like you have a big crew here," she said. I could feel the pressure of her friends' eyes as they pretended to talk amongst themselves. I wondered if they knew. "I have no idea what I just saw. I feel like Caesar should be here to wag his thumb." Véronique's speech was fast. "Anyway, what's new with you? Did you drop your phone in the bathtub, Teddy?"

"I don't know," I stammered. "Sorry. I've been busy with all of this for a while."

She looked around in subtle disapproval. "We can still hang out," she said, now out of their range. "It's okay."

"Okay, V."

"I'll message you," she said, sensing a need to take control of future interaction.

Not knowing what else to do, I leaned in to hug her. She seemed surprised, tensing slightly as I put my arms around her shoulders. After we pulled away, I watched Véronique exit behind her two friends before turning back to the game.

Verdun won 5-3, but I only found this out later: we left midway through the period, when I was carried away by a drunken wave to a LaSalle bar with Maxime and his teammates. I would check our website after to see how many bets had been wagered, but the final tally didn't matter: I had just exposed thirty young guys to a world they fell in love with. They would be back to bet.

Across the bar, Maxime and his teammates loomed over a corner rail, laughing about the game. Some of the bikers from the concourse came in, with their leather jackets and goatees, and controlled another fifteen feet of bar space. Someone in their group (a prospect, probably) ordered one hundred drinks and started passing them out.

We continued to drink and smoke and dip, and at around one thirty, one of the bikers mandated that we all go to the nearest strip club. A cheer followed when two of the Verdun heavyweights picked up the smallest of Patty's friends, hoisting him in the air like the Stanley Cup. He was passed along the bar and had a look of strained humiliation when they put him down. I placed a drink into his hand, wrapped in a twenty dollar bill. He finished it in three sips.

Over two thousand left my pocket that night as I paid for Patty's friends to take a tour in the backroom. I also spoke to several of the other fighters on Maxime's team, including a guy who came from the same region as my mother, and chatted with the bikers — Serge, Benoit and Rene — before Maxime pulled me in for a half dozen drunken embraces.

The guys Patty brought made boozy promises to wager the following week. I looked around for my oldest friend, but he was somewhere in a back room, doing coke with one of the three strippers he needed money to get a team dance from. I didn't go back myself and instead moved between the groups, telling the younger guys about our betting options, offering to provide them with logins and free credits if they wished to start. They were receptive to my pitch (as people usually are when they're speaking to the person financing their night). Knowing this, I would get Patty to follow up with them.

Past two, I was tired and wanted to leave. Maxime, some teammates and a few bikers had gone into a back room with a half dozen strippers, while several other hockey players were still on the main floor, sitting with the bikers (some now wearing their patches). Winners of the nineties war, they were now the only club that mattered and could wear colours in public without worrying someone may have placed a bomb underneath their car.

Otherwise, my kids were mostly still here, either sitting around pervert's row or fumbling with the ATM machine. One of the back doors swung open and Maxime and his teammates re-emerged. From my seat at the table, I saw several of Patty's friends staring at the Woodchipper with a reverence that teenage girls showed pop stars.

Maybe it was a moment of clarity, induced by the several liters of alcohol I consumed, but in this moment, I realized that Maxime, who lived beyond the social parameters that so many young men made a public show of rejecting, embodied the experience I was selling: not violence, *per se*, but wildness and the possibility of a conclusive result. We all *had* to find out who'd win, and the savagery that provided our answer, distasteful insofar as that it might be sustained, donated a brief reprieve from the banality of our lives, one sanctioned by the people and press as an excusable interest by a species barely removed from its origins.

12.

"**My old man got deported** a few years ago," Karim said. "There wasn't much cash to go around, you know?" On a clear night in mid-October, the falling sun cast a wounded glow over downtown. Karim was slightly ahead of me, moving around several Chinese families walking in the opposite direction, the muscles in his neck tensing on each step. I'd forgotten my question, and then remembered we were talking about his pregnant girlfriend, and how Karim had to start making more money.

"So how'd you get in with Ed?" I asked.

"Worked as a busboy at one of his bars as a kid."

"Was he ever allowed back? Your dad, I mean," I asked, side-stepping a tourist.

"Nope," Karim answered, pulling out a cigarette. We walked in silence as he pulled out a lighter.

"Sorry that happened," I said. "I guess I kind of know where you're coming from. Different circumstances, but you know what I mean."

"All good, man. And yeah, that's fucking awful what happened to your parents, bro." Karim shook his head and lit the dart.

"I'm only asking because you mentioned it, but what'd they say he did?"

"You know — involved in some terrorist lies. It was some security bullshit over 9/11 that caught a lot of people up. But we didn't have any money for a lawyer."

"When's the last time you saw him?" I asked. Karim paused and looked up, trying to remember.

"Been a while. Couple years ago, something like that. In Jordan." Ahead of us, a bylaw officer prepared to ticket an illegally parked car. Karim snorted as we passed. "Imagine making a living doing that shit?" he asked. We continued to walk for a bit as Karim became philosophical.

"Probably why I'm here," he said. "Only way I could get anything was from hustling. My mom worked her ass off, but you can't pay for kids making minimum at a grocery store, you know? Every lunch was pulled from the expired aisle."

"So it's you, and…"

"Got two sisters and a brother. Sisters are at school."

"And your brother?"

"Z. Zinedine, he's a wild fuck. Five years younger than me. Lives with his hands cocked. Smart, too."

"How old is he?" I asked.

"Nineteen. You'll meet him sometime." Karim's attention focused on something down the street.

"What's this?" he asked.

Two blocks from our destination, a group of police cars had overtaken Saint-Laurent. There were three on each side of the street, as well as several unmarked vehicles in the near distance. At least ten people were standing around a business, including five or six officers, several detectives and a news truck. There was yellow police tape across the sidewalk and as we approached a female officer directed us to the street's other side. When we passed, I could see that in the middle of the taped enclosure was a boutique called Caribe Blanc. There was no obvious damage to the store but something terrible had occurred to justify the security.

"What happened here?" I asked a teenage boy, leaning on his skateboard. He responded in French.

"Somebody got lit up," he said. "Maybe a couple." Across the street, young black men were leaning against a red sedan.

"You ever been in there?" I asked Karim, motioning to the store.

"No, but fuck me bro, I know who owns this spot…" Karim pulled out his phone and began to text.

"Who?"

"This Haitian dude. Pierre something. They call him Prince. A crazy fuck. They've tried to get him like five times. Always got away."

"Until now?" I asked.

"Who knows, bro." Karim looked on with interest. "Whoever did it though…" he said, shaking his head and smiling.

"Yeah?"

"Whoever did it had to be a heavyweight. Because Prince has guys all over the place."

"Was he taking bets, too?" I asked Karim.

"No, but entrepreneurial."

I looked across the street to where the Haitians stood together. Each ornamented with gold, they whispered into one another's ears. I assumed they were connected to whoever owned the boutique.

"Know any of those guys?" I asked Karim.

"Don't think so."

Two more police cars arrived. A dour female officer got out from one of the cruisers and stared at Karim, giving him a hard look before turning to speak with one of the detectives.

"What was that?" I asked. Karim laughed again.

"She cuffed me a few years ago. Probably doesn't even remember, just sees my face and thinks I'm a shithead."

"You are." Karim laughed.

"Come on," he said, motioning towards the Vietnamese restaurant, "we'll know what happened before the hour's out, guarantee."

Once we sat down for dinner, Karim and I continued to speculate on what had happened. When the waiter arrived and overheard our conversation, he told us that a friend witnessed the getaway and gave a description of what he saw to the police. He shook his head and said, "Crazy." When our meal was finished, we walked back down the street. Three police cars remained, and the area was cordoned off by yellow tape. Several locals stood around, speculating on the shooters' motives.

"Yo," I said, tapping Karim from behind. He was waiting in line to buy ice cream. Behind him, a father argued with his two young children on the size of cone they were allowed.

"That dude Sil, his cousins just got out, right?" I said, motioning behind me and up the block to where the shooting happened.

"Yeah…" Karim said, nodding his head.

"Did Prince ever have a problem with the Italians?"

"No fucking clue, bro," Karim said, shaking his head. He turned around and ordered two cones. As the attendee worked her forearm in retrieval of some hard ice cream at the bucket's bottom, Karim looked skyward (his habit, whenever he thought something over), and then returned to me.

"He might have! Yeah…" Karim said, smiling as he remembered something. "There was a problem a couple of years ago, that's right! Over a shylock debt or some shit. Who the fuck told me that, bro?" he asked himself, snapping his fingers to stimulate a memory.

"Prince owed money to some of the Italians," Karim went on, his mind now lucid. "That's right! That's what happened! Guys got called in to mediate but he never paid it back 'cause the I-ties got locked up for something else. And he probably figured, 'fuck the debt, I'll deal with it later.'"

"And this is 'that' later."

Karim laughed. "I guess. Maybe?" He could see that I didn't find it funny.

"What's the matter?" he asked.

"If it *was* them, do I have something to worry about?" I asked, backing up against a wall beside the storefront.

"Why?"

"K! Turn your memory on, bud: Sil! Outside the strip club!" How could he have forgotten this already?

"Oh! Right. I don't know. Probably not."

"No?"

"That goof came at *you*. He owed *you*. But we'll talk to Eddy. It's worth bringing it up with him."

"Yeah…" I said. "Well, he already knows about Sil. But this," I said, pointing back towards the crime scene.

"Sometimes people get their number dialed. And remember, T," Karim said, taking a luxurious lick, "we don't even know who did it."

Each SLSPL team played on Fridays and Sundays. There were two teams in Montreal, two more within an hour's drive and the remaining four on both sides of the St. Lawrence. I couldn't offer betting on the entire league yet, and expanding our options to Saint-Jean or Sorel made little sense because the people on my sheets were all in the city. For now, everything had to be local. But if the operation continued to grow, we'd be stupid not to expand our betting options.

Because it was a small league, figuring things out came fast. I had several long conversations with Maxime about its culture of fighting and how it was decided amongst a team's tough guys who would fight whom (usually with a short huddle before the game), and how to predict the likelihood of a brawl (which was hard, unless, like in Verdun, there was something outstanding that hadn't been avenged). Once I had a grasp of this, handicapping became easier, especially with the prop betting on possible matchups, since fights were often random: the byproduct of guys being on the ice together at specific times (with the exception of preordained scraps between "number 1s" — league nomenclature for a team's premiere heavy).

As I'd explained to Eddy, unless someone was knocked out or badly beaten, deciding who won a hockey fight was subjective. Unlike in boxing, there were no judges and things often ended in a clumsy wrestling match. For this reason, I didn't take bets on who won, and while it didn't escape me that gamblers could offer fighters money to ensure the outcomes they wanted, here I'd have Maxime as my mole. If I found out that guys were fixing outcomes, they'd be permanently removed from our betting options (and maybe worse, depending on the financial damage, their overall contrition and — if Andre agreed — whether the player was expendable).

In the second week, I had a dozen new bettors. By week three, I had over thirty. They were mostly university-aged kids, many of them Anglo, who knew the league existed but never paid attention until they had a reason to. This point was important: in sports, a cultural divide existed in Montreal. Boxing and semi-pro hockey were dominated by the French community, and it was only the myopia of those in control which prevented their events from reaching a wider audience.

As for the new bettors, Patty would be responsible for their conduct, since his vouch had brought them in (he would get a small percentage of whatever we made from those he turned my way). I also had Patty create a document of files for each new bettor: if they had a job, notable assets, outstanding debts and limits on their betting sizes. After the first game in Verdun, which birthed a dozen new bettors, he was given the responsibility for collecting and paying out. So far, we hadn't had any issues, in part because they had a sense of who stood atop the gambling ring, and in part because I'd capped the bet sizes (unless I knew they came from a wealthy family or already had a job). So far, the only guy who wasn't forthcoming with his debts was Stu Boudreau, whom Maxime had called a pussy when we met him a couple of weeks ago. He'd lost on consecutive weeks and had a new excuse each time we went to collect. Beyond Stu, I knew some of the other young guys would slip, so Patty and I figured out a payment template we'd rely on.

Since I had hockey now, in addition to football and baseball, the sheet started taking in more money. In the third weekend of October, I made over eighteen thousand, an amount three times that of my first week.

"I'm surprised at the amount of action coming in, bud," Eddy told me, the Monday after the shooting on Saint-Laurent. He was looking at a printout of the betting receipts (always shredded by early Monday afternoon). "There's gotta be other shit we can do with this. Drive the fans towards our bars after the games. Put them in the strip clubs. All that." Eddy's body language was open and bountiful today. Gone was his usual cool detachment, as he seemed less guarded in his glee. He had smiled when I walked into the gym.

"I've never seen anything like this league," I said. "You get young guys into these games and it's like introducing a kid to Santa." Eddy smirked, and I asked whether Andre would take more money to bring in other heavyweights. There were hundreds of recruitable guys — graduates, all, of the same junior hockey system that made a paying spectacle of teenage boys having bare knuckled fistfights. This would drive ticket sales and bring in more bettors.

"How much do you think it costs to bring a top guy in?" I asked. "Somebody with a reputation? Like Maxime? For one game?"

"A top guy like that, probably a grand?" Eddy said. "Less for others. But you gotta cover their flight, accommodations, all that. May go as high as a couple dimes but you can probably negotiate down. How else are these guys gonna make cash that easy?"

"I got my eyes on a few guys from out west," I said. "Two from Ontario, two from Alberta. Legit heavies squeezed out of pro hockey because the AHL and Coast got flooded with the lockout. I wanna give their names to Andre, and I'll pay for everything."

"In exchange for what?" Eddy asked.

"It'll drive betting through the roof, Ed. And I'll make back more than I invested." Eddy smiled and sat back in the booth.

"You becoming a sports fixer now?" he asked.

"There's a documentary going around. It's about minor league tough guys. Some of them are out of work. We bring these guys in and there'll be a whackload of dudes wanting to bet on their tilts." Eddy considered the idea.

"How much money is being moved through this league, anyway?" I asked.

"There's some."

"Your buddy ever have cash flow problems?"

"He shouldn't, Verdun's full every game. Why? You want to get into ownership, too?"

I smiled. "Maybe. In due time." Eddy leaned back in his seat and looked out the window. There were groups of university students moving in both directions on the street. I was so happy not to be in school anymore. How could I receive a better education in a university classroom — with the gassy digressions of students desperate to assert their superiority — than through my current work?

"You asked me before about Prince," Eddy said, "the Haitian who got it on Saint-Laurent?"

"Yeah?" I sat upright in my chair.

"He had a problem with the Italians years ago, before they

went in. They got out and he got it."

"You know it was them?" I asked.

"That's what I hear." I took a long sip of coffee and stared across the street. The students had passed. A father was leading his two young children into an expensive toy store.

"You nervous, T?" he asked me. My heart surged when he said this.

"Should I be?"

Eddy smiled and shook his head. "Sil came at you, right?"

"He did, I told you that."

"I know what you told me, ostie," Eddy said.

"Well, do I gotta start looking over my shoulder now?" I asked.

"I don't think so," Eddy said, "just keep your head down and the money coming. Only protection a guy ever needs."

13.

That same night, Véronique and I went to the Museum of Fine Arts. We spent two hours walking between the paintings, our feet in that comfortable, swaying rhythm where your attention can linger just long enough to process images of lone peasant women moving through rural French towns.

We sat down on one of the leather backless sofas in a corner room where an elderly couple was slowly chatting by an image of Maximilien Robespierre. Behind us, a wall-sized tapestry depicted the forward sweep of a European army, its movements set against an apoplectic sky.

Something about Robespierre's face reminded me of rifling through my dad's dresser in search of a lighter (Patty had acquired some fireworks we were going to explode in the park). In the disorganized small upper drawer, I found a sketchbook of drawings he'd done. I struggled now, to remember what they were, but there was perhaps a park scene, then one of me playing hockey outside, and, I think, a sketch of a woman's face, likely my mother's. I never asked him about it and not once did he comment on his interest in drawing or art.

"What paintings do you like the best?" I asked. Véronique was sitting close to me. Our shoulders were touching.

"I don't know how good my judgments are—" she responded, staring into an impressionistic pond. Ladies in large hats were walking across a bridge.

"That doesn't matter. Neither are mine. So, which?"

"The one by the French painter, with that woman on the narrow street. I like the way she was walking. It looked like something nice had happened to her and she was remembering it as she went along."

"Pretty damn pretty," I said. She laughed and shook her head.

"Who are you, man?"

"Somebody just trying to spread his wings." I asked Véronique about her school and work. She would graduate in June but was still at her co-op placement. It was unclear whether her office was still plagued by a sex scandal. She didn't reference it, though, and instead talked of essays and Excel spreadsheets.

"How's everything going with your stuff?" she asked, turning to face me. A Chinese couple had entered the room. The toothy older woman looked at me and said something to her husband.

"I'm getting into sports management," I said. "Long term." I had no idea where this came from, not having even thought of it before. Maybe I didn't want Véronique to think I was a degenerate. But it made sense, at least superficially, so I kept talking.

"Really?"

"Yes. They're doing a lot of stuff wrong, no imagination. I've been thinking about it a lot. Across hockey, boxing, there are huge opportunities there that aren't being taken advantage of. The English market is there to be taken. You were in that business too, at least to some extent, and you must have seen things that could be improved, no?"

"I did. I saw a lot of ambition but little vision."

"Right! Exactly! Like what I'm doing with hockey right now."

She smiled and shook her head in the way people do when they're uncomfortable with another's enthusiasm for something distasteful.

"I guess."

"By the way," I continued, "what were you doing at that game? I thought you didn't even like hockey. That story you told me about being traumatized as a kid...."

"My friends and I were bored and wanted to do something," she said, measuring her speech.

"Ahhhh."

"And," Véronique continued, more slowly, "I thought you might be there."

It was nearing nine when we stepped onto Sherbrooke. Unsettled by recent history, my stomach felt like curdled cheese: it had been a fine date, and I was content to leave it that way.

"Want to go for a drink somewhere?" she asked. "If you need to get home, no problem."

"Sure, I could do one. Where?"

"There's a place around the corner." I followed Véronique to a small English pub where we sat on highchairs in the back corner. We ordered two pints of beer.

"How are you doing?" she asked after a short silence.

"With everything?" Véronique nodded, yes. "I'm okay," I said, stumbling to locate a vocabulary. I didn't want to dwell on things, and she recognized it.

"We don't have to talk about this," she said. "I just wanted to ask in case, you know."

"It's fine, thanks."

Véronique cupped her beer and watched the bubbles rise.

"What can I do?" I said, finally, my lone declaration on the subject. Véronique looked up and we made eye contact. "They're gone," I said, "their bedroom's empty."

"I can't imagine how hard that is."

"I don't know. To tell you the truth, I hardly think about it.

I'll keep them in my heart but... again, what can I do beyond not let them get assfucked by having their house snatched?"

Véronique looked at me for a moment and then paused. "I get that," she started, "and I have no idea how you must feel, but you need to think about it, maybe, no? If things stay bottled up..." I didn't answer, staring instead at my beer. "I don't want to overstep," she said.

"Everything can go like this," I said, snapping my finger. "A person's life, I mean. It's over, just like that..." Véronique squeezed the top of my hand. "So how do I feel, sometimes? Like my toes are over a cliff."

"How often are you drinking?" Véronique asked.

"What, why?" I asked, surprised by the question. "What do you mean, like partying?"

"Partying, getting drunk..." she said.

"Well, you party *too*," I said, embarrassed by my accusatory tone of voice. "We're at a bar right now."

"Yes, but I'm not doing that every weekend," she said. "I'm not doing it multiple times per week."

"What's with this? A big part of my life is being in the clubs, talking to people," I said. "And everything social centers around alcohol. And you know *that*." Véronique appeared to bite her tongue. She wanted to say something but relented. I knew it would be about going back to school or taking myself in some other direction.

"You know," she started, "I'm going to take off for a little bit. I want to spend some time out of Canada."

"For how long?"

"I don't know yet. Maybe a few months. Maybe a little more. Depends on whether I find something interesting."

I could immediately see her new life and was diminished by this vision: one of cafes, sun-drenched walks on cliff-side Italian towns and Véronique's frequent seduction. I would be here, handicapping hockey fights for hapless gamblers desperate to bet on men giving one another brain damage.

"You could come," she said, smiling.

"You don't want to say here with me?" I asked. She shook her head.

"No. There are worlds beyond Montreal." One more thing," she began. My heart fell. "What happened when I went to your place a few weeks ago. It's okay, it happens. You had a lot on your mind. There's no pressure, okay?"

"I know," I said, now an ant before an elephant. "I'm sorry, it had nothing to do with you." Véronique nodded.

"You know, you could be good at a lot of things," she said.

"Like what?" I asked.

"Whatever you want. Things that don't involve what you're doing."

"But I have a reason for doing this," I answered. Véronique looked from me to a painting on the pub wall. It showed an English country town where frocked noblemen gossiped in a town square.

"Would *they* want you to be doing what you're doing?" she asked, turning to make eye contact, a drip of judgment appearing in her voice for the first time.

"What do you mean?"

"Well, people are getting hurt, no?"

"Who?"

"The players who are taking these punches. The people who lose to you guys."

"Would *who* want me to be doing what I'm doing? What do you know about it?" I asked, now somewhat shrill. "There's no one left to offend."

Véronique took another sip of her drink and looked down. There was nothing else to say so I asked for the bill. After an uneasy goodbye, we stopped talking to one another.

14.

I wasn't ignorant to how dramatically my life had turned. I sometimes had these realizations whenever a banal duty — like verifying whether I had enough cash for drop-offs to our winners — crystallized the strangeness of my new position. My brain would start associating the causal things that led me here, but I didn't dwell on them. After all, the source of these events justified all that I was now doing, and comforted by this belief I would invariably return to my business. It was especially useful to have so much to do when there was an equal number of things I didn't want to think about. And so while Véronique retained some space in my head, I kept sufficiently busy to where any shame I felt through our association would be quickly forgotten whenever an indolent debtor needed reintroducing to reality.

Unless in exceptional circumstances, we always collected on Fridays. When a bettor didn't pay on consecutive weeks or if they stopped answering our messages, the protocol changed. Today, I was set to meet two avoidants and Karim came along to help.

"How do you want to handle this, bro?" he asked. We were walking downtown, towards a spot where I arranged to meet the first bettor. Karim was wearing a purple Louis Vuitton tracksuit, one I'd seen on an NFL player captured drunkenly outside of a Hollywood club. I didn't know how much Karim made every week, but his growing wardrobe was a source of amazement. If he was concerned about paying for a kid, there was an obvious place to start saving.

"If he doesn't have it — and he probably doesn't — we're putting him on a plan," I said.

"You don't think he'll have it?" Karim asked, pulling out a cigarette.

"His head's already underwater. I doubt he can even pay the vig."

"He a goof?"

"A suburb kid," I said. "Nice guy, but can't help himself."

"Just make him your bitch, bro," Karim said, looking at me with a coy smile. "I got a solution."

We continued walking as the wrinkles of Karim's velvet suit folded in on each other. I wasn't dressed for the cold temperature, my hands hardening in the frigid air. When we arrived at the parking lot, I checked to see if there were security cameras that might record our conversation. We waited for a minute in silence.

Smitty — a slight guy about my age with wispy black hair that fell sideways across his forehead — emerged from around the corner. He looked like any one of the guys I grew up with, in his faded jeans, white sneakers and black hoodie. Smitty's eyes were moving to the ground and back again as he looked from Karim to me. I said hello and nothing more: deliberate silence placed a burden on the bettor.

"I just need a bit more time, man," he said in a small voice, shaking his head.

"You're too far behind," I said. "Three weeks, Smit."

"I'm sorry Teddy, it's not like I'm betting anywhere else, I just got bills and my car fucking broke down and—"

"Not good enough," Karim said. "This is how things are gonna go, okay?" Smitty was startled by the intervention.

"You're going to pay us back, there's no getting out of the principle. You bet. You lost. You owe." Karim said this in a practiced, percussive rhythm. "We'll talk about the exact amount and put you on a plan." Smitty looked down and nodded. "But you also owe Teddy a vig. So you're gonna work that off and part of the principle."

"How?" he asked, bewildered.

"Giving us rides," Karim said, "and whatever else we need. Nothing crazy, but if we need to get somewhere, have something picked up, whatever, you do it. Understand?" Smitty didn't say anything and sighed.

"Depending on how much you do," I added, "I'll start shaving off part of the debt."

"Come on, Teddy, I'll get some money soon—"

"Nope," Karim said, his tone sharpening. "And don't give us the shelter puppy eyes. You got nothing for three straight weeks, bro. We gotta send money up and you're fucking with the flow. You don't like this option, we'll set you up with someone else." Smitty looked down and nodded. I didn't want to involve a goon, but nor did I offer an alternative.

"Alright Smit," I said, "I'll be in touch with you." Smitty turned around and slunk away. I looked at Karim.

"We gotta go over to Crescent," I said. "Second guy's from my neighbourhood. He's older. Could be a cunt."

"I ain't worried," Karim said, smiling. "Not after what you did to that hippo in Laval, bro. Where's he work?"

"Full time for the city but serves in one of Eddy's bars so he can take down. He's there now. Stu."

We made our way west towards Crescent and walked up some wrought iron stairs to a second floor restaurant that became a bar at night. Late-afternoon, it was half-empty, and towards the back I could see Stu pretending to clean pint glasses. When he saw us come in, perhaps noticing that Maxime wasn't with me today, Stu held up a finger to indicate we'd wait. Karim and I stood by the bar, declining the server's offer for a drink. Stu came back two minutes later, looking at Karim as he tried to process his face.

"I'm done in two minutes" he told me. "Want to meet out back?"

"Two minutes," I said. Stu turned around and disappeared into the kitchen.

"This dude has that 'you'd-be-lucky-to-suck-me' face," Karim said. "If he tries something out there, he ain't making another bet with anyone." I didn't know whether Karim had a weapon.

Stu came back out and motioned towards the back door. We followed him past a concerned waitress and down a flight of stairs that led to the back alley, where there were dumpsters but no cameras. Stu turned to face me, his face taut. I waited for him to start talking.

"I need another week," he said.

"Why?"

"Because…" he began, shaking his head. "My parents, man — I needed to help them out 'cause my dad's sick—"

"What do you have now?" I asked, uninterested in the explanation.

"Can you just put me on a schedule?" Stu's blue eyes were bloodshot. He may have gotten drunk last night.

"Ship's sailed, bro. You couldn't even meet the plan we had."

"Come on, Teddy."

"Nope," I said. "Sorry, dude, no more slipping." I could see Stu becoming angry. At his situation. At his fatigue. That I — his physical inferior — was the person he was answering to.

"No?" he asked, blood collecting in his temples. "What are you gonna do about it, bud?" I could feel Karim tensing beside me, but he was still content to let me lead.

"What else you got?" I asked.

"What do you mean?"

"You got a watch, laptop?"

"Fuck that," he said.

"Huh?" Karim asked. Stu sneered at him before looking back at me.

"That site's a piece of shit anyway, doesn't recognize my credits, always entering the bets wrong!" I laughed in his face. This incensed Stu even more.

"And you think I'm going to start selling shit off to pay *you* back?" he asked. "You were a fucking *nobody* in high school," he said. Stu's voice was breaking.

"I'm just trying to give you an out," I answered.

"Your parents forgot to turn the stove off and now you're a tough guy? Give me a fucking bre—"

I leapt forward and threw a punch that landed on his forehead. Stu staggered backwards and grunted, preparing to steady himself so he could fight back. I hit him with another right hand and could feel the skin of my knuckles peel back against Stu's teeth. He lurched forward in a drunken shimmy, grabbing my shoulders with hypertrophied arms, but Karim punched him in the side and I heard a short pop when his hand rebounded off Stu's rib bone. He fell to the ground and Karim began kicking him in the same place. Stu screamed and tried to armor his stomach as blood emerged in his mouth. Already a bruise had formed on his forehead.

"Give this twat a fucking kick, bro," Karim said, "talkin' about your parents like that. Fucking cunt!"

Karim's face demanded another blow. I stared at Stu, near hyperventilation as he braced for a boot. It wasn't out of compassion, but perhaps some forgotten moral instruction, somewhere in the back of my brain, that prevented me from doing it.

"Let's go," I said to Karim, pulling him by the arm.

"You're paying tomorrow," Karim said, looking back at Stu, who whimpered on the concrete. "The guy we send won't leave without it." He delivered a final blow to Stu's stomach before we left the alley.

When I looked back, just as we were turning onto Crescent, Stu was still horizontal. The same door we used to exit the restaurant had opened and I heard a shriek from the waitress. Maybe she would tell the police, I didn't know, but the prospect of trouble meant nothing to me now. The only sensation I experienced was relief over how little any of this registered with me.

15.

The Count of Westmount wanted to talk. This is what I'd started calling the sharp who won thirty-five thousand in my second week. He messaged earlier to ask that I stop by his house, but I had to see Eddy that afternoon and requested that he come downtown instead. I still didn't know what he looked like as we'd never spoken in person (though he had obviously seen me put money through the mail slot of his house), and I was in a shoe store on Sainte-Catherine, being helped by a robust, frizzy-haired Arab — who had on one those store-uniform referee jerseys that stretched over belly — when I felt a tap on the shoulder. I turned and was met by a small, thin man with black hair and a pronounced jaw. He had the same facial detachment as Ferdinand Guillot.

I knew that his name was Allan, which seemed banal for so mysterious a person. He had on navy pants, and a tight, powder blue sweater over top of his white dress shirt. Allan smiled at me without opening his mouth but looked uncomfortable being in the store. Of course, no one took any notice of him.

"How are you?" he asked in the small, self-assured voice of someone who knows exactly what they're about to say, reaching out to shake my hand. Allan's bony palm contained a wiry strength, and from up close I could see the black centers of his eyes. His face was not unkind, but when he smiled, subtly, as he was doing now, his teeth were jagged for someone of obvious wealth.

"Nice to meet you in person. What's going on?" I asked, turning away from the shoe rack. Behind me two young boys were directing homophonic insults at a Nike ad. I took him away from the corner where they were talking.

"There's a problem with the site," he said, his voice low. "It's not registering any of my bets."

"That's got nothing to do with me," I said, "I don't chase people off who win."

"I'm not saying you do, but I tried to register two this weekend and the site wouldn't take them. Both games hit."

"Did you place those bets elsewhere?" I asked. While he didn't answer, Allan's eyes never left mine. They had turned harder. His lips were now a tight line.

"Alright," I said, "well if that's true, I'm sorry. I'll get your account set right."

"Thank you. I'm not suggesting you're responsible, Teddy, but it's bad business to shut down people who win," he said, crossing his arms. "I've been with you guys for a while and don't want to leave, but I will. They've made a lot of money off of me, too."

"I agree, Allan, and I'll take care of it."

I promised to get back to him, and Allan shook my hand and left the store. Wherever the hell he went, I had no idea. What was the source of his income, I wondered? Who was this man and what was he doing with us?

"First time I ever got laid," Eddy started, "was at my buddy's house in Hochelaga, about a block from where I lived. We were young, ostie, fourteen probably, and got some liquor. Anyway, a girl we went to school with came by. JF passed out upstairs but we were still going. Before I know it, she jumps on top of me.

Next thing I know my life changes. Everything since has been about getting more of *that*." I smiled at his story. The life-changing experience Eddy narrated happened a couple of years later for me.

He had asked me to meet him at a cafe in the Old Port. With no sign outside, I didn't know it existed and had to push into the unknown through a heavy front door. Inside, the large open space felt old world, with dark ceilings and leather wingbacks in a corner area walled by colourless photos.

"I loved that fucking street for that reason man, I never forgot it, you know? Always made me happy to be on that street. Like it parted all the clouds."

"What street?" I asked. He told me the name, but I'd never heard of it. The city's east-side neighbourhoods were almost exclusively French and largely unknown to me.

"I loved that street man," he repeated, looking away again.

"I can tell."

"That's why I just bought the house," he said, smiling. "I also bought a couple more on that block."

"Congratulations," I said. "Probably a good idea."

"The parties we used to have there, man," he started. "My buddy's parents were always away. It was wild man, ostie. Everything that could have happened, happened in that house."

"And now you own it," I said.

"Yes sir."

"You're going to own the whole city soon," I said. He smiled and looked away but offered no self-effacing remark. Eddy had an ego that wouldn't dismiss even the smallest complement, and it seemed that he did, in fact, want to own the city. Every time we spoke, our conversation bent back towards real estate. He spent hours every day scouring the internet for new listings. But what about his other businesses? What space was left for them?

"So," I asked, "what'd you want to talk about?"

"The book's changing hands," Eddy said. "Those ostie fucks bought out a bunch of people. They want a piece of what we're doing, too." He took a sip of his coffee and waited for my reaction.

"But you're independent," I said. "Why do they have a claim to what we're doing?" Eddy didn't answer my question and stared past me. "If you say no, are they going to make a problem?" I asked.

"That depends."

"On?" Eddy took another sip of his coffee, looking out towards the port. Tourist families were taking pictures before the harbor.

"These are that piggy's cousins?" I asked.

"Yeah," he said, "two cannolis. They call Genny 'the Benz.' Got the name taking a dealership from a guy who bet against the eighty-six Habs."

"So what can we do?"

"I'm gonna talk to them."

"And they're just buying out everyone who has a piece?" I asked.

"They want it for themselves, and they want people to know."

"Why can they dictate?" I asked, remembering at once what they did to Pierre Jacqueline.

"Because they got guys."

"What do we have?" I asked, eager to finally know how strong our group was.

"We're a small shop and some of my guys may be going on vacation." I didn't ask who they were, but knew that Pierre-Andre and Jean-Marc had been arrested. Without their influence Eddy may have been reluctant to resist the Italians.

"So what do you want *me* to do?" I asked him.

"I want you to start making more money," he said. I didn't

remind Eddy that my sheet already was. This weekend it took in nearly twenty-five thousand. The overall volume of wagers had quadrupled from my first week, as word about the SLSPL market was finding new ears. Patty was getting more messages from guys connected to the people he brought in, and there was no reason to expect the rate of expansion wouldn't continue.

But there was another way to make money, one I'd been resisting until now. I told Eddy of an idea whose success was contingent on Andre's ignorance. He agreed with the proposal. "But one more thing," Eddy said.

"Yeah?"

"I heard about the beating you laid on that kid, the one from the restaurant. One of the waitresses had to be paid not to call the fucking cops. No more of that shit, especially outside of one of my spots. Calice, T, you can't be cracking people too often."

"I don't want to, but you heard what he said?" I asked, my voice rising. Immediately I thought about Sil and the strip club. This could have implications now that Genny had formally entered our business.

"He's a fucking idiot, sacrament. But stay in the shadows, T, always."

"One more thing," I started. "The sharp from Westmount, Allan, came to see me. Said his account wasn't working. We're not chasing guys off if they're winning, are we?"

"No, of course not," he said, staring past me and across the bar. I wasn't convinced but Eddy pre-empted my follow-up question.

"Your idea, T. Might be something there," he said. Do it."

16.

I came from hockey, and though my talent for the sport was modest I understood its machinery. There was a system in Canada, one mythologized by the media and made real in rinks across the country, where promising young hockey players were removed from their homes during teenage hood, forced to live in a sealed value system that answered only to itself, and taught to skate, hit and fight by humourless men who saw coaching as an approximation of military generalship. From childhood on, I followed the careers of players I'd seen during trips with my dad to Longueuil Collège Français games. The hockey ecosystem was substantial: under the NHL there was the American Hockey League, the East Coast Hockey League, and various circuits scattered across the American southwest, where fringe professionals could spend a few years before returning to small Canadian towns and using their minor celebrity for some type of sales position.

The abundance of leagues created a demand for tough guys, many of whom moved from one place to another (particularly in the lower tier circuits, where players were constantly looking for opportunities to make more money). Since the SLSPL paid in cash, it was easy to bring in new players on the promise of a lucrative weekend. As a self-appointed representative of the Verdun team (Andre had previously agreed that I could contact people on the team's behalf), I leveraged Maxime for a way into this world. He knew people everywhere in hockey and provided me numbers of former teammates who could be coaxed into coming into Montreal. Most didn't want to say no because we were offering real money for weekend work. All it took was an introduction over text, "I got your number from Maxime Doucette, would you be interested in…", a fast phone call, and from there, my network of contacts expanded by the dozens.

Even if they said no outright, I had the means to change opinions. If I wanted a particular player — one with a hard-won reputation who fans would pay to watch — they'd get one thousand per game. I would cover half of this expense and Andre would pay the rest. This sort of tax-free profit was far more than any of these fighters would make during a weekend in the Coast.

"A fucking grand bud?" was the response I got from Jamie Afelski, a well-known AHL heavyweight who'd returned to a life of farming in the Ottawa Valley. He was the perfect candidate for our purposes, in that he lived close enough to drive himself into Montreal (meaning we wouldn't have to pay for airfare, although some teams did for players who lived elsewhere in Canada and were popular enough to justify the expense) and was a darling of internet fight footage.

"Yeah, for one game. If things go well that could be regular," I promised him.

"I heard about this from a buddy," he said. "Is it all fightin' or what? I've already had a lifetime of tilts…"

"There's a bit of that," I started. "Nah, fuck it, who am I kidding, there's a *lot* of that. The fans like a certain type of player. Your type."

There was a pause on the other end of the line as Afelski considered returning to the ring. But one thousand tax free dollars for a farmer still likely struggling with his operation's debt load was too tantalizing to say no. I re-emphasized the money.

"If things go well, that rate will rise," I said. "Some of the heavies in this league are cleaning up. It's not the guys who score that get paid the most. It's the guys our fans care about. You do your part, and we're happy to re-negotiate, even though what I just offered you is a lot more than first-timers get. And that's because of your reputation."

This wasn't a lie. Less accomplished tough guys were offered smaller amounts, but Afelski was known: he'd beaten up several respected heavyweights during a career in the minors and would have played for the Blackhawks had he not snapped his leg in half at twenty-four.

"I'll give it a shot," he said in a lilting Valley accent, "tough to turn down that kinda money."

Beyond whichever phone numbers Maxime provided, to find players like Afelski I spent hours every day scouring the hockey message boards. They detailed which guys were no longer eligible to enter the United States because of legal trouble (leaving us as their best available option), who had made a name for themselves lower down in the hockey hierarchy and wanted their shot in the best fighting league in the world, and players who, for whatever reason — injuries, trades or the infinite number of variables that dictate someone's success in any given profession — needed a place to play. Some of the SLSPL's current heavyweights were guys who hadn't prospered in any of the main professional circuits, but who could nonetheless scrap and understood the SLSPL's premium on pageantry. Our fans loved guys with elaborate pre-fight rituals, and this was who I pursued: those fearsome and game enough to be taken seriously, but who, crucially, could entertain. Even players whose styles were more sedate often bought into these expectations once they arrived in Quebec and saw how money followed mania.

Beyond player acquisition, I had to figure out who was likely to fight whom. This mostly involved a mental calculation that took into account which players on the other team approximated a given fighter's size and experience. Of course, if I thought there was another interesting matchup that bettors might want to wager on (regardless of its implausibility), I created wider lines to provide these betting options. Prior to our home games in Verdun, I even distributed a pamphlet of suggested matchups, making sure that our website's developer updated the league's gambling page with a new feature that spotlighted possible tilts and corresponding odds.

The administrative side of this work was an effort I hadn't anticipated, but my operation had to keep pace with demand. Patty had put aside his enthusiasm for daytime talk shows to help out with the organizing. He started spending more time on his laptop and frequently came to me with player names I'd forgotten or never heard of. I would then find their contact information and make an offer. There was a staggering number of guys to pursue, which was perfect because my sheet needed to start making more money. After all, there were opportunities I wasn't taking advantage of. It was time to start engineering fights.

I received another email from the registrar's office about whether returning to university was in my future. It wasn't a generic message, either, as a woman's name appeared at the bottom. There was a date I needed to reply by, but rather than consider her question I opened a hockey rumours website to see who'd recently been moved in the minor professional ranks.

One of players I acquired through this research had just arrived in Montreal. On Friday afternoon I met Chanse McDougall before his first SLSPL game. He'd just flown in from Regina and was staying in a motel close to the rink where, two years ago, two addicts fell from a second floor balcony in a fight over contested meth. I received his number from Marc, the Verdun GM, in part because I'd financed the player's airfare and since Marc believed we wanted to speak with McDougall about a pro-am boxing opportunity (he had fought as an amateur in Saskatchewan). When I showed up to his room with a case of beer, McDougall opened the door in bleary-eyed disorientation.

Our conversation started with an apology for interrupting his nap. He wasn't much taller than me, but broader, with a hockey player's lower half, and shook my hand with a fast smile, asking that I follow him in. The room was small, with an old carpet and antiquated television set over which his clothes were drying. There was some open luggage by the bathroom, and on his nightstand a murky spittoon. McDougall sat on the edge of the bed and rubbed his eyes. I took a seat on the small chair beside his TV.

"So," he started, still trying to organize his thoughts, "you got something in boxing, right?"

"There may be a pro-am opportunity here this summer. You know," I went on, "if you make a name for yourself here, people here are gonna come watch you box. That's how it works with this stuff. You plan on playing here for a bit?"

"If the money's there." He spoke in the flat manner of people from Western Canada. "So what's with this fight card?" he asked. "Why do you want to talk now if it's after the season?"

"It takes a while to find the right people. You have actual experience and we're looking to fill a show with guys from the league. That way we can promote it during the season," I lied. McDougall nodded, interested in the idea.

"Yeah, well maybe," he said, yawning. "We'll see how things go. Do French fans even cheer for English guys?"

"If they punch with some poison, you're fucking right they do. Anyway, big game tonight," I went on. "You got Sammy Lajeunesse making his debut."

"I know," he said, stretching his arms and hamstrings, too groggy to care. I pulled a tin out of my pocket and handed it to him. McDougall thanked me and began to pack it.

"Who's going him?" I asked, smiling.

"Lajeunesse? I dunno. Somebody…" he said, fitting a pinch into his lower lip.

"Good scalp," I said, "for a guy looking to make his name."

"Everybody'll want that guy."

I didn't want to state my intention, but he had to be aware of the reward. "I'm a friend of the team's," I answered, getting up to leave. "If you're the one who gets him, I'll make sure they up your game rate, but keep that between us, as I don't want the other guys getting pissy. We're happy to have you here." I put two hundred dollars down on the table. "This is for food, and whatever else you need."

"You don't have to do that, man," he said.

"All good. I know what you did in the Dub, the two-minute Tompkins tilt in the Coast, and I told Marc he needed to sign you. Just want to make sure you have what you need. I think you're going to do well, and if I'm right, there's gonna be a lot more money coming your way. The fans here want a show above all and you're a guy who brings the pop they pay for. Anyway, I just wanted to say hello and gauge your interest in the card. Who knows — you take out a few number ones and may end up headlining it. But we can talk about that later."

McDougall smiled, perhaps out of relief that he could go back to sleep. I wished him a restful nap and left.

Sammy Lajeunesse was an NHL heavyweight made stateless by the lockout. All of the lucrative European contracts for enforcers had been taken, and the SLSPL paid more than the

AHL (with nearly all of this money in cash). With nowhere else to play, Lajeunesse signed with his hometown Quebec City team, whose arrival in Verdun was teased on the daily sports radio shows, their jackal hosts laughing at the prospect of Lajeunesse fending off a whack-a-mole of anonymous toughs. The game had sold out and at least fifty of my bettors were going, everyone wagering on who he'd fight first.

I put McDougall as a longshot because the most obvious candidate was Lachapelle, the heavyweight Maxime fought prior to their circus a few weeks ago. Most of the early action tilted towards him and some of my bettors thought there'd be a brawl. I wasn't sure about this, only hopeful that McDougall would get to the NHLer first.

Patty and Karim stood beside me through the warmup. Lachapelle skated back and forth across the red line, trying to intimidate Quebec, but Lajeunesse appeared not to notice, going through the regular drills as an assertion that, in this lowly sideshow league, he would do more than fight. As usual, mulleted Verdun fans swore at him from behind the glass, but again, the enforcer barely noticed, stickhandling in and around an archipelago of pucks by the blue line. He was listed at 238 pounds and, as an active NHL player, Lajeunesse was in far better shape than most tough guys in this league, many of whom were twenty pounds overweight, some with fat faces and visible stomachs. He either wasn't wearing shoulder pads or had on very small ones, but Lajeunesse's jersey stretched over his rounded shoulders. Towards the end of the warmup, after he had been taunted for the past twenty minutes, Lajeunesse skated off the ice; before he could disappear into the tunnel, one of the fan's threw a glass of water on him. The heavyweight pointed upwards, and security apprehended his tormenter.

The crowd was bigger than a few weeks ago. We stood in the same section on a full concourse, our bodies wedged as we competed for a clear view of the rink. When the game began, Quebec skated out to a concord of boos. Verdun was next, and horns blasted as a lineup of fighters took their laps before the national anthem. McDougall pumped his legs, skating between teammates.

On the second shift, Lajeunesse was playing with two skilled forwards. He looked serviceable, too, making basic passes and maneuvering himself into open ice before the net, where Lajeunesse almost batted in a lazy rebound.

Midway through his shift, Lachapelle was sent out and the crowd began to cry. The Laval heavy skated up to the NHL enforcer and started wagging his gloves, but Lajeunesse skated away.

"Drop your fucking gloves you fucking pussy!" a teenage boy yelled.

This interaction happened several times in the first period: one of the Verdun heavyweights would challenge Lajeunesse, but in each instance the NHLer declined. He didn't want to fight yet, and every 'no' enraged the fans. When Lajeunesse walked back to his dressing room after the first period, a gang of teens gave him the finger. Poor Chanse McDougall, however, only played two shifts. He didn't share the ice with Lajeunesse as his line was pulled off twice before defensive zone faceoffs.

My attention was called to a group now standing with the bikers, not far from our position on the concourse. Sil was among them, wearing a black sweater that accented his potbelly. I hadn't seen him since the strip club. He was with three other Italians, one of whom had a muscular face and was clearly being deferred to. This man wore a leather jacket, brown slacks and the sort of expensive dress shoes that only rich people could afford to waste in the winter salt.

"Fuck," I said, to no one.

"What?" Karim asked beside me.

"That clown from Laval outside the strip club, he's down the concourse. Don't look now," I said. Karim waited a moment before glancing in their direction.

"Yeah, I see that dumb tubby," he said.

"Fuck do I do?" I asked.

"What do you mean?"

"The guys with him hit those Haitians on Saint-Laurent."

"They're not doing jack shit in here," Karim said.

"Still…" I began.

"Still what?" he said. "You gonna Forrest Gump out of here?"

"No, of course not."

Eddy was at the game, too. He had spent the first period in the owner's box, emerging during the intermission to mingle with the dozens of people he knew here. As if to put a spotlight on me, he came over to say hello. Andre, the Verdun owner, walked over to speak with the other group. Some I recognized from the strip club on opening night.

"Got some company," I said to Eddy. He was sipping on what appeared to be rum and coke.

"I know, I was just talking to them."

"That clown Sil is there."

"I *know*, tabernak, I was just talking to them."

"And?"

"And what?" he asked, annoyed.

"They going to cause a problem?"

"Why would they? He's their retarded relative, ostie. Just outta jail, they're going to cause a problem for *him*, in front of four thousand witnesses?"

"And in time?" I asked.

"Are you worried, Teddy?" he asked, smiling.

"I just want to be ready."

"Just keep your eye on the money. How we doing tonight, anyway?"

Everything looked good, but the major determinant of our success would hinge on who got to Lajeunesse. From the corner of my eye, I could see Sil listening to the more important people speak. I knew he wouldn't forget me, since no man fails to remember the face of someone who hurt them. The humiliation that follows getting beaten up — especially when the loser initiates contact — exposes a truth that self-regarding men rarely acknowledge: that we're really not all that hard.

"Fucking guy's gotta go somebody at some point," Patty said, beer in hand. We were looking down towards Quebec's bench as the team had returned for period two. Lajeunesse was stretching his hamstring. Eddy nodded silently as he prepared to leave.

"Somebody can't let him say no," I said.

"How much came in on this game?" Patty asked.

"A lot."

"How many of those are bets on Lajeunesse-Lachapelle?"

"A lot."

When the second began, Verdun scored two goals in five minutes. Lajeunesse was still getting a regular shift but doing little offensively. Booed every time he touched the puck, no one came to see him stickhandle.

"Drop the gloves and get your team going, you fucking loser!" a drunk man in his mid-twenties yelled in French. Everyone around him laughed.

With Verdun up by two goals, McDougall's line came on. Lajeunesse was still out, and McDougall skated over to challenge him by the Quebec bench. The fans screamed for Lajeunesse to consent, even though, from Quebec's perspective, answering McDougall's aggression made little sense when it was leading. Lajeunesse hesitated, still unwilling, but McDougall — fully alert after his long afternoon slumber, his obstinacy buoyed by the knowledge of how rare this opportunity was — wouldn't get out of his way and pushed him again. As Lajeunesse tried to skate on, McDougall punched him in the chest. The entire rink started chanting.

"Dougy! Dougy! Dougy!"

Knowing he had but one choice, Lajeunesse dropped his gloves and grabbed McDougall by the shoulders, using his longer body to secure leverage. McDougall scrambled to free his hand from Lajeunesse's grip but couldn't as the bigger man dominated his wrists.

Lajeunesse was situating McDougall's body to where it became an accessible target. Once the NHLer had his head within his punching range, he threw three overhand rights. The third punch smashed McDougall's forehead, buckling his knees. As he fell, Lajeunesse threw an uppercut that hammered off the smaller man's jaw. But rather than let go, Lajeunesse continued punching an unconscious McDougall, whose knees were on the ice. The crowd began screaming as the referees wrestled the NHL heavyweight away, but Lajeunesse still pounded the limp body. One of the other players from Verdun jumped in and started punching Lajeunesse. A line brawl broke out.

Lajeunesse was being punched by a Verdun forward as the head referee grabbed his arm. I looked down to the Verdun bench to see if anyone was set to jump over, but its coach was holding the players back. The NHLer was now standing against the glass, subdued by the ref, while the fans yelled for justice. Elsewhere, there was pushing but no active fighting. Lajeunesse was led off the ice, pelted by emptying beer cups as he vanished.

On the ice, McDougall was being assisted by his team's trainers, who called for an ambulance. The entrance at the other end was opened and a stretcher appeared. Once raucous, the rink had become a wake, as paramedics carefully made their way to the opposite blue line and loaded McDougall, now somewhat conscious, onto the stretcher. Both benches banged their sticks against the boards as he was wheeled off the ice. The crowd's applause was sedate.

"You made a down payment worth of cash, eh," Patty said. "Everybody took Cote or Lachapelle, no?" I'd forgotten about the sheet, but he was right.

"That dude nearly got introduced to Allah," Karim joked, motioning to where McDougall's stretcher had exited through a tunnel. "He one of the guys you brought in?"

"Yeah," I said, "I talked to him today…" My entire body felt hot as the game resumed and Quebec tied it near the period's end. There was no more fighting as the crowd became invested in the score. At the next intermission, I went down to the players area and asked a trainer about McDougall's condition. He shrugged underneath his mustache. McDougall had been sent to the hospital, he said. This was his only update.

I went back up to the concourse. Patty had bought a new round of drinks as more bar friends arrived. I looked over to where Sil and his cousins were standing with one of the strip club bikers. Shorter than Silvio, they started walking in my direction.

There's a full-body sense of dread one experiences when something very bad is set to happen, and a wash of hot anxiety came over me. Sil was at the back of a line led by some block-jawed leopard with a manicured goatee. My legs felt like they had grown roots deep beneath the concourse's foundation. There was nothing I could do but deal with this.

The leader came to within a foot of my face and addressed me in a cadence particular to Italian-Montrealers.

"How ya doin' bro?" he asked, staring unblinkingly into my eyes. There were muscular creases on each side of his goatee. His voice was soft.

"I'm good," I said, "liking the game?"

He laughed, surprised I came back with a question. "You're the young guy working for Eddy now, eh?"

"Yes."

"And you know my friend at the back of the line here," he said, motioning behind him to Sil.

"I do." The man let my confirmation hang for a moment. It felt like I could have impregnated a girl and had her come to full term before he answered.

"I heard you guys had a disagreement a little while ago." His eyes were hazel brown and devoid of emotion. I didn't say anything. "You did or am I being told some shit?" he asked, employing interrogation tactics mastered over a lifetime.

"We did, but it's done," I said, "water under the bridge." At the back of the line, I could see Sil look down.

"That's good," he said, beginning to smile. "If you make a bet, you need to pay, right?" I nodded in silence.

"Well, fuck it, bro, shit happens," he said. He leaned in closer to my ear. "But you're not playing the tough guy anymore, right?"

"No," I answered. "I'm not."

"How'd you do tonight, anyway?" a thin, taller man behind him asked. He was bald, with a wide mouth and pronounced cheekbones.

"Sheet's doing pretty good," I said, relieved to be speaking with someone else. "Pretty good," I repeated, trying not to look back at the leader.

"This was a good fucking idea," the leader interjected, "taking action on this shit. How'd you find out how to handicap this?"

"Just been watching the league," I said.

"You're a smart kid," the lead man said.

"Thank you."

"You're going to keep this going, right?" he asked.

"Yes sir." At this, the first three men burst out laughing.

"Respectful too, the kid," the second man said.

"I'm Gennaro," the leader said. "Now listen," he bent forward and put his hand on my shoulder. "This shit between you guys is over, you understand? Nothing's gonna happen, but he's my cousin, so no getting back in the ring again, you understand, bro?"

"I do."

"Good. Keep those lines tight, bro." He pulled his hand back and offered it for me to shake. I did, looking him directly in the eye. Gennaro moved on, his three men trailing behind him. When Sil passed he did so without acknowledging me. It took several minutes for my breathing to get back under control. A few moments later, Eddy appeared.

"You make some new friends?" he asked.

"Don't know about that."

"I smoothed things over with Sil. What'd they say to you?"

"Only that whatever happened was done."

"That it?" he asked.

"They asked about the sheet. Gennaro, whatever his name is, liked the idea."

"He thinks we're his subjects, sacrament," Eddy said, a hard note in his voice.

"Are we?"

"What the fuck do you mean?"

"Well, what if he squeezes us?" I asked.

"He doesn't get to own everything," Eddy said, motioning to the rink. "Why'd you tell him how the sheet was doing, anyway?" he asked.

"He asked — what am I supposed to say?" Eddy looked down in contemplation of this new reality.

"What are you going to do?" I asked.

Eddy paused for a moment before responding. "I'm gonna talk to him again. How's the sheet doing?"

I didn't have the numbers but knew it was our best night.

Despite the volume of bets, no one had taken McDougall, and while it didn't feel good to acknowledge this, his beating would serve me well. Why? My debt to Eddy had just been paid off. I was now making money.

17.

"**He didn't have the experience** to go that guy. I respect his balls. But that was too big of a step up."

Maxime and I were having a beer in St. Henri. His daughter, Angélique, had only just been picked up by her mother. Tall for her age with long brown hair, she spent most of dinner reading one of those teenage magazines that covered the trajectory of Nickelodeon stars who went on to pop stardom. When Maxime introduced us, proud of what he'd produced but uncomfortable with exposing her to someone from his other professional circle, she smiled with the open, good-natured face of someone whose identity wasn't predicated on aggression. We talked about her elementary school's soccer team, where she'd spent the season playing goalie. Though she delighted in her father's company, I didn't think Angélique knew the degree to which Maxime was revered across Quebec. She seemed disappointed to leave.

When she left, our talk turned to business. The incident with McDougall had made its way onto the mainstream sports media channels that otherwise didn't pay attention to the SLSPL. This was partly because of the event's viciousness (McDougall's face was broken and his brain a mess, and it was possible he would never play again), and that Simon Lajeunesse was involved. I changed the subject.

"I ran into Sil's cousins at the game. Just got out of jail. You know a guy named Gennaro?"

"Know *of* him. Think he used to own a piece of the league. What he say to you?" Maxime's knowing response reminded me that he knew almost everyone in Montreal who worked in the milieu and had some connection to hockey.

"That what happened between me and Sil was over. He was interested in our sheet."

Maxime wore a brown turtleneck under his black North Face vest. His hair had been gelled back, and though he'd likely shaved that morning a thick shadow was forming on his cheeks. "It only comes back to cash, bud. Some of the guys in this wouldn't care about who killed their brother, tabernak, you know?"

"Is Eddy—" I started.

"Eddy ain't on the same level as them. There's an establishment that he ain't a part of."

"What do they own?" I asked.

"Everything that everybody wants a piece of." Maxime took a sip of his beer and glanced over to a table of women looking at him.

"So what's this mean for Ed?"

"No idea yet," Maxime said, looking down. "Depends on whether Eddy gets defensive." Though I trusted Maxime instinctively (he never interrupted me and appeared to internalize most of what I said, since, unlike Eddy, he wasn't preoccupied by other things during our conversations), I didn't want to speak to candidly about our boss. But this wasn't necessary. Maxime had misgivings of his own.

"He needs to make a decision," Maxime went on. "I don't know if he put enough fucking interest into this business, ostie. You don't do this shit part time. It's full time or you don't do it at all. You can take action and you can do real estate, whatever. But the legit stuff needs the other stuff if you want enough to stay above board."

"So what's going to happen?"

"He's in a bad spot now, ostie, Ed. I've seen it happen. Some guy like him does okay, bigger guys come in and want the pie. Smaller guy has to decide how much to give up."

"What happens when the smaller guy says no?" I asked.

Maxime smiled and shook his head. "A pitbull doesn't back off when a poodle hogs the dish. This is just how it starts, bud. They show themselves, start asking for shit and the demands get bigger. Works the same way every time," he said.

"So where does that leave me?" I asked.

"With a decision bud," he said. "Build a pile of money and get out. Nobody's got any loyalty in this shit. In anything." Maxime took a sip of beer and continued. "My first contract in semi-pro. I had a name back then, but still had to establish myself in the league. I got injured in the offseason, between playing in the American league, East Coast league, then I got in trouble and was off for some time. People thought I was done. I came back to play in Richelieu, first time in the league. The owner was an asshole and wants me to prove myself. It was nice at first, but I never trusted him. I signed a contract on a per-game basis, played five games in the league and didn't get any money. Not one fuckin' dollar, tabernak. And this after I fought ten times against toughest number ones in the league. So I go and see the owner and he gives me half of what I was owed, tells me to keep proving myself. I told him to fuck off. He eventually paid me and was never late afterwards. He was a fuckin' asshole, sacrament, even though he paid up. It taught me something: you need to get your money. Always. You do work for someone, and they profit from it — you need to get your money. Every time. Every fucking time."

"To do that, I gotta continue taking bets for a while."

"I know, just be sure about where you step. Conflict," he said, pausing, "it's coming."

A waitress came over and Maxime asked for another beer. When she left, his attention was absorbed by a table of giggling women sitting across from us. Maxime sent them all a shot. After a vigorous hug to end the night, I called Smitty to pick me up and he arrived within ten minutes, silent in the driver's seat on our drive back to NDG. I woke up the next morning, exhausted and confused before I remembered our conversation. Everything I was doing had now become real. So too would be the consequences.

"You see this?" I asked Eddy, pushing a paper in his direction. It was the Montreal Gazette's sports section. "Violence in Verdun: On Loan from the Locked Out NHL, Simon Lajeunesse Hospitalizes Opponent." The article's description made it sound as if McDougall was almost beaten to death. Now out of the hospital, he was healing a brain hemorrhage and done for at least this season. The article questioned whether charges were coming against Lajeunesse. Eddy laughed when he saw the headline.

"What a fucking joke," he said.

"You think this will impact the league?" I asked him.

"Yeah, in a good way. Friday was Andre's biggest gate ever. This is the best attention the league could hope for, ostie. The fans come looking for a fight. All this media attention just confirms they'll get a bone to chew on." He wasn't wrong: our profits had grown to nearly forty thousand a week.

"Just look at your numbers," he said. "Look how many of these young guys wanna come to the games and bet. It's a great fucking business, man, and *you* recognized this first," he said. "Everybody benefits."

"I have a guy that wants to get on," Patty would say to me, often several times a week, throughout November and early December. They were all bar or university friends who wanted to spend their spare dollars gambling.

Only when someone showed they had money did I allow them to bet in bigger amounts. The guys older than us, just out of university and employed, had different limits. Some were capped at five hundred, others at a thousand. The more established bettors had higher ceilings. Some, like the Count of Westmount, had none.

With semi-pro hockey, it was mostly younger guys wagering, so the profits I made from individual bets were smaller. But with so many more bettors, the aggregated SLSPL action added up to more than I would have had if the NHL season was on. Of course, more bettors brought increased excuses for why they couldn't pay, so whenever guys didn't come up with the money, we put them on a plan. If they didn't pay after repeated weeks, we cut them off. If they caused trouble, there was always the possibility of dealing with someone like Maxime. Stu's beating was whispered between the bettors, and those on my sheet knew that consequences would attend cuntish behaviour. But there was a hierarchy of suffering. With me, things *could* end badly (and it would be a lie to say I disliked being known as someone not to short). With Maxime, an irresponsible bettor could spend their next few months in a dark room. And since dealing with their lies and deciding how much credit to lend was exhausting, I paid Patty to help with this. A practiced excuse-maker, he was well-placed to detect deceit, and Patty suddenly had some money for a twenty-one year old.

By December, my number of bettors approached one hundred and fifty, which meant that a hundred and twenty-five had been added since I took ownership of the sheet. The old gamblers were still wagering on football and, to a lesser extent, basketball, but since the NFL would be done by February, if we didn't have the SLSPL, paying off my debt would be impossible.

The speed at which the sheet grew meant my operation had to expand. Karim was also helping make collections and paying out — work that I compensated him for. I also had to spend more so that Maurice could make sure the envelopes were in order every Friday for those owed money. He was a careful person, and each week provided a list of debts we were owed, including vig calculations. All amounts were associated with the log-in numbers assigned to each person. Personal names never appeared.

I was also having more influence over who Verdun brought in. After the disaster with McDougall, I became more selective in the heavyweights Andre acquired. He needed money (why, I didn't know, given how successful the league had become) and leaned on Eddy whenever the till went empty. While it was possible he was taxing us by suggesting we pay more for players than their market values warranted, the phony receipts Andre provided Eddy (whose holding company had officially become a "team sponsor") for costs associated with running his team, like purchasing equipment, allowed us to more easily move cash through his team. It was a perfectly closed system, since we were taking action on games whose participants we'd paid for.

It would be overblown to say people became more concerned about violence in hockey after McDougall's hospitalization. There were the usual complaints from writers who trafficked in public moralizing. Some called for an investigation into the league, others for criminal charges, but most just laughed it off as just another violent incident in a history of many. The SLSPL's popularity — in light of the NHL lockout, and given the press it received via Simon Lajeunesse — meant increased ticket sales, more cash, and a greater capacity for teams to bring in tough guys from other provinces. This made for more violent hockey, and the number of fights per game never dipped during the first four months of the season. There was no money without the brawling, because while the league had some excellent players, few would care if the circus element didn't exist.

I often wondered if this league would be possible without the bikers' influence. In the 1990s they'd brought bombs to Montreal. What remained was bombast. To me, the SLSPL served to fill a void left by the biker war's conclusion, because with its pageantry and violence, the league functioned as a natural extension of the alpha male, outlaw culture made famous by the same people now using it to launder their money. And so in a very practical sense, the bikers were fundamental to its governance, pushing money through the various teams. Put more circularly, this allowed for the purchase of more tough guys, which resulted in more violence, and increased fan interest, and more money, and more tough guys, and…

To make sure we got the right people, I spoke frequently with Maxime about fighters he knew from other leagues who could step in and meet the threshold of savagery and showmanship our fans demanded. I paid the Woodchipper for his advice, and while he always made a show of protesting, not once did he refuse my money.

He was having a strong season, too, fighting every game, and had already registered a knockout. (It was rare that a hockey fight put someone to sleep. In a top year, the most lethal heavyweights might get two or three of these in a season where they fought every game.) Maxime was also talking about getting back into the boxing ring. He had fought twenty times as an amateur and wanted to appear on at least one pro card before retirement. His athletic career couldn't pass without appearing in a prizefight.

"I want a shot," he told me on a Saturday at Eddy's boxing

gym, when Maxime had come in for a short workout between his Friday and Sunday games. "No better time than now. The league's hot as shit. We're on RDS, on TVA. Everybody knows us, and I ain't getting any younger, sacrament," he said, taking a sip of water. "Tell Eddy. Tell him to make that tanned fuck Calix put me on. He's gonna make money, and he knows that."

"You don't like Calix?" I asked him.

"I've been asking him for years," he said. "Guy's got his head up his ass."

"I'll talk to them. But there's still another company in this city," I said, referencing Boxe Montreal. "You ever reach out?"

Maxime took a long sip of his protein shake, smirked and shook his head. "They're never giving me a fight, T," he said, shaking his head.

"Why not?"

"Long story, bro. But it ain't happening."

18.

I hadn't had sex in months. I wasn't bothered by its absence, only that other people may find out. In truth, my body was undisturbed, to the point where I could hardly even remember what it felt like.

Without a relationship to fall back on, I'd gauge my willingness — without the fear that an incapacity to continue could be exposed — with a lap dance. So at the end of a long Sunday, where our sheet made another thirty-seven grand, I left Karim at the sports bar and went for a solo drink at Corp Célestes.

The club was still full as groups of men who'd spent Sunday afternoon watching football made their day's final stop. Dana, a bartender I'd come to know over the past few months, took my order and handed over a cold rye and ginger. Behind her, NFL footage recounted the day's highlights.

While I already had several drinks, the two pounds of wings festering in my stomach ensured drunkenness would be impossible. But I wanted to have one more before venturing up for a dance, and took the first glass quickly before ordering a second. When Dana started telling me about her time at the club (starting in university to pay tuition), I noticed in the TV's reflection that Gennaro had entered with a few other men. I pretended not to see him and stared at the sports highlights, hopeful his group would move towards one of the back booths.

On television, one of the smirking TSN personalities was

recapping a dramatic NFL result when I felt a recognizable hand on my shoulder.

"Teddy," Gennaro said, "how ya doing, bro?" I saw the bartender look at him before smiling in the way people do when they're afraid.

"Hey Gennaro, how are ya?"

"Good day today?" he asked. "And call me Genny, bro."

"Good day," I said, nodding. "A lot of action broke our way."

"That's good to hear, bro," he said. "I'm happy to hear that. You by yourself?"

"I am, yeah, just going to have a quick one and head home."

"Come have a seat with us, bro. Have one on me and go."

He wasn't used to hearing no, so I picked up my drink and paid the bartender.

Over at their table, Genny introduced me to his group. One of the men, Ali, taller and heavyset with an untrimmed beard, looked Lebanese, and shook my hand without smiling. The other, Fortunato, I had seen at the game. He smiled, pumping my fist. When I sat down, Genny provided some justification for why a twenty-one year old had a seat at their table.

"Met this guy recently, he's working for Eddy. Doing real well. Started taking action on semi-pro hockey. Who's gonna drop the gloves and shit. More money than god, this kid," he said. I laughed.

"Eddy, eh?" Ali asked. "How's he doing?"

Genny interjected. "Same old Ed," he said. "'The Executive.' A lone fucking wolf, the guy. You like it over there?" he asked me.

"He's been good to me," I answered, uncomfortable.

"He's a competent guy," Genny answered. "Good guy to show you how shit works. Some of his business plays..." He trailed off, content to let me speculate. "Oh yeah, by the way!" he said, smiling now for the first time as he pointed to me. "This guy gave Sil a fucking beating. Fuck sakes!" he said, laughing. I could see Ali's eyes become large.

"What'd you do, bro?" he asked me.

"Ah, it was nothing," I answered.

"Wasn't nothing" Genny said, "he was embarrassed as shit about it. I love the guy but he's a big dummy sometimes. Probably didn't want to look you in the eye at the game, the goof."

"No hard feelings on my end," I said. "Shit happens."

Fortunato nodded. "That's right, bro."

"I just want the sheet to run smooth," I said. "Don't want a problem with anyone." Genny appeared satisfied and ordered a round of drinks when the waitress came over.

"One more Teddy, come on, bro," he said, slapping me on the shoulder again.

"Sounds good." What else could I say?

"So yeah, Eddy," Gennaro said, intent on having a conversation only he was interested in. "He's a good guy. Doing some good things out there, the guy. He's got a good little book, some loans, some girls. I don't want to start no issues neither. I don't need that shit right now."

The waiter returned with another tray of drinks. Genny had ordered an expensive brand of scotch. I tried to maintain a poker face as it coated my stomach.

"Good, eh?" Genny said, motioning to the booze. "You got your eyes on any of the girls in here?" he asked.

"Not really," I said, embarrassed, "just hanging out."

"Sure," he said. "Want me to set something up?"

"Thanks, but I'm okay for now," I answered. "You guys here a lot?"

"One of our spots," Genny said. The group laughed. "One of many." Fortunato referenced a friend from Laval who had his car stolen. Genny was certain it was midway to the Middle East right now. "Straight to the port and somebody in Brunei," he said. It couldn't tell whether his glee indicated involvement.

Several minutes later, two men came into the club and sat down at a table close to us.

"Watch the fuck out," Genny whispered to me, amused. "Two undercovers, right there. I recognize the one guy from a trial ten years ago. Little pencil neck. You'd think the fucking cops would send somebody I didn't know." I looked over at them. They were speaking amongst themselves. Not once did either look in our direction.

"Fucking goofs," he went on. "What are they doing here? I got no restrictions right now, me."

"They want to see who you're meeting with," Fortunato said.

"Only my man Teddy," he said. "This guy's gonna become number one out here. I can see it."

"I don't know about that," I said.

"It's in you," Genny said, his hand on my shoulder. "You just may not know it yet." I looked over again at the two undercover police officers, both of whom were staring at me.

19.

"What were you doing last night at Célestes?" Eddy asked at our Monday lunch. I was at the gym, texting about the SLSPL from behind the front desk, when he came in at the usual time. Eddy had gone into his office to look at real estate listings and yelled for me to come in.

"I went in for a drink by myself after I left Karim. Wanted to get a lapper. Genny came in and then invited me for one. How'd you know?"

"Genny? I talk to Ali sometimes," he said. "He used to bounce at one of my clubs."

A long silence followed. "I just went in to get a drink. It wasn't to meet those guys — I had no idea they'd even be there. He just saw me and then, you know, asked — or told — me to come for a drink. What was I supposed to do, say no?" Eddy looked at me with hard eyes and took a sip of his coffee.

"He say anything about me?" he asked.

"Just that you were a competent guy," I said. Eddy nearly snorted and lanced a large piece of salad.

"I go back with that guy," he said. "We both started out doing some things together." It occurred to me that I knew very little of Eddy's past.

"What?"

"You know what he went in for?" he asked. I shook my head, no. "Conspiracy to murder. Tried to take someone out in

Laval. Cops had a phone tapped."

"He mentioned last night how there were undercovers in the bar watching him."

"Watching all of *you*," Eddy said. "Now they know who you are, too, tabernak."

"Why would they care who I am?"

Eddy laughed. "Give your head a shake, T. You don't think they asked themselves, 'who the fuck's the kid at their table?'"

"They don't know my name," I argued.

"Don't matter bud, they know your face" he said. "And now you're on their radar. Lemme tell you something," he went on. "That guy's a snake. He says one thing to your face and another thing behind your back. He sees what I saw: a smart young guy who's got a mind for this. But the minute he thinks something's off, you'll get a knife in the neck."

"Is he in the mob?" I asked, at once feeling stupid for using the word.

"It doesn't matter what he's in, only who he has."

"I still don't understand how this shit works," I said. "We're independent, no? Can't we do whatever we want?"

"Just keep your head down and run that sheet the way it's supposed to." Eddy stopped short of asking me to confirm my loyalty. "These guys don't give a fuck," he went on. "Yeah, nobody wants to go to jail, but it's the cost of doing business for them. If somebody gets in their way... You understand, bud? But there's no reason to get testy, not right now. We're gonna keep going how we are."

"Okay," I said.

"Genny wants the whole book," he went on. "He wants it for the money, but he wants it for the ego. Best thing's to fly under the fucking radar, bud. You understand?"

"I do."

"The guy who had it before, Albie, owned it for years, but

he was a greedy motherfucker and wanted to keep everything for himself, tabernak. Guys were pissed and for good reason: why should one guy control everything? There's plenty of money for all. Anyway, some guys who used to lick Albie's ass started moving against him, but he was too full of himself to realize it. A few years ago, he got called to a meeting in St. Leonard and somebody came outta the closet with a shotgun."

"Who did it?" I asked.

"A lot of theories, but the guys who pulled the trigger were connected to the guy who bought you that drink."

"Oh yeah?" I asked.

"That brought a ton of heat. Guys had to come in from Toronto and New York to settle it. A few meetings and it got ironed out. I'm telling you this so you know, tabernak: it's a dangerous fucking thing to own, the book, everybody who gets it gets a problem. So we're just going to hold onto our piece and keep making money, you understand?"

"Okay, Ed," I said.

"I'm looking out for you with those guys, you know that, right? They don't have your interests in mind."

"I know." Eddy sat back, satisfied, and returned to his laptop.

"Now, numbers..." he started.

We went through our accounting for the weekend and discussed the Monday Night Football matchup. Eddy was concerned about our risk exposure, but I assured him we could move the line back in our favour depending on what came in during the afternoon. Risk management was becoming easier, but I wasn't concerned about the game: there were other things now causing me anxiety.

Winter arrived in Montreal and cold winds claimed my

street throughout December. I didn't have plans for Christmas or anyone to celebrate with, and despite receiving an invitation from Patty's family, I lied about having the flu.

I woke up late on Christmas morning and spent most of the day watching movies. A few celebratory texts came in from friends, but I heard nothing of Véronique. We were taking action on the two NBA games and a few losing bets were placed that I barely paid attention to. Instead, I ordered some Chinese food, which arrived, lukewarm and soggy two hours after placing my order. I microwaved the mishmash of fried rice, egg and chicken rolls, but became hungry again immediately afterwards, pacifying my appetite with an entire bag of salt and vinegar chips. I felt like utter shit and remained on my back for over an hour as an unfunny comedy played in the background.

Around eight, I dressed myself and went outside for a walk. The streets were vacant, and a thin film of fresh snow coated the ground. At regular intervals one of the neighbourhood houses hosted a parking lot of cars belonging to family members visiting for Christmas dinner. Even in instances where the homes were desolate, most had some form of red, blue and fuchsia lights twisted around their leafless trees. The snow pushed down under my feet as I walked down a hilly side street towards Sherbrooke and turned right.

I passed an old bakery. My mom always seemed to take me there at the same time on Saturday mornings, and I suspected she had a secret liking for the young man who worked behind its counter. I would sit in the distance, watching her cheeks glow brighter with each of his compliments. He was likely in his early twenties, then, and would be in his late thirties today. I asked my mom about him once and remember her face going red during our walk home.

Passing a window into one of the popular local bars, I saw several drinkers inside, leaning over their pints. I checked my pants to verify whether I had any money, finding sixty forgotten dollars lodged in the crease of my jean pocket. This would buy a few rounds, and so I went inside and took a seat at the bar, several feet away from the closest drinker. There were no TVs inside and over the stereo system a Beatles playlist had settled on *Something*. I ordered a pint of Guinness from the blonde bartender and took two cold gulps when she returned with the drink. The alcohol soothed a belly that was only starting to digest the glut of garbage it contained. I sat alone, staring at pictures on the wall.

I could feel the bartender looking at me. She returned to ask if I wanted another beer, and then paused, as though debating another question before returning to the tap. Black Guinness flowed smoothly into a clean glass. My interest in the pour encouraged her conversation.

"Christmas festivities over?" she asked. Maybe twenty-seven, tall and thin, with wide hips and a flat upper body, she wasn't beautiful but had the bright face of someone to whom no bad deed was ever done.

"I guess," I said. "Pretty lowkey."

"Just a family dinner or something like that?" she asked. I liked the pop in her speech.

"Chinese takeout," I said. "How about you?"

"We had a big meal earlier this afternoon," she said. "I went over to my parents. Ate so much that I didn't think I'd fit behind the bar tonight." She laughed.

"Probably no better way to work it off."

"No doubt!" I focused again on the pictures as she filled another order. Moments later the bartender returned.

"Did you at least get some good presents?" she asked.

"I didn't get anything," I said.

"Why not?"

"I'm on my own this Christmas."

"Did you just move to Montreal or something?" she asked.

"Nope, I'm from NDG." The conversation stalled. My mind went through a number of calculations about whether to keep talking, but something pressed me to keep on. What was the point of staying mute? "I'm by myself," I said, my throat closing.

"Oh!" she said. "I'm sorry."

"It's no problem."

She wore the face of someone who regretted their question. "I didn't mean to pry or anything," she said.

"You're not prying, don't give it another thought."

"Do you want another drink?" she asked. "It's on me."

"Sure, please. Thank you."

She returned with another Guinness, my third, and placed it down on the bartop. There were only two drinkers left, neither making demands for her attention. She came back to introduce herself.

"I'm Sarah," she said.

"Teddy, nice to meet you, Sarah." We shook hands over the wet bartop. "Merry Christmas," I said.

"Merry Christmas. So why are you alone, Teddy?"

I drew a breath before responding. "My parents died earlier this year."

"Oh my god!" she exclaimed. "I'm sorry!"

"Thank you, it's okay."

"What happened?" she asked, her voice trailing into an ellipsis.

"They were killed in a fire at our family cottage. Back in April." Sarah shook her head, overwhelmed.

"What the hell, man? I don't even know what to say." She appeared frozen. It was hard to tell whether Sarah believed what I told her.

"It's okay," I said. "I mean…" I didn't know what to say. "It fucking sucks," I went on, "but there's nothing I can do about it."

"Yeah…" she said. Fifteen feet from me, unsteady hands waved a bill. "Sorry, one second," she said.

"Of course."

I could see Sarah fumbling for change as a drunkard leaned over the bar, a wet smile forming on his face. When she handed him two bills, he leaned in for a sloppy hug. Sarah put away a few dirty pint glasses before returning.

"So how are you doing?" she asked me.

"I'm okay."

"I remember hearing about that in the paper," she said.

"Yeah, it was in the Gazette."

"Do you want another beer?" she asked.

"Sure," I said.

She poured me a lager. I then had a shot of whiskey, a couple of vodka sodas, two more shots, two beers, and finally a Guinness as the room began to blur. I didn't think there was anyone left when Sarah told me she was closing for the night, and reached into my pocket to produce whatever money I had, retrieving the wrinkled sixty dollars.

"This is all I got," I said. "I'm sorry." I couldn't register the reaction on her face, but she took the money, quickly retracting her hand when I put mine on top.

Upon waking the next morning, I was afraid of having done something inappropriate (my memory of the night's final hour was gone) — a possibility strengthened by a jagged cut across my palm and bloodstained sheet. When I went downstairs, it wasn't the unnaturally cold temperature of the main floor that alarmed me (I had left the front door open), but the sight, strewn across my main floor and living room, of the family pictures that once rested on the mantelpiece. All of them had been smashed.

My mother lay in pieces on the living room floor. It was a picture of us both, taken on a mountaintop in northern Haiti.

As a sixteen year old on a school trip, I went to Cap-Haitien to help build homes in a village north of the city. I will never forget the jolty, serpentine ride from the airport (whose battered runway was nestled into a valley) to our destination northwest of the city. Our van was surrounded on all sides with motorcycles commandeered by helmetless drivers and taxis where dozens of people sat wedged within a small wooden box. We snaked our way beside Cap-Haitien's appallingly dirty beach, over a bridge whose water below was filled by garbage, and through a battered, colourful French colonial town populated by more people than I had ever seen.

Overhead, the February sun poured in through the bus windows. Everywhere on the road were potholes, and each time one of our wheels fell into one we were jolted upwards, our heads touching the ceiling of the cramped van. During the entire ride my eyes never once left the window, so desperate was I to absorb every sight and colour. There were groups of small children walking from church in their immaculate catholic outfits. One girl, probably no older than ten, smiled at me as our bus drove slowly by.

We drove across the broken road and through the mountain towards Ducroix. The nicer homes, tucked into nooks along bends in the road, were invariably barred at the windows. Elsewhere, rural villagers lived in concrete huts and small children washed themselves outside, where they drew water from wells and played soccer in abandoned dusty parking lots. When we turned the corner at the end of a long hill and in the direction of Ducroix, the full Atlantic Ocean came into view, blue and sparkling, and I looked at the coastline that continued on to Labadie. In the background, muscular mountains cascaded to the sea.

Everywhere there were goats — alert and anthropomorphic with their tiny human jaws — and I marveled at how easily they navigated the steep rock faces. When the bus paused by a pothole, I saw a slim green salamander scurry from underneath one rock to the next, and I longed for the same freedom — to get off the bus and absorb some Caribbean air for the first time (I had never been on an island vacation before).

Where it was not deforested, the mountains were carpeted by a lush green treeline. There were whispers among the students that to walk into the hills was to risk your safety, but no evidence substantiated this rumour. During our stay, we helped build a small home in the hills outside of town. The structure's continuing viability didn't bother those we were helping, whose daily existence was too precarious to worry about the long term.

On our final night we saw a voodoo ceremony. This came after a fine meal in downtown Cap-Haitien, when we drove back to the hotel in Labadie — above and across the mountainous road on whose shoulder we built the house, where we came upon a party of people singing and dancing underneath one of the small houses beside the road. It looked no different from any random Saturday night gathering, and its significance was lost on me until the bus stopped and our guide, Mirlande, who had spent her entire life in Cap-Haitien, instructed us to get off and observe. My mother stood beside me, and we watched across the darkness as sparks flew skywards from the small fire. As dancers moved around the singer's drum, my body became trapped by its rhythm, and time passed without me being aware of it.

I realized, staring down at the frame's broken shards, how the memory's sense of timelessness preceded what I experienced so many weeks ago at Métropolis. Grossly intoxicated, could I even have remembered this yesterday? Is that why I'd smashed the picture? I strained for an answer but there was no revelation: I had blacked out and couldn't remember anything.

I passed an inebriated after Christmas, drinking with different groups I'd known in high school and university. Each day was an exercise in coming back to life: a groggy morning would yield to a lazy afternoon, bitter acknowledgements at the cold, and then incoming texts from friends who wished to get away from their families and forget themselves under a tidal wave of alcohol. I was frequently with Karim, who had a vigorous appetite for going out and appeared to know every bartender in Montreal. Otherwise, I spent the rest of my time with old friends, who — after I'd purchased another round for the group — would make sentimental missives about my situation. I bore these with acceptance, but they did nothing for me. Instead, I drank even more energetically and twice within the span of a week woke up disoriented on unknown couches. While I could mostly do as I pleased, given the excessive empathy afforded to me by people familiar with my story, not everyone was so accepting. The sad eyes of a friend's father confirmed obvious disapproval when I climbed the stairs in his basement late one morning. He offered me coffee as a way to start a conversation about how a better way was still possible, but I made an excuse about meeting a nonexistent aunt and slipped out the door. He invited me back for dinner and I accepted despite having no intention of returning.

At the beginning of January I took a sustained break from drinking (four days). I hadn't read a book in months and bought one from the local store on the roving killing groups Hitler employed in Poland. But I quickly put it down, unable to withstand further descriptions of murder and mass graves, before returning to my work. We were near the end of the college bowl season, with only the national championship remaining, and hundreds of wagers were coming in. On the night of USC-Oklahoma, Eddy was called for a meeting.

20.

Genny wanted to buy us out. I learned this from Karim, who relayed the details with breathless precision when I met him in a Westmount parking lot. Eddy had been called to a Laval cafe where Genny met people. He was offered a number for our operation.

"Genny tells Eddy he owns it," Karim said, wide-eyed. "The book only got farmed out when he went in, and other people were allowed to run independently, but now everything's back under his banner."

Karim said Eddy didn't agree and was told any dissent would be dealt with. He left promising to think about the mandate, and then spent several stressful days at home debating what to do.

Our boss had no leverage. The two brothers Eddy relied on, Pierre-Alexandre and Jean-Marc, were facing drug charges and hadn't been to the gym in months. Without their leverage, any negotiation with Eddy became less daunting. Genny held more influence and to run afoul of him would jeopardize us. But what could Eddy do? If he allowed himself to be bought out, Eddy would not only give up a primary source of his income, but absorb reputational damage in a business where weakness wrought ruin. Who could take him seriously if Eddy allowed his stake to be seized? There would have to be some negotiation, but how would this work?

"What the fuck do we do now, then?" I asked Karim.

"Just wait and see," he said. "Whatever happens, I got a new thing on the go I can get you into. Easy cash, nobody coming back on us." Karim provided no more information on his new business.

"If the Italians take all of our action, what are they gonna do to me?" I asked. "They gotta still be pissed at me about that shitkicking." Karim laughed at the memory.

"Just stay away from them for a bit."

"It's them not staying away from me," I answered.

Before I had the opportunity to meet Eddy in person and speak about this, I went to Maxime's game in Laval. He was looking to damage Laval's heavyweight — a tattooed cementhead whose family was sitting close to the home team's bench. Two minutes into the game, both men squared off. Maxime punched Renald Laplante fifteen times in the face before Laplante fell, waving his hands in sad protest when the referees came in to save him from a premature onset of Alzheimer's.

After the game, I waited for Maxime to talk about an upcoming boxing opportunity. There was talk in the gym that Pugilistica would stage a Bell Centre show sometime in the spring. I wanted Maxime to be on it. Not wanting to stay late, I pulled him away from a conversation with some Saint-Jean fans who made the trip into Laval.

"Easy show tonight, eh?" I said to him.

"That guy wasn't ready for this level," he said. "They find them in fucking bars, ostie, and expect them to go a number one."

"Reason I'm here: sounds like Calix is gonna start booking fights for a spring show. You want to do it, right?"

"Fuck yeah, I'm interested. When?"

"Probably sometime in early May. Your season should be done by then. That way, you can get a proper training camp and come in ready."

"Who am I gonna fight?" he asked. "Or I guess you don't know yet?"

"Who knows, some tomato can, probably. I'm going to talk to Calix about it tomorrow 'cause he knows you're interested and that would help drive ticket sales a bit."

"That sounds good, ostie," he said. Behind Maxime, I could see a group of people waiting to speak with him. There was also a taller man who may have been Maxime's dad. But I needed his opinion on something and moved in closer.

"You know what's going on right now?" I asked, softly.

"I heard some things."

"What do you think?"

"It's a bad spot for Ed. Nothing you can do. Just stay out of shit," he said, nodding slowly. "Could be an earthquake coming, I've seen it before."

"I know, and I don't want to get fucked. If I lose this…," I said, pointing to the rink. "Somebody's buying our place as an investment property."

"Just protect yourself," he said. "Let's talk tomorrow."

Calix wasn't at the gym on the following morning, so I couldn't ask whether Maxime would be on the card. Eddy was also absent, and I spent the first couple of hours reading a magazine from behind the front desk as people came out of their cardio kickboxing classes. Around eleven, I went outside for a coffee and walked to a Starbucks down the street. The city was about to enter a cold spell and when I reached the shop, my face was immobile. I was warming my hands in line when someone tapped me on the shoulder. It was Fortunato.

"What's up bro?" he asked, smiling. His teeth were flawless for someone recently in jail.

"Oh hey, how are ya?" Fortunato looked down at me through his nose.

"I'm good bro, need some caffeine."

"What are you after?" I asked. "I'm buying."

"No, no, no!" he said. "Of course not, bro!" When it was my turn to order, I asked for two coffees and passed one over to him.

"Thanks," he said, "but I have to grab another one. Big man's in the car." I looked outside and saw a black SUV parked beside the curb.

"He didn't want to come in?"

"Hates the cold," Fortunato said, fixing his brown eyes on mine.

"So do I. I gotta get back to the gym, Fortune, enjoy the coffee."

"Teddy, one sec, buddy," he said, holding onto my shoulder. "Genny wants to see you. Five minutes, okay?" I resisted the urge to say something sarcastic about the odds of him seeing me here.

"Right now?"

"Five minutes, bro. I promise."

I followed Fortunato outside, where he opened the SUV's back door. I climbed up and inside, sitting down on one of its plush leather chairs. Genny leaned back to look at me. He wore an expensive winter jacket whose hood was countered by feathers. The car was sauna-hot.

"Teddy! How ya doing, bro?"

"I'm good, Genny, how are you?"

"Good. Good, bro, I'm good. Anyway, this won't take long," he said. "I got an offer for you."

"Yeah?"

"I want to give you a piece of the book." Genny looked back at me when he said this.

"What, really?" Shocked, I sat upright.

"Really bro, a little piece, one and a half percent, but that little piece is worth a hell of a fucking lot, okay?"

"For sure."

"Fucking right, bro." Genny took a sip of his coffee.

"Why?" I asked.

"'Cause what you've done with the league takes vision, it's impressive, bro."

"Thank you," I said.

"Do you understand how big this is?" he asked, looking back at me. "Guys spend three lifetimes out here and never get this chance."

"Yes, yes, of course, Genny, thanks for thinking of me."

"Nobody this young's ever gotten a piece."

"I'm honoured."

"So what do you say?" he asked, flatly. I wasn't sure how to answer.

"What about Eddy?" I asked. "I still work for him, you know?" Genny took a deep breath.

"Eddy's good, the guy, but…" he paused for a moment, "he's limited, bro, the way he thinks about things, you know, and we got the biggest show in town now. I also might be getting into that league," he said. "If I do, there could be overlap, which I can't have. But if you come in under me, we can make that market ten times as big. Taking action on each team, every game." It was a fine proposition, but any excitement was tempered by a rotting feeling of disloyalty.

"Listen buddy," Genny said, "I know you got work, so think about it. The offer won't be here for long. I respect what you're doing, but I only have so much patience, you understand? Get back to me soon, bro."

"Thank you, Genny, I will."

My discomfort at what Genny proposed was offset by its promise. If I went with him, I would have access to more bettors, endless muscle and an affiliation with the milieu's ruling class. I would also almost certainly become rich. Having even the book's smallest piece would guarantee more than I could ever spend, and whatever debt I had would be cleared right away.

That night, Patty came over for dinner. We were going to watch hockey and discuss our plans for the coming weekend.

"How are things going with V?" he asked me. I didn't know what information Patty was privy to. His question bothered me, though not because he'd dared to ask it.

"Nothing's happening. We tilted a little while ago. Haven't talked to her since."

"She was messaging me about you," he said. "Wanted to know what the deal was."

My heart had begun to pound. "And what'd you tell her?"

"That you're a busy guy."

"Good answer." I thought about Véronique every day but wasn't going to admit this. "How about you with the girls?"

"So yesterday, I'm downtown doing some shopping at Les Ailes. I see that chick from Célestes, she's there in the women's section. You know who I'm talking about. Short girl, brown hair. The one who told me about the piss payers."

"You talk to her?"

"I tried to but a couple of the young guys connected to Genny's crew were there. What's the one dude's name, Alessandro? He comes over and takes her away. Gives me a real dirty look. And like, he *knew* me. Knew who I was. Seems like a twat."

"Well that guy could be working for us soon because Genny offered me a piece of the book," I said.

Patty sat up in his chair. "Come the fuck on." He said this with a shock I wasn't used to. Patty was often performative in his reactions, but the surprise was real. "How much? When?"

"Today. A point, but that point's worth a ton."

"Yeah, you're fucking right it is," he said. There was envy in his eyes, and I didn't want to gloat.

"So what are you gonna do?" he asked.

"It's a tough spot, Pad, because regardless of whichever decision I make, someone's gonna get pissed off."

"Exactly. So who are you more afraid of offending?" I didn't know how to answer.

"No idea." I pulled Chinese food from the containers and made plates for both of us, passing one to Patty. He didn't say anything, taking scoops of the chicken-fried rice purchased from a spot on Sherbrooke.

"Well, I don't know what to tell you, man," he started. "That's a hard call. Like, if you went with Genny, Ed couldn't really do much. He'd have to take it. But can you trust that cunt, Genny? What if he sells you out or reverses things.? Prolly real slippery, that guy."

He was right, and this seemed so obvious once Patty said it. What would Eddy do if I defected? He didn't have the muscle or interest to challenge Genny's group. But was it not naïve to believe everything Genny said? A cinematic scene premiered in my mind, in which I told Patty that whatever happened, I was doing this only to pay my debt, and once this task was complete, I would hand my operation to him. A tear formed in Patty's eye during this imagined conversation, which concluded with a solemn hug in my empty house. In reality I said nothing. No such offer was tendered because I didn't want to give anything up. I liked my work too much, and now needed to make a decision.

Later that night, I was watching a Canadiens game at home when someone knocked on the door. This never happened, and so I made my way to the front, where, hidden out of view, was a baseball bat my father gave me. I looked through the peephole and saw it was Eddy. He'd never come here, and I couldn't remember giving him my address. Eddy looked alone, so I opened the doorway.

"Ed, what's up?" I asked.

"How are you, Teddy?" He appeared stoic and in his left hand was an SAQ bag, which he handed to me. I knew there was an expensive bottle somewhere inside it.

"Good, do you want to come in?" I asked. Eddy entered the front door, taking his shoes off before walking into the kitchen.

"Do you want a drink or something?" I asked.

"No. So this is it, eh?" He looked around the living room. "Nice spot, bud. Where are the pictures of your parents, tabernak?"

"Getting cleaned," I lied.

"Fucking sad, man" he said, shaking his head. "I'm sorry for all that. How much of that debt you paid off?" I had already provided the bank thirty-three grand (having just made another of our quarterly payments), and Eddy nodded in the grave manner he used to express approval over something serious.

"How long's it been now?" he asked.

"Since they passed? About nine months. Your parents still here?" Eddy shook his head and sat down on a kitchen table, looking around to the backyard, where mounds of snow had piled against the fence. I had cut out a path leading to the alleyway. It reminded me of the tunnels we built as kids.

Eddy was here for a reason. I had spent the whole afternoon thinking about this. If Genny was being honest, I stood to become rich by working underneath him, but then Eddy could seek retribution later. If I stayed with Eddy, Genny could turn my lights off.

"I got a question for you," he began, facing me with his resolute eyes.

"Genny approached me downtown today," I said, before he could get there. "I was getting a coffee and Fortunato pulled me out of line. He offered me part of the book. A point and a half." Eddy stared at me, saying nothing. "I didn't accept," I said, hoping this would provide some reassurance.

"Why am I only finding out about this now?" he asked, gripping the table's edge.

"Because it only happened a few hours ago. Why? What'd you hear?"

Eddy's smile was joyless. "No offense, T, but he's going through you to hurt me. And you'll never get those points. Never in a million years. Not because you aren't capable, but because the guy's a selfish cunt who makes the same ostie pitch to everyone he wants to get over on. When it suits him, he'll pitchfork you. He doesn't care about loyalty, tabernak. Doesn't understand the word."

"Well, that's all we talked about," I said, raising my hands like someone accused of a crime. "I swear."

"I believe you. Come sit down for a second," he said, pointing to the opposite kitchen chair. I took my seat. Eddy leaned forward, hands clasped between his legs.

"Are you unhappy with our arrangement, T?" he asked.

"Of course not."

"But does that mean you're going to stick with me?"

"Yes." What else could I say? My analysis had been made obsolete by the pressure of conversation.

"You've been doing real well, fucking exceptionally well, so I want to reward you, okay? I got another business I'm going to cut you in on."

"What is it?" Eddy's phone buzzed on the tabletop, but he didn't look at it.

"ATMs. I'm gonna give you a couple because you're making more than enough and need to start cleaning your shit. It's the easiest way. But I need your commitment, right? Are you with me?"

"I am. But what about Genny?" I asked. "Is he going to come back on me if I tell him no?"

"I'll handle that," he answered, without revealing how. I told him about Genny's threat to get involved in the league. If he did, and made a problem about us taking bets on it, our hockey profits would diminish. Eddy mumbled something about looking into this. He didn't appear to have thought about the possibility.

"So, the ATMs?" I started.

"I've got 'em all over downtown. You stock them and make money off the surcharge. Easy as it gets." Eddy seemed to have forgotten my question. "Like we talked about, you'll always be okay moving low-key. Genny will hit people, and that's what the cops get their periods over. But remember, it's not what they know, only what they can show in court, you understand? If they can't prove jack shit, they can't go forward with anything." Eddy rose from the kitchen table and walked around to where he was only a foot from my face.

"Are you with me, Teddy?" he asked again.

"I'm with you, Ed." He put his hand on my shoulder.

"You miss your parents, bud?"

"Yeah, I do," I said, looking him in the eye. He brought me into a hug, holding on before releasing my body with a squeeze of both shoulders.

"I'll be in touch with you tomorrow about what we talked about," he said.

I watched Eddy put his jacket on and close the door. After he left, I realized he was the first adult in this house since my parents left for the cottage. At once I felt alone, any upsurge in my finances having been offset by the realization that I'd last experienced a twinge of warmth in the same spot where I now stood, when, at seventeen, my mother consoled me after being let go by a high school girlfriend.

Hours later, after a snowless night had turned silent, the day ended in a musical lament within the closed universe of my headphones. Ghostface yearned for a simpler time. His concerns seemed appropriate for the moment.

21.

Why were my parents dead? The police determined that a baseboard heating system misfired, causing the propane tank to explode. I read this on the morning after Eddy's visit, looking through a long-ignored report that sat underneath some forgotten books on the coffee table.

The cottage had been a central feature of my childhood. Each summer I spent several weeks lounging on its deck when I wasn't ankle deep in the water, casting a long fishing line into the calm lake. My mother would sit behind me, absorbed in a novel (rarely did she venture in), as my father fished alongside me, shooting his own line deeper into the water. One of the most lasting memories of my young life came from the friendly smiles of older cottagers who congratulated me on my first catch (and, afterwards, the rotting stench of fish as it hung from a line my father hung). I cried when he took it down.

After dinner, usually taken on the deck, we would sit outside while my parents entertained a neighbouring cottager or whichever family friend joined us for a short stay. There were rarely any children there, unless someone I didn't know brought along a son or daughter. In these instances, I was of course obligated to entertain them, and depending on the athleticism of the visiting child we might play baseball in the little field beside the house (or chase each other throughout the adjacent woods, which always resulted in the crying child being consoled by their parents because I had either hidden myself too expertly or abandoned them somewhere in the forest). My mother would scold me in these instances and demand that I apologize. I would, abandoning this cruel practice long before I turned nine.

The amount of time I spent there necessitated much time alone. I read whatever books my mom brought home from the library and shot a tennis ball against an abandoned garage with the lone hockey stick we had on the property. One summer, a girl around my age from Montreal came to stay at the cottage across our yard. When my father saw us catch eyes from across the lawn, I became so embarrassed that I didn't venture out again for the entire afternoon. We finally met over hot dogs and salad on the back deck, and she asked several questions about my school, talking about her friends in Westmount. Melanie had a boyfriend, but said this only after I first lied about having a girlfriend. I could sense my mother's eyes pressing against the window screen as we talked, and when I returned to the kitchen in search of some juice, she smiled.

"How are things going out there?"

"Good," I said.

"Does Melanie want a drink?"

"Yes."

"What's the matter, Teddy?" she asked, giggling.

"Your questions."

"Oh, come on," she said, her eyes twinkling. My mother went into the fridge and removed two juices. When I returned outside, Melanie was sitting on the deck's edge, her dangling legs in metronomic swing. I sat down beside her, to where our thighs wedged together under the hot sun. Behind me, I could hear the screen strain.

I never saw Melanie again (it was possible we were in the same bar on Crescent one night a few years ago), but we developed a closer relationship over the two weeks her family spent at the lake. Board games turned into long walks and smiles from our parents whenever we returned.

It went on like this each summer, until, in my late teens, cottage time became less frequent as I wanted to stay in Montreal and spend summer nights with friends. My mother would always launch a filibuster to lure me back, but quiet nights in the Eastern Townships during a Montreal summer were less enticing than getting drunk downtown.

I was last at our cottage the previous summer, and only for a weekend — one cut short by an argument I had with my mother about some federal election topic. An excess of alcohol sharpened my tongue, and the inconclusive debate, which my father avoided with a premature exit to bed, ended with my mother calling me "nasty." I left the next morning and apologized to her later, but my final memory of being there was one of angry humiliation.

The previous year, there had been cooling problems at the cottage and my father had a local electrician come in to look at the heating system. Dad was meticulous with safety upgrades and had scheduled for someone to come back that June.

I hadn't even called them during this final week. Why not? Why wasn't I there, too? Why didn't I understand my mother's wish to have me there? Why hadn't I spent more time with them?

After a nightmarish sleep, where I dreamt of crawling away from a burning house (a bloodless hitman was walking after me with a cocked handgun pointed at my head), I woke up to a late text from Karim. He needed to talk.

Karim wanted me to meet him at Lenny's, a downtown strip club no one from our circle ever went to. I accepted on the condition it would be fast. I was tired and hated the place. Patronized by some of the city's worst people, one year ago a university student was shot to death outside after getting into an argument with some drug dealer, now on the run.

I showed up alone, bypassing the two African bouncers standing outside. Inside the front door, fluorescent lights illuminated the face of a girl taking cover charge, and having no connections I paid the ten dollars and walked into a depressed strip club. Karim was sitting in the back.

"You get some bad news?" I asked. Karim didn't say anything. "What's the matter?"

"This stays between us, eh?" He was fumbling with his cigarettes, looking from the table to me.

"Of course."

"I need some cash." Karim spent haphazardly but I sensed his hole had become a mine shaft.

"Who do you owe?" I asked.

"Another bookie."

"Who?" I asked, rubbing my temple.

"A couple of fucking bad finishes last weekend, T, and…" he stopped himself, knowing I didn't care.

"And you can't go to Eddy because he told us not to bet unless we're laying off?" I said, finishing his thought.

"Yep." A group of bikers came into the bar, but I didn't recognize any of them.

"How much do you owe?" I looked at Karim's eyes, in a staring contest with the table.

"Sixty-five," he said, glancing in the other direction.

"Hundred?"

"No." I exhaled and had to stop myself from punching the table. "Jesus Christ. Who's the bookie?" He looked down again, embarrassed.

"Fucking Genny."

"What? Oh for fucks sake — why?"

"Was talking to him at the last game and he gave me a good fucking line," he said, raising his voice. "And because I got a kid coming, I wanted her to have a house, and I thought I saw an edge." I took another deep breath. It made no sense to get upset, even though I knew what his solution would be.

"When's he need it by?" I asked.

"He got me on a plan. Five grand a week plus the vig."

"How much do you need help with?"

"All of it." Karim couldn't look me in the eye.

"What about that other thing you were talking about?" I asked. "I thought you were getting rich. What happened there?"

Karim shook his head and looked down. "Not doing that shit anymore." I had read a recent Gazette article about Montreal criminals defrauding seniors through a charity email scan. I didn't ask if he was involved.

"I can help," I said, "but five's a lot because I need to keep paying Ed. I know you probably don't want to pay less or you're gonna be into this guy forever."

"I know, Jesus Christ, bro, I know." Karim was frustrated but knew better than to vent.

"How are we going to make sure you stay on top of it?" I asked.

"Teddy," he said, his tone now conspiratorial, "you're taking action on hockey. Fix a fucking outcome, man."

"How the fuck am I going to do that?"

"What do you mean?" Karim asked, surprised. "Don't tell me that you haven't done it before." I explained to him, half-honestly, that you couldn't fix a fight, only try to maneuver certain outcomes into existence, but even this was hard. And if you started fixing matchups, everything would go to shit, given how talkative the league's tough guys were. Chewing on an ice cube, Karim didn't want to hear it.

"I came with you to pick up when you were short, right? Put

myself in harm's way for you. Didn't I?"

"Yes, you did." I remembered Karim jumping out of the car when Sil grabbed me from behind.

"Who showed you shit at the beginning?" he asked.

"I know, man! I know you did. And I'm gonna help you, but stop with that shit. You're the one who fucked up," I said. Karim didn't respond and sipped his drink. "I'll give you the five K tomorrow and help from there, but you're paying points."

"What the fuck man?" he asked, shocked.

"He's giving you three, right, so you actually owe sixty-nine fifty per week, not five. I'll get you to sixty-five grand, but you're going to have to pay me back at a point and a half, you understand?"

Karim started to protest. "Come on, Teddy, I got a baby coming and you're rich as fuck right now!"

"No I'm not!" I said, trying not to yell. "I'll try and get you settled up with Genny soon so you're not paying juice forever," I went on, "but that's all I can do. *All* I'm doing right now is paying off debt. I'm not profiting shit. Everything I make is going to that house. Everything. Who would you rather owe money to, me or him?"

"When can you make a fight?" he asked.

"Make a fight?"

"When you can you fix a fight, like we talked about?"

"*You* said that," I almost screamed. "*You* talked about that." A waitress came by to ask if we wanted another drink. I declined but Karim motioned that he wanted one more.

"You gotta help me, bro, come on," Karim said. "You don't know how lucky you've been so far on this run. That shit at the strip club, that would have gotten most guys killed, you know that, right?" I couldn't argue.

"But you're still here because you're making money. That's the best sort of protection. If you weren't earning like that it's possible somebody woulda popped you. Or somebody would have torched your house or some shit like that." These suspicions had been in the back of my mind. Karim's words confirmed them.

"You're not going to tell anyone about this, right?" he asked me.

"Of course not."

"Thanks, T." I got up, eager to leave.

"You're going already?" he asked.

"I'm tired and I hate this place. Meet me tomorrow at the regular spot."

"Thanks again, Teddy."

"Don't mention it."

The following day, I met Karim at the brasserie and gave him nearly seven thousand dollars. He thanked me with the hangdog face of a guilty man, and then left for Laval where Genny was expecting him. I watched his sorry, swinging hips exit the back door, seething at this new responsibility. It wasn't obvious that he'd pay me back, only that Karim's implosion just made my life harder, and I wondered if Eddy knew how big of a mistake one of his primary employees had made, and more, whether I should tell him.

22.

Per Eddy's promise, I owned three ATM machines. Two were at downtown strip clubs, while the other sat wedged into a bathroom alcove at the same Crescent St. bar where Stu had served (he had taken time away from work, I was told, and was unlikely to return). I had to make sure they were stocked with cash every day, but this involved no more than using an intermediary I provided (bills taken from our gambling activities). For a service charge, he took my cash and supplied the ATMs with clean bills.

Karim wanted me to start fixing hockey fights, but I told him that we'd remain on the current payment plan instead. At this he pouted like a boy denied desert. Otherwise, I still owed an answer to the man he was indebted to.

On a frigid Tuesday morning, I met Genny at a coffee shop south of Jarry Park. He was sitting near the back and didn't rise when I arrived, pointing to the chair beside him. Since I'd first seen him at the hockey game two months ago, Genny had put some weight on. His face didn't appear as taut, perhaps because of a ready access to carbs denied to him in prison. Genny's olive skin seemed sun-drenched for a Montreal winter. I remembered someone told me he owned tanning salons.

"What's going on, bro?" he asked. He may have been coming from a meeting, because Gennaro's black hair, thinning in the middle of his forehead, had been gelled carefully. A heavy overcoat hung over the adjoining chair, and he had on black slacks and an argyle, cream-coloured sweater. On his pinkie was a gobstopper-shaped ring. Unlike the younger guys, I don't think he ever went out in public with a tracksuit on.

"Same old. You excited for the Super Bowl?"

"I don't give a fuck. You going to get away this winter, bro?" he asked. I hadn't even thought about it.

"I'd like to. Are you?"

"Dominican, two weeks, leaving Thursday," he said, taking a sip of his coffee. Genny sat motionlessly in his chair, waiting for me to respond.

"That's aweso—" I started.

"So, bro, haven't heard from you in a while?" I drew a breath and then recited an answer constructed between the traffic light and parking space.

"I'm going to stick with what I'm doing for now," I said. "I'm sorry, Genny, I appreciate the offer, I really do, but I can't turn my back..."

Genny was unperturbed. "I get that," he said, "and Ed's a good guy, but you're leaving a lot of money on the table, bro."

"I know, but..."

"So that's it, my pile of cash ain't big enough?" Genny didn't sound angry, taking another sip of his coffee. He seemed to enjoy extracting difficult answers.

"Genny, I like you, I respect you—" I started.

"But you don't want the work..." he said.

"It's not that at all. Like I said, I respect you..."

"With me, there are no limits," he said. "No limits and nobody's ever going to look at you cross-eyed, bro."

I didn't know what else to say and sat in place like a moron. Genny waved his hands in the air, standing up to indicate the meeting was over. I didn't want to leave without some assurance things wouldn't become hostile.

"Are we alright?" I asked.

"You're a young guy, I like you," he said. "By the way," he went on, "I'm buying into Laval." His hard eyes had turned triumphant.

"So where does that leave us?" I asked, understanding the implication.

"We'll talk about that later," he said. "When I get back from vacation, bro." Genny's tone had become declarative, but I wasn't in a position to argue. He reached out to shake my hand and I paused for a moment before wishing him an excellent trip, escaping into the cold morning air.

Businesses were being firebombed, and before the end of January, gangsters had started killing each other in Montreal. Five people had been shot, and their murders, according to the grave police official who provided details to the press, were the result of reshuffling amongst black gangs in the northeast part of the city. With the release of so many criminals following their acquittal on charges from the nineties biker war, a force had returned to the street and wished to exert its influence. Some of the bikers and Italians didn't respect the black street gang members, whom they saw as useful only for muscle and drug peddling, and wanted to reclaim the downtown drug market.

One of the men featured extensively in the article was not like the others. The only black man to have become a full-patch member of Les Diables, Frederique Ducasse, whose name pushed the milieu's needle, served as a bridge between Montreal's established groups and the black gangs they coveted as endless sources of criminal labour. Divided by colours, Ducasse had recently tried to unite the two primary factions under his control.

According to the newspaper story, which I had devoured that morning, a meeting was held between Ducasse and his underlings at which this new arrangement was proposed. Ducasse's new position was still one of implicit subordination to the whites, which didn't appeal to the more senior gangsters, one of whom reportedly spat at him and walked out. This man, Peppy Jean-Gaston, was the first to die. His body was found dumped in a city park: two shots entered his back and one had removed the back part of his skull. The killer was unknown, but it was suspected that he'd been lured into a safe place by someone he trusted.

The following day, the body of Jean-Gaston's business partner, a man named Maxime Depute, was found slumped over the steering wheel of his car in a Hochelaga garage. He had been shot several times, and it was believed that both men died on the same day, which suggested coordination in the killings.

Then, at the end of January, two low-ranking soldiers from rival gangs fought in a St. Michel bar. Their confrontation escalated, a knife was pulled, and one of the men stabbed his opponent in the neck, which tore through his larynx and killed him instantly. The murderer ran off, but not before his face was captured by local security cameras. Police immediately issued a warrant for Kenny Paul of Rosemont—La Petite-Patrie. Paul didn't remain a fugitive for long, because three days later his body was found on a Prairies riverbank. He had probably been given up by his gang, which concluded that to prevent further killing it had to divest itself of an impulsive murderer.

The threads of this web spread outward, seemingly in every direction, but it was the story's final paragraph that rocked me. It said that police investigators feared further violence, as Ducasse had been seen meeting a known shot caller at a Saint-Laurent cafe, with whom he was forming a consortium. His new partner? A man conveniently away when all of this transpired: Gennaro Moriarti.

Having said no to Genny, I didn't want Sil's beating to provide an excuse for retribution. I thought about this on Super Bowl morning. It was a time-consuming anxiety because this was the most important day of our year.

Unlike Genny, I liked the Philadelphia-New England Super Bowl matchup. So did my bettors, who registered all sorts of senseless wagers. Beyond our usual offerings, we opened lines on most of the props provided by Vegas books. I wanted Philly to win (and somewhat despised football, though not because I didn't like the game, whose athleticism was matchless; rather, I hated the knowledge-monologues guys my age made at sports bars), but I wasn't setting the line and our football handicappers thought New England a stronger bet. As usual, we'd wait to see where the sharps placed their money and adjust our line from there.

Money immediately started coming in on New England, and our book was exposed several days before the game. To reconcile, we made the line on Philly more attractive, and this helped readjust things.

The two weeks that preceded the Super Bowl were torturous. Every sports media channel devoted most of its coverage to debates between hyperventilating experts. These conversations were idiotic, but I became convinced of their influence on betting opinions. Regardless of how dumb something was, just by hearing it enough times (i.e., X team's pass rush will be too much for Y team's offensive line), a strain of poison took root in the minds of sports bettors, who — not being experts themselves — would adjust their opinions according to whatever they heard on TV. In truth, they had no real knowledge but wanted to bet nonetheless, both in order to satiate their need for action, and since, if they lost using the "experts" prediction, it would be easier to justify the bad wager by reminding others of the conventional wisdom "at the time". In reality, it was just a feedback loop of bullshit that created a false understanding of how the game would go.

Outside of the few, most people had no idea how a game would unfold. They didn't understand what they were betting on and justified their wagers by a line's attractiveness ("we kinda have to do it," I often heard when a longshot was presented, and small bets could result in big returns). Those who prospered had an advanced understanding of matchups (a stylistic clash in boxing, for example, that might favour one fighter over another). Those who failed were tantalized by betting lines they didn't grasp.

Super Bowl week was frenetic. In the small moments I had to myself, I began to plan for a trip to the Dominican Republic. I didn't want to go with anyone from work and invited Patty, who accepted on the pretext that I would finance his flight and hotel (he had very little extra money to spend, he said). Our plan was to fly into Santo Domingo and spend a few days before going to Punta Cana.

But I had football matters to resolve. One of Eddy's friends was hosting a Super Bowl party at a club he owned downtown. I arrived an hour or so before kickoff and shook hands with the twenty or so people there, taking my seat in the back at a circular table that had been reserved for Eddy. He was sitting with a couple of other people, including a woman I'd seen before but was meeting now only for the first time. She was thin, with globular implants and the etched features of a plastic surgery veteran. Eddy introduced her as Juliet. She extended a creased hand for me to shake. There was no wedding ring.

"Nice to meet you," I said. "How do you two know one another?"

"Proposed to her decades ago and she told me to fuck off,"

Eddy said. Juliet laughed and began asking Eddy about Terrell Owens' ankle, one of the game's talking points.

"I think he might be a bit fucked up," Eddy said. "Talked to Ephy in Vegas this morning and he said it's moving all the books down there. How's it gonna impact the game? We'll see. What do you think, T?" he asked.

"I think his ego's so big that he's not going to be anything but great tonight."

"That's why all our money's coming in on New England," Eddy said. I looked at him and he nodded to indicate that it was okay to speak about the business before Juliet.

"We're exposed there," I said to Eddy. "The teeter totter isn't level." There were numerous screens throughout the club, including an enormous projector that faced most of the seating area. Our booth had its own television. On it, a female reporter discussed an injury with the gravity of someone revealing a terminal diagnosis. She assured an overweight studio host that this emerging story would be monitored until game time. I could see gamblers in the club watching.

Several minutes later, Calix King sauntered in with Ferdinand Guillot, the boxer I'd first seen at Métropolis. Everyone in the bar moved out of his way as Calix walked towards our booth. Eddy rose to meet him. They walked towards the other side of the club and began speaking about something, Calix leaning down as he whispered something into Eddy's ear. Ferdinand slid into the empty space before me. I wanted to ask him about boxing, but Juliet had questions.

"Do you have a girlfriend, Teddy?" Juliet asked, leaning in to where her breasts pushed through the open shirt, wedging against one another.

"I don't," I answered. "Not right now, anyway."

"And the reason for this is, what?"

"Just doing my own thing."

"He's married to his work," Eddy said, having returned in time to hear her question.

"I'm sure you wouldn't have trouble finding one," Juliet said, smiling.

"Sometime soon," I said.

"Teddy's had a tough year, tabernak," Eddy said, "but he's coming through like a boss." This was the last thing I wanted to discuss. In two months we'd be approaching its anniversary, but I had no plan for how to memorialize the event and tried to move outside my mind whenever its ghouls escaped the basement.

"Oh yeah?" Juliet asked.

"No more questions, J," Eddy said, "let him enjoy himself."

"I'm sorry," Juliet said, putting her hand on my wrist.

"What do you do, Juliet?" I asked.

"I own a dance studio," she said, rising to perform a pirouette in the booth. She had the uncaring confidence of a drunk person but didn't seem inebriated.

"What kind?"

"Everything," she answered, smiling.

"Pole dancing!" Eddy said.

"Oh yeah?"

"We do that," Juliet said, nodding, "among other things. Ballet, ballroom, I'm Russian, you know. You should come into the studio sometime," she said. "We'll make a dancer out of you."

"I got two left feet," I said. Both genders had told me so.

"Leave that to me." Juliet's smile conveyed perhaps more than an interest in teaching.

Closer to the game, more heart attack-inducing food was placed on our table. A diet of deep fried pickles, wings and bucket-sized beers turned my stomach into a vaporous mess. The Super Bowl's pre-game pageantry was relentless, and I wanted nothing more than for the game to start.

Before kickoff, several more bets came in on New England

and we were heavily exposed on one side. I mentioned this to Eddy, but he said we'd cover ourselves with prop wagers the gamblers would bite on. We opened the line on Philly even further, to where it was now five to one. When I asked if it made sense to lay some of our risk off with another bookie, he shook his head, no. I couldn't understand his reluctance.

I spoke to Ferdinand Guillot, long absorbed by the TV, and told him that I had an idea for him (it came to me when I was cleaning up the picture I'd smashed of my trip). When — without using these words — I told him to move beyond his lame and forgettable 'Technician' persona to build something around his Haitian heritage, Ferdinand giggled. My pride in the notion evaporated at his laughter.

"What's so funny about it? You think it's stupid?" I asked, hopeful the others weren't listening.

"No, I don't think it's stupid. It's good. I'm just surprised you thought of it."

"What about Bossou? He's the god of…"

"…power and aggression and force. I know who he is. Somebody's done his research," he said, laughing.

"What do you think?"

"I'm no brawler. But what do you know about voodoo?" he asked.

"Well, who are some of the other gods you could use?"

Again Guillot laughed, as though he couldn't take my question seriously. I could see Juliet listening to our conversation.

"Damballa," he said.

"Damballa?"

"He's the creator of all life. Master of the intellect."

"What does he look like?"

"A snake."

"You want to align yourself with a snake?"

"Just look it up. Damballa is dope. That's who I am."

"If that works better, I think it's a good way to go," I said. "One more thing—you're closer to Haitian culture than me. Will this piss people off?"

"Why would it piss people off?"

"I don't know—"

"Who gives a fuck?" Guillot's voice then softened. "No one's going to care."

Ten minutes before kickoff (and just before time would expire for wagering on the final outcome), someone registered the two biggest bets I'd seen yet: twenty-five thousand on my sheet, and one hundred on Eddy's (where, unlike for most of my bettors, there was no limit). He took the under with me and bet against the spread on Eddy's. These wagers would pay half a million dollars if they won. I showed this to my boss.

"Who the fuck bet that?" he asked. It was my man from Westmount. The Count.

"What's our exposure if he wins?"

"Big," I said.

"Well, what is it, tabernak?" he asked, impatient. "What's the dollar value?"

"Five hundred minus what we're taking from whoever loses. We could be out over half a rock."

"Jesus fucking Christ," he said and looked at his watch. Kickoff was in thirty seconds and there was no time to lay off with someone else.

"I never thought we'd see a bet that big," I said. Eddy sneered and looked away.

"Alright, let's just see what happens," he said. "I need to make a couple of calls." Eddy left somewhere down the hallway.

With Eddy gone, Karim arrived with his brother, Zinedine — medium sized and thin, his hair tied back in a bun — whom I was meeting now for the first time. After shaking my hand he sat down on the outside of the table, his pale eyes searching the room.

In a new outfit for the game, Karim (whom I'd given money to pay Genny that morning) introduced himself to Juliet. She said hello and looked away. When our waitress came over, the brothers ordered wings, but Zinedine wasn't drinking. Eddy returned several minutes later to sit down at the table. I didn't know who he was talking to.

"What's up K?" he asked, looking at the television.

We turned our attention to Jacksonville, Florida, where thousands of flashbulbs documented the opening kickoff. Donovan McNabb was taken down on the game's first drive, only to have the play overruled with a replay challenge. From there, the first quarter became a comedy of Philly squandering its opportunities. McNabb was sacked and then threw an interception in the red zone. After the Eagles defense held the Patriots, its offense fumbled the ball on the following possession. In the second quarter, both teams scored receiving touchdowns to make it 7-7 before the half. Both of the heavy wagers looked good from the Count's view: since the over/under was 46.5, I needed over 33 points scored in the second or there'd be another punishing debt to account for.

Chosen because of the unlikelihood he would reveal a breast, Paul McCartney played at halftime. I didn't care about the show and went to the bathroom. People who made their living in real estate and restaurants were getting drunk, and I could see Eddy taking calls at the bar's other end, trying to move risk around.

In the third quarter, both teams scored short passing touchdowns. It was 14-14 at the beginning of the fourth quarter, and Eddy rubbed his eyes while, beside me, Karim stole subtle looks at his boss, perhaps happy at our growing misfortune.

"You're still not in bad shape," I said to Eddy. "Spread's four and a half and the Pats are a fourth quarter team, they just need a TD and a few stops on D."

"Yeah, but you could be fucked here," he said, turning to me. "You need, what, nineteen points for the over?" I nodded.

I could see Eddy forming calculations in his head, pushing money around on an imaginary spreadsheet to ensure he'd have enough to pay. Early in the fourth quarter, Corey Dillon rushed for a short touchdown. This brought immediate relief to our table and a roar in the bar. Nearly five minutes later, the Patriots kicked a field goal, which put them up by ten points and created space so they could cover the spread. Eddy relaxed somewhat but he was too experienced to announce victory. Meanwhile, I needed nine points to prevent paying out, but the Eagles — those stupid, unsteady fucks — were botching things. Despite the superb play of Terrell Owens, McNabb threw an interception with only seven minutes left. The Eagles defense then stopped New England, which gave Philly possession again, and its four minute drive resulted in a touchdown to make the score 24-21. Eddy said nothing and stared ahead. I could see Juliet gauging his stress level.

As the Eagles prepared for an onside kick, I needed them to recover and at least tie the game in its last two minutes. Otherwise, the Patriots would run out the clock, creating a disaster for Eddy, since they were up by three points, not seven, and wouldn't cover the spread unless New England did something risky in the most important moment of its season. Of course, this didn't happen as New England ran the ball on three consecutive plays, requiring Philly to spend its final timeouts and stop the clock. A Patriots punt ensured Eddy would likely be beaten on the money, but there was still another opportunity for the Eagles to score and push the total points past 46.5. But Philly fucked it up again, wasting their first two downs and turning it over on the third when Rodney Harrison intercepted McNabb.

A knee by Tom Brady to end the game made sure no more points would be scored and that I, too, had an iceberg-sized debt. My hands began to shake.

Beside me, Eddy stared at the television. He had money, of course, but wasn't rich enough to laugh off several hundred thousand dollars. This would necessitate an inventory of his finances. Karim wasn't as subtle.

"What's the matter Ed?" he asked. Eddy said nothing and looked down. Not realizing his boss didn't care for compassion, Karim went forward. "Don't matter, you can handle it." Eddy looked up, his eyes fierce.

"What the fuck do you know what I can handle?" he asked. "What the fuck do you know, tabernak ostie de criss? Fucking dummy placing bets all over town. What the fuck do you know?" Zinedine's features tightened as the table went silent.

"Come on," Juliet said, putting her hand on Eddy's wrist. Several of the adjacent tables looked over to see what was happening.

"Sorry Ed, sorry man," Karim said, looking down.

"You should be sorry," Eddy shot back. "Fucking retard, you think I don't know about *that*?" Karim's face had turned from its regular olive shade to white. Juliet — practiced in de-escalating male anger — was tapping Eddy on the wrist in the way a parent might pat a disgruntled child. Eddy threw a bunch of money down on the table to pay for our tab and Juliet rose with him. Before they left, she smiled and waved to me before turning around, avoiding Karim.

"We're meeting tomorrow morning," Eddy said to me. "Gotta get our hands around this, sacrament." Eddy walked out without acknowledging the dozen or so people motioning for his attention.

"Don't think I ever saw Ed like that," Karim said.

"He just lost a shitload," I said. "So did I."

"How much?" Karim's brow pushed over top of his eyes.

"A ton." The Count created a hole that would keep me in the red for at least a month. Karim either hadn't considered this or didn't care.

"Well what about my piece to Genny?"

"What about it? I've got no money, dude," I said. "You know how much I just got taken for?"

Panic showed on Karim's face. "Don't you have the ATMs going?" he asked.

"That's a small bit of income, it's not gonna pay back a hundred dimes," I said.

"So what does that mean?" He didn't seem capable of internalizing what I was trying to convey.

"That we're all gonna be squeezed," I answered. "I was set to get some sun in the Dominican but that's over now." Karim appeared lost, while his brother, who hadn't said a word in over an hour, looked down in angry silence. I told Karim we'd talk about it tomorrow after our total balance sheet was computed. He left with Zinedine, who didn't say goodbye when they walked off.

Calix King, who had been speaking to a woman in the far corner for most of the fourth quarter, came over to where I was standing. He knew I wanted to talk about the spring show and said there might be a spot for Maxime. I attempted some rehearsed bullet points, but Calix was going on vacation for two weeks, so I'd have to wait for a more formal conversation. When the promoter got up to leave, Ferdinand Guillot trailed behind him. The fighter gave me a peace sign as they exited.

I went to bed depressed and woke up hyperventilating at four in the morning. Sometime during the night my brain constructed a scenario which memory replayed upon waking: I was half-drunk in the middle of Patty's shabby kitchen while a party raged in the apartment's living room, fumbling with my dad's number on a broken cell phone. Each time, I pressed the wrong button, dialed someone else or a lubricated finger slipped from the keypad. I did this five, ten, one thousand times and became so frustrated that I threw the phone against the floor. It refused to break and when a kick missed, I fell to the floor where my face smashed against a cement slab. Party-goers ran from the living room into the kitchen, where I lay quadriplegic-like and screamed.

"My parents are fucking dy—" I couldn't make out their faces but there was unmistakable laughter. Someone I didn't know squatted overtop of me and dangled his cock close to my face. I reached up to rip it off but grabbed only air.

23.

The next morning, Ferdinand Guillot was punching a heavy bag when I met Eddy at the gym.
"You know how much we're on the hook for, right?" he asked from behind his desk. Eddy looked better today than I expected, but I didn't know why he chose to say "we," as the majority of this was his debt. "After all is said and done, I owe this guy over four hundred." His speech was deadpan. I thought about the indifferent reactions of Patty's partygoers in my nightmare.
"Do you have that, or will you pay in installments?" I asked.
"We're not renting furniture here, tabernak, we don't pay in installments," Eddy said, shaking his head at the question, "especially with that sardine acting like he's the Cigar. I'm going to settle up with this guy on Friday."
"So will I." I wanted to talk about the various murders, hardly spoken of in recent days (and undiscussed yesterday, despite the number of Super Bowl watchers whose incomes were made illegally). While the milieu's gossiping never stopped, lips closed when people turned distrustful of their peers.
"What about all the guys who got it recently?"
"I don't know," he said, "some guys crossed a line, who cares. What the fuck did he know about this game that nobody else did?" Eddy asked, bringing things back to our debt.
"He's the sharpest guy we have," I said.
"We should make him our handicapper," he answered.

"This guy's a lone wolf. He's like the Wizard of Oz in that townhouse."

"Be a bad thing if people knew how much he was holding," Eddy said, smiling. He sensed my unease. "I'm kidding, bud. I'm not sending somebody to his house, come on." Even if Eddy wasn't, the Count didn't seem like he might be caught unaware.

"So how's this gonna go?" I asked.

"I have the money, so this guy's getting paid. But that's a lot of cash, bud. I need to rearrange a few things and put some more loans out. I got my eyes on a couple new businesses."

"What other businesses?" I asked, still with only a vague idea of everything Eddy did. Beyond the boxing gym, he owned bars and restaurants downtown, and kept an obsessive watch over local real estate. But most of this was still unknown to me: I could only ever sniff around the edges.

"Juliet liked you," he said, smiling. "Talked the whole way home."

"She your girlfriend or something?" I asked. At this, Eddy laughed more genuinely than I'd ever heard.

"Just a friend. We've done some business together. You been laid recently?" he asked. I looked up, surprised by the question. "You know," he went on, "I've never seen you with a girl, not once. I know you like chicks — that rip told me." At this, he laughed again. "But do you got anything regular in your life? A broad you can at least call on to hang out, bud?"

"I was seeing a girl for a little bit some time ago, but not anymore."

"'Some time ago'?" Eddy asked, laughing. "You could get any girl, man, especially with all that cash." I was starting to get mad.

"Cash?" I started, "everything goes towards—"

"So what's the matter?" he asked, "your dick can't get horizontal?"

"It works. How am I supposed to have time when my days are spent dealing with excuses?" This was a bad answer I hated myself for making.

"You make time, T. There's no life without it." I wasn't sure whether men in their forties lied as much about having sex as those my age did, but it seemed plausible that Eddy was still active.

"I guess not."

"When's the last time you did it, anyway?" he asked. I sighed, exasperated. "Okay," he said, sensing my frustration, "don't pull the tampon out."

"What's the next step with this?" I asked. Eddy had returned to his laptop, transfixed by a new listing. He tapped his mouse, straining to read who the agent was.

"We pay this guy out on Friday. You have the cash on hand?" I nodded, yes, even though this would cut what I was holding nearly in half.

"What about K?" I asked.

"What about him?" Eddy looked up.

"Even with the ATM money coming I can't afford to hand over seven dimes every week."

He sneered and shook his head. "Of course you can't. It's his problem, not yours. Tell him to rob a fucking bank." This seemed a contradiction of Eddy's advice to keep a low profile.

"If Karim isn't good for it, things might go bad."

"They might," Eddy said, shrugging his shoulders.

"Wouldn't that be bad for you, too?" I asked.

"We'll cross that bridge," Eddy said, plagiarizing one of my lines. He had returned to the listing and started writing an email of inquiry.

All throughout January I had thought about Véronique. What was she up to? Who was she seeing? I was too proud, even, to ask Patty about her. I suspected they were still in contact, and while it was doubtless platonic, I knew that he wouldn't hesitate to escalate their friendship if the opportunity arose.

It was hard for me to admit that feelings existed which needed reciprocation. Why, I didn't know. When I finally found the courage to text her, my excitement swirled with anxiety. But she never responded.

That Friday, I was in Laval to watch Maxime and Saint-Jean. This was another anticipated game since Laval had brought in Garnett Bone from somewhere deep in the British Columbia interior. A man with developmental problems who spent the warmup yelling, "Fuck youuuuuuuu, fuck youuuuuuuuu," to the Saint-Jean team held a sign showing Bone feeding Maxime into a woodchipper. Over seven thousand had come in on the probability of this being the game's first fight, but I did nothing to dissuade Maxime from accepting Bone's challenge. If it happened, it happened.

(Like many of the players in this league, Bone's past was a problem. He had once been a high draft pick and played a little over a season in the NHL, winning against some of its most established heavyweights until a motorcycle accident reduced his mobility. From there, alcoholism pushed him to the margins of professional hockey, where he fought in eight different leagues over the last ten seasons. He was twenty-five pounds overweight but retained an anvil jaw.)

To Maxime's despair and my benefit, he and Bone wouldn't meet. In the first period, Maxime was forechecking when the puck rimmed behind the net and was picked up by a Laval defenseman. When Maxime arrived to throw his hit, the player turned to avoid a two hundred and fifty two pound cannonball, but the Woodchipper's momentum was so great that he couldn't stop and hammered the player into the boards, making contact with the numbers of his jersey. The defenseman's upper half whipped backwards before his head rebounded off the glass. He lay face down on the ice, as though he'd been shot. The fans began to scream.

"Fucking guy turned his back," Karim said, who was standing beside me.

Maxime was jumped by the closest approximation of a tough guy Laval had on the ice, whom he punched out. Laval's trainers began their careful run towards the fallen player. There was pushing and shoving on the periphery of where his body lay but it didn't look as if there'd be a brawl. Everyone was too focused on the player, who still wasn't moving.

"I don't know what Max is supposed to do there," I said. "Nobody wants to see a guy hurt, but don't show your numbers when the train arrives."

The referee was pulling Maxime towards the penalty box. I imagined he'd be ejected for hitting from behind, if only to tone down the game's temperature. Maxime was standing in the penalty box, looking back towards the fallen player as the Laval fans shouted at him. At first, he didn't respond, but one man came down and dumped a glass of beer on his head. The Woodchipper turned around and punched the glass behind him, which brought more catcalling from the fans.

"Fucking murderer!" they yelled in French. I looked over to the corner. The Laval defenseman was starting to move a bit.

"Fucking useless pussy sacrament, Doucette, ostie calice!"

As the paramedics unfolded a stretcher, the head referee pulled Maxime out of the penalty box. Fans saluted his ejection, and, shoulders sunk, he skated towards the dressing room tunnel behind his bench. A bald, pot-bellied fan standing overtop, and who was jacking off an airhorn, blew it directly in the Woodchipper's face when he walked underneath him. Maxime grabbed the instrument, but the fatty wouldn't let it go: he toppled over the tunnel and onto Maxime, his round, limp body falling like that of an overweight bear whose girth defeated a tree branch. Players and personnel from the Saint-Jean team jumped in to separate them. I could see the fat man come to his feet, unsteady, his confused face covered in blood. The referee leapt over the boards and pushed Maxime back towards the dressing room.

Meanwhile, Laval's defenseman was only now being loaded onto the stretcher. Surrounded by paramedics, I couldn't see his face from where I was standing. The arena remained hushed as he was taken off, navigated towards a waiting ambulance.

I left Karim to check on Maxime, walking down to the dressing room area, where I showed my pass to the security attendant. There were two people associated with the Saint-Jean team there, but otherwise the space was empty. With ten minutes left in the first period, everyone was still paying attention to the game.

I knocked on the dressing room door. Maxime was sitting at the other end, leaning back against the wall, a shamed rhinoceros. He was about to insert a dip and looked up, surprised, when I appeared.

"I didn't mean for that to happen!" he said, shaking his head.

"Guy turned at the last minute," I said.

"Is he okay?" Maxime asked, his concern real. He didn't care about hurting people if their injuries came from crossing the behavioural norms that regulated activity in the streets or on the ice. Transgressions like these precluded pangs of conscience. But if Maxime harmed someone who was playing by the rules, it bothered him.

"Got taken away just now," I said.

"You think they're gonna suspend me?" he asked.

I shrugged my shoulders. "Either way, it's going to be okay," I said. "I'll make sure of that." Though I did love Maxime, it occurred to me that having him close was in my interest, both because of the protection he provided, and since he could be a good conduit of useful information. Maxime only cared for Eddy insofar as he could provide a source of income, and I needed his loyalty to remain with me.

"Thanks, T."

"What happened when that marshmallow fell? He burp up a Big Mac?" I asked, giggling.

We laughed together and I threw Maxime an unopened tin, promising to call him later. When I got back to our seats, I could see the police had arrived. They were speaking with some of the Laval officials. I nudged Karim, who looked over, lost in his thoughts.

Maxime was suspended for the regular season. This amounted to twenty games and a substantial loss in salary since he didn't have a contract and was paid by appearance. The league rationalized its harsh punishment by the victim's degree of injury: he had broken his back and orbital bone, lost seven teeth and had a serious concussion, requiring his banishment to a dark room. After the event, there was more media grandstanding about the league's need to stem its violence, and in response to the firestorm (and sensitive to its souring perception after what happened to McDougal), the SLSPL levied the biggest suspension in league history.

Further, there were also legal considerations. Some people speculated that Maxime might be charged. The police were investigating, but Eddy's source in the department suspected it wouldn't go anywhere. What more could they determine?

Everyone had seen what happened. It was documented and on camera. How could they establish that Maxime tried to hurt him? Where was the premeditation? The guy turned his back at the wrong moment. Still, there was a sword over Maxime's head.

Because much of his income had been taken away, I provided Maxime with an interest free loan and would cover the money he would have otherwise made playing. This put even further stress on my finances, but I couldn't allow him to go bankrupt. A disgruntled Woodchipper was dangerous.

Prior to the Super Bowl, I had over one hundred and thirty thousand in cash (a secret ledger of each week's profits and losses was hidden in my laundry room). I kept most of this money behind two false walls I'd constructed. One was behind a toilet in the upstairs master bathroom. The other I placed behind our basement furnace (which I deliberately obscured with a mess of hockey sticks, rakes and other miscellanea that would make the space look forgotten if anyone broke into our house and was trying to figure out where my money was hidden). Otherwise, every few weeks I put a couple thousand of this stash into my bank account. These deposits were always well below reporting thresholds so as not to arouse suspicion. That way, if things ever did go badly and I was robbed by someone with inside knowledge of my operation, I would at least have a modest nest egg with which to rebuild.

During the last week of January, my sheet had started to take in more wagers, to where, on the latest weekend, sixteen hundred bets resulted in nearly fifty thousand in profit, of which I would keep half. As our action on the league came alive, my half-sheet had gone from only a couple hundred bets per week to nearly two thousand. This was the case on Super Bowl weekend when nearly nineteen hundred bets netted me almost twenty-nine grand (which would have been excellent had Allan not destroyed my weekend). Of course, I still had other money going out, like the installments I had to pay on our house, the cash I spent each week on the fighters we wanted to bring in (a number that had been climbing recently as we needed new tough guys to keep up with demand), and money to maintain a lifestyle that had me in bars and restaurants on most nights, buying expensive dinners and offering free appetizers to people in drunken consideration of wading into my world. There was an abstract, paradoxical point to this, since my success helped legitimize their vice. Moths to a flame, it was the golden light my gamblers wished to bask in.

One bartender who worked at an expensive downtown restaurant, Geordie McLain, sidled up beside Patty and me one night after his shift ended. He had just won the week before.

"I'm hot right now, bud. Real hot. Feel like I can predict things in advance." He said this with a laugh, aware of how ridiculous his boast was. Geordie wanted my friendship and respect — to be seen by me and my associates as someone with enough guile and juice to make it in our circle — as much as he did a gambling win. From there he spent recklessly, losing thirty-five hundred in the two weeks that followed our conversation.

Loud talk like his was often purposefully made in front of the others: when a group of young guys would congregate by a Saint-Laurent supper club bartop and make a show of buying dozens of drinks, the talk always turned to gambling. In these scenarios, it was important that any of the women on the circle's periphery could hear their boasting and see them living dangerously (though it never occurred to my gamblers how little this did to impress them). I was always in the middle of these clusters, both a sympathetic ear and facilitator of fun. "Teddy-Boy," they'd start:

"No line's too tight for me, lad!"

"Yeah, I'm a fucking degen but so are all of these guys. I want five bills on Toronto, five on Edmonton."

"With the football, I'm like Nostrademus… Nicodamus… whatever the fuck that old bearded cunt's name is. Ted, gimme a dime each on…"

"I need another week with the principle, bud. But can you give me some more credits? I'll get you the vig tomorrow, you know I'm never late with that…"

Whenever those on my sheet found me at a bar, they loved introducing me to their friends. They loved buying drinks for me. They loved paying fealty to the person indulging their worst instincts. They loved, in short, being seen with their bookie. Why? Because it showed they were down.

The loan I gave Karim took a sizeable chunk of my money away, as did the one hundred thousand I owed the Count of Westmount. With the NFL season over and my new weekly loan arrangement for Maxime, I needed to start taking even more action on hockey.

Meanwhile, the Woodchipper appealed his suspension, but the process was slow. As always, things had turned political, and the league wanted to make an example before the government's flashlight reached some dark corners.

After spending a couple of depressed days on his couch, I convinced Maxime to get back into the boxing gym, reminding him of Calix's interest for the May card. It made no sense to stay at home, drinking beer as his stomach expanded. After some aggressive prodding by me, Maxime returned to training on Monday.

Back in the ring, Maxime looked okay, too, and while his skills were still rudimentary, the Woodchipper began transferring his weight like an actual boxer during sparring with a chubby local heavyweight. When he finished, Maxime came over to where I was sitting, panting from exhaustion. I handed him a towel and some water. He took a long gulp and matted down his face. Behind him, Maxime's training partner tapped him to say goodbye. They hugged.

"How are you feeling? I asked.

"Every day I gotta get a little better, a little better," he said. "You got someone for me yet?"

"No. Gotta talk to Calix again."

"Who could we get?"

"I don't know yet, Max."

"Ask him then, manager" he said, smiling. We had agreed on a formal arrangement where he would enter the professional ranks under my direction. I just needed to finalize some paperwork and submit it to the Commission. Max would do the same.

"It's probably going to be some Eastern Euro cab driver," I said.

"I don't care where he's from."

I wanted to see his progress but had other motivations. With my debt to the Count, I couldn't afford any breaks this week and wanted Maxime to come for the collections.

(Violence was my preferred last resort when dealing with someone who couldn't pay. There were so many other arrangements to use: from deferring payments, to asking that debtors pay a percentage, to taking something they owned, to cutting off gamblers who were behind on the money so that they couldn't wager with other bookies across town. The oversight from law enforcement that came with hurting people wasn't worth it.)

"I may have some work for you this week," I said. "Just need you to ride with me, nothing more."

"When?" he asked.

"The usual, Friday. Three hundred for a few hours. Something happens, like you have to look at a guy, I up the fee."

"Alright," he said. There was hesitancy in his voice.

"What's the matter?"

"I heard they're going after your people." Maxime's eyes were those of someone revealing a girlfriend's infidelity.

"Who's saying that?"

"Remember Anthony, the kid I played with in Thetford?" Anthony Bertrand had been an NHL draft pick whose NHL career didn't materialize because of a domestic violence charge that was later dismissed. His talent didn't warrant the NHL justifying a contract to its fans.

"His cousin bets in Laval. Knows Genny. Said Genny was promising free credits to anyone who went with them."

"Well," I began, alarmed, "I never heard that."

"Yeah, well, I don't imagine you did, sacrament. Say they're taking bets on the league now too."

"What?" I said. "Genny just bought into the league?"

"Yeah, and that's why he's Gary Bettman now." Maxime wiped his face and looked down. He began stretching his shoulders, quads and hamstrings, making elastics of the overworked muscles on his long body.

I was still trying to understand this. "In any case," I started, "I still need to collect this week, and I'd like you there. I'll pick you up at around one on Friday afternoon, okay?"

"Okay, T."

24.

I received fewer bets this week. The NFL season was over, which meant that a major source of income was gone for the next seven months. But the SLSPL was still on, and in Montreal, which worshiped hockey in lieu of religion, this was an anomaly I couldn't explain. Teams were still playing. Guys were still fighting. So why weren't people betting in the same volume? Was Maxime right?

By Friday morning the missing wagers still hadn't come through. At eleven, I picked up Maxime from the gym downtown, where he just completed another morning training session. He came through the gym doors, a cloud of condensation forming around his head in the cold air, and sat down in the front seat.

"Jesus H," I said. "Couldn't get clean or what, bud?"

"Sorry T, I just finished," he said. "Didn't have any time." I maneuvered our way out of the downtown mess and towards the West Island.

"How'd everything go today?" I asked. Maxime described the morning's training session, which focused on speed and explosiveness. He wanted a real test, he said, looking out towards the stalled highway traffic.

"Well, you may be right," I said, changing the subject.

"About?"

"Somebody taking our action."

"I'm hearing this shit third-hand, but that's what they're saying." Maxime pulled a protein shake out of his gym bag and began drinking.

Where would Maxime have heard this? I tried not to glance at him out of the corner of my eye so as not to seem paranoid. Who else was he speaking with? Was this one of the gossipy conversations people were constantly having in the milieu? Or was he meeting with people whose plans opposed mine? No, I told myself, that couldn't be.

We arrived at the first stop. The bettor, Gabriel, was a friend of Stu's, and they both worked together for the City. He was having a cigarette outside, its smoke spiraling into the cold air. Gabe owed a couple thousand and was sullen when I appeared.

"How are ya Gabe?" I asked. He handed over an envelope. Inside, I could see there were twenty one hundred dollar bills neatly arranged. I had become so well-versed with cash that I knew at once it was the right amount and didn't have to count.

"Not gonna get it back this week?" I asked.

"Nah, taking a week off, Teddy," he said, never having done so with me. "Gotta take my foot off the gas a bit." I wasn't in a mood to pussyfoot.

"Taking your foot...? You going somewhere else or just pissed about Stu? You hear what that guy said to me?" I asked, invoking Stu's insult to my parents. Gabe appeared nervous, looking into my car where Maxime was staring back at him.

"Come on," he said, holding up his hands to ridicule my question.

"You've bet with me every week this year, one of the most reliable guys I have and you're pretty much even, and all of a sudden you wanna step back?"

"My wife's on me." I couldn't resist laughing at this explanation. The idea that someone's wife — that anyone's wife — could prevent their husband from gambling was so absurd that it didn't merit an earnest rebuttal.

"Oh, I bet she is," I said.

"Come on, Teddy. I don't need this."

"Neither do I. You don't want to bet, you don't want to bet, but don't give me that runaround about your wife. Do I look like a fucking idiot?" The more I talked through his excuse, the angrier I became. I wanted to smack him but knew this was pointless to prolong. Gabe looked down, embarrassed by his weak excuse, but I didn't say anything else and got back in the car, where I turned to Maxime.

"He's giving his action to somebody else," I said.

"Genny?" Maxime asked.

"How the fuck would they poach him so easily?" I looked back to Gabe's house, with its new, oversized pickup truck outside. This guy was probably paying a grand every month for that piece of shit truck, but now he couldn't bet anymore.

"Everybody knows everybody in this city," Maxime said. "You think you're the only ostie guy he's dealing with?"

"What do you think they're offering over there? Better credit? Better lines?"

"Probably."

We left to make my other collections. Everyone paid and so Maxime had no purpose but to remain in the car. But only half the gamblers acted as if they were going to wager on the weekend's game, and while I didn't want to appear desperate by offering free credits, it was obvious something had changed. Was their relaxed apathy (none of them could just *stop*) about placing future bets the result of my bettors becoming aware of other options? I didn't know, but it felt as though my business was being taken. So, too, would my house, if this continued.

25.

"You need to talk with those guys," I told Eddy later that afternoon. "I'm a shepherd whose flock got poached." It wasn't lost on me that taking our action was part of a longer strategy that concluded with my removal.

"I told you he's a motherfucker, tabernak. But we'll wait a week, bud. If it's still slow, I'll arrange a meeting. We might need someone to broker. These guys have people who don't like 'em, too, don't forget that," he said. "A lot of people think Genny's a cunt and if he's too aggressive that'll scare other guys in the city. He can try this with one book, but he can't do it with everyone, you understand?"

"So we wait a week?" I asked. "I can't afford this Ed. The Super Bowl fleeced me."

"It'll be fine," he said. "Don't worry about it."

"I do worry about it," I said. "You have pipelines of cash flowing all over. I don't."

"Then maybe you gotta think of some new ways make money, ostie."

"New ways?" I said, furious with his answer. "I *did* think of new ways! I created a whole new market! My ideas are making everybody a ton of money. *I did* what I was supposed to." I could feel my chest and shoulders tensing. Eddy noticed this.

"Don't start getting heavy, calice," he answered, first slowly, and then soothingly. "You've done a lot, I know you have."

"So where does that leave us?"

"Like I said," he started, irritated, "we'll wait a week and if it keeps up I'll talk to someone." He returned to his laptop, and I got up to leave.

"Leaving so quick?" he asked.

"Need to get back out there," I said, under my breath.

"Thanks buddddd," he called out as I left. Eddy did this whenever he didn't want me to leave in anger.

"Alright," I said, hateful at my submissiveness. I didn't know what to think as I stepped outside and got into my car. It didn't appear that Eddy cared about my situation, and was I then not an idiot for refusing Genny's offer? Had I defected, my half-sheet would be flourishing with the range and resources he would have provided. Or was Eddy initially right: that even if I had accepted his offer, Genny would have inevitably suffocated me in his quest for control?

I didn't know what to believe, only that the circumstances of my work had become uncontrollable.

I woke up at three on six consecutive nights, each time with an imaginary phone in my hand. During one of these nightmares, a giant without irises came into my room and dumped a tangled goo of concentration camp bodies on me. Their flesh tore away as it fell against mine, and I could see my mother's gaping mouth drop towards my face. I woke up yelling, too afraid to fall back asleep, and when I finally did, an hour and a half later, I slept until noon the next day. There were less messages than usual on my phone in the morning. I answered only those that wanted action.

After another down week, Eddy told me to appear at the meeting with Genny. It had been arranged by an old-timer I was told not to make eye contact with, in an industrial part of Verdun where someone owned a warehouse (Eddy had also told me to dress warmly, as Genny would try and take advantage of some fast compromise — one hastened by the urge to go back inside on a cold winter's day). Eddy wanted to make a show of arriving together, picking me up in his Escalade, driven today by a silent giant nicknamed "Little Craig." My boss said nothing for the entire ride, and when we arrived there was another SUV parked at the lot's other end. Alongside it was a smaller luxury sedan. Eddy told Craig to park some distance away, and when we stopped, I could see the doors open and Genny step out, Fortunato behind him. An older man in a long coat emerged from the sedan.

"Okay, let's go," Eddy said, stepping out of the car, where he provided the final instructions. "Keep quiet unless you need to jump in for something specific."

"Yep," I said.

Still tanned from his vacation, Genny walked towards us in hard, purposeful strides. Fortunato and the mediator followed. Genny offered a hand to Ed.

"How ya doin' Ed? How ya doin', bro?" he said, turning to face me. I smiled, close-mouthed, and nodded.

Behind Genny, the older man addressed everyone. I had no idea where he derived his influence from, which reminded me how little I knew of the milieu — who its principal players were, where power was concentrated, what decades-old problems created the invisible backdrop that we were all acting against. No, I hardly knew anything beyond the necessity of keeping my mouth closed.

"So, we're all here," the man said, making eye contact with each of us. "Let's get into it. Eddy raised an issue about you taking some of his customers," he said, looking at Genny.

"Yes," Eddy answered.

"I don't control where people want to place their bets," Genny said.

"Unless you're poaching."

"How the fuck I'd do that?"

"You're giving guys free credits to jump ship," Eddy argued, his voice still under control. There were no formal rules for any of this, only the interpretations of those involved, and while it was common to carve out geographical borders, especially where drugs were involved, this was different.

"Says who?" Genny asked.

"Everybody."

"Fucking degenerate gamblers playing telephone? Who's everybody?" Genny asked. He possessed the pointed aggression I'd seen from so many bullies at high school parties, who would show up in groups, not knowing anyone, and pour beer in the fish tank before starting a fight.

"Genny," Eddy began, in a tone that was conciliatory but firm, "there are more guys out there than any one of us can handle. But somehow my guys — for the first time ever, ostie — are going somewhere else. Why's that?"

"Maybe your service ain't what it used to be," Genny said, glancing out of the side of his eye to gauge my reaction. I didn't say anything and looked to the mediator.

Eddy tried to respond but was cut off. "Besides," Genny said, "I bought into that league now. It's a conflict if this kid's taking bets on something I have a piece of, right?" Here, Genny turned to face me. "You can do it under me, bro, and kick up twice if you continue," he said, pointing to himself and Eddy.

"We have the same arrangement in Verdun," I said, speaking up for the first time. "Thousands every week, so we got skin in the game, too." For two months I'd given the team between three and six grand a week to bring in new fighters. Everyone benefited from this investment, and it was ludicrous to suggest that I was somehow an interloper. Eddy put his hand on my shoulder.

Genny turned to the mediator. "Georgy, this don't work for me. I own the book and part of the league now, but we have two sheets taking bets on it? That don't make any sense. Let's centralize the hockey stuff and halve the profit."

The older man paused for a moment and considered his point. "Ed's guys are his," he said in an old voice, "but anybody else is open season. Let's agree to this, because it don't make sense for things to go in a bad way. One more thing," he said, turning to me.

"You're the one handicapping this league so well, right?" he asked me. I nodded.

"You set the lines for everyone," he said. "That way, Genny gets the right numbers." He turned to Eddy. "What's your ownership stake in Verdun?" he asked.

"We're helping them bring guys in," Eddy said. "But we've put a mortgage worth of money into that league. Guys are taking vacations off the market we created." Georgy considered this and then explained that Genny's formal ownership meant he had a right to our action.

"Owning and paying into have different privileges," the old man reasoned. He looked at me when I said this.

"What? I created this market and—" I started, before Eddy put his hand on my shoulder again.

"I'm not speaking Alzheimer's, kid," the old-timer said. Genny almost smiled beside him. I didn't answer.

"One more thing," Genny said. "I want that little carpet flier to settle up with me." I'd forgotten about Karim. After I stopped giving him money, he'd been slow to answer my messages. We usually spoke every day about our lines and whose debts had grown, but he hadn't been in the gym. Patty told me that Zinedine stabbed someone in a Saint-Laurent club (his crew was causing problems), but that was the only recent news.

"Isn't he on a plan?" Eddy asked.

"Yeah, but I need it now, Ed," Genny said. "I'm tired of that little fuck forking over installments when he's got enough to pay in full, the guy. He's running goddamn romance scams for widows and screens my calls like I'm fucking CRA." I turned to Eddy, expecting him to defend Karim. He said nothing.

"I guess that's it," Genny said, turning to Fortunato before looking back at me. He then extended his hand for Eddy to shake, thanked the mediator and walked back to his car. Georgy said goodbye to Eddy and nodded at me, turning back towards his sedan, while Eddy and I walked back to the Escalade. Craig drove out of the industrial area towards downtown.

"What the fuck?" I said.

"He owns a piece of the league now," Eddy said, as if I didn't already understand that.

"So does Andre. You know what's going to happen, right? He's going to cut our feet out with credits. So I'm going to be setting lines that he profits from?"

"Yeah, I don't know," Eddy said, looking out the window. "How much of that debt does Karim have left?" I said nothing, seething beside him.

"How much?" Eddy asked, his tone sharp.

"Probably around thirty-five." Eddy shook his head in disgust.

"Fucking grocery clerk, tabernak."

"I'm going to fall behind on my own payments, Ed. I'm not even treading water."

"We'll figure out another way," he said. I'd heard this before.

"What are you going to do with Karim?"

"I'll pay his way out of the hole," he said from the front seat. "But he's done with me. I'm going to fold his sheet into yours," he said. "He ain't doing shit with it right now anyway. Eventually somebody else can can take it over." I looked at Little Craig, who was staring through the windshield.

"How's he going to take that?" I asked.

"Who the fuck cares, sacrament? What's he going to do about it?" Eddy leaned back in the bucket seat, absorbed now by a newspaper. "Genny comes out of that ahead and then gets even more leverage," Eddy said, shaking his head. "All because that little ostie shit can't control himself."

"He doesn't deserve to get hurt," I said. In the driver's seat, Little Craig's ears came alive.

"Nobody's getting hurt," Eddy answered.

26.

Outside of our family home, the first investment property I ever owned came through paperwork Eddy put in my name without asking. It was a townhouse close to McGill that cost over eight hundred thousand ("an absolute steal" the coked-up real estate agent later gasped), which Eddy's construction crew immediately set upon fixing. Three weeks later, the house had internal finishes that belied its low list price. The countertops were quartz, there were ornate finishings along its walls and the house had been outfitted with new furniture. On its ownership papers, the agent put "businessman" beside my name, deliberately omitting which business I was involved in. The objective was to rent it, and this too had already been arranged: one of Eddy's friends was going to pay cash.

"You don't have to do jack shit for this place," Eddy said. "And I'll give you a cut when we sell it."

"When will that be?"

"Year or two. When prices spike, we'll offload it. With all the renos, we may be able to get double for this — or more — in a better market."

"I wish you would have told me," I said. "I didn't want my name on this house."

"It's a gift bud, don't be a child. Market's in the shitter so it's the right time to buy. No better investment than a spot like this." His rationale did nothing to improve my financial position *right now*. I still needed cash to make the quarterly payments, and even with Karim's sheet I'd be making less now that Genny was our new master.

The week before our tenant moved in, Eddy threw a party. I barely knew any of these people, recognizing a few of them from the Super Bowl party, and stood behind a white countertop in the kitchen as strangers pretended like they were all best friends. Some of the girls here were probably strippers or escorts. One was being encouraged to flaunt a nipple, and after much prodding by both sexes she pulled down a sequined top. Her reward was a glass of Grey Goose.

Soon after, Karim appeared with his brother, who investigated the room when he walked through the front door. I wasn't sure whether Karim had been told his sheet would be taken. His carefree bearing indicated that he hadn't.

"Waddup Ted?" Karim said. "You know Z," he went on, pointing to his brother, who reached out to shake my hand.

"How ya doing, Z?" I asked.

"Waddup Teddy Knox?" Zinedine said, his voice flat.

"Maaaaan," Karim said in a low, conspiratorial voice, drawing out the lone vowel as he opened a new bottle of vodka, "remember that debt to Genny?"

"Of course" I said, already eager for this to be over.

"He fucked me on that, bro." Karim's eyes were wide, like he'd discovered a shocking fact it was his duty to inform the world about.

"How?" I asked, uninterested in what would surely be a lie.

"He never counted all my payments." I couldn't think he expected me to believe this. "When he told Eddy about the overall, he didn't include what I already gave."

"Why didn't you say anything then?"

"Cause I didn't know about it until recently!" Karim looked at me with expressive shock.

"You gonna tell Ed?" I shouldn't have even asked this. Karim didn't need any new thoughts in his head.

"Yeah — he's gonna get some of his money back."

"You'll kick a hornet's nest," I warned him. "I wouldn't."

"It's Ed's money! He has to know, no?" Karim said, trying to sound rational. I shrugged my shoulders. On the room's other side, Eddy was speaking to a girl in the living room.

"Do you want a drink, Z?" I asked.

"Don't drink, bro, but thank you," he answered. Zinedine was looking at his phone and didn't appear to care about anyone in the room. I poured myself a gin and soda as new partygoers arrived, and Karim began speaking to a girl I may have once seen at Célestes. Hulking gym devotees in condom-tight shirts pulled bottles out of SAQ bags. On the room's other side I could sense Eddy moving towards me. Karim also noticed and ended his conversation.

"Hey Ed, how are ya?" Karim asked. Eddy slapped his shoulder perfunctorily.

"You're owed a bit of money, you know that, eh?" Karim warned.

"For what?" Eddy asked. He was looking at a message on his phone, not making eye contact with Karim.

"The debt to Genny — we overpaid — he didn't count some of my payments, Ed."

"Come on," I said to Karim, "not here."

"What?" Eddy asked. "How much?" He was staring at Karim now, his phone having fallen to the side. Eddy's body had assumed the same posture it flattened into after the Super Bowl party.

"The fucking guy's a snake," Karim began. "He owes you at least ten dimes."

Eddy's eyes had become scopes. "We'll talk about this later," he said.

"But I want to get that money back for you." Two guys across the countertop looked over to see what we were talking about, their buzzed eyes focusing on Eddy, waiting for his reaction. I told Karim we could talk about this outside.

"You're not going to do anything," Eddy said to him.

"Why?" Karim asked, looking down.

"You're also not going to talk about this — with anyone," Eddy said. "I don't need backstage chatter, ostie."

"Alright Ed, alright," Karim said, ashamed. "I won't say shit. No problem. We're going for a smoke." He went with Zinedine to have a cigarette outside.

"Fucking dummy," Eddy said as he watched Karim walk outside. "I'm done with this idiot."

"What are you going to do?" I asked.

"Send him back to the grocery store," he said. Soon after, Juliet appeared at the doorway with two girls in their early-twenties. They had brown hair, peaked cheekbones and spoke with European accents. Poland maybe. Juliet hugged Eddy before turning towards me.

"Teddy! How are you?" she asked. "Come and meet two of my friends," she said, introducing Anna and Ivana. Both smiled as their eyes searched the room.

"Nice to meet both of you," I said. Neither appeared interested in speaking with me so I went back in search of a drink.

"What's the matter?" Juliet asked, sliding over to where her body wedged against mine. "You don't want to talk to them?"

"They don't seem to want to talk to me," I said. Eddy showed up at my side, shaking his head.

"This guy could have any girl in the room, but I never know where his head's at," he said.

"He just needs the right one," Juliet said, squeezing my hand as she looked at me for a second before returning to Eddy. Karim and Zinedine were back in the kitchen and had noticed Juliet's girls. At once Karim drew them into a conversation neither wanted to prolong. I don't know what he was talking about — some European beach town, maybe — but they were looking through him as he described partying on ecstasy. An hour later, I had become somewhat drunk when one of the girls accused Karim of getting too close to her. Juliet intervened and some nasty words were exchanged between Zinedine and Anna.

Eddy was watching from a corner of the room. He walked over to where Karim was standing and told him to leave. Karim protested and Ed, now also somewhat drunk (a rarity), came closer to his face, his pupils containing separate bonfires. I walked over and pulled Karim away, but he continued to complain ("Ed, I didn't do shit, come on, bro!"). Zinedine stepped in to push my hand away.

"Fuck outta there!" he said.

"I'm just trying to calm things down," I answered.

"Relax Z," Karim said, his voice one of resigned shame.

"Tabernak, hit the road, boys," Eddy told the two brothers.

"Fuck you, playdoh fuckin' tough guy!" Zinedine shot back, eager to be berserk. Eddy stepped forward but I held my arms out to prevent Zinedine from starting a situation only he was fit to finish. His face remained hard when Karim pulled him out the door. After both brothers left, Eddy shook his head and spat into the sink.

"Fucking goofs!" he said, turning to Juliet, who rolled her eyes. The other partygoers who'd stopped to watch were now discussing the outburst.

I knew and liked no one in the room, making an excuse about having to leave. Smitty picked me up and drove us back to NDG, where I climbed into bed and passed out with my clothes still on. When I rose the next morning, my face creased by a crumpled pillow, I hated myself for being so hungover. Booze did nothing to improve relations with others because I'd spent the party isolated within my cold cave. Instead of the clarity boasted of by seasoned drinkers, alcohol brought only blur, and the lone lesson I learned from its consumption was how incapable I was from resisting the release. It wasn't about enjoying others because I didn't care about any of these people, and wondered briefly if this apathy extended to myself. Each night out became an escape into blackness. Why? I didn't know. What the fuck was I doing with myself?

27.

At the gym on Monday, I waited for Maxime to finish his last bit of sparring. In the final round he dropped his left hand and walked into a power shot. The Woodchipper winced but kept fighting.

While he was getting better, even I, an unsophisticated boxing watcher, could identify shortcomings that would doom him against better competition. Maxime's habit — forged over so many hockey fights — was to answer an opponent's success with more violence of his own. But in boxing, where a fighter had to plot his way around the ring, this wasn't enough, and how soon he'd meet someone capable of exploiting this weakness was a question his first professional fight would answer.

Despite these criticisms, watching Maxime spar reinforced my self-loathing. He was past his physical prime but pushing his body to its limit, while I — vastly younger and not having absorbed one tenth of his damage — could barely stand for two minutes without sitting. I gulped down a Gatorade and marvelled at the size of his back, tattooed the entire way across. Maxime was no longer svelte, only big, but he'd managed to work his way into shape over the past couple of weeks and had far better cardio than he did for hockey, where his hardest exertions came during the brief bursts when he threw his hands.

"You fucking hungover again, Ted?" Maxime yelled from the ring mat. I shook my head, no, and thought I could see his eyes roll.

Elsewhere, the gym was filling up, as pro, amateur and white collar fighters were moving through their paces. Boys from Montreal North shot their fists into heavy bags beside the lawyers from René-Lévesque.

"Big T!" Maxime said once he'd dismounted the ring. He seemed to have lost some weight and I could see his cheekbones again. Since his suspension, Maxime had been in the gym every day.

"What are you checking in at?" I asked, motioning towards the corner scale.

"Two forty-two," he said. This was over ten pounds less than his hockey weight, where he didn't need endurance beyond the forty-five seconds required to fight or take a physical shift. To make a start in boxing, Maxime needed energy for eight rounds. He had made a fine start.

"Feeling good?" I asked.

"Yes sir." The upper reaches of his abs were starting to show themselves.

"Feeling quick?"

"Yes fucking sir."

"Good," I said, "'cause you're looking like Tommy Morrison, I like it. How'd it feel to get popped like that?"

"Fucking mistake by me, calice," he said, shaking his head, "but if you want to spar with the big boys…"

"I'd say never drop your left hand, but I've never fought a round in my life," I said, "so what do I know."

"Hopefully who I'm getting in May." Maxime leaned on the ring rope and looked towards Calix's office.

"I'm gonna talk to him now," I said.

"He's busy. Genny's in there," Maxime said, motioning to the closed door.

"You saw him?"

"He was here earlier," Maxime said, "watching me spar."

Genny had never been to the gym before. Why was he here now?

"I need this fucking fight to pay my bills, man," Maxime went on. "You hear what happened?"

Maxime's construction job, where he worked as a union labourer four days a week, had just been closed for financial misconduct. He didn't know why, though the usual charges of bid-rigging had surfaced. Maxime took another sip of water, his mind distant, and sat down on the ring mat. A couple of minutes later the door to Calix's office opened and Genny emerged. He shook hands with the promoter and from the other side of the gym I could see a young, olive-skinned Italian — Alessandro, whom Patty had seen at Les Ailes — get up. Before he could leave, Genny saw me.

"There he is," Genny said, smiling as he came over to shake hands with Maxime. It was the first time I'd seen him in a tracksuit. "I've watched this guy throw down for decades."

"Hi Genny," I said.

"He looks good, this guy," he said, pointing to Maxime. "The Big Chipper." Max appeared to blush at the compliment: even an experienced tough guy wasn't immune to a prideful surge.

"He does," I said, "we just need to find him somebody to fight."

"I got a guy," Genny said. Maxime looked up. "Yeah," Genny continued, seeing his intrigue register, "that's what I was just talking to Calix about. I'm managing a kid coming in from Jonquière. Heavyweight."

"What's his name?" I asked. Genny told me but it didn't register. "How experienced is he?"

"Good amateur, the kid," he said. "Making his debut at pro." Genny looked from me to Maxime.

"Interesting," I said, glancing at Maxime.

"This guy don't give a fuck," Genny said, smiling. "So what do you say?" he asked. "You're his advisor, right?"

"I'll get in there with anyone," Maxime replied before I could answer. "I just need somebody to commit."

"Yeah, I guess," I stammered, "we'll have to check your kid out."

"Come on, bro," Genny said to me. "The Chipper's a legend, my kid's a kid."

"Why so eager to give him Max, then?" I asked. Genny didn't hesitate before responding.

"Because I want him tested, see what he's about," he said. "Purse will be ten K a piece — that's fucking unheard of for two guys making their debut here."

Maxime came alive at the amount and then looked away: his trainer was calling him from across the gym.

"I gotta clean up, boys," Maxime said. "Genny, good to see you." They shook hands and Maxime departed for the shower. I knew Genny wouldn't propose a boxing match whose outcome wasn't preordained. Hidden within his goodwill was another motive.

"And maybe we can wager," he said to me.

"What are you thinking?"

"Let's just make it interesting, a little fun for everybody. We'll talk about it later," he said, "when Eddy's around. But it's gotta be something we're gonna sweat, or else what's the fucking point, eh?"

"I don't have a lot of cash right now," I said, hopeful the subtext was obvious. "And I got debts."

"The percentage," Genny started. "The shit you owe by taking action on the league. I'll wipe that for the rest of the season." This wasn't nearly the tantalizing proposition his tone suggested it was.

"How much are you thinking?" I asked.

"A hundred."

"There's only a few weeks left in the SP," I said. "A hundred

K's a lot more than the amount I'd be paying you."

"Make the bet bro. Your boy needs the money," he said, speaking about Maxime. "Guy gets suspended then his job gets snatched. No luck on the guy. You get him into the ring and the Chipper's getting paid." Genny paused for a second, his eyes icicles. "But he's only fighting if he takes on my guy. I talked to Calix. We have the one open spot." I considered the offer. "You ain't got nothing to say?" he asked.

"I'll talk to Eddy," I said.

"I guess you can, but the wager's between us. That other kid," he started, "the one who worships Muhammad."

"Karim."

"He's been talking a lot, bro," he said. "Saying I'm spreading fiction about his debt," Genny leaned into me as he said this. "Is he fucking stupid, the goof, or what?"

"Well I haven't heard anything," I said. "And nobody listens to him anyway."

"Not like you'd tell me."

"A hundred K?" I asked.

"Yeah, bro."

"I'll get back to you."

28.

Now, an accounting of my finances. I still had a quarterly home payment to make in the middle of May. By making the bet, I'd have less than twenty-five grand in cash on hand. Since the number of wagers I was taking continued to decline, if I lost and couldn't take action anymore (because, in addition to Genny squeezing us out, I wouldn't have enough money in reserve to run my own sheet) there would be nothing left to pay future installments. But if I won, I could pay the entire remaining debt outright.

"A hundred k?" Eddy asked, chin on his fists, after I met him to discuss the proposition. We were at an Italian restaurant in St. Leonard, not far from where some of Genny's men owned cafes. He had a plate of cheese cappelletti in front of him. It was barely touched.

"Yeah."

"Who's he got?" Eddy asked.

"Some kid from Jonquière, I don't know him," I said.

"Thought you were the boxing expert." Eddy was staring at his phone.

"I'm going to look into it," I said. Eddy took a measured bite of his pasta. The waitress came over to ask if I wanted something.

"Get something," Eddy said. "It's on me."

"What he's having," I told her. I sat back in the chair and looked around to where, in one corner of the restaurant, a large Italian family was celebrating. A short man held up a smiling little girl, kissing her on the cheek.

"So?" I asked.

"What do *you* think?" he asked back.

"I think he might try to Don King me. But Maxime's fucked if he doesn't get the fight, so that's another thing. And *I'm* going to be fucked if he loses." Eddy didn't respond as he continued to look at his pasta. "Plus I'm not exactly printing money since my business got taken away," I said, looking at him. "Wagers are way down, you saw that, right?"

"Of course I saw that." Eddy didn't seem concerned. "Is that all he had to say," he asked, "about the bet?"

"Nope." I let this linger for a moment.

"Well?"

"He referenced Karim talking about him. I denied it, but..."

"There ain't much I can do about that," he responded. "Karim talks too much. If he's lying — and he probably is — Genny's got a right to be pissed."

"Is he going to do something about it?" I asked.

"I don't know," Eddy answered. "Why? Karim's a nobody." I had last spoken to him the morning after the party. He sounded desperate, eager for me to tell him a different version of the night he feigned being unable to remember. Later that day, Eddy told him that his sheet was gone. I hadn't seen Karim since.

"Even if it fucks with his reputation?"

Eddy smiled and winked at me. "Sounds like you want something to happen."

"No, fuck no," I said. "The opposite!"

"In any case," he went on, shrugging his shoulders as he forked another mound of pasta, "it's out of your control. And mine."

"How's it out of *your* control? You can stop this shit, no?"

"K's an ungrateful little prick." I said nothing and stared at a plate of hot bread the waitress had just put down. "What's the matter, not hungry?" he asked.

"Thought I had more of an appetite."

"Yep," he responded, staring at his cell phone again. "So listen, Teddy," he said, looking up. "I got another property we gotta grab. Once in a lifetime. By the Old Port."

"What about the bet, Ed?"

"What about it?"

"Well how do I protect myself?" Eddy laughed.

"It's like you've said before calice, there's a million fucking ways to make an outcome." What did Eddy expect me to do, pay someone off? I wasn't opposed to this but if Genny found out he would kill me.

"If Genny ever got a whiff of that…" I started, exasperated with his lack of interest.

"You scared?" he asked, smiling. What was the matter with this guy?

"I'm just saying, there'll be consequences."

"There's always consequences," Eddy continued. "So stay in the shadows. You're good at that."

I started researching Genny's prospect. There was footage online that showed Xavier Laliberté fighting in a dingy hotel before a dozen people. In the first video, he looked tall and inexperienced. In the second, taken a few years later, his technique had improved but it was difficult to know how much power he had. I couldn't find anything else online and would have to see him in person, but I'd heard through a contact that Laliberté was training at a gym off the forty. When I arrived on a Tuesday morning, a young man who occupied the same position I pretended to at Eddy's gym looked at me suspiciously.

"What you doing here?" he asked in French.

"Genny told me I could stop by, he's the kid's manager," I said. "That fine?" The tone of his face changed.

"They're in the back," he said, gesturing towards the open gym where two fighters were warming up. There were several men at ringside who looked at me when I came in. The space seemed new by boxing standards, with fresh equipment, a ring that wasn't stained by decades of sweat and heavy bags that weren't criss-crossed by a patchwork of duct tape. Windows to the outside provided a view of the highway. It appeared as if someone had made an investment in local boxing.

"Who are you?" an older, white-haired Québécois asked me in French.

"A friend of Genny's," I said.

"He tell you to come?"

"Yes."

"I don't know about that," he said.

"Well, why don't you ask him?" I said, indifferent to this walking corpse.

"Who the fuck are you?" his partner — a short, bowlegged doofus — asked.

"Ask this guy's fucking manager," I yelled. Laliberté looked over and the group turned around.

The shorter man didn't respond, returning to the two fighters. I stayed back from the ring as he rang a bell and sparring began. The boxers circled one another during the opening round, moving their shoulders in mutual attempts to goad the other into making a mistake. It was only training, and each man took a noticeable zip off their punches. Still, it didn't appear as though Laliberté was a puncher. Skilled, maybe, but not capable of putting someone into a coma, and while Laliberté at least looked like a boxer it was impossible to know whether he'd be too much for Maxime.

The men at ringside began shouting instructions, pushing Laliberté to close the distance. He began ordering his opponent with the lead foot, moving him towards the corner where his punches found the other man's midsection. A familiar hand slapped my shoulder. It was Genny.

"They let a guy like you in?" he asked. Genny appeared to be coming from a meeting.

"Mandelbaum wanted to check me," I said, gesturing to the old man.

"So what do you think, bro?" he asked, pointing towards the ring.

"He looks like a fighter," I said, talking about Laliberté.

"He does, the kid," Genny says. "It's a good fit: young, up-and-coming skilled guy and an older heavy that everybody knows. Both guys got followings, both guys'll draw."

"And what do *you* think?" I asked, trying to catch him off-guard.

"I just told you. I *think* I want to make this fucking bet," he said, smiling.

"A lot of risk for a young guy coming out of the gate, no?" I asked. "Maxime's legit tough. He's tested." Genny looked on at the ring, unperturbed, as Laliberté became entangled with his opponent in the corner. He lost the battle in tight, pushed back by his older, overweight sparring partner. Maybe Laliberté wasn't that strong.

"If he can't handle someone like Maxime, the kid's got no future in this," Genny said.

"Fair enough." I looked out of the corner of my eye, where a large SUV had just parked. There were two men in the front seat staring at the gym. Weathered and rimless, it didn't look like something driven by anyone in the milieu.

"It's a hundred K," he went on, "that's nothing, bro."

Laliberté's opponent was starting to exert a little more pressure. Successive jabs concluded in a flush right hand that landed on the prospect's chin, throwing his head back. I couldn't be sure if his legs wobbled but it wasn't a concussive shot. Laliberté shook his head and continued to box, re-establishing control of the ring's center.

"You see?" Genny said, elbowing me gently. "He's a gamer. Right style clash for the Chipper."

"If he doesn't take Maxime, who's he going to fight?" I asked.

"He's fighting Maxime," Genny said. "That's what everybody wants. I'm already getting calls from guys wanting tickets to this. The Chipper's only getting on if Lally gets him, bro. So we got a wager or what? Come on, bro," he prompted, smiling, live a little." What other choice did I have?

"We do," I said, reaching out to shake Genny's hand.

"Fight's in five weeks," he said. "One more thing. You're a trustworthy young guy, but you gotta put the cash up first, understand? We'll both put it in escrow."

"How?" I asked.

"I got a third party. Eddy knows him. He'll hold the cash until after the fight." I stared at Genny, distrustful, and he recognized this.

"You think I'm gonna fuck you for a hundred dimes, bro?" he said. "I don't give a fuck about a hundred dimes. But if you bet, it's gotta be serious. You gotta put a stake up first. I'll be in touch on that," he said.

The gnome who yelled at me earlier was staring again. "Look at this drawbridge troll," I said to Genny. "Everybody thinks they're a spider, standing on an anthill."

As I was leaving the gym there was some energetic applause. Laliberté must have done something productive. When I got outside, the SUV was still parked. I made eye contact with the driver — a uniformed white guy in his late thirties. Beside him was another man, older, whose eyes investigated me from knee to neck as I moved towards my sedan. The police weren't even trying to disguise themselves.

I called Maxime after meeting with Genny and he asked that I come by for dinner. When I arrived, he was having a pasta with his daughter.

"What's up, Teddy?" Maxime yelled when I walked in the front door. I came up to the main level, which opened to his kitchen. Seated beside Angélique, whom I said hello to, was an older man at the head of the table. The Woodchipper introduced me to father, Daniele. We shook hands. Maxime's father was tall and thin. He looked at me with a mistrust that bordered on arrogance when I accepted his bony hand.

"This is the guy," Maxime said to his daughter and father, "who made it happen."

"Not true," I responded in French. "You got the spot 'cause you deserve it."

"What do you think of Laliberté?" his father asked.

"Watched him this morning. He has skills but Max will take him if he fights with some pepper…" Maxime's father returned to his pasta.

"What do you do for a living?" Daniele asked, looking up again. Max stared across the table to his father.

"Teddy's involved in boxing," he said.

"I asked *him*," he said.

"Max's right" I responded. "I've been working at the boxing gym, doing stuff like that."

"Stuff like… you're a young guy," his father said, "to have connections like this."

"Just got lucky," I said.

"That all you're involved in?" he asked.

"Dad!" Maxime said. "Leave this guy alone, ostie. He's my buddy." Maxime's daughter looked down at her dinner.

"Yes," I said, "that's it."

His father motioned to the food. "Do you want something to eat?"

"Yes!" Maxime said, "have a seat, bud."

"It's okay—" I answered, "I'm going to meet someone for dinner later—"

"Then at least have a beer!" Maxime replied, getting up to walk over to his fridge, where he pulled out a cold bottle and handed it to me.

"Sure," I said, now indifferent to endearing myself to his father. "So," I began, looking at Maxime. "Christmas is coming…"

"It's going to be a fucking beautiful day, man," he said. "A beautiful day."

29.

Where was Karim? He wasn't answering my messages and when I stopped by his Griffintown apartment, no one was home. I didn't know where his mother lived but stopping in was inconceivable. His girlfriend, too, was unknown to me: despite spending nearly every day with him for five months, I'd never even met her.

This question was on my mind the following morning, when, after a lackadaisical shoulder workout at the gym, I showered and walked to the nearby Starbucks. I was sitting by myself in the corner, reading a baseball preview, when someone called my name.

"Teddy!" I turned around to see Gabriel, who weeks earlier had told me he wasn't going to bet anymore. He was with another man who looked to be in his late twenties.

"Gabe!" I said. "What are you doing here?" After Gabe made his excuse that day, I heard he lost to one of Genny's half-sheet guys, who had him beaten when a debt went unpaid. There was no evidence of the assault on his face, but he looked more crouched than I remembered.

"Good, man," he said, nervous, "what's up?"

"Just finished a workout," I answered, paying no attention to his friend.

"You mind if we sit down?" he asked.

"Nope, of course not," I said. "I have to take off soon, so you can have the table." His friend, tall and in good shape, stood by in silence, nodding along to our conversation.

"Got someone to meet?" Gabe asked.

"Doctor's appointment," I said, a lie. Gabe's friend went to the cashier to buy their coffees, asking first whether I wanted anything.

"How are the lines this weekend?" Gabe asked. I'd never ever run into one of our bettors like this in public and felt a twinge in my stomach. I knew that he worked for the City and had been suspended from work before, though for what I couldn't be sure. There was a recent Journal article about municipal employees being charged over a bid-rigging scheme for road contracts. What was he doing here now?

"No idea, man," I said, staring forward. "What are you doing this weekend?"

"Just my usual," he said. "I'm gonna watch some sports, maybe toss some cash in." His smile was conspiratorial. "Want to jump back in on hockey. Must be some good tilts to wager on this week?" I shrugged my shoulders and looked down.

"Are you playing any hockey these days, you know, men's league?" I asked. "Weren't you into that?"

"Nope, took the year off," he said, impatient. "Look," he continued, "while I have ya, I want you to meet my buddy. He's tired of that bullshit government parlay."

"You just ran into me here?" I asked.

"Yeah, how does that happen, eh? Sorry about how we left things, by the way. I just needed to take a step back for a second. Nothing to do with Stu." Gabe looked down when he said this and then back at me. Two women with short haircuts sat down at the table beside us. They began speaking in French about seeing retired NHL players at a restaurant on Saint-Laurent. I couldn't be sure if one of them was looking at me out of the corner of her eye.

"I'm here at this time every week," I answered, leaning in so my speech wouldn't be audible to anyone with a recording device. "Not here," I said. He nodded and looked back at me.

"Yeah, of course," Gabe said, "no problem." His friend reappeared with two coffees.

"I'm Teddy," I said, reaching out to shake the other man's hand. "What's going on?"

"Alex," he said, "nice to meet you." His hands were hard and calloused near the fingers. Tattooed underneath his wrist was a cross. He had a defenseman's body, long, with an overdeveloped butt, and bent slightly forward as he stood there.

"What do you guys have on for the rest of the day?" I asked. Gabe was flummoxed.

"I think we're going to get a workout in, too," he said.

"You have some time off or something?" I asked. "Don't you work for the City?"

"Had some vacation I'm going to lose if I don't use it."

"On a rainy Wednesday, like this…?" Gabe made a sad sigh.

"End of fiscal's coming up," he said, improvising. Having failed at the introduction, he was frustrated but I could see him rallying for another attempt.

"Do you guys work together?" I asked, looking to Alex, who remained stoic, standing beside the table. He, too, appeared to sense that something had gone wrong.

"Nope, just buddies," Alex said. "But I have some time off right now."

"What do you do?" I asked him.

"This and that," he said. "I landscape for a big chunk of the year."

"Good to know," I replied. "I may need to get my parents' place done later this summer. Do you have a card or something?" Caught off guard by my question, Alex's posture straightened.

"No business card on me," he said, "but I'll get you some info."

"Sounds great." I made a show of checking the time. Gabe could see that I was attempting to leave and intervened.

"Teddy," he started, raising his eyebrows at me. I could feel Alex's focus intensifying. "Is there no way I can hook my man up?" The world seemed to slow down, and I resisted looking over at the two women beside me, who had stopped talking. This stupid, dumb cunt, asking me this in public.

"With what?" I said. I then looked over to Alex, who had the face of someone exposed for cheating. After a pause, the two women resumed their conversation.

"Gotta go guys," I said, "no benefits at the boxing gym, so I can't get billed for a missed appointment. Nice to meet you Alex, send me that info when you have it. See you Gabe."

"See ya," they both said together.

When I exited the coffee shop and walked towards my car, I noticed a sedan parked across the street. The driver stared ahead with a nonchalance that seemed engineered. It strengthened a suspicion that began in my stomach when they both entered the coffee shop: Gabe had stolen municipal money to pay his debts, and owing to some deal he'd arrived at with the police, was now trying to get details on the operation he was indebted to. It seemed probable to me that Alex wasn't a landscaper, but a cop.

Eddy was in his office when I got back to the gym, looking at something on the computer. I waited outside as a high-pitched businessman talked about some development opportunity close to the waterfront. I could only hear bits of conversation, but it sounded like a plot of land where a factory existed was being sold. I could hear Eddy laughing, and then both chairs grinding against the floor as they prepared to sign off. When I walked in, past the overweight fellow who had to shift his stomach so we could simultaneously pass through the door, Ed was smiling more broadly than I was used to.

"What are you so happy about?" I asked him.

"Remember I told you about that plot by the port?" he asked. I didn't. Eddy began describing his tentative purchase of a piece of land that he would turn into a condo. He said it would cost five million.

"This kind of piece never comes up for sale. Like getting a shot at Angelina Jolie. It's like winning the fucking lottery, man."

"How are you going to pay for that?" I asked him.

"I got some irons," he said, looking back down at the paperwork and then to his laptop.

"You know Gabriel, the City worker on my sheet?" Eddy shook his head. I told him about my interaction at the coffee shop and Gabe asking that his friend be put on. This had never happened before, but Eddy seemed indifferent.

"Action comes to you, you know that." He paused, ordering his thoughts. "Funny you say that," he went on, "because I heard something I didn't like the other day."

"What?"

"My guy told me the league's getting talked about behind closed doors. 'Cause everything got so big over the winter, and because of all the incidents, a lot of people know about it." Eddy's 'guy' was someone in the SPVM who would provide information relevant to whatever he was doing. I didn't even know the source's name.

"What does that mean?"

"We have to shut it down, calice," he said. "At least temporarily, and then open a new site."

"What? That's gonna set us back weeks. The season's almost done."

"I know, but no one saw this coming. That's a credit to you," he said, smiling.

"Are they gonna make an arrest?" I asked, my temperature hot. Eddy shrugged and returned to his laptop.

"We got other ways to cover your nut," he said, not looking at me. "I got lots more real estate to get into."

"Yeah, but that's not *my* thing. I just have to shut everything down? How am I gonna make any money?" Eddy looked back in my direction.

"How many of the guys betting do you know personally?" he asked. "Cause somebody's talking. Blame them, not me, tabernak. This shit happens in this business, bud. We always have to adjust." I thought back to who among those Patty brought in may have been a risk. I didn't know any of them that well. It could be anyone. Why was Eddy only telling me this now?

"This fucks me, Ed," I said. "We can start taking bets the old way, then. Set up an office over the phone..."

Eddy paused for a moment and appeared to think about something. "No, 'cause guys at the league are getting mad. They think it's influencing the games."

"What? How?" I asked. "They think guys are placing bets on themselves?"

"Yeah," he said, staring at the screen. I started to protest before Eddy cut me off. "You want to put a bullseye on you?" he asked.

"And the cops," I went on, "I thought 'they were always watching us'?"

"You gonna argue with me?" he asked, incensed, turning to rise slightly in his chair.

"No. I didn't mean any disrespect, Ed," I said, my neck starting to burn. "But—"

"Karim started talking like that. Now, he ain't around no more."

"What's that mean?"

"He ain't working with us, is what the fuck I mean. Look,"

his tone now soft again, "I'm not comparing both of you, you're a lot smarter than him, but you don't know everything, bud. When are you going to realize that?" I was furious but didn't say anything.

"Listen," Eddy started, his tone smooth and understanding. "I might as well tell you now. I'm getting out of this shit, for good."

"What? As in, everything?"

"Yeah." Eddy paused and stared at me. "I'm selling my book to Genny."

"What? When?"

"Couple weeks. He's gotta get the money together, which I'll need to buy this property." Eddy stared at me with the triumphant face of someone whose life's work was being completed.

"I *also* have a property to take care of. Ed, I can't afford to stop now."

"Hockey's done," he said, "Genny and I talked. It's bringing too much heat."

"When'd you decide? Why didn't you—"

"Stop," he said, shaking his head. "It's done."

"So what happens to me?" I asked.

"I'll give you another loan if you want. But you're a star, bud," he said. "What do you wanna do?"

I didn't need a loan, but autonomy. I didn't want patronizing compliments but support from a man I'd made more than four hundred thousand for in seven months. Eddy had told me of his plan to sell the book almost as an afterthought — the sort of detail a skilled liar slips in late during a conversation, hopeful his cavalier messaging will blunt its impact. The casual way in which he communicated this detail infuriated me each time I thought about it. It was as though I was a shmuck, a clown, an interchangeable cog or afterthought he didn't consider important enough to worry about. Eddy didn't care whether his movements impacted me, nor — it was becoming clear — did he care about me at all.

It would be a lie to say my feelings weren't bruised, but I had more practical matters to consider. Having made a modest profit after setting up the bet with Genny, I had only about thirty grand in cash remaining, and I had no idea what sort of future earning potential there would be with Genny now in control. Eddy's development plans were long term, and did nothing to help me in the interim. I could borrow money but what would be the point if I had to pay a vig?

I learned from Maurice (who did our envelopes) that Eddy wouldn't get full payment for his sportsbook until after the card. Genny was going to pay him on retainer, give Ed a piece of whatever he made in the meantime and then transfer the full amount sometime by the middle of May. Their deal was being overseen by the old-timer who mediated our conversation behind the warehouse, with an underlying bond of some sort. Now Genny would have a few hundred new regular gamblers, a number arrived at (and almost entirely expanded) by my work.

They had no right to take this from me. I created a market no one had ever conceived of, and they were just going to shut it down without my consultation? Why could they tell me no?

I looked at our website. The SLSPL option had already been taken off and I was getting messages from gamblers wondering why they couldn't wager. Our baseball and NBA options were still there, however. Why would those still be up if the hockey lines had been taken off? If the police were on to us for bookmaking, why was the site still operational? Taking unlicensed bets on other sports was still illegal, so the argument about laying low made no sense.

At our apartment, I told Patty about my conversation with Eddy and how we weren't going to comply. He leaned back in the battered La-Z-Boy and stared at the ceiling, nervous about what I was proposing.

"We could get heat for this," he said.

"I can't afford to stop now, but I'll take whatever comes our way and leave you out of it. Why do they get to shut us down?"

I promised him a new arrangement, where Patty would receive a greater cut of whatever we made over the next few weeks. There was only a month left in the SLSPL season, now in the playoffs (where there was less fighting anyway). Laval and Verdun might realistically be eliminated within the next ten days but there were still at least a couple of betting weekends left. I made an arrangement with Patty to set up a satellite office at his apartment. We would only accept bets from people we knew, and I would ensure the risk was balanced, since there wasn't enough cash in reserve to pay off any huge wins (and since I couldn't go to Eddy, as we'd be doing this behind his back).

To accomplish this, I set up a physical board in Patty's living room to mark our bets on. We still had about thirty-five guys wagering through this system and while there were questions about what happened to the website, I answered only in the most indirect way.

The problem, now, is that we didn't have a website to ensure there were no mistakes. Patty had a spreadsheet to account for the bets, risk, profits and lines, and I made sure to verify his work as he could be haphazard (to date he'd done what I asked of him, so his work was beyond criticism). I just had to ensure he kept quiet. With only a fraction of our earlier bettors still with us, I was making far less than before, only now I didn't have to send any of it up. But with games during the week, since it was the playoffs, there was more to do, and our little venture brought some water to what had been a desert.

It didn't escape me that this could create consequences. What would happen if anyone found out?

30.

It didn't turn into a period of triumph. We were only making fair returns with the pop-up book, which kept me alive but made little overall difference on my debt. A week or so later, I was lying on my couch watching a hockey game, plotting about other ways to make money, when Patty messaged me to call him. At once I thought something happened with our operation and anxiety compacted my chest. I called him and Patty answered right away.

"Karim got shot downtown," he said. "By the metro in Hochelaga."

"What the fuck?" I said, out of breath. "Who told you this?"

"Remember Dom, we met one time downtown?"

"No…"

"He tends bar down there. Said Karim came in for a couple of drinks, stepped outside and somebody popped him. One in the head, one in the neck, and they took off on a bike."

"Is he fucking dead?" I yelled into my empty house.

Patty hiccupped on the other line, afraid to state the obvious. "Well fuck, I don't know, dude, but doesn't look good, ya know? Anyway…" I fell back onto the couch.

"You there?" he asked. Time had stopped and it felt as though every liter of blood had collected in my head.

"What? Sorry, yeah" I said, slowly. "Cops are obviously there?"

"It's all cordoned off. Probably be on the late news tonight. Who woulda got him?"

"I have no idea," I said.

"Could it—"

"Not on the phone!"

"Sorry, yeah."

"Fucking goddamnit!" I screamed to no one. "Guy's got a kid coming for fucks sake! I gotta go. Let me know what you hear." Patty assured me that he would.

I sat down on the couch, exhausted, and then got up in search of my baseball bat, walking around my house to confirm everything was closed and locked. I knew this couldn't happen without the approval of someone with clout, because while Karim was a bit player, he once answered to people who weren't.

My phone was full of messages, but I answered none of them. At eleven I turned on the local news, which had a short feature on the murder. The reporter said that a "twenty-four year old man" was shot exiting a restaurant earlier that evening. It didn't mention whether he was known to police, as these reports usually did, and the segment gave way to a piece on a toothless municipal ruling.

I went downstairs to verify whether my doors were locked (they were, I had already checked three times previously), and then went back upstairs, bat in hand.

I sat with my laptop propped up on my knees, scrolling through every available local website. There was nothing, so I messaged a few question marks to Eddy. He answered back and asked that I meet at his house the following morning.

Near midnight, I couldn't sleep. Rain fell outside my window and when one of the infrequent cars passed, I could hear water geysering out from the treads. When I had almost fallen asleep, I heard a car stop close to my house, where it loitered for a moment. I reached underneath my bed for the rifle Dad had kept at the cottage — one of the lone artifacts that survived the fire. I pulled it out, edged closer to the sill and looked outside, but the car was gone.

When I woke up the next morning, forgetful of when exactly I'd fallen asleep, I felt once more like I'd passed from a nocturnal nightmare into a waking one. The gun lay in place on the floor beside me, pointed towards an open door.

It was still raining the following morning when I drove to Eddy's house in Laval. I didn't know this community and had a faint memory of my father taking me to a birthday party here sometime in elementary school, hopeful I would become friends with the son of a colleague. Eddy lived at the end of a cul-de-sac that wound its way through a wooded part of the borough. When my car pulled up to his house — a two-story, five-bedroom house indistinguishable from the street's other homes — there were two cars in the driveway: Eddy's Escalade and a smaller Mercedes sedan that must have belonged to his wife. I parked my car along the curb by his front lawn and texted to say I was here. He instructed that I enter through the backyard gate.

I walked around to the house's other side, stepping over wet grass, and under a wrought iron arch that led to his backyard. Beside the garage I could see small security cameras pointed towards the lot's four corners. Eddy's yard opened behind his house towards a wooded area at the back, where there was a covered space with a large pizza oven. He'd built an elaborate new deck behind the kidney-shaped pool. A hot tub sat close to the kitchen's bay window. As I made my way in, the door slid open and Eddy stepped out, dressed in a tracksuit. He had two coffees and gave one to me, pointing towards the pizza oven. I followed behind and we sat down on chairs opposite of one another. It was cool out and I wasn't dressed for the temperature.

Eddy stared into the woods and exhaled. "You're down a buddy," he said, taking a sip of his coffee.

"I know…"

"I know you were friends. We'll find out what happened, calice." He looked at his cellphone when a message came in. Behind Eddy, I could see a woman tending to a small child in the kitchen.

"Who do you think it was?" I asked.

"Could be anyone," he said. "Pay a Haitian and they'll do it for a dollar."

"You think it was a Haitian?" I asked.

"I have no idea, T."

"I have a decent sense of who it may have been," I said.

Eddy stiffened and made himself bigger, as he always did whenever I challenged him. "I had nothing to do with this shit, if that's what you're getting at."

"Not you, Gen—" Eddy cut me off.

"He was running around with different groups, doing shit with his brother, who's a little psycho. That crew's having problems everywhere."

"Ed…" I started.

"A lot of people didn't like K, talked way too much. Too fucking full of himself, ostie." Karim was scatterbrained but never arrogant. Eddy looked at his nails, newly manicured.

"Are you going to the funeral?" I asked.

"I'll see," he said. "Probably be a lot of cops watching that thing. You ever find out more about Gabriel?" he asked.

"No, I haven't had the chance."

"He's a clown," Eddy said, looking downwards. He seemed

mad, maybe put off by my presence.

"Is anyone else going to get it?" I asked. He smirked and shook his head.

"Like?"

"Well, Karim did." Eddy looked back towards his kitchen where a little girl was banging on the window.

"What about me now?" I asked him. "They hate me too, ever since Sil."

"You shouldn't have done that," Eddy said. I looked at him with hatred.

"You fucking laughed when I told you!" I started.

Eddy looked towards his house. "My daughter wants to say goodbye before her appointment." He turned to me. "Anyway, about Karim, when people don't play their cards right, this happens. You know that. There's nothing anybody could do."

"What are you going to do when you find out?"

"We'll see," Eddy said, looking once more at the kitchen window. He got up, motioning to the house where an attractive woman with a modified body, wearing leisurewear similar to Eddy's, was holding up the little girl. She waved at her father.

"I talked to Andre the other day," Eddy said, shaking his head as he looked back at the house. He smiled. "You don't know half of what the guy deals with, ostie."

"What's he dealing with?" I asked.

Eddy shook his head again. "The business, man, all this bullshit."

"What, like his actual business?" I asked. Andre had a construction company, but I knew nothing of how it worked.

"Yeah, that and other shit. He's getting pressed by a lot of people, you know," Eddy said.

He wanted my intrigue, revelling in his power to withhold information he correctly suspected I wanted. But I didn't wish to satisfy him, and instead, looked for another way to get it.

"Well he's making a lot more money through the league right now," I said. "Attendance skyrocketed since we started our thing."

"Yeah, but he's getting pressed by these nosey ostie fucks who know what you guys are up to."

"Who? Which guys?"

"Other owners."

"Which owners?"

"You got a lot of questions."

"Well, you're alluding to something that I may have to be prepared for."

Eddy smiled. "Don't worry about it," he said, "it's really not a big deal. Anyway, I gotta deal with this," he said, "we'll be in touch." Eddy stood up to shake my hand before heading back inside. I walked out of his backyard, almost tripping on a stray toy squished into the wet grass, and got back into my car. I looked back at his house, but blinds veiled Eddy's living room.

I turned my car back on, fixated on the insensibility of our conversation: regardless of whether his biker friends were out of pocket, Eddy had enough power within the milieu to stop most things from happening. If he'd known Karim was about to be killed, Eddy could have prevented it. But Karim had little material impact on Eddy's financial interests anymore and this made him expendable. Now that he was getting out of gambling, maybe I was, too.

"Verily we belong to Allah, and truly to Him shall we return."

I attended a celebration for Karim, held at an Islamic community centre in east Montreal. There were a few dozen people there, uneven in their level of mourning, and towards the back

I saw his mother receiving family members who attempted to pacify her with pats on the back. She appeared to be in her late fifties and nodded between eye dabs whenever a well-wisher appeared. I sipped tasteless coffee near the back, waiting for my opportunity to say I was sorry.

Seeing an opening, I walked over to his mother. She was a small, fine-featured woman, with large, attractive eyes and a sharp mouth that pointed downward. Her olive skin was creased at the eyes, now wet with tears.

"I was a friend of Karim's, I'm sorry for your loss," I said. She investigated me while a younger woman (Karim's sister, perhaps) held up her mother's arm.

"Who are you?" she asked in a small voice.

"My name is Theodore. Teddy, actually."

"I've never met you before." I could see that she was trying to deduce whether I was one of the criminals he ran with.

"I knew Karim from the restaurants," I said, embarrassed. She nodded in quiet disapproval.

"Thank you," his mother answered, looking behind me towards an older man shuffling in her direction.

I moved on and looked to see if anyone familiar was here. None of the bar people I'd met with Karim (there were too many grinning, flushed faces to remember) had arrived, and nor did I see his girlfriend. Talking to an older man at the back was Zinedine, who saw me and raised his hand. I walked over and the older gentleman disappeared.

"I'm sorry, Z," I said, leaning in to hug him. His embrace felt stiff.

"Thank you." He wasn't crying: Zinedine's eyes were the colour of diluting heroin.

"I don't know how this happened," I said. He stared back at me silently. "I—I really don't know man. I kept trying to reach K and…."

"We're going to find out," he said.

"Did anything happen that I wouldn't know about?"

"Fuck no," he said. "He was laying low. Working to pay off that debt. Doing regular work, too, drywall and shit."

"So, why?"

"I got no idea, but this don't have nothing to do with you, you were good with him." The muscles along Zinedine's usually tense jaw had relaxed. He looked behind me towards some new arrivals.

"Well," I began, "let me know if there's anything I can do to help," I said, gesturing towards his mother.

"If I call on you, it won't be to help *her*," he said. I had no idea what this meant. Some of his friends were standing together in the corner. Zinedine nodded to them. One came over and introduced himself as Sénèque. He was muscular, with wide shoulders that challenged the confines of his shirt.

Another woman came over to say hello. As I walked out, I noticed a poster by the hall's entrance that provided a summary of Karim's short life.

It described his upbringing in Montreal North, love for his mother and family, and Karim's teenage immersion in sports. The picture, taken several years ago at a wedding, shows a smiling young man in a rented tuxedo, his arms stretched over two sets of disembodied shoulders. Karim played football in high school and once dreamt of becoming an engineer. It concluded strangely, not with the promise of eternal life, but a callback to one of his childhood interests: "Karim," it read, "loved Power Rangers."

My car jostled over the wet, beaten streets on the drive home. The city's neighbourhoods had an ugly lifelessness, and when I stopped at a light and saw a group of young people moving towards McGill, I longed to walk with them. When I turned onto my street, a hollowness began its annexation of my chest. Despite having no destination, I wanted to continue driving.

I passed the baseball diamond in our neighbourhood, unkempt and made wet by the weather. In late teenagehood, Dad often tried to pull me away from my room to throw the ball around, but I never wanted to. I could now more clearly hear his voice fall from the other side of my door than I ever did then.

When I got home, I called Patty (who hadn't come with me today because of an altercation he'd had with one of Zinedine's friends) to see if he was doing anything tonight. He was, of course, and I arrived at his apartment just after eight with a bottle of scotch. At the door, Patty welcomed me with a hug.

"Fucked up, eh?" he said.

"Went to the event today. Brutal."

He introduced me to three guys who were drinking beer and watching the lone SLSPL game on RDS. All were in university and shook my hand with a vigor that made me at once forget the afternoon. Darren, maybe, asked who I liked.

"Quebec," I said, "best team in the league all year."

"Fuck," he said, "should have bet on it." Some of these guys may have wagered with us this year, I wasn't sure, but I didn't grant him the opening he obviously wanted. Two wingers, both middleweights, dropped their gloves off the opening draw.

"Here we go," one of Patty's friends said. Everyone leaned forward but the fight climaxed in a frustrated grapple.

"Open up, fuck!" another snarled. Our conversation became more liberal as the alcohol consumption surged. Patty started slapping me on the back in compassionate solidarity, his eyes two circular blue, wet stones.

We sat around drinking for the next hour or so. Conversation never steered far from sports, unless Patty wanted to discuss whichever girl he planned on meeting. He was probably talking to five or six at once, but I didn't care to hear about his conquests.

"How you feeling, bud?" he asked, when his three friends left to go outside for a smoke.

"Not bad."

"Rough week?" he said.

"Not good."

"Any idea why?"

I shook my head, not even looking at him. "No idea," I said finally, "but nothing to do with me. Genny hated K. Could have been him. Probably was."

"Fucking weird," Patty began, as his friends came back inside. "I mean, Karim was there when Eddy first taught you about—"

"Pad!" I said, shaking my head. He said nothing and took a sip of his beer. "Where we going anyway?" I asked.

"Électronique," he said, smiling. "You got connections there?"

"I'll text one of the bouncers," I said, messaging Claude to ask for VIP. Twenty minutes passed but he didn't answer. The boys were eager to get more drunk and so we passed out shots of Macallan. The bottle was gone five minutes later.

"I'll buy you a couple drinks at the bar," the quietest of the three said.

"Don't worry about it."

"You're a hell of a guy" he said, squeezing my shoulder.

"Anytime, bud."

"You hear back?" Patty asked.

"Hasn't responded, but it doesn't matter. We can go wherever and grease." I couldn't help but think that Claude should have answered regardless of whether he was working. It didn't escape me that he'd gone silent out of fear.

"Your girl might be there," Patty said. I looked up, nervous. "Just letting you know. I got a text from her friend. They're going." I immediately went to the bathroom and combed my hair.

When we arrived at Électronique, I paid our way past a large line quivering in the cold night. Inside, the bar was saturated with drunk, gyrating bodies, each escaping whatever they wished to forget about the week. Patty sliced through the crowd vying for the bartender's attention and ordered two drinks each for us, looking back to me for money. I found a few bills in my pocket and passed them over some bare shoulders. When Patty received the drinks, there were two more on the crowded bar top. He gave them to two girls standing on the outside of our group, pulling us into a conversation where I was introduced to Amelie, who leaned in to whisper something in French, her grapefruit-sized implants encroaching on my shoulder. The music muted her soft speech to where I couldn't understand a word.

I felt a tug on my shirt from behind. It was Véronique. I hadn't seen her since we left the pub that night, and while Patty had teased her appearance, I was too off-guard to be nervous.

"Teddy!" she said, "what are you doing talking to her?" Véronique looked as though she'd lost weight, and wore a red dress that didn't seem to fit right.

"Sorry, what?" I said.

"Come talk to me," she said, pulling me towards her with a rocky hand. "What have you been up to?"

"Not much," I stumbled. "You keep popping up when I'm out. You been following me or what?"

"Patty was talking to my friend, I don't know…" she said. I wondered whether he told her I would be at that hockey game, so many weeks ago.

"Tell me some good news," I said.

"I'm going traveling for the next six months. Europe!"

I remembered this from our night at the museum and didn't ask where she was going. "Who are you here with?"

"Some friends." She pointed to a group standing about fifteen feet away. They turned to look at us when she gestured in their direction. In the group were two guys my age. One was handsome and stared at me with a level of distrust that I enjoyed. I didn't know where else to take this conversation.

"Last time we ran into each other you were giving me shit for drinking too much. Bit of a role reversal," I said.

"I'm just out with my friend." She gestured haphazardly towards the group, where the same unintimidating fellow glowered.

"We should get together sometime," she responded, fingering the collar of my shirt. "Would you want to?" I looked to the bar, where Patty was dispensing drinks, and then back to Véronique, whose eyes were trained on mine.

"Let's go for a coffee," I said. Véronique nodded and kissed me on the cheek before returning to her group. Patty was talking to some other people I didn't know, so I scanned the crowd to see if anyone else was here.

The crowd became increasingly drunk, and past one a fight broke out on the dancefloor. Two guys began throwing punches. A third person cannonballed into the scrum with a beer bottle and cracked it over somebody's head. The glass shattered and two girls standing nearby, one of whom may have had shards of glass in her hair, began screaming as the two groups struggled. An army of bouncers attacked the floor.

"Ahh shit!" Patty said, delighted. This somewhat sobered me, and I took a step away from the melee. I wanted to leave but was scared to seem a coward, so I stayed for a moment, drinking from a watery vodka soda.

"What the fuck just happened there?" one of Teddy's friends asked.

"Two guys tilted over some broad," Patty responded. "Fucking meatsauces."

Dancing resumed once the brawl was broken up and those involved were dismissed. Patty ordered another round and looked to me for more money. "I'm tapped out," I lied. "Need to get some more cash."

"Come on dude!" he said, laughing, "you own the fucking ATM machines!"

"Not in here."

Some of the other guys started pooling money that had been absent until now, and a battered wad was placed into Patty's hand. He paid the bartender and handed drinks to two more girls standing nearby.

Past drunk, one of Patty's friends started asking me about gambling and whether we were still taking wagers. I don't think he'd bet with us before and told him no.

As I waited for Patty to produce my drink, a group of unsmiling twenty-somethings entered the bar. I didn't know them, but posture and appearance marked them as connected to the milieu, and they appeared to be in search of someone. I couldn't be sure whether Alessandro – the same person I saw with Genny at Maxime's training session – was out front, as a Yankees hat was pulled down over the leader's eyes. I watched them move to the bar's other side and could feel Patty's eyes on me. He passed me a drink.

"You see a ghost?"

"Some guys came in."

"Who? Fucking full patches?"

"Just went around to the other side of the bar."

"What's the matter with you? Who is it?"

"I dunno, somebody, but why take a chance?"

"You're getting paranoid bro," he said, smiling.

"Let's grab a cab," I said. "This place is trash anyway."

"I'm talking to this broad right here!" Patty replied. "They don't know me anyway, whoever it is."

"You're talking to ten every day, Pad!"

"I'll say goodbye to her first. Then I'll bounce," he said. I wanted to go at once and he sensed it.

"It's fine, T. They don't know me bud. I'll be out soon."

"Alright," I said. I maneuvered through the amoeba towards the door. When I stepped onto the street, where the threat was non-existent, I took a relieved breath and climbed into the nearest cab.

I spent the following day's first few hours underneath my duvet. It took a supernatural act of will to pee, shuffle downstairs and fill up a glass of water. When I lied in this state as a teenager, my mother would deliberately vacuum outside my door, knocking against it to sow regret over my partying. Every effort to soundproof my bed with a fortress of blankets failed.

Back in bed, I slept for another two hours. When I finally woke up there were a number of messages on my phone. One was from Véronique.

"Patty got beat up last night." The text seemed so matter-of-fact. I lurched upwards and called her.

"What? What happened" I asked, my voice rising.

She was tired and hungover, taking her time to answer. "I don't know how it started. You were gone at this point. But there was a big fight over at the bar. Another one. I looked over and saw him on the ground. He was bleeding."

"Jesus fucking Christ."

"Does this have anything to do with you?" Véronique's voice sounded small.

"I don't know," I said, knowing that it almost certainly did.

"Are you going to visit him in the hospital?" she asked.

"Fuck! He's in the hospital? Yeah, I guess, if he's still there." The phone went silent for a few seconds.

"Teddy, are you okay, man? Where are you?"

"I'm at home. I'm fine, but I gotta go," I said. "I'll get in touch with you soon." Véronique began to speak but my head had fallen off its shoulders and was rolling towards the open bedroom door. I hung up the phone.

Patty wasn't in the hospital anymore and had gone home to his parents. He messaged me back that morning, so I walked over to their place around three and knocked on the door. His father answered and stepped outside, closing the door behind him. I hadn't seen him since the funerals. Donny's creased eyes were sad, but I couldn't tell whether he was also angry.

"What happened last night?" he asked.

"I left early, so I didn't see what happened."

"He's got a broken orbital bone and cracked ribs." I sighed and looked skyward. "He just fell asleep," Donny said, sensing that I wanted to go in.

"I'm sorry this happened, I'll come back when he's awake." I felt like an imbecile, standing on his front stoop and likely in part responsible for what happened to his son. Donny stared down at me from his elevated position.

"I'd call the police if I didn't think it would get you both into trouble," Donny said, staring at me. "What the fuck are you guys up to?"

Frozen in place, I didn't say anything and looked back at him. I had known Donny my whole life, and he continued to exert a paternal control that prevented me responding in the manner I would have to Eddy. We were too familiar for me to posture.

"What are you guys up to?" he said again, slowly.

"I had a debt to pay, our house — my parents' house — and I started doing some things to pay it off. But Patty isn't on the hook for any of this," I said.

"He *is* on the hook. What kind of things?" I didn't answer. Donny's eyes turned from hard to understanding.

"If you need help…"

"It's okay, but thanks."

"Be careful, Ted," he said to me "it's been a long left turn."

"Well what was I supposed to—" I nearly started to yell and then stopped myself. "I'm sorry," I said. "I'm sorry."

"You let me know." With that, Donny closed the door. I turned around and walked home through the neighbouring streets. On my way, I got a call from Eddy. I debated whether to answer but picked up.

"We gotta meet," he said. I didn't answer but he kept talking anyway. "I'm coming to pick you up. I'm not far, anyway. Can you be ready in fifteen?"

"Why?" I asked.

"Why the fuck why, tabernak? So?"

"Yeah," I said after a long pause, "sure." I started swearing in the street and a woman passing looked at me in fear. I remembered, then, how near this spot ten years ago we taped a boy to a pole. He didn't play sports, was gentle in the way that unathletic, good-natured boys not yet inured by the playground pressures are, and trying desperately to break into our group. As we ran away laughing, he cried and flailed. I shook my head at the memory with a loathing that seemed particularly acute today. Maybe it was because his mother had tried everything to help us like him.

When I got home, Eddy's Escalade was already in the driveway.

"Look at the goddamn state of you, calice," he said. "Drunker than a fucking dockworker yesterday."

"I wasn't that bad," I said, shaking my head. "Went home early. Where we going?"

"Around the block." Eddy drove to a sports bar nearby that I hadn't been to in years. Two guys who used to maintain the local rink were having beers on the bartop. The hostess seated us in a booth near the washrooms, and when the waitress came over Eddy ordered drinks for both of us.

"You're going to feel better," he said. When she returned, the cold beer cooled my throat. Eddy's tone darkened.

"You still taking action on hockey?"

"What?"

"Don't fucking lie to me," he said. "I got a call from Genny this morning. He heard through that fuck Gabe — who went to him looking to get a buddy of his on a sheet — and said you set up an independent office. Genny sent his boys out to investigate and one of his guys had a run-in with your little buddy last night. Said he was bragging to some douchebag about still taking wagers." I didn't say anything and looked at Eddy from over top of my beer.

"You know how fucking dangerous that is?" he asked.

"Evidently, it can cause problems," I said.

"Don't get sarcastic, sacrament."

"What the fuck was I supposed to do?" I almost yelled, rising in my chair. "My fucking hand was forced! How the fuck am I going to pay back this debt if I don't have any money? I created all of this, and then it was just taken from me!"

"You know how fucking lucky you are to have two legs right now? Don't ever raise your fucking—"

"What the fuck was I supposed to do?"

"Why care so much about this house anyway?"

"What?" I asked, stunned by his question.

"That house. It worth getting killed over?" he said.

"Somebody's gonna kill me?"

"Well, no, I'm just saying… you've done well in this shit so far, why risk everything?" I exhaled, seething, and gripped the table with maximum force so as to resist smashing my beer glass over his face.

"You just don't want your deal with Genny to go belly up," I said, challenging him for the first time.

"What?"

"You heard me," I said. "You're worried about pissing off a guy that probably — no, definitely — killed one of ours, and whose guys jumped my best buddy last night. But there's no limits, right Ed, to the compromising? He can just do what he wants?" Eddy looked like he wanted to hit me, but I didn't care anymore.

Instead, Eddy took a sip of his beer. Sitting across from me he seemed smaller than usual. "No, there are no limits," he finally said, drawing out a breath. "There's only what's practical, the sand's always shifting, bud: you'll stay on your feet once you realize this." I hated him more in this moment than anyone I'd ever known, and when Eddy offered to drive me home, I lied about going on a date at a nearby restaurant, resolving never to work with him again.

One of the girls from the bank on that day I first learned of our debt was walking down Sherbrooke, near the turnoff to my street. I made a sad show of pretending to study the ground when we passed. As my feet shuffled on, I remembered a high school party when one of my friends called her "fucking ugly" before a group of snickering buddies. She pretended not to hear and looked down, her pallid skin having turned almost brown, and I recalled the heavy breathing that followed her fragile self-worth being destroyed. I remembered watching this and how I didn't say anything to offset the moment's cruelty. Despair seized my body as I tried to find something else to think about in the two minutes it took to get home.

31.

I woke up late on the anniversary of my parents' deaths. Not knowing how to feel, I proceeded as normal, with coffee and Sportscentre in the morning. Later I received a text from Véronique. "How are you doing?" she asked, proposing that we meet up that night.

Around noon I went outside and looked at the mailbox, newly stuffed with junk mail. Inside was a letter from the bank. I stared at it for a moment, doing a quick inventory of my debt. There would be another payment in the second week of May. I still owed $180,000 — a number that would be cleared if Maxime won his fight.

I went back inside and opened the letter. There was no outstanding balance in the top right corner, but a series of paragraphs that concluded with the bank's intent to repossess the house. The terms had changed, it said, as the initial loan — wrongfully calculated — was now legally obsolete, and being a callable debt, the bank had recourse to demand full payment whenever it wished. It felt like someone had spat on my face after grinding it into the carpet. I screamed inside the living room and threw the letter against my wall.

I fell back against the couch. From my position I stared into the backyard, where two birds fought for the possession of a walnut. They circled one another, wings an orchestra of struggle, before disappearing out of view. The sky into which they escaped was overcast, alternately obscuring and then providing an opening for the sun. I returned my eyes to the ceiling, pale and cracked by dying paint, and couldn't escape the house's silence.

That afternoon I received a knock at home. I got up slowly and walked over to the door, where through the peephole I saw two men in poor suits standing outside. They weren't members of the milieu but law enforcement, and the shorter man, his combover laced with gray, gave another impatient knock. (I had been in this position before. Four years ago my parents had vacationed to Cape Cod and I hosted a packed party in their house. Even the master bathroom got hotboxed. The next day, two female police officers showed up to address the concerns of a paranoid neighbour.)

I opened the door and stared at the officers.

"Theodore Knox?" he said. He had a direct bearing and unimpressive face, which sloped inward near the chin. Behind him, the impassive taller partner looked on.

"Yes?" I asked, aware that each of my answers had to be succinct. They looked tired and I disliked both of them.

"We need to speak with you."

"About?"

"I'm Detective Poehler, this is Detective Brisebois, we're from the SPVM."

"Okay?" I could feel my chest tightening. We were in full view of my neighbours and though no one was outside I didn't want anyone to see us.

"Can we go into the backyard?" I asked, pointing towards the gate.

"This will only take a minute," Poehler said. "We have a legal obligation to warn people whenever there's a threat on their life."

"What threat?"

"We've heard your name's been floated as a target."

"By who?" I wanted to yell 'stop speaking in fucking parables.'

"That we can't say."

"Then what's the purpose of this?" I asked, looking into the eyes of each one.

"We know what you're doing," Poehler said.

"What do you know?"

Here, the detective smiled. "Get your head out of your ass. You don't think Eddy Robichaud isn't under constant surveillance? You think we don't know about the sportsbook, who's betting, how the cash is getting routed? What you're doing in hockey?"

"If you want to arrest me, I'm right here." For the second time today, I felt momentarily free of all anxiety. What were the police going to do, charge me with illegal gambling? The penalty for this would be less finite than someone from the milieu learning I had provided information against them. Confronted by these two dullards on my doorstep, it occurred to me that this could have been a ruse. Eddy had contacts in the police force, and it was possible that after our last meeting he might have sent someone over to test my loyalty. But there was something funny about the idiocy of this: me, breaking my ass to conduct illegal activity so I could hold onto a house the bank could take back whenever it wished. I wanted to laugh — at this, and at their obvious belief that fear might prompt my legs to spread. Everything was over, anyway. What did I care anymore?

"We know you've had a bad year," Brisebois said, looking at me, "with everything that's happened. And we know you're a smart kid. This can be over."

"How's that?" I asked.

"If you work with us, we can protect you," Brisebois said.

"Protect me how?" Brisebois looked to Poehler for an answer. Before he could begin speaking, I interrupted.

"I don't know what you're talking about, and I don't think you can help me," I said, motioning for the officers to leave my property.

"Cut the shit," Poehler said. "You're gonna get killed or you're gonna get arrested. Pick option C." He handed me a card, turned around and walked off our property. From inside the living room I watched their unmarked car move down my quiet street.

32.

Véronique still wanted to come over, and after some messaging that afternoon I called her a cab. I hadn't cleaned the dishes in a week and plates of congealed Kraft dinner were stacked beside the sink. Despite my warning, she said that a messy house wouldn't bother her and when the doorbell rang, I answered, still in my sweatpants, finding Véronique with a package of food at the front door. She hugged me.

"How are you doing today?" she asked.

"I'm fine," I said, swallowing. "Come on in." We walked towards the kitchen, where she put her things down on the table. "Have a seat," I said, pointing to the table. "What do you got there?" I asked, pointing to the package.

"Macaroni and cheese, with some sausage, onion and parsley mixed in." I asked whether it should be microwaved or baked.

"Depends on how hungry you are."

"I haven't eaten all day, so microwave," I said. I placed the package inside and set it for two minutes. We stood in quiet silence as the machine spun our heating food. She looked at the living room mess and ignored my direction to leave it alone, shaking her head with sad disapproval. I watched Véronique pick up one of the pizza boxes near my fireplace, moving from there towards a heap of clothing in front of the television. I walked over and began to help her.

"How's Patty?" she asked as we worked together.

"He's messed up," I answered, describing my visit to his parent's house earlier. "I left early because I thought there could be an issue. Told Patty to come, but he wanted to stay." Véronique looked from me to the microwave.

"What do you think happened?" she asked.

"Somebody was probably talking too much at the bar and guys got into it, I don't know."

"About your business?"

"Yes."

"How are *you* doing?"

I looked at Véronique for a moment before catching my reflection in the darkened window. Blood was gathering in my neck. I sensed but didn't *know* that she was trustworthy, because while Véronique had all the hallmarks of a genuine person, or at least, of someone who was interested in others, the source of our meeting at that Métropolis fight cast an unfair shade over her loyalty to me. But while I had thought about this before, now, in this moment, I no longer cared.

"I don't know," I said. She looked back at me and said nothing. "It sucks, obviously," I went on, "but, you know, as I said to you before... there's nothing I can do about it."

"I know," she said, "and I'm sorry." Véronique came over and put her arms around my neck, drawing me into a hug.

"It's alright, man," she said, in a calm voice I remembered from my mother, "don't resist." I relaxed my shoulders in her embrace.

"You just need to continue thinking about them," Véronique said, oblivious to her power. Something began to happen inside me. A colourless mist, shifting in tone and shape, spread outward from my stomach, saturating every cell of my body as it moved upwards, paralyzing my limbs and demanding its release. For the first time in years, I started to cry.

"Oh, woah," she said. "I'm sorry Teddy!" I started to quiver, shaking my head to indicate it wasn't her fault. Véronique seized me by the shoulders as I leaned over the countertop. I continued to cry, no longer in control of my body.

"It's okay, it's okay, it's okay," she said, rubbing my shoulders. "It's okay, take it easy, take it easy, take it easy, man." I was humiliated by my blubbering.

"I can't honour them," I said, still sobbing. "I can't, I can't, I can't."

"Yes, you can, of course—" she began.

"No!" I yelled. "I can't! Look at my life! I can't!"

"What do you mean?" she asked, taking a step back to look into my eyes. Her speech was deliberate. "I know you're involved in—"

"I don't even care if I get caught," I said, "I don't fucking care anymore. I was good once, as a kid, you know, I wasn't hard or mean or…and now…all I can think about is everything bad that I've done. The bank, the fucking cops…" I couldn't go on and stood there, panting like an exhausted child. "It's all over anyway. You don't know what I've done…" I said, shaking my head.

"What have you done?" Véronique had become nervous. "Did you hurt someone?" I shook my head and looked down, snot dripping from my nose.

"It's okay…" she said.

"You can't say jack shit about this," I said to Véronique. "I'm serious…"

"I won't."

I collapsed on the kitchen chair, panting as I tried to reclaim my breath. Véronique pulled a tissue from out of her bag, and I used it to wipe my eyes. I took a long breath and exhaled, apologizing for my state. She sat down in the opposite chair, extending her hands over the table for me to grab. "You already know the first bit: last year," I started, "I found out my parents owed a bunch of money to the bank…"

I told her everything, from starting with a half-sheet to my confrontation with Sil, creating the hockey market, Karim's death, the bank's intention to repossess the house and finally, today's warning by the police. After finishing, I sat back against a hard chair and looked at the ceiling, purged for a moment of the disease festering in my chest. Véronique looked down.

"I don't know what to say," she began. "That's quite a story. Wow."

"Yeah…" I exhaled and stared out the window, where I could see my reflection in the black glass. My cheeks were flushed with colour.

"Are you afraid of what could happen now?" she asked.

"I really don't give a fuck what happens," I said, having finally disclosed everything to someone. I recognized the concern on her face and explained to Véronique that she wasn't in danger here. Nothing was going to happen at my house.

"Still, come on Teddy," she said, perhaps afraid I wanted to hurt myself.

"I can't be involved in this anymore." I said. "What would my mom say if she knew I was involved in this shit?"

"You were in a bad spot," she began. "That's how this happens."

I looked down at my hands, sweaty and tense, and found they contained a twisted blanket, which I had been contorting throughout the confession.

"So what are you going to do?" she asked. I shrugged my shoulders, not knowing what to say or do. "Do you at least feel better, now that you talked about it?"

"Yeah, I guess, but saying it out loud just reinforces everything." Véronique took a sip of water.

"Is that why you didn't want to be with me?" she asked. I didn't know what she was asking about.

"When we hung out before," she said. "And we never had sex. Is this why? Was your mind elsewhere? Or…"

I began to stammer, intimidated by so personal a question. "I don't know. Maybe I felt blocked, or I couldn't relax around you because I just didn't feel like myself or something. I don't know…"

"How do you feel right now?" she asked me.

"About sex?" She nodded. I hadn't even considered it.

"Yeah, well I'd like to…" I began. Véronique slowly came over to where I was sitting, her eyes never leaving mine, and sat down on top of my legs. She wrapped her arms around my back and kissed me, putting her hand up my shirt.

"Just relax," she whispered. "If you want to stop, we'll stop." Véronique's eyes contained oceans of goodwill, and this recognition produced a twinge within some forgotten cave of my heart — where a stagnant pool of water started to heat, bubbling with renewed energy as it pushed against the constricting walls to where, almost imperceptibly, there was a breach.

Without being conscious of it, my body started to relax, ridding itself of the tension in my shoulders, hips, legs, arms, and finally my groin. I picked Véronique up and brought her over to the couch, where we kissed horizontally, pulling her pants down to massage in between her legs. When she was sufficiently wet and — finally, wonderfully, affirmingly — enough blood had moved through a tunnel whose wall of fallen rock had once made its passage impossible, I slipped myself inside of her. From there, we remained connected for the next fifteen minutes.

I had a couple glasses of wine afterwards, but Véronique didn't take a drop. She was the first person to sleep in our house since my parents left for their cottage trip, and remained pressed against me for the nine hours we were attached: peacefully asleep, her blond curls formed a golden nest that rose above my blanket. When I got up the next morning, Véronique was already awake. She smiled at me.

"How are you feeling today?" she asked.

"A lot better. How are you?"

"I feel great," she said, extending her arms outwards as she yawned. "Busy day today?"

"Yeah, I have stuff to do."

"I'd ask what, but..."

I looked out the window, where everything was wet. A spring breeze entered the open window of my bedroom, cooling a shirtless chest.

"I'm sorry," she said, squeezing my arm. "What I meant was—"

"I don't have that much going on. Do you want something to eat?" I asked, "Some breakfast?"

"No thanks." Véronique got up from bed and walked naked over to the washroom, where her pepper shaker backside jutted out as she bent over the counter to wash her face and mouth. When Véronique returned, she got back on top of me, and once more our bodies came alive.

We remained connected underneath the covers. I wanted to clean myself and invited her to shower with me. When we were both clean and dry, I offered to drive her home. Véronique initially refused but broke down under my coaxing. Fresh and feeling natural again, we drove east towards her apartment near McGill.

"Do you think you'll get a place in the city" she asked, "if the bank won't back down?"

"I don't know yet," I answered, not having considered it. When I dropped her off, Véronique hesitated for a moment in the front seat.

"What's going on?" I asked. She motioned for me to step outside of the vehicle. I did, and we stood for a moment on the sidewalk.

"What?" I asked her, taking her by the hand.

"You can get out of this," she said to me. "Go into that bank. They'll work with you. And then get all of the way out."

Véronique leaned in and kissed me on the cheek, squeezing my hand before disappearing into her apartment. On my way home, a Kinks song played in the car beside mine. In other circumstances I may not have noticed it overtop the melody of tires and engines, but my hearing was more acute this morning. *"I will follow you wherever you go…"* And while part of me remained embarrassed by my breakdown, and unsure of whether I'd erred in confessing my mistakes, I sang along with the lyrics, more open to the world than I had been in memory.

33.

Before I could pull into our driveway, I noticed for the first time a neighbourhood family having lunch through the front bay window of their house They were Indian, and a girl, maybe ten, was reading a book beside her father. She was without concern, deeply immersed in her story, as though it confirmed the world's potential for frictionless joy and a future of infinite possibility.

Back inside our house I packed a bag, taking with me some clothing and a brick of cash hidden behind the living room television. One hour later I was in Maxime's living room. I had already told him everything. He was sitting back at the kitchen table, an empty water bottle beside him, listening as I went through the details chronologically.

"So they just show up at your place?" he asked. Maxime pulled a can of dip out from his pocket and stuck a black wad between his gum and lip.

"Said I'm going to get killed or arrested. What do you think?"

"They always say shit like that," he said. "I heard the same thing when I went through all my bullshit years ago, ostie. You never know with cops. They could just be trying to fuck your head up. On the other hand, they may be telling the truth." Maxime pulled the water bottle to his mouth and spat a small brown pool into its nozzle. The spit clung to the bottle's side as it cascaded to the bottom.

"But that's the thing," I said. "Either I get fucked by Ed and

Gen, who find some excuse to put me in cement, or the cops, who chuck me in jail where one of their guys has me biting my ankles. Eddy's got police buddies too. I don't know who they are, but he could be using them to test me."

Maxime took a sip of water, roofing the lower lip with his tongue so as to avoid ingesting any dip spit.

"I haven't heard jack shit about anything," he said. "Fuck I wish you were my manager for this," he said, referencing his fight in a week. Maxime still didn't know about the size of my bet on him. "You brought me here, T."

"Thanks, Max." I took a sip of the beer he gave me.

"If I hear something first, you hear it next. I'm with you before any of those cunts. But I don't know, ostie man," he said. "You might want to talk to the cop again, feel him out a bit. Then make a call, you know?"

"I thought you didn't like cops?" I asked him.

Maxime shrugged his shoulders. "You gotta look at this shit, how do you say, situational," he said. "You know what I mean? What's the lesser of the evils?"

"I don't know."

"So what are you gonna do?" he asked. Maxime was beginning to stretch his shoulder.

"I'm going to lay low for a bit," I said. "And step away from my house."

"You can stay here," he said, motioning around his apartment. "I give you all the free dip you want." I laughed.

"Thanks, but no," I responded. "I don't want to complicate your life before the card."

"Fuck that!" Maxime yelled. "What the fuck are they going to do to me? I'm ten feet tall right now. Every gangster's scary 'cause of who they're with, not what they'll do alone." I looked over to a picture on his fridge. Standing in between his daughter and girlfriend, Maxime was holding a fish, smiling.

"I'm gonna find a way out of this," I said. "Just worry about that fight, Maxy." His eyes were unconvinced. I gave Maxime a hug and left.

That night I found refuge at a two-story motel in a forgotten community on the south shore. It was on one of those streets someone might close their eyes to if misfortune placed them here: a fallen domino link of failed businesses, pawn shops, abominable food chains and abandoned lumber yards. People bought rooms here to pay for prostitutes or sell wholesale qualities of coke.

My new home — rented to me by an unshaven man who barely spoke English and answered none of my questions — had no view beyond the parking lot's broken asphalt, and the room merits scant description: cracked walls, faded paintings of pristine sailboats, a television with four channels and, occupying its usual place in the drawer, a lone, battered bible with several of its pages stuck together.

Near midnight, I sat on the edge of the hard mattress, with its worn sheets and fraying lace. If I escaped to Toronto (or elsewhere), someone would look for me. If I stayed around, someone might kill me. If I fled the country, I would likely be arrested upon my return.

But still, the air felt lighter after my night with Véronique, and I suddenly cared about foregoing future breaths. What choice did I have, then, but to play each side against the other?

First, I still had to speak with the bank. The next morning I drove back into NDG, taking a circuitous route away from the streets close to our house. I was received by the same man who made my case hopeless in September. He appeared to have put on weight.

"What's this?" I asked, holding up the letter that communicated the bank's intention to repossess our house.

"I'm sorry, but there was a clerical error with the loan," he said. "The interest was never calculated correctly. So, you actually owe more, unfortunately."

"How is this even legal?" I asked. He mumbled something about it being a "callable debt" and looked away.

"So now," I began, "I owe you $250,000, payable in full by the middle of the month?"

"Yes."

"I'm going to call my lawyer," I said, despite not having one.

"Of course, it's your right to do so." His voice was flat and disinterested. What did he care about legal action? The bank had an army of lawyers to refute whatever argument I put forth.

Aware of the maneuvering required to pay in full, I promised to do so if he agreed to extend the deadline by a month.

"I can do that on a one-time basis, but there's going to be interest and if you can't make the payment there's nothing more I can do," he said, talking as though he were doing me a grand favour.

I agreed to his terms and instructed him to finalize the paperwork. He gave a subtle, lazy sigh and took an hour to get the documentation in order. I left without signing the documents, promising to return the following day. It seemed unwise to agree without first getting a legal opinion.

The next meeting deserves no description. I quickly got a phone consultation with a lawyer specializing in real estate law.

The young woman, likely in her late twenties, spent fifteen minutes using convoluted language to explain how the bank retained all power in a callable lending scenario — a power it could exercise at any time. She suggested an in-person consultation to review the paperwork and see whether there were caveats I could exploit. I promised to think about it and hung up, allergic to further monetary enslavement by the other half of a system I'd rejected.

I didn't want to enter into an expensive, drawn-out legal process, but how was I going to pay this debt? It was more than I would make if Maxime won, and I didn't want to ask any of the street guys for a loan.

On my way back to the motel I turned on the radio. The local sports radio hosts were discussing the upcoming card and speaking about Olivier Rioux's chances in its main event. The lead host was convinced that Rioux's power would be enough to overcome Sammy Watkins' educated boxing skills.

"If he just catches him with one shot, you know, I think that might be enough to discourage Watkins," he said, with a mouthful of hard consonants. "Talking Olivier Rioux versus Sammy Watkins at the Bell Centre in just over a week, if you want to weigh in, the number is…"

This line of reasoning was ludicrous. A boxer almost always beat a puncher, but this was the sort of meatheaded speculation that controlled boxing analysis. Ignorance was the foundation of all wagering, especially in combat sports where diminished variables imbued bettors with a deluded sense of expertise. It would also power much of the betting over the next week. Realizing this, I knew there was an opportunity here.

The Count of Westmount messaged that he wanted to talk. I turned around before reaching the bridge, replying with a lie about already being in his neighborhood.

When I drove up the windy street towards the hill his townhouse sat on, I could see a delivery truck blocking the driveway. Two workmen in blue overalls stood outside, ready to transport a new refrigerator through the front door. Allan held the door open as the workmen moved past him, their tight movements choreographed so as not to mark the trim along his front door.

I saw his head move in the direction of my car. He held up a finger, instructing me to wait. After five minutes, the workmen came back out and climbed into their truck. The front door remained open, and the man reappeared to wave me over. I got out of my car and met him in the middle of the driveway. He looked at me with the expressionless face of someone for whom human interaction required an analysis of its worth to decide whether it should be prolonged.

"Sorry about that, how are you doing?" he asked.

"Not as good as you," I said, "given the year you had."

"A lot broke my way," he said, "it's mostly luck."

"Modest too," I said. He smiled with a closed mouth.

"You're a good guy to deal with, Teddy," he said. "Sometimes people aren't prompt with the payments. With you it's on time, every week."

"When you win, you need to get paid," I said. Allan met my eyes and seemed to be working through something as he looked at me.

"Some of the guys who do this…" he said, shaking his head.

"What?"

"I've dealt with most of them," he began. "I'm not going to say who, but it can be like pulling teeth to get paid." The conversation stalled for a moment as I waited for his question. "Anyway," he began, "the site, what's going on with it? It's been down all day."

"I'm surprised no one talked to you," I said. "You might not be seeing much of me anymore, because — between you and I — the guy I work for is thinking about getting out. I guess they already shut the site down because Eddy's book is getting transferred."

"To who?" I told him about Genny.

"So where does that leave you?" Allan asked.

"In search of a new life, maybe," I said. An idea came into my head, but this wasn't the right time to discuss it. I told Allan to get back to me if he had any other questions. We shook hands again and I left.

On my way back to the motel, Maxime messaged to say that Olivier Rioux would be training at the gym today. Before I could take advantage of a chance to watch Rioux so close the fight, I wanted to drive by my house to see if there were any unusual cars on our street. When I looked down from Monkland, a dark sedan was parked near the stop sign at its other end. It was just far enough that I couldn't tell whether someone was in the front seat but, as though aware that I was watching, the invisible driver escaped towards Sherbrooke.

Eddy was in New York for the week and wouldn't be at the gym today, so I drove next to the boxing club, aware that he might have installed someone to meet me. I couldn't pass the opportunity up; a plan was forming in my mind whose success was dependent on appraising the main eventer.

It was also the first time I would see Maxime train in weeks. I entered the gym, noticing the cautious eyes of a younger guy sitting on a corner chair, and Maxime motioned to me from the ring apron before going through a few rounds of sparring. While his footwork was lighter, and although his punches appeared straighter, it was impossible to tell whether sufficient improvement would make good on my wager. When it was over, the Woodchipper dismounted from the ring and put a drenched arm around my shoulder.

"Real good, bud," I said.

"I want you in my corner on fight night, okay?" he said, panting.

"I wouldn't miss it." Maxime took a sip of water and started to compose himself.

"What's your fight plan?" I asked.

"I'm going fucking hard at this guy, you know? All pressure. Volume. Punches in bunches." He took a long sip of water and wiped sweat from the top of his brow, reaching into his bag for a tin. Post-exercise was the best time to dip, he said — Maxime's reward for such a difficult hobby.

"He can't punch and may not have a chin," I said, only confident in my first claim. "Spark out, you'll knock him."

"I can't wait for this opportunity, calice, Teddy…" Maxime shook his head, wondrous of this good fortune.

As the ring was cleaned, I could see Olivier Rioux enter from a back room. He waved to all of us before sliding through the ropes, where Rioux began to move around the ring's four corners. His partner arrived next — a younger fighter brought in from Philadelphia to mimic Sammy Watkins — and both men bumped gloves before beginning the first round.

Olivier was trying to load up on his punches. He wasn't boxing in a traditional sense, because rather than trying to control the ring's center and push his opponent towards its ropes, Rioux was throwing artless power shots. Watkins, his eventual opponent, who had never been knocked out and employed a telephone pole jab, wasn't someone who'd walk into a right hand, so was there not a smarter way for Rioux to prepare? Power was important, of course, but it should never be privileged over plot.

The fighters sparred eight rounds, but Olivier demonstrated no variety in his attack. One member of his team, whom I'd seen here and at the fights, came over to say hello. Younger even than me, Etienne had grown up in boxing.

"Confident?" I asked him.

"As long as we don't lose the centre of the ring."

"He's slick, Watkins. Real slick." I said.

"Does he have a chin though?" Etienne asked, rhetorically. If Watkins was smart enough to stay away from Rioux's power, it wouldn't matter, though the American (who was a conservative fighter), *did* have a chin. I'd seen him hit but never hurt.

"How's he feeling, Olivier?" I asked.

"Confident as all hell, man," Etienne said. "Biggest moment of his career, you know?"

"So his power's gonna win out?" I asked.

"If Oli's smart with it, yes."

But despite being the betting favourite, Olivier wasn't smart. It would be harsh to call Etienne delusional — he was a sharp boxing person who understood how things worked, but what was he supposed to say? That he thought Rioux might *lose*? Olivier was his fighter, and it was Etienne's duty to ensure the mental scaffolding stayed upright. But I wasn't in the business of respecting illogical loyalty. Rather, it was my job to exploit delusion. Everything became clear.

34.

Rioux wouldn't throw the fight. Boxing at home on the biggest card of his career, he was too proud to consider this, and I wouldn't entertain the notion of proposing it, both because he would tell someone and I'd be ruined, and since I didn't have enough money to make the risk worth it. The referee hadn't been announced yet, but this would only be important insofar as he needed to keep the fight from devolving into clutching and grabbing (as that would benefit only Rioux). Since Olivier would likely not stop Watkins (as I've said, the American was just too slick), I wouldn't need to worry about an overzealous local man stopping things if the visiting fighter got caught. No, the referee wasn't important.

Sammy Watkins was going to win on points, but I had to make this a certainty. To do this, I needed a judge. Then I needed a head fake. But first, I needed the police.

———

"Who wants to get me?" I asked Poehler the next day. Standing bench-side in a Brossard park, we were surrounded by trees in the corner of a soccer field where it was unlikely anyone could see us. I was still spending my nights at the motel, and knew it best to arrange something on the river's south side.

"What did I tell you last time?" he asked. Poehler seemed annoyed he had to meet on what was likely a day off. He was dressed in a poor-fitting tracksuit the Italians would have laughed at.

"Well, don't you have a legal obligation to tell me?" I asked.

"Not the who. We don't give names so the person being threatened doesn't try and find the threat."

"Or you don't know…" I said.

"Excuse me?"

"No offense, but how do I know you're not making this up?" I asked.

"What reason would I have to do that?" A vein filled with blood on the left side of Poehler's neck, pushing out from underneath its pockmarks.

"You obviously know why," I said, hopeful Poehler would intuit my suspicion that he may have been doing things with Eddy.

"No I don't," he said, shaking his head. "I can bring you in on bookmaking charges any time I want. That charge is in the can. But I'm giving you an out here. If you're half as smart as you think you are, wise up."

"Prove you're not trying to fuck me," I said.

"How would you like me to do that?" he asked, straightening. Behind Poehler's head, a maintenance crew was beginning to work over the field, still bruised by patches of dirty snow.

"Do you have any idea of how hard your life will be if you get charged?" he asked.

"My life's already hard, so that depends on what I get charged for." I wasn't trafficking people or selling drugs. I hadn't killed anyone. The possibility of a long jail sentence was non-existent.

"Regardless of what the charge is, you'll get time. You know what kind of shit goes on in the Montreal Detention Centre? You ever been to a jail, bud?" he asked, now more slowly than before.

"I haven't."

"Good place to find out who you're not."

I stared back at Poehler, who perhaps believed his logic had won out. He was too confident in this assessment.

"What do you think I did, anyway?" He smirked and I held my hands up to suggest confusion.

"We know all about the site." But what did he know about me?

"So what do you say?" he asked.

"I'm going to think about it."

"You're not in charge here, so don't think too long," Poehler said, frustrated as he rose to leave, "or I'm bringing you in. At the very least I have you on making book. You got a week."

I had bought myself some time at least, and correctly divined that he had almost nothing. Poehler wouldn't have the opportunity to arrest me because I'd be gone by then, whether through my own escape, or by the hands of those I planned to ruin.

After downing a revolting strip mall cheeseburger near the park, I texted Allan and told him we needed to speak. An hour later, he messaged back, asking to come by his house at eight. When I arrived, parking between lights on the street's hedge-lined side, it didn't appear as if anyone was home. I knocked on the door and Allan answered immediately.

"What's going on?" he asked, unsmiling. Straw-like veins ran down his thin arms.

"I have something you might be interested in."

"What's that?" Allan looked behind me towards a couple walking their dog.

"Can we talk in private?" I asked. He stared at me before moving to the side.

"Come on in," Allan said, turning around as he walked towards the kitchen. His house was expensively decorated in an austere way — the sort of space occupied by a well-heeled bachelor with fair taste but little female influence. Free of pictures or any revealing personal information, the kitchen was full of black and chrome appliances, and Allan pointed me towards a circular, high-topped table where I sat down. The kitchen opened to a living room where a theater-sized television faced the large sectional couch. On the mantelpiece I could see a picture of Allan holding a small girl. Outside was a small backyard with pricey patio furniture and a hot tub. It seemed like a good place to smoke and drink.

"This is a nice spot," I said, "I'm happy to have contributed to it." He smiled. "Anyway," I went on, "I have a bet you may be interested in," I said.

"Yeah?" Allan looked amused by the suggestion.

"Rioux-Watkins." Allan cocked his head upwards.

"What's the bet?" His face had returned to its usual impassivity.

"You take Watkins. He's the dog, but he's gonna win."

"How do you know?"

"I just saw Rioux spar. He's moving like a guy after last call. Olivier's gonna get eaten." Allan paused and looked outside.

"Why are you telling me?" he asked, leaning back against the fridge, arms folded.

"Because I want you to work with me on this."

"But *why* are you telling me?"

"I'll make an early bet on Rioux to widen the line and move the action his way. You come in late with a big bet on Watkins. It's a fuckton of free money."

"Are you asking me to wager on sheets you're associated with?" His smile was near invisible.

"No. Ed's selling to Genny. We'd be doing this through Genny's office."

"Why?"

"Because I want to make money." He didn't seem to believe what I was saying.

"But why can't *you* make the big bet?" Allan asked.

"Because when we win, I'm afraid Genny'll fuck me. But he won't fuck *you*."

"What do you know about this fight that no one else does?"

"Beyond who owns the stylistic matchup? Beyond Rioux being a limited puncher who'll get outboxed over twelve rounds?"

"Yes. What do you *know*?"

"I know how to get to a judge," I said.

"Is that right?" Allan's eyebrows raised.

"Too much?" I asked. He shrugged, waiting for my explanation.

"It's insurance. We shouldn't need it."

"Why are you so confident?"

"Our boxing lines hammered everyone all year," I said. "I know where the edges are. Our book's shown that."

"That may be," he said, "but why would I want to go in on this sort of thing with you?"

"Because it'll be the easiest cash you'll ever make."

"If I did something like this, I'd want assurance…" he began.

"One bet, two hundred K. If we push the line enough early, we may get ten to one on Watkins, maybe more. You have an account with Genny, right?"

"I do *now*. I only wish you'd given this more thought." He said this with a level of sarcasm that annoyed me.

"Do you want to do it?" I asked.

"Two hundred thousand is a big wager," he began. "It draws attention. I haven't gone that big before."

"You were half that at the Super Bowl and everyone knows you're a sharp. That's why it *has* to be you." He was indifferent to the compliment and looked down at the kitchen floor.

"I don't know," he said, slowly, "I don't think so, but thanks."

"I'll give you twenty-five K up front," I told him. "And ten percent of our winnings. If the bet goes belly up — which it won't — I have a house in NDG that I'll liquidate." Allan smiled. "Twenty-five grand up front," I reiterated. "The bet's contingent on the outcome of another fight, which, if it goes my way, will free up the money to place the bet on Watkins. Either way, you get twenty-five dimes no strings attached." Allan didn't break eye contact.

"Think it over and get back to me," I said, preparing to leave. "But keep this between us."

"Why do you think I will?" His sarcasm had become nonchalance, and I was getting mad.

I straightened myself in the way Eddy did when prefacing a declaration. "I respect you as a bettor, and if you say no, it stays between us, and we'll never talk about it again. But one other guy knows about this. If there's any blowback on me, he's gonna be hanging out at the bottom of your driveway, you understand?"

"I'll get back to you," he said.

For my plan to work, Allan had to make the bet. If he did and the odds became ten to one, forcing Genny to pay out over two million, this would prevent him from buying Eddy out. He was rich, sure, but couldn't cover a loss this size in cash. If Eddy didn't get the money, he couldn't buy his property.

What would I do with our winnings? I'd pay the debt, install security cameras at my house and meet Véronique in France. It made no sense to stay.

But what if things fell apart? If I gave Allan twenty-five thousand and put ten towards the head fake on Genny's book, I'd be out of money. If we lost the main event, I would owe Allan one hundred and seventy-five thousand and be out of our house.

I couldn't lose. This had to work. There was one more piece to line up.

The following morning, I met Véronique in the parking behind her apartment. She came outside in sweatpants, holding on when she hugged me. Foregoing small talk, she asked what I needed from her.

"I need the pictures," I said to her. "From the judge." She paused for a moment.

"Oh, what, those? Why?" The topic made her anxious.

I explained why, lowering my voice. There would be no digital trace of her sending anything, as I created a fake email account she could access from her Blackberry to upload the image. A young family departing for what looked like a vacation appeared in the parking lot.

"What if he comes after me?" she asked.

"For what? He's going to come after *you* for sending a picture of his dick? No one's coming after anyone, you can bet on that," I told her. "Besides, you're leaving on Tuesday." Véronique had an early flight that would take first to Paris, and from there to Nice. She looked from me to a parking lot puddle, where in a pool of murky water the gray sky appeared.

"What are you going to do with the picture?" she asked.

"Use it as insurance." She looked away, uncomfortable with the prospect of becoming involved.

"If you do this for me, I can get out of this shit for good," I said. "I'll have enough cash to meet you in Europe. But I need the picture. It's not coming back on you, V."

She nodded and handed me her Blackberry. I used it to upload the image, thanking her as we stood for a moment in silence, each of us unwilling to acknowledge the obvious.

Véronique smiled, her mouth closed, and leaned in to hug me, pressing her palm against the top of my back as though reaching into my body to extract a piece of it for herself. Fighting my beating breath, I noticed when we pulled away that her eyes had become wet. She didn't cry, but force and feeling paralyzed her speech, and I, too, was incapable of saying anything, aware that we wouldn't meet again in Canada, and that the coming week would determine if we'd meet again at all. I said goodbye, running my hand along her cheek in a clumsy attempt at poetry as I promised a fine dinner on some Mediterranean terrace. When I remembered how she looked down, lips quivering, as I got back into my car, it felt as though a fist was lodged in my throat when I crossed the bridge towards the south shore.

"He's here." Dana, one of the bartenders at Corps Célestes, texted me. Dal Bertrand, who would judge the Rioux-Watkins main event, was in the club again, boring the dancers with complaints about his finances. I drove back downtown and parked a few streets away from the strip club. When I arrived, the bartender who messaged me was busy making a drink.

"He's drunk in the VIP room," she said, nodding towards the other side of the club, where men were paying stacks of money to not cum.

"How long has he been in there?" I asked.

"Almost an hour." I laughed when I heard this. "He can afford that shit? What's he do for a living, anyway, own a bar that no one goes to?"

"No idea what he does," she said, smiling, "but just because he can pay for it doesn't mean he can afford it."

"Exactly." She passed me a rye and ginger. I took a sip and looked around to see if anyone was here I may have known. As

I waited for Bertrand to appear, a younger man around my age, Alessandro, who ran under Genny and may have been the one who led Patty's shitkicking, had entered the club. I watched him from my seat, careful not to make eye contact, looking away when his head turned in my direction.

Alessandro and his friends sat down on the opposite side of the stage, where they could see everyone coming out of the VIP room. I tried to remain inconspicuous, turning my head every few minutes as a procession of men, young and old, moved up and down the stairs. I was worried Bertrand had passed unnoticed, but Dana shook her head (she'd been monitoring the stairway's movements when my back was turned).

"There he is," she said, pointing to the VIP room's entrance. I turned around and saw Bertrand waddling towards a chair that faced the stage, where he was directly in Alessandro's view. To move down and speak with him would have exposed me. I had to wait.

"Are you going to go talk to him?" she asked.

"Need a minute," I said. Dana poured another drink for a customer. From the corner of my eye, I saw Alessandro get up and walk towards the exit, a cigarette in his mouth. I couldn't make a confident pitch in five minutes, so I waited to see if he had left. Alessandro came back in and motioned for his friends (soldiers, all, in the small platoon he commanded) to leave, and at once they got up and left the cabaret. I rose from my seat and walked down to where Bertrand was sitting, putting my hand on his shoulder. He looked at me, surprised.

"Hey," he said, trying to place me.

"Let's go to the back booth," I said, "I have something you gotta see."

"What? Why—"

"It's just going to take a minute," I said, "but if I were you, I'd want a look. No one's over there."

Like he was being led to the gallows, Bertrand got up slowly and moved towards the booth. When one of the doormen came over to wag his finger, I gave him fifty dollars to go away. With some effort, the judge tucked his stomach underneath the table.

"How are things going?" I asked him.

"What is this?" he asked, nervous for my answer. I held up the phone.

"You sent this picture to someone. That's your number. That's your face. That's your cock."

"Where'd you get that?" he asked. Bertrand tried to get up from the booth, but I put my hand on his shoulder.

"There's no sense in leaving yet," I said. "I'm going to make this right." Bertrand stared at me but didn't say anything. "You're going to be judging Rioux-Watkins next week," I went on.

"And?" he sighed, having some sense of where this was going.

"Don't worry about it," I said, "not asking you to fix anything. But you have to turn in the right scorecard."

Bertrand stared at me for ten seconds without saying anything. "Which is?" he asked.

"Watkins on points. And he's going to win anyway, so it's not like anyone's going to question you. But I don't want Rioux getting a bullshit hometown score from the only Montreal judge. Do you understand?"

"What if Rioux knocks him out?" he asked me.

"He sucks. He won't. But if he does, that ain't your problem."

"And if Rioux wins a legitimate decision?"

"Again, he won't. But in the off-chance Rioux beats him on points, score your card for Olivier, I don't give a fuck. I'm just trying to keep you honest."

"Ten grand," he said, flatly. I became enraged and edged closer to him.

"Listen to me, you fat goof. You're sending a twenty-year-old pics of your twizzler and want money?" He started to speak but I cut him off, in shaky control of my growing rage.

"I know you have cash problems and if this picture gets out, you're done as a judge and will probably be investigated for sexual harassment. All you gotta do is stay honest and it dies. There's no risk or downside. But if you act like a fucking clown, *this*'ll go the way you thought it was gonna go."

He looked around the club to see if anyone was watching us. Patrons ogled the stage, but no one looked in our direction. Bertrand nodded at me through beaten eyes.

"Do the right thing, and I may make it worth your while," I said, placing some money down on the table to help pay his tab. "If you don't…" I started before trailing off. He said nothing and leaned back in the booth as I got up to leave. Back on the street, I saw Alessandro talking to some girls. I couldn't be sure, but I thought he may have seen me.

I received a text message from Allan on my way back to the motel from Célestes. He agreed to place the bet. The next morning, I drove over to his house with the initial twenty-five thousand, and then left right away.

35.

Fight week came to Montreal. I called Fortunato before noon and told him I wanted to put ten thousand on Rioux. He laughed when I said this, asking what I knew that others didn't. "I have a good feeling, that's all." He marked it down.

That morning I met Patty in a Côte-des-Neiges coffee shop. It was the first time he'd left his parents' house since being discharged from the hospital. While he wasn't walking gingerly, Patty, who usually floated, moved through the front door with a subtle caution (this, even though I had already messaged him to indicate everything was safe). There was still bruising on the right side of his face, which looked more rigid than the left and still puffy. He sat down in the booth opposite of me and, reduced of his usual bravado, still had enough self-awareness to smile.

"My parents want me to press charges," he said, laughing sadly.

"How you feeling?" I asked him.

"Getting better. Those cunts went to work on me."

"I know, I'm sorry," I answered. Patty had offended his share of people but deserved none of what happened to him. I seethed each time I thought about it.

"You warned me. You saw it coming. Puss did me in again."

"So they want you to press charges, eh?" His parents were reasonable people who usually let things go, but this was a higher level of drama for a boy who'd spent his life creating it.

"Yeah, every day Mom's in my ear. 'Why you gonna let them get away with that'?"

"You'd be shining a light where we don't want one," I answered.

"I know, T, I'm not a dummy."

There was a larger problem I needed to speak with him about. Patty was in a bad place. If my plan worked, he would get pressed by the people I was getting over on. On his own, he wouldn't last.

"Listen Pad," I said, "I called you here for a reason. You gotta go bud. You gotta leave the city for a while."

"What? Why?" He knew the answer but asked it anyway.

"I'm going to get us out of this, but you gotta go," I said. "Go to TO, go to Van, but get the fuck outta here. I'm gonna give you some cash to get set up, okay?"

"What are you planning?" he asked. I didn't want to tell him. Though I trusted Patty, divulging this would benefit no one.

"No violence, nothing like that, but I do have a plan. Just promise me you'll get outta here. ASAP bud. You have enough to get to Van, right?"

"Yeah, but I don't know anyone out there—"

"Doesn't matter. It's far and it's safe. Tell your parents you want to go in another direction and visit UBC or some shit. They'll like that. Stay there for a bit. It's a good spot. But go now, like this week."

"Where are you gonna go?" I told him about Europe but didn't specify a location.

"This whole situation dude," he said, shaking his head. "I can hardly believe this shit. All from that fucking night at Métropolis. And now we both gotta jet. Fucking ostie de calice tabernak."

Patty wasn't smiling anymore. He looked up at the ceiling, overcome by the situation and his inability to impose order on it. I could see he felt powerless. The milieu's indifference had finally registered. We had to leave our hometown.

"I know, bud," I said. "I know."

Later that week, there were press conferences and fighter meetings, weigh-ins and interviews by the journalists who owned boxing coverage. The event dominated sports media: the Journal provided its usually comprehensive coverage and even the Gazette had a decent preview. RDS ran a feature each day on one of the matchups, ending its week of coverage with a piece on Olivier Rioux. It felt as though there was a palpable belief among Montreal fight fans that he would win. This was perfect for my purposes.

I was still in contact with Maxime, who was happier than I'd ever seen him. We had a smoothie together at his house after a training session on Tuesday (as Eddy was back in town, I was still staying away from the gym). Still perspiring, he told me that at least one hundred and fifty family and friends had bought tickets. The Saint-Jean paper had also featured a longform piece about his journey from hockey also-ran to professional boxer.

"No, I am not anxious," he said, in response to my question about his nerves. "This is a great opportunity for me. I don't care about losses, you know? I don't have ten years to build a career."

"Are you going to rough this guy up?" I asked.

"Yes Teddy! Exactly. Exactly, man! That's the only chance I have. But it's possible, man. I know it's possible!"

"You've been watching tape on this guy?" I asked.

"Yes, but there's only so much you can learn in a week, you know? I just need to know when he drops his hands and prepare for that. That is all I can do…" Maxime was becoming emotional as he spoke. I wanted to change topics, but the Chipper had become carried away.

"I know what's happening here," he said. "I'm not fucking stupid. Calix thinks I'm going to get banged up. Use me to build this kid. But I'm not. I'm bringing a fucking fight on Saturday night. You'll see."

"I know you will. That's never been in doubt, buddy," I said, smiling.

"I hope not!" he said. "You helped make this possible, everything in boxing. You know that right?"

"I've played a small part, Max. You did the rest." I almost wanted to cry when he said this.

"Are you doing okay, too, Ted? Still at the motel?"

"Yep, and I'm doing fine."

"Good, because you're too young to be living this way, you know?" Maxime said, his voice searching.

"I appreciate that, but I'll be okay, Max. Just think about Saturday." He smiled and squeezed my shoulder.

His concern was heartfelt, but it was me who should have been worried. Two weeks before the fight we submitted CT scans to the Régie des alcools. This was a formality that almost always passed without incident, until the doctors said they discovered something worrisome on his brain. It was a strange mark, almost like a void, between the bridge that separated its two hemispheres. Neither doctor knew what to make of it.

While they discouraged his involvement, it wasn't enough to prevent him from fighting. Of course, Maxime was indifferent: "This fucking thing has probably been there for ten years, tabernak. Fuck do I care?" The Woodchipper maintained that he felt excellent, and since there was no way he wouldn't fight, it would be counterproductive to create doubt so close to Saturday.

The press conference was held on Thursday but nothing interesting happened. Long-winded promotional speeches ceded to uninteresting comments by the fighters. All of the regular local news teams were there, including representatives from several American publications. Maxime was on-hand, sitting in the front row. He was called up towards the end to answer questions, and when Maxime was asked if he'd box with the same abandon he showed in hockey, the Woodchipper demurred. "No, you can't box that way. You can't. I need to be patient, to stay calm, and if I do that, I can be successful. People who know me from hockey know what I bring to a fight. I bring my fuckin' — pardon my language — nuts to a fight. And I'm going to bring them to the ring. There's no doubt about that. No doubt."

The press loved Maxime, especially those publications from outside of Quebec, for whom he was an exotic entity — the sort of legend you may have heard of over a beer but never considered meeting in person. Laliberté, his opponent, was also present, and seemed confident (though less charismatic) about his chances. His wife, who also sat in the front row, had just given birth to a girl. He promised victory for both of them.

Watkins and Rioux took to the podium last and promised to knock one another out. Rioux seemed so certain of his chances, shaking his head when asked if there was anyone in the division who could withstand his power. Watkins didn't seem to care. "Nobody at middle can move with me, none of ya'll can box with me. This dude's gettin' it tomorrow. Ya'll see." There was no pushing and little swearing for the sports highlight shows to tease their viewers with. Rioux was certain he would win. I had wagered everything on the opposite.

On Thursday night, I was sitting on the edge of my motel bed, researching hotels in Europe, when I received a call from Eddy. I didn't pick up and continued my intelligence gathering. He rang again. I sighed and stared at the ceiling. What did this guy want? I answered the phone.

"T, you're a hard man to get in touch with."

"What do you want, Ed?"

"That's a new tone, bud. I just heard you placed a big bet with Genny." I didn't answer and looked out the window.

"I like Rioux," I said, after a long silence.

"Appears so." Eddy paused before continuing. "That's a lot of cash, bud," he said.

"What do you want?" I asked.

"What's with the attitude, T?"

"I'm tired, that's all. So yeah, what do you want?"

"Couple things. Somebody told me that your ATMs haven't been stocked in a while. Then Little Craig said he passed by your house the other day — he's dating some broad in NDG — and the front window looked broken in." I sat up in bed.

"He was just 'passing by my place'?"

"Yep, that's what he said." I looked at the television. "I take it you haven't been home," he continued.

"Been staying with someone I met for a bit."

"Who's that?" Eddy asked.

"A girl, doesn't matter."

"Are you gonna be at the weigh-in tomorrow?" he asked me.

"I might."

"We'll talk. See ya then."

Why would Eddy tell me this unless he was trying to create a problem? Did he want to induce me to go home because someone would be waiting? What would be his motivation for wanting me hurt? Was Eddy nervous that I was talking to the police? What if someone had broken in? What if they fucked with our house?

The next morning I checked out of the motel and rented a car on the south shore. If anyone was in my neighborhood, I didn't want them to see me return, and so I picked a small SUV and crossed the bridge back into the city. Underneath a gray sky, downtown looked quiet from the distance. I turned off the highway and drove a back way into my neighbourhood, peering out at NDG from behind the tinted windows of my rental. I passed the same doors and driveways I'd known all my life, recognizing no one. Pulling up to my street, I made a right turn. It was free of cars.

I wasn't going to stop at our house in case someone was there waiting and drove by instead, where I could see that one of the smaller side windows had been broken. It was subtle enough that most people wouldn't have noticed it, so why did Craig? There didn't appear to be anyone around and the house was otherwise untouched.

I parked on a parallel street and walked over to the alleyway leading to our backdoor. Deserted and wet from recent rain, fallen leaves clung to the soles of my shoes. Bat in hand, I walked through the gate behind our house and approached the back door. I opened it at first slowly and then fast, walking into our empty kitchen. Someone had been inside. Books had been knocked off the shelf and a few photos smashed. I could see footprints on the floor. They belonged to a medium-sized shoe and were old, mud having fossilized on the carpet (it had rained two days ago). I stopped, thinking there was a sound, but it was only a man yelling at his dog on the street's other side. I went upstairs where the shoe marks climbed towards our bedrooms. The doors to both were open and I feared there'd be a coiled lump of shit in one of the beds. But there was nothing, just a few open drawers but no obvious theft (my mother was never into jewelry). When I went downstairs, after checking every room in the house, there was something I previously missed in the kitchen that ruled out any belief this may have been a random break-in. Pinned to the fridge was a note in uneven lettering: "get a security system Teddy."

I remembered something and walked back upstairs, into my

room, where the footprints had paused in front of my bed. I crouched down and looked underneath the box spring, where I had taped my father's rifle. It was still there, untouched by the motherfucker who broke in. I pried the rifle away from the tape and held it against my chest, looking out my bedroom window onto the street below. There was no one outside, and so I sat on the edge of the bed, debating what to do.

If I left for a hotel, someone could come back. But if I stayed, someone could hurt me. Who could this have been? Where was the threat coming from? It couldn't be Genny, who would want to resolve our bet before he did something bad to me. Zinedine? He couldn't believe I had anything to do with his brother's death. Was someone feeding him false information? (It occurred to me that, at least for now, it was in Eddy's interest to obscure Genny's role in Karim's death. Why would he want Zinedine to make problems before Eddy could complete his deal?) Or was Eddy trying to scare me into coming back so they'd know my location and could do something about it?

I went back downstairs, got out a bucket and mop, filled it with hot, soapy water, and began to clean off the mud: throughout the living room, on the stairs and in our bedrooms. I put our books back on the shelves, hung the fallen pictures and taped over the broken window, placing a block of wood from the basement behind it.

It was Friday morning. The weigh-in was later this afternoon. I had promised Maxime that I'd be there on the understanding that nothing could happen in a public place. Before, there were other steps to finalize.

That afternoon, a day-before weigh-in was held at the Montreal Casino. Each fighter approached the slave block, where they disrobed, preened and got naked in instances where they were an ounce or two over the limit. The Casino turnout came alive when two welterweights got into a shoving match, forcing the mediation of both camps. Otherwise, the biggest crowd gathered to watch Olivier Rioux and Sammy Watkins faceoff. Both fighters looked emaciated, their stomachs taut keyboards. After some initial jockeying for position before dozens of cameras, the pretend aggression relented, and they retreated into their respective camps.

When it was Maxime's time, he glared at Laliberté and brought their heads together in an aggressive show of respect. His physique was that of a thirty-eight year old man, in that he still had a paunch below his shaven chest, and his vaunted muscularity—hilariously captured in a picture of him in the stands after a senior league fight, shirtless, lats flexed, eyes psychotic—was mostly gone. He was now simply big, but still meaner looking than his young opponent.

Before I could reach Maxime, I saw Eddy standing with Little Craig. They were involved in an escalating conversation with a group whose backs were to me. When I walked over, I could see it was Zinedine who was gesticulating before Eddy. I came up and inserted myself into the circle. Zinedine had three other guys with him. I recognized them from Karim's celebration.

"What's going on?" I asked, looking around the circle.

"I'm chatting with Z," Eddy said. "He's a bit worked up."

"I'm just asking for answers," Zinedine said, his pale eyes flickering.

"You guys watch the weigh-in?" I asked.

"Fuck that," Zinedine said. "Who cares? This guy's been lying to me for weeks."

"Calm the fuck down," Eddy said, asserting himself for the first time. "There's twenty cameras and ten security guards watching." Zinedine laughed.

"You think I give a fuck?" Zinedine asked. "Let 'em come over." Little Craig shifted his weight, unsure of how to handle things.

"Let's talk about it somewhere else," I said. "This ain't the spot."

"No point," Zinedine said. "This over-the-hill fuck's just gonna keep feeding me bullshit."

"I don't know how many different ways I can say the same thing," Eddy said. "I had nothing to do with what happened. Nothing. What the fuck would I gain from that?"

"Yeah fucking right!" Zinedine said, moving forward to where he was only inches from Eddy's face. Little Craig wedged in to block Eddy. If physical contact occurred, someone was going to get smashed.

"Who do you got left?" Zinedine asked him, almost as a whisper.

"Alright guys that's enough" I said. Zinedine looked at me out of the corner of his eye. "Come on," I said, now more slowly. "Not here." Zinedine exhaled as he stared at Eddy. He then turned to me.

"You going to the fight tomorrow?" he asked.

"I am. Are you?" Zinedine snorted and looked behind me towards the bouncers, reluctant to insert themselves.

"What's up big man?" he asked the head bouncer. "Nothing happening here. Just chatting." Zinedine turned around and motioned to his group. "They want us out," he said. "Anyway it's no problem, lots of time to sort things out later." He turned and left through the front door, his crew following.

"Been a while, T," Eddy said. Little Craig stared at me with uneasy eyes. His face, bloated by a bad diet, was stressed, and I could see him looking out of the corner of his eye towards Eddy.

"You were right, Ed, somebody did break into my place," I answered. Eddy said nothing. "Some piece of shit smashed the window," I went on. "Left a note for me on the fridge."

"What it say?" he asked.

"Doesn't matter. I'm back there now. I've got a .22, cameras and a good view of both sides of the house from the top floor…"

Eddy looked from me and towards the stage. Genny had appeared and was talking to Laliberté.

"That kid's gonna get it eventually," he said, almost absent-mindedly in reference to Zinedine. I looked over to Genny, who was moving in our direction. Fortunato was behind him.

"How you guys doing?" he asked, smiling. A gold cross stood out against Genny's black shirt. "Big day tomorrow, how's your man?"

"Ready to go," I said. "Laliberté?"

"He's a lion. I heard you got some other action too," Genny said, alluding to my bet.

"I think we're going to see something tomorrow night."

"Time will tell," Genny replied.

After leaving the weigh-in, I got takeout from an Italian shop on Monkland. When I arrived home there were no new cars on my street, but still I stepped through my backyard in cautious observance of the bushes and hidden areas where someone could be waiting. But there was no one around, and I sat down on the couch, where I ate my spaghetti and meatballs. The meal was large and stretched my stomach. I turned on the television.

I thought about Olivier Rioux, twenty four hours before he'd disappoint twelve thousand fans at the Bell Centre. My attempt to forecast the fight was interrupted by a call. I thought it might be Eddy or Allan. It was Zinedine. I had no idea where he got my number from.

"Yeah, Z, what's up?" I asked.

"Where are you, I'm in your neighbourhood, can we meet to talk quick?"

"I'm not home," I said, "and won't be for a while." I could hear a sigh of disappointment on the line's other side.

"We're cool, Teddy…" Zinedine said, as though to pacify my concern.

"I know we are…" I replied, looking towards the window, covered by blinds, thankful that I parked the rental several streets away.

"What we all talked about today—" he said.

"Z, the phone," I cautioned.

"I know," he said. "Was that bullshit, what he said to me?"

"About K? No, I don't think so," I said. "He would have had no reason…" I began.

"Yeah…" Zinedine seemed unconvinced.

"Are you going to the fight tomorrow?" I asked.

"I'll be there," he said. "We'll see ya then." He hung up the phone and I sat back on the couch.

If Zinedine went after Eddy, there would be no evading a response: he was known to the police and would be suspected first if something happened. But Zinedine — who carried himself like someone whose behaviour wasn't constrained by consequence because he knew that it was unlikely he'd meet a harder man — didn't seem to care.

How strong was Eddy, anyway? What would happen if the wrong fight came his way? What did I even care?

I wasn't scared about tomorrow's main event, it was Maxime that concerned me. Though he promised for the fight to be on the level, Genny's word meant nothing. Why was he so eager to bet, beyond the possibility of my financial ruin if Maxime lost? He wouldn't do that without being sure of the outcome.

Maxime *had* to win. Allan had to place his bet at the right time. Watkins had to defeat Rioux. I had to get my money and leave the city. The consideration of these necessities (and what could happen if they didn't come to pass) kept me awake as I stared at the ceiling, closing my eyes every two minutes in a failed attempt to find rest. At some point past two in the morning, physiology won out. Secure in the knowledge that our darkest worries rarely come to fruition, I finally fell asleep.

Noise woke me at 4:47. I looked outside the window (too skittish for a deep sleep, I wasn't disoriented upon waking) and saw a car outside our house. I reached under the bed and pulled out the rifle, holding it beside my head as I stared down at the sedan. If someone took a step towards the house, they would get a warning bullet. If this method of deterrence failed, they would get shot. It looked as if the passenger door had started to open. I cocked the gun, rushed to the bottom of the stairs and turned a light on that illuminated the driveway. I ran back upstairs and looked outside where the car remained, its doors still closed. It was a small sedan, one I hadn't seen before, and likely belonged to a young hitter someone paid to be here. My heart in a full sprint, I couldn't tell whether a door was opening when lights from another car appeared in the distance, pulling up to a stop on the street's other side. I could see two drunk girls stepping out of a cab. As they stumbled hand-in-hand towards a darkened doorway, the car outside my house drove off.

36.

The following morning, I packed my bag in preparation for leaving after the fight. I would drive to Ottawa and spend the night at a hotel. That way, I could avoid any entanglements if a bad result put me in someone's crosshairs. If Maxime won, I would call Allan right away and instruct him to place two hundred thousand on Rioux. If this worked, I would stay in Ottawa and drive back to Montreal only after Allan received the cash from Genny. From there, I would move the money back into my bank account, likely by putting it through a casino first (cash in, cash out after losing a couple bets), pay the debt and leave Canada.

That afternoon, after dropping off the rental car and stopping at the local army surplus store, I installed fake security cameras on the front and back doors, so it at least looked like someone was watching if an aspiring fire bomber approached our place.

I walked into Maxime's dressing room at six-thirty that night. The Bell Centre was beginning to fill, and Maxime's bout would be one of the final introductory matches. I found the heavyweight with his trainer, father and girlfriend. He was pacing the dressing room, eyes wild.

The Woodchipper extended his glove when I entered, his gaze transfixed by the ground. Maxime's trainer, a local Jamaican named Bruny Johnson, acknowledged me, and I sat down in the corner, content to watch them prepare. The fighter was manic, walking forwards and back, stopping to throw a series of punches, sweating and grunting and locking heads with his trainer every minute or so.

His girlfriend smiled at me. Raven-haired and intensely tanned, she didn't seem nervous, perhaps inured to danger because of the hundred previous times she watched him fight in hockey. Maxime's father made little notice of me when I entered, nodding as one would at a wake. I couldn't have cared less about him and returned to Maxime.

"Five minutes," I said to them. "Let's do it, big fella."

Johnson nodded and Maxime started throwing combinations at his pads. Soon a knock came on the door via the arena staff member whose job was to escort Maxime to the ring. The boxer turned to his trainer, and they locked heads once more as Johnson said a few calming words. The pair then turned and walked out the door. Maxime slammed his boxing glove into my palm when he passed.

I followed Maxime out of the room but didn't accompany him on the ring walk. Instead, I entered the Bell Centre's bright blue and red lights, and walked over to the media table where reporters looked at the ring from over top of their laptops. An old, bearded man who wrote for one of the leading French papers smiled at me.

"*C'est ton homme ici!*" he said, smiling as he motioned to Maxime, now in the ring.

Xavier Laliberté came next. Genny wasn't part of his entourage, made up of a few beefy farm boys from northeastern Quebec, his old, wrinkled trainer, and a shorter, fatter person I assumed was Laliberté's brother. The fighter received a fine applause from the few dozen people who'd driven down from Jonquière to watch; energized by the stage, he hopped to the ring.

I looked over the Bell Centre's lower bowl — from the fans in the first level to those at ringside, and the people clustered around the ring, most of whom had some sort of position in the event's administration, but I didn't see Genny. It was then that I noticed the judges. There were two men and a woman, but they weren't who I expected (Jean-Philippe Lagasse had been replaced by an older man whose identity it took me a second to process). I couldn't remember where I'd seen him.

As the two fighters began their in-ring preparation, I noticed Laliberté's stretching routine, and his habit of leaning far on either side to draw out his groin. This triggered a memory from his sparring session so many weeks ago. This older judge had been at the training session that day! I remembered his arrogant face when I walked in and our exchange. What the fuck was he doing here?

I turned to the reporter again. "What's this guy doing judging?" I asked him. "Who is he? I thought it was going to be that other guy, Lagasse?"

"Last minute change, I think," he said. "Lagasse might be doing the main event. One of those judges got taken out."

"What? Which judge?"

"There was some issue," he said, shaking his head. "I don't know, but somebody got switched out." I looked at the ring, where the announcer was introducing both fighters. Doucette received a huge applause from his fans at ringside, some of whom wore his hockey jerseys and swayed drunkenly. Both men were brought together by the ref and Maxime glared at Laliberté.

I had to know which judge was removed. But before I could find another reporter, the bell rang, and both fighters started squaring off. Maxime was boxing with more restraint than I expected, throwing jabs to the body and keeping himself out of Laliberté's range. He didn't seem overwhelmed by the stage, and this comforted me somewhat, but Laliberté could fight a little and twice caught Maxime with flush jabs to his chin. The punches shot Doucette's head back, but he continued to plot his way around as Bruny yelled at Maxime from the corner, warning him about letting Laliberté fight behind his left hand. When the round ended, he walked back to his corner, still breathing through his nose and in full emotional control.

"Hey," I said between rounds to one of the blond TVA reporters at ringside who sometimes wrote about what was happening at the Régie des alcools, "did one of the judges get pulled for the main event?"

"Yes," she said.

"Which?"

"Dal Bertrand."

"What? Why?"

"He's being investigated for something" she said, shrugging her shoulders as she refocused her attention on the ring.

I moved closer to the ring for the second round. When a security guard tried to intervene, I told him I was part of Maxime's team. Bruny verified this when I shouted to him from behind the guard's outstretched arm. "You see!" I said, "I'm part of the fucking corner!" The man nodded and moved out of my way. I edged up close to Bruny and whispered into his ear.

"They bought a judge. He needs a stoppage." Bruny's calm eyes turned to the ring, where Maxime was having a few strong moments. Twice he landed combinations that stung Laliberté, but each time the younger man regrouped by retreating into a shell and moving out of range. Every time Maxime made any progress, Laliberté fought back, tagging him with flush punches to the side of his head. The degree to which subjectivity informs how one processes a boxing match that involves a friend is near indescribable: every punch absorbed is a confirmation that your instincts were wrong, that your friend should never have put himself in this position, that he's being clearly outclassed by a superior opponent, and you were stupid for being delusional enough to think him capable of winning. And each time Maxime got hit, the crowd, now around four thousand, grew quiet. I thought of his brain absorbing more damage.

But the Woodchipper hadn't lasted twenty years in semi-professional hockey without fighting his way through some difficult moments. Laliberté landed a power shot near the end of round three, but undaunted, Maxime came back to mount a sloppy, late round flurry where he pushed Laliberté into the corner and unloaded a series of imprecise punches, only the last clearly landing on his face. This brought some members of the crowd to their feet, but the younger fighter wouldn't go away, and at the beginning of the fourth he landed a snappy jab on Maxime's nose, forcing a trickle of blood. I was becoming nervous and thought of how, only two months before, I told Eddy that Max "wouldn't face much on his way up." The reality was that his technical prowess was so far behind his peers that however tough or violent a man he was, it didn't really matter if he encountered a higher degree of skill.

When Maxime got back to his corner, I got up right underneath where he was sitting.

"You need a fucking KO here Maxy!" I yelled. "They ain't giving it to you on the cards! Knock this guy the fuck out!" Maxime nodded and looked back towards Laliberté, who was taking heavy breaths and listening to the instructions of his trainer. Behind Laliberté, I could see Genny sitting in a front row chair to the fighter's left. He was with three other men, including Sil. They were staring in our direction.

In the fifth, things got precarious. Maxime looked exhausted and started taking more punches, while Laliberté had grown stronger and began throwing four and five-blow combinations. With a minute left he dazed Maxime with a right hook that pushed him back into the corner. Laliberté came forward in an attempt to finish him, but the Woodchipper held on and forced the referee to intervene. Badly hurt, Maxime was met with an uppercut upon the referee's release, which dropped him to the mat. He collected himself on one knee, near hyperventilation as a ten count was administered and my heart rate multiplied. But the Woodchipper got to his feet, which drew a modest applause and the ref asked if he wanted to continue. Maxime nodded and went into a protective shell until the bell sounded.

Between rounds Johnson implored Maxime to box more intelligently. We needed a knockout, but much juice did he have left? Obviously exhausted, with an opponent good enough to pose even bigger problems and still relatively fresh, I began to feel sick. This wasn't a hockey fight, which lasted forty-five seconds and demanded only balance and total aggression. Rather, boxing required that a fighter draw upon reservoirs of strength in situations where one's original plan wasn't working.

I tried to create urgency in the corner. Behind me, I could see Eddy looking on from his seat in the front row. Juliet and the two girls she brought to the party were beside him. "Max," I said, now yelling, "they're trying to take this from you. Knock this motherfucker on his ass! He has no chin! No fucking chin at all. Send this kid packing! He hasn't been in half the wars you have. You got four fucking rounds man! KNOCK HIM THE FUCK OUT!" In the other corner I could see Genny giving encouragement to Laliberté. Sick of this cunt, I hoped each of my words reached him.

Maxime appeared to refocus and get his breathing under control. When the bell rang, he was already on his feet. Maxime walked into the ring's middle and launched a few wild power shots that missed Laliberté's forehead. Maxime was at least trying to stop him, but I was frightened that his recklessness might leave him vulnerable. But while Laliberté was just good enough to provide problems, he was weak enough to make mistakes of his own. One minute into the round he threw a lame jab that missed, and Maxime countered with a straight right which landed flush on Laliberté's eye socket. Sensing blood, Doucette marched forward and threw three more power shots. One of these tagged Laliberté on the chin. He fell to his knees and the referee counted to ten. The Jonquière man rose, and Doucette set himself upon Laliberté, pounding his midsection and jaw. Laliberté absorbed five undefended punches but managed to hang on long enough so that the referee could move in to separate both fighters and give him a reprieve. But Maxime continued applying pressure, using a simple jab-power right combination he now believed Laliberté couldn't stop. Near the end of the round, Laliberté appeared far more fatigued than at any previous point. When Maxime got back to the corner, I slapped him on the back.

"Fucking right! Fucking right Maxy boy!" I yelled. Beneath us, Eddy was looking on with interest. On the other side, I could see Genny clapping behind Laliberté, yelling at his fighter to access the same reserve of energy that Maxime tapped.

"Let's go, bud!" I yelled again, carried away in the excitement. "You're going to stop this guy right now, he's fucking dead in there!"

Maxime got up from his stool and returned to the ring's centre. Laliberté at least tried to begin the round strong, even catching Maxime with a sharp jab to his cheek, but his energy was now only superficial. The Woodchipper had been reborn and brushed off Laliberté's offense by throwing a hard overhand right that knocked him to the mat.

"Fucking right!" I yelled. I could feel Genny looking at me.

Laliberté was given a ten-count and rose to his feet at four. Certain only that he had to keep fighting, when the referee grabbed his hands to see if he was capable of continuing, Laliberté prepared himself to box. The referee released him, and Maxime threw consecutive overhand rights that Laliberté couldn't defend. The Woodchipper then pushed his opponent — who by now, looked like someone who'd been administered an anesthetic — into the ropes, and launched repeated uppercuts that smashed against his cheek. Laliberté fell close to where I was standing. There was nothing behind his eyes, and while he was in no shape to continue the referee nonetheless started another count. In the opposite corner I could see his trainer leaning over the ropes, towel in hand, prepared to throw it, but Laliberté got to his feet and the ref again asked him if he wanted to continue. He said yes and the ref stepped out of the way only so that Maxime — poised in the opposite corner and prepared to attack — nearly ran to the other side of the ring. The Woodchipper delivered a sharp jap-right-cross that Laliberté didn't see and knocked him out on his feet. Now unconscious, Laliberté was still upright and Maxime — desperate to avoid ambiguity — threw an undefended overhand right that smashed Laliberté's face. He fell to the mat face first, with limp arms incapable of bracing his fall, and Laliberté's nose (and then, by order, his forehead) absorbed the force of his tumble. He laid motionless on the ground as the crowd gasped and several doctors jumped into the ring. Maxime launched himself into the air and then came over to hug Bruny and I, drenching us in his sweat. He was breathing maniacally, and I strained to look around his back where the doctors were working on his opponent. Genny was now angling to get into the ring but one of the security guards pushed him back. My face was lubricated by Maxime's body, but I realized it wasn't only sweat: he was crying.

The Bell Centre went quiet as medics demanded we leave the ring. Maxime went over to where Laliberté lay and extended a fist to him. He then climbed through the ropes, while I remained on the outside, watching the paramedics take their time with the beaten fighter, whom I could see now somewhat returning to life. They began loading him onto a stretcher, carried by six men. After the initial struggle to get him over the ropes, Laliberté gave a drunken thumbs up to the crowd. He was then brought into the arena's bowels where a waiting ambulance would take him to the hospital. Remembering my obligation, I texted Allan and told him to place the bet. Out of the corner of my eye, Eddy was walking towards me. Juliet and her girls were behind him.

"Jesus fucking Christ," he said, "what a fight."

"Yeah… it was," I said, my eyes still trained on the disappearing stretcher.

Behind Ed, I could see Genny moving in our direction. He walked up to me and made an aggressive stop. Genny stared for several seconds without saying anything.

"He okay?" Eddy said, in reference to Laliberté.

"He's cooked," Genny said.

"Well," Eddy started, "I hope he's alright, sacrament. Gave that thumbs up—"

"—That fucking Chipper load his gloves?" Genny asked me.

"What?" I asked, squinting in disbelief. Alessandro was now standing behind him, his face that of a stupid dog eager to bite on behalf of its owner.

"He don't punch like that," Genny said, a vein beginning to emerge in his forehead. "I've seen every one of his amateur fights." Genny was almost yelling now. "Now, all of a sudden he's fucking George Foreman, are you shitting me, bro?"

"The athletic commission watched the fucking gloves getting wrapped!" I said. People beside us were looking over.

"Don't talk back to me, you stupid little fuck," Genny said, moving towards me. "I'm not making good on that bet before we figure out what happened."

"Figure out what?" I asked. "Are you for real? Funny hearing that when one of the judges was at his training session!"

"Fuck your mother's cunt!" Genny nearly grabbed me, but Juliet intervened.

"Come on guys," she said, trying to calm things down.

"Find a finger to fuck, you discount madam," Genny said, sneering at her. Startled, Juliet moved back in front of Anna and Ivana. Genny moved on, brushing my shoulder as he passed. Thirty feet from us, I could see Maxime speaking to his father and coworkers.

"What about the hand wrapping?" Eddy asked after Genny walked by. I didn't answer.

"Teddy! Hello!" Little Craig said, leaning into me.

"What?" I asked, not paying attention.

"You forget where you are bud?" Eddy asked. There was something about his appearance — he had a new suit on, tailored and tacky — that angered me.

"What? I don't know?" I responded. "Go ask him. Ask your business partner."

"Take it easy, Teddy," he warned.

"Why don't you get outta here, ass licker." Eddy's eyes expanded but I continued. "Some fucking clown rolled up to my house at almost five in the morning yesterday."

"That had nothing to do with me, T."

"Fuck off," I said.

Juliet stepped forward again, her voice soft. "Teddy..." I ignored her. Zinedine was coming our way.

"Looks like somebody wants to see you," I said. Eddy turned.

"What do you want *now*?" he asked Zinedine.

"I wanted to see what you're talking about." He had five guys behind him, including Sénèque, whom I'd met at Karim's celebration of life. I could see Juliet wince. Zinedine turned to her.

"You don't seem as sour today," he said to her. "But we got no interest in your property here." Juliet didn't answer. Anna and Ivana looked down.

"Watch it, Z," Eddy said to him. "Last time I'm saying this. It had *nothing* to do with me." Eddy's voice was rising. I could feel the eyes of people watching us but didn't care whether Zinedine popped Eddy. It was only my bets that mattered.

"Well it's either you or him," Zinedine said, pointing his finger towards the direction Genny had left in. Security arrived and Zinedine backed away slowly, his eyes still on Eddy. "Not leaving without the answer and if your boy steps forward at any point (here, he pointed to Little Craig), we're gonna split his stomach."

Eddy turned to me when Zinedine left. "We'll deal with each other later."

I laughed at him. "Our dealings are done."

I left Eddy for Max on the main floor's other side. During the fight he was on the verge of passing out, and when Laliberté fell he appeared more relieved than happy (once he realized it was over, after hugging us, Maxime climbed the turnbuckle, pointed to his friends in the audience and flexed his biceps). He was in love with the esteem of his construction friends, most of whom were drunk and had shirts that said 'Woodchipper' on them. When the fighter turned to face me, I noticed Maxime's father put his head down.

"Hey Teddy boy!" he said, grabbing me by the shoulder.

"Congrats again!" I said. "Fucking eh plus, bud." Maxime was still in disbelief over what had just happened.

"How's he doing?" he asked. "My opponent, Lally, how's he doing? Tabernak, that didn't fucking look good, but I had to make sure I took it, you know?"

"I think he's okay," I said, "I don't know. He's on his way to the hospital. Hopefully nothing too serious." Maxime nodded.

"Of course, I don't want to see no one hurt," Maxime said. I wanted to ask where the power came from tonight, but a new man came cannonballing into the group and spilled his drink on

Maxime's trunks. The Woodchipper laughed, while behind him loitered a few heavily made up women, one of whom looked familiar. Initially I couldn't place her and then remembered she was among the group I first noticed at the Métropolis fight a year earlier. It wasn't Maxime's girlfriend, but someone devoted in some measure to the Montreal boxing scene. She looked at me but only briefly, because her attention became absorbed by the fighter once he turned in her direction. They walked off to speak in the corner. No longer anyone's focus, I looked around the arena.

The turnout was excellent. While there were some unoccupied seats at ringside, the lower bowl was full. Cocktail-carrying people were taking their seats beside me. I couldn't see either Genny or Zinedine's crews anywhere. I walked over to where some of the event's officials were standing.

"So, what happened to Dal Bertrand?" I asked one of the elderly officials standing near the ring — an arrogant fuck who hated me despite my efforts to speak with him in French (he sometimes came to the gym, walking past the front booth without saying hello).

"He got pulled," the official said, not even looking my way as he consulted a sheet of the fights.

"Why?"

"Probably because he fucked up somewhere, you know?"

"Who's in his spot?"

"Somebody else, I don't know."

"Thanks for the valuable information," I said. I looked down at my phone. Véronique had texted me to see how everything was going. It was past two a.m. in France. She was out partying, likely drunk. I messaged back but didn't expect an answer.

About twenty feet away, I could see the television crew speaking into a camera. They were filming the introductory portion of the broadcast in advance of the show going live.

I alternatively loved and loathed this group, which alternated between expert commentary and fellatio for whichever fighter it thought would advance the network's business interests. I wasn't sure whether Poehler was on the floor, but there was someone who approximated his size and shabby clothing standing around fifty feet away. Close to him I could see Stu, whom Karim and I had left in that alley. He was with Gabe. They were talking to Eddy. I hadn't seen Stu since we hurt him.

They were looking in my direction when a new voice assaulted my ear. "You tell Maxime to kill him you fucking piece of shit?"

"What? What are you talking about?" I asked, turning around to see Alessandro staring at me.

"He's fucking in intensive care. Massive fucking brain bleed."

"Jesus Christ," I said, alarmed.

"And you were screaming for the knockout!" Alessandro was getting closer to my face as a group of fans started looking at us.

"That's cause I knew we needed a knockout to fucking win! This is brutal news, but how the fuck is that my fault?" I yelled back. My shock was fast replaced by anger.

"You ain't getting your two hundred K either. There's gonna be an investigation. Something got fucked up here," he said.

I said nothing and looked back towards the ring. "And this ain't over" he said, getting closer to my face. "Some fucking rat shit here. You want to go out like your buddy? He was a tough guy until we caught him."

"What?" I said. "Get the fuck out of my face, you meathead." He was poised to strike but I welcomed everything. "What the fuck did I tell you?" I yelled, now even more angry, "get the fuck out of my face you fucking pussy! Who the fuck are you anyway? You useless, lacky fucking cunt. Fucking wannabe roid-slut muscle. What the fuck are you gonna do about it? Fucking loser! Fuck right off!" Other people beside me were becoming concerned.

Alessandro seemed to grow smaller, sneering before turning around and disappearing into the crowd. I took a long breath and then apologized to the people around me. Xavier Laliberté was on life support?

"What's going on?" Maxime asked.

"It's nothing," I started. "It's not your fault. But Laliberté's in trouble. He's got a brain bleed." Maxime's face went white.

"What the fuck, Ted?"

"That's all I know. I was just told that, but I don't know if it's confirmed." Maxime shook his head and looked down. "It's not your fault," I told him. "It's not your fucking fault. Not one bit."

"Oh fuck," he said. "Fuck man, what the hell." I grabbed Maxime and squeezed him by the shoulders, speaking in slow, deliberate sentences.

"This is boxing. You didn't fuck up." He looked scared. I wasn't used to this.

"What? What do you mean? They're going to come for me?" he asked.

"No. For what? It was a fight. This shit happens. It's terrible, but it happens. You didn't break a rule."

"I ain't talking about the rules," he said.

"Promoter wants to speak with you," I said, pointing to Calix King, who was standing nearby. "Probably wants to give you another fight, go see him." I could see Calix glaring at me.

I leaned in closer to Maxime, slipping some money into his pocket. "Go to a hotel and pay cash," I said. "Skip out soon while the main event is on. I'll call you later."

"I thought you said…"

"Let's just be safe," I said.

"What about you?" he said to me.

"I'm getting out of here early too. They're circling."

He stared at me for a moment as Calix pulled on his arm.

I nodded at him. "Get the fuck outta here, leave through the basement," I said — pointing towards the dressing room area. "I'll call you in a bit."

When Maxime left, Zinedine came back over to see me.

"The shit's swirling around you tonight," he said. "What'd that guy say to you, bro?" I made a mental calculation of whether to tell Zinedine what Alessandro had alluded to. If I did, Zinedine would likely attack him in here. This could put by bet in jeopardy.

"He's somebody we gotta watch," I said. "May have been involved, I don't know."

I glanced over to where Genny and Eddy were still talking. They were looking at us. I went back to my seat in the front row.

Another fight started. Two Latinos fought five feverish rounds before the network-backed man scored a vicious combination knockout in the fifth. Our Montreal fans, who adored a firefight above all else, stood and cheered as the pint-sized featherweight mounted the turnbuckle in salutation. It was perfect matchmaking, enlivening an arena in which entertainment had been scarce for the last hour.

Next it was Ferdinand Guillot's turn, who walked to the ring in a new, Damballa-inspired outfit I had suggested for him. Through the first four rounds, Guillot always kept himself *just* out of his Japanese opponent's reach, maneuvering his shoulders to avoid Hideki Ueno's power punches and ducking underneath his hardest shots.

As Ferdinand began to score, the damage to Ueno was mounting. His face had become lumpy and its side profile, once rounded, showed a protuberant bump in the sixth round. But in no way was he deterred: despite a deluge of abuse Ueno continued to move forward with a messianic guile, only to be punished each time for his bravery. In the seventh Ferdinand hit him with a shot so flush it snapped Ueno's head back and sent him backpedaling towards the corner.

Between rounds, I could see the ring doctor shake his head at the referee, who walked back into the center of the ring to wave it off. Ten thousand fans cheered as Ferdinand climbed the turnbuckle closest to where I was sitting. He then walked over to Ueno's corner and hugged the beaten man, into whose eyes the doctors shone a flashlight. Devoid of energy and a shell of the person who began this fight, he put a groggy, sportsmanlike hand over Guillot's shoulder.

Our local tuxedoed ring announcer provided the official scoring — a twelfth round technical knockout victory — and the referee held Ferdinand's hand skyward. Guillot, smiling openly for the first time, was soon joined by the television commentator who asked him to describe this victory. Guillot gave an articulate answer and the Bell Centre applauded when he spoke about his wish to unify the belts and become Montreal's first undisputed welterweight champion. It was the finishing touch on his swift ascent.

The Bell Centre went dark when the main event came on. To remain any longer would be a mistake, but I didn't want to leave without first determining whether our bet might work. Sammy Watkins was introduced first and booed as 50 Cent's *What Up Gangsta* played in the background. He had a small group with him, perhaps five or six people, and bounced towards the ring in white shorts with blue trim. When he moved between the ropes and traversed its four corners, Watkins held his hand skyward as he saluted the Bell Centre crowd. The more respectful fans applauded. A group of goons in tight clothing hissed.

Rioux came next, wearing purple trunks, his walk scored by an understated Bob Dylan song that seemed at odds with the moment's magnitude. He received a large cheer from the Montreal boxing fans and entered the ring trailed by an entourage that included Calix King.

Rioux saluted his fans and then disrobed in preparation of

the fighter introductions. It would be an exaggeration to suggest the Bell Centre exploded when his name and record were announced, but there was an impressive roar, and I could feel my stomach flutter as I remembered the stakes and temporarily forgot the several belligerents at ringside. I had no idea where Genny was (likely talking to someone else on the other side of the ring), and so I sat back to watch the action.

When the bell rang to start round one, Rioux came out of his corner with both hands blazing, pushing Watkins back towards the corner where he unloaded a series of punches the American only barely maneuvered around. Sensing a fast, explosive stoppage, the crowd began to scream as Rioux pushed forward, abandoning technique as he attempted to sever Watkins's head from his shoulders.

With a minute left in the first round, and after it had become obvious that Watkins had underestimated Rioux's power, Rioux threw a concussive shot that just barely missed Watkins' face. Had the punch connected, the fight would have been over. Feeling idiotic for underestimating the concussive possibilities in Rioux's right hand, my heart began to murmur.

I couldn't openly cheer for Watkins and so I sat back with my entire body flexed as the round moved towards its end. Rioux continued to box aggressively while the American appeared to find his way around in the last thirty seconds, having learned to anticipate Rioux's forward movement. There was little he could do when the rules were broken, however, and with ten seconds left they both tied up in the corner. The referee broke their clinch and Rioux simultaneously pushed and tripped Watkins, who fell back towards the corner, imbalanced. Rioux used this opportunity to throw a right hand that caught Watkins flush on the chin. The American fell as the crowd became frenzied, and the idiot referee — who refused to call it a slip or reprimand Rioux — began to administer a ten count. Watkins complained from his knee as he waited for the count to become eight before rising, and from my perspective at ringside, it was hard to tell whether he was hurt. When the action resumed, Rioux pressed forward in the last five seconds as he tried to end things. The arena had become euphoric.

The bell rang to end round one. Rioux had Watkins pressed against the back ropes, unable to move, and when the referee wedged himself between them Watkins made his way back to his corner with his head down. I wondered whether it was as obvious to him (as it was to me), that he was already down 10-8 and — though it was still early in the fight — he couldn't afford another round like this.

I tried to read Watkins' body language and see if he was composed enough to box his way back. But I knew that it would have been stupid to stay if the fight ended with an early Rioux knockout, and so I prepared my escape, looking around to determine whether Genny's men were still here. Silvio was walking in my direction. I pretended not to see him until he was inches from my face.

"Genny wants to see you on the concourse. Right now," he said.

"What? The fight's still on?"

"It's just gonna take a minute."

"You got a bit more juice tonight, eh Sil? Fuck off," I told him.

"It's just going to take a minute," he said, again, inching towards me. "He just wants to talk. You don't come now, bro, and we're putting a cocktail through the bay window of that house."

On the other side of Silvio I could see Zinedine. I tried motioning in Zinedine's direction, but he didn't notice me. I then glanced back to Silvio, paused for a moment and nodded.

"That kid ain't doing anything for ya," he said. When I got up to leave, he pushed his hand into my lower back. I swatted it away. On our way out, we passed Sénèque, who was looking at us. As we moved by him, I whispered in French, wagering that Silvio wouldn't understand.

"These are the guys who got K."

Sénèque seemed to hear me but nothing registered on his face.

We left the floor area and walked up the long flight of stairs leading to the concourse, passing the thousands of people entranced by the fight. My feet felt as though every step was an extraction from the mud, and when I reached the top of the stairs, Silvio's hand had reappeared on my shoulder, directing me to a remote part of the concourse where Genny was waiting. He was with Alessandro and Ali — whom I had once met at Célestes. Genny took a step in my direction.

"My guy's fucking on a respirator," he said to me. "Just had a kid."

"I know," I responded. "It's terrible."

"Shut the fuck up," he said. "There was fucking plaster in those wraps."

"What?" I asked, dumbfounded by the accusation. "Are you fucking kidding?"

"Watch your fucking mouth." Ali moved closer to me.

"Fuck you," I said to him. "Nobody plastered anything!" My voice was rising. "Do you think I'm insane?"

"We're going for a walk," Genny said, grabbing me by the wrist. "We're gonna find your buddy next."

"Let fucking go of me," I said, pulling my arm back from Genny's right hand. I began to walk away when Ali grabbed my neck, lurching me backwards. In the arena I could hear the crowd roar, presumably because of an offensive surge by Rioux.

I tried to resist but Ali was too strong, maneuvering me to his liking. There was no one on the concourse to witness my exit. Escape was now impossible, and I realized, being pushed through the front door, that I wouldn't get away with any of it: our bet would lose, and I wouldn't get my money. But what difference did it make? Genny's anger would make these concerns obsolete.

37.

Outside, my body controlled by the cyclops behind me, I used a free hand to pull out my phone and tried to call Maxime.

"Put that fucking thing away," he said, slapping it out of my hand.

As Genny's group shuffled me towards a parking garage, I could see one of Zinedine's men watching from a distance. He was pretending to have a smoke, looking in our direction. One of the security guards outside was staring at us, too intimidated to intervene (and grateful, the coward, that nothing was happening to justify his intervention). I turned around to face Ali.

"Get your hand off me you fucking goof." He didn't want to lose face but wasn't prepared to get violent.

"That's enough," Genny said. I didn't know where we were going, but there was an SUV idling nearby.

"There are cameras everywhere," I said to Genny. "Something happens to me, they'll know who did it."

"Do you think I give a fuck about a security camera, bro?" he asked. Sil stood behind Genny but remained silent. As we neared the truck, I could hear a voice yelling from behind.

"Teddy!" I turned and saw Maxime walking in our direction.

"Get your fucking hand off him!" he yelled. Ali looked at Genny and then released his grip.

"What's going on here?" he said. "You alright, T? I saw that big dummy we picked up from following you out. What the fuck do you want with him?" he said to Genny.

"Our kid's on life support," Genny answered. "What'd you put in your gloves?"

"Tabernak ostie de criss, I didn't put jack shit in my gloves!" Maxime started moving towards Genny, whose group steadied itself. They were five against our two, but Maxime didn't care. Buoyed by grief and testosterone, his eyes were wild.

"Calm down, Chipper," Genny said. He had a smile that made me nervous.

"Look what the fuck you're accusing me of," Maxime answered, turning to Ali. "You make a move and I'll put *you* in the fucking hospital." Behind Genny, Alessandro was consulting his cell phone. He'd just got a text. His face shot up.

"He's fucking dead," he said. "Xavier's fucking dead! Just pronounced it. Dead on arrival at the hospital, he fucking stopped breathing."

"What?" Genny said. "What the fuck?" He turned around to stare at Maxime, whose face had gone from red to white.

"What?" Maxime said. "I didn't try to kill that kid!" he yelled. "You think I wanted that?"

Genny advanced towards Maxime, who tensed his body in anticipation. Behind Genny, Ali readied himself.

"You better fucking relax!" Maxime yelled. I could see one of Genny's men reaching into his jacket for something. My legs were drained of blood. I couldn't move them.

Before a gun could be drawn, a car hammered to a stop beside us. Karim's brother and his crew leapt out and began taking baseball bats to Genny and his men. We were now on the inside of the parking garage and our prior confrontation had turned into a bacchanal of screaming and swearing: bodies were being flung and smashed against concrete. Aluminum bats made hollow sounds as they bounced off backs.

Zinedine was screaming incoherently as several of his friends clubbed and kicked Genny's men in the stomach. Maxime and

I were entangled with Genny and Alessandro, who I grabbed by the collar and started punching in the stomach as he attempted to gouge my eye. I landed one blow on his rib and could hear him gasp and double over. When he did, I found his eye socket with an uppercut. He fell back against the asphalt, and I stomped his chest to prevent him from rising. Maxime was punching Genny in the eye. On his own, he had no chance against the Chipper.

Lights illuminated the fight, and I could see that security guards had arrived. One of Zinedine's men screamed at them and the guards turned around.

"Cops'll be coming," Zinedine yelled. He grabbed the baseball bat and struck Ali on the kneecap. He then turned and smashed Sil across the chest. The fat man fell. He was now holding his forearm on the ground, broken from defending himself against the blow. Behind me, Zinedine ran over to Genny, bleeding on the ground after Maxime's beating. He pulled a gun from inside his pants and pointed it at him. My mind began to blur. I looked down at Genny, beaten nearly to unconsciousness by Maxime.

"Whoa," Maxime said to Zinedine. "No, come on."

"This guy got my brother."

"No I didn't!" Genny screamed.

"You're not giving me the right answer!" Zinedine yelled, bringing his pistol down on the side of Genny's face.

"There's cameras down here, Z," I said. "Don't do it man!"

"No there ain't," he responded. "Look around."

Genny's other men whimpered on the pavement. Suddenly, Alessandro got up and launched himself at Maxime, thrusting his hand into Max's stomach. The big man exhaled and fell forward, almost silently, where his body began to spasm on the ground. I could see that a knife was sticking out of his abdomen and jumped on Alessandro, who'd fallen backwards from his effort to stab Max. I kicked him in the face and he began to blubber. My brain frenzied, I turned around and attended to Maxime. The knife remained lodged in his stomach as Maxime continued to seizure. I tried to stabilize him, but the violent movement of his huge body was too great for me to subdue and when Maxime turned on his belly the knife punched in even deeper. Maxime's eyes became wide as he gasped for air. I had no idea what to do and began to hyperventilate. Beside me, Zinedine raged.

"What the fuck!" he screamed. "Shoot this fucking cunt," he said to me, passing a gun. I stared at it for a second, and then at the man lying half-conscious on his face.

"This guy killed your boy!" he said, making reference to Maxime, who was taking short, urgent breaths. I looked back at Alessandro, still lying on his face, but I couldn't take the gun from Zinedine. In a panic, I ran over to retrieve my phone from the ground and started dialing 911.

"Who the fuck are you calling?"

"An ambulance, he's gonna fucking die!" Zinedine looked at me and then turned around to point his gun at Genny's head. I grabbed him by the hand.

"Don't do it man. It's not worth it."

"Are you kidding?" he asked me, enraged.

"All hell's gonna break loose."

"I don't give a fuck." Zinedine put his gun down momentarily and the same SUV stopped beside us. Its doors were thrust open.

"What the fuck are we gonna do about him?" Sénèque asked from the front seat, motioning to Genny.

"Let's get him in the car. Piece of shit took my brother," Zinedine said, almost to no one as he stared down at Genny. "Your buddy Ed gave you up by the ring."

Two of Zinedine's other men jumped out, picked up a half-conscious Genny and dragged him into the SUV's backseat. Without acknowledging me, Zinedine leapt into the front. Like a horse stung on its ass, the truck lurched out of the parking garage and vanished.

I turned back to Maxime, remembering I hadn't called the ambulance yet and dialed 911. The operator came on and I gave her our location. She instructed me on what to do. But when I leaned in to verify Maxime's condition, it was already too late. So I ran.

EPILOGUE

The investigations started immediately. Genny wasn't found, and it felt like there was a gathering storm of violence between members of his crew and those of Zinedine's brother — with both sides waiting for the police attention to relent before launching their rockets. Everyone knew what happened: the security guards saw Genny's men lead me out and multiple witnesses reported watching Zinedine's SUV fly through the Drummond and René-Lévesque intersection, turning left on its way to the highway.

There were no security cameras where our brawl unfolded, so the police didn't see Zinedine pull Genny away, and because his body disappeared there was no evidence, yet, with which to charge him for murder. Otherwise, a toothless Alessandro was arrested for killing Maxime, his fingerprints found on the blade that ended my friend's life.

And what happened in the fight, for which we laid out so much money to bankrupt Genny's book? After a bad first round, Sammy Watkins regained his composure and won the next eleven. The roar I heard in the second came after a skirmish on the ring mat when Watkins' corner launched a protest over Rioux's roughhousing. By then Watkins had taken control, which forced Olivier to repeatedly punch the back of his head during a clinch — a violation the referee didn't see fit to penalize. When Watkins' cutman appealed, one of Rioux's supporters confronted him and some shoving followed. Rioux's friend was ejected, after which the fight resumed and Watkins established a level of control he didn't relinquish.

Since Genny wasn't around to pay what he owed, Fortunato was now in charge and starting from a great financial disadvantage, given the money he owed Allan (he never found out that I was the bet's originator). In turn, this meant Eddy wouldn't get his money to buy the property, but what could he do about it? With Genny dead the deal was off, and if he pressed the issue Fortunato would kill him. Otherwise, Fortunato took over the book and honoured all debts from the fight, including the two million he owed Allan. (I was content to let the one hundred thousand I had in escrow be lost, for to attempt its retrieval would have committed me to a meeting whose escape was doubtful.)

I wasn't around for the police inquisition and cared nothing for a bookmaking rap, which I could deal with in time. The possibility of even temporary imprisonment in a city jail — and having my head broken by one of Genny's loyalists, angered by the belief that I was tied to his death — seemed a risk worth avoiding.

After the fight I spent twelve interminable days in Ottawa, paying cash at a Kanata hotel until I received word from Allan that he'd gotten our money. He wired the cash to an account I set up, and from there, I moved — on one fast night, with the help of a sympathetic teller receptive to my proposal that his life could change with some easy help — enough of it through a local casino to ensure my debt could be paid off through legitimate ends. From there, I sent Patty enough money to last a year, and then filled the hole that first brought me into Eddy's orbit with a transfer at the bank branch close to my hotel.

My necessary absence from Montreal meant that I couldn't attend Maxime's funeral on the following Friday. The night's events dominated local news coverage for a few days, with faulty speculations about street loyalties that erupted in murder, but not once was my name mentioned: I was neither puppeteer nor puppet, but thread in some coarse fabric, and had Maxime not intervened to save me he wouldn't haven't been smothered in its folds. While there is no demiurge, only conflict born of self-interest, I will never escape that his life ended through my machinations.

It is two weeks later. I am standing in the middle of my parents' hallway, facing the door as I wait for a cab to arrive. In the dead of night I snuck in through the backdoor, aware that police may be stationed on our street. Beside me is a suitcase filled with what I'll need in the coming days or years. I have money in an overseas account that Allan wired for me, which will sustain whatever lifestyle I choose for some finite time. Having turned off every electrical appliance in the house and verified that no water is running, I move from my bedroom to that of my parents' — untouched since they last left it — and then close the door, walking softly down the creaking stairs, my steps monitored by faces immortalized in the wall-side pictures. When I get to the bottom of the stairs, I verify that everything is closed, that everything is quiet, and take a long breath to calm my anxious stomach. The car has arrived and will take me to the airport where I'll escape into the sky. I stand in silence and stare into the empty living room, picking up my suitcase so I can walk out the back door, which I close behind me and lock. There's no one in the alley to see me leave, nor will any witnesses capture my return. It is time to go. The house isn't mine. Véronique was right. It is tying me to Montreal, a city now sepulchral, and I will now move into the world, towards Nice, the Mediterranean and her. The sky lightens as dawn breaks and I move through the backyard, turning right onto the alley where a car waits at its mouth. Portals to memory, the house's windows watch me leave, and if death subverts my doubt that in some unknown realm I'll reunite with all those who occupied its rooms, I will cleanse myself, first, before time forces a confrontation with this riddle.

ACKNOWLEDGEMENTS

Thank you to Kieran Devaney for his excellent editing, to David Provolo for his wonderful design, and to all those whose feedback encouraged the story's completion.

And a sincere thanks to you, the reader, for your interest and time spent with the story. As reviews are invaluable for indie authors, please consider leaving one on the preferred platform of your choice. Further, you can find news related to upcoming projects and links to other writing on www.eliottmccormick.com.

Manufactured by Amazon.ca
Bolton, ON

40146339R00192